CAT IN A TOPAZ TANGO

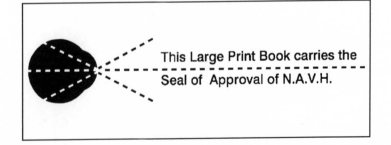

This Large Print Book carries the
Seal of Approval of N.A.V.H.

A MIDNIGHT LOUIE MYSTERY

CAT IN A TOPAZ TANGO

CAROLE NELSON DOUGLAS

THORNDIKE PRESS
A part of Gale, Cengage Learning

GALE
CENGAGE Learning·

Detroit • New York • San Francisco • New Haven, Conn • Waterville, Maine • London

GALE
CENGAGE Learning

Copyright © 2009 by Carole Nelson Douglas.
Thorndike Press, a part of Gale, Cengage Learning.

Thorndike Press® Large Print Mystery.
The text of this Large Print edition is unabridged.
Other aspects of the book may vary from the original edition.
Set in 16 pt. Plantin.
Printed on permanent paper.

LIBRARY OF CONGRESS CATALOGING-IN-PUBLICATION DATA

Douglas, Carole Nelson.
  Cat in a topaz tango : a Midnight Louie mystery / by Carole Nelson Douglas.
    p. cm. — (Thorndike Press large print mystery)
  ISBN-13: 978-1-4104-2119-7 (alk. paper)
  ISBN-10: 1-4104-2119-8 (alk. paper)
    1. Midnight Louie (Fictitious character)—Fiction. 2. Barr, Temple (Fictitious character)—Fiction. 3. Women cat owners—Fiction. 4. Cats—Fiction. 5. Las Vegas (Nev.)—Fiction. 6. Large type books. I. Title.
  PS3554.O8237C27698 2010
  813'.54—dc22   2009034720

Published in 2010 by arrangement with Tom Doherty Associates, LLC.

Printed in the United States of America
1 2 3 4 5 6 7 13 12 11 10 09

For the late Mary Katherine Marion,
a friend
who was fun, fearless, and fashionable,
clever, creative, and supportive,
and for all the great times
we had together

CONTENTS

Previously in Midnight Louie's
    Lives and Times 11
Chapter 1: Nervous Nuptials 17
Chapter 2: Louie Left Out 27
Chapter 3: House of Max 32
Chapter 4: Alpine Do-si-do 54
Chapter 5: Missing in Action 62
Chapter 6: Lost in Cyberspace 76
Chapter 7: Duty Call 83
Chapter 8: Police Premises 96
Chapter 9: Twinkle, Twinkle,
    Little Star 100
Chapter 10: Grilled Crawfish 108
Chapter 11: Wolverine Dreams . . . 114
Chapter 12: Shotgun Reunion . . . 117
Chapter 13: Car Chase 129
Chapter 14: Road Scholars 133
Chapter 15: Emerald City Express . . 146
Chapter 16: Text for Two 151
Chapter 17: Leaving Laughlin . . . 164
Chapter 18: The Bus Fume Boogie
    Blues 175

Chapter 19: Unhappy Hoofer 180
Chapter 20: Dancing with Danger . . 195
Chapter 21: Celebrity Is the
    Cat's Pajamas 202
Chapter 22: Pool Shark 204
Chapter 23: Shaken, Not Stirred . . 216
Chapter 24: En Sweet 221
Chapter 25: Everybody Undercover,
    Quick! 235
Chapter 26: Insecure Security 244
Chapter 27: Reinvention Waltz . . . 250
Chapter 28: Precious Topaz 255
Chapter 29: Brothers, Where Art
    Thou? 266
Chapter 30: Undressed Rehearsal . . 277
Chapter 31: Hot Stuff 289
Chapter 32: Wardrobe
    Malfunction II 294
Chapter 33: Hotfooting It 311
Chapter 34: Mama's Girls 315
Chapter 35: Purse Pussycat Prowl . . 323
Chapter 36: Red Hot Chili Peppers . 329
Chapter 37: The Shoe Must Go On . 334
Chapter 38: Mercedes Pasodoble . . 346
Chapter 39: Chef du Jour 351
Chapter 40: Rapid Recovery 359
Chapter 41: Too Dead to Dance? . . 365
Chapter 42: Pasodoble Double
    Cross 377
Chapter 43: Stomp 'Em If You
    Got 'Em 395

Chapter 44: Too Hot to Handle . . . 400
Chapter 45: Postmortem on
    a Pasodoble. 405
Chapter 46: A Perfect Barbie Doll . . 410
Chapter 47: Madness in His
    Method Dancing. 416
Chapter 48: Paso de Deux 425
Chapter 49: Another Opening,
    Another Blow 436
Chapter 50: One-armed Bandit . . . 448
Chapter 51: Crime Seen. 455
Chapter 52: Rehearsed to Death. . . 464
Chapter 53: Fighting Form. 482
Chapter 54: Rest and Recreation . . 493
Chapter 55: Last Tango in Zurich . . 498
Chapter 56: On the Topaz Trail . . . 514
Chapter 57: An Open and Shut Case . 520
Chapter 58: Fenced In 526
Chapter 59: Terminal Tango 531
Chapter 60: Curtain Calls 552
Chapter 61: Dial M for Motive . . . 559
Chapter 62: Topaz Tango 572
Chapter 63: Ciao Ciao Ciao 576
Chapter 64: For Her Eyes Only . . . 587
Chapter 65: Cane Dance 599
Chapter 66: Dancing in the Dark . . 607
Chapter 67: No Good Dude
    Goes Unpunished 612
Tailpiece: Midnight Louie Mulls
    Many Matters. 621
Carole Nelson Douglas Plays the
    Dance Card. 627

9

Previously in
MIDNIGHT LOUIE'S
LIVES AND TIMES . . .

There are a lot of fat cats in Las Vegas.

These glitzy media-blitzed streets host almost forty million tourists each year and a ton of camera crews. If cameras are not recording background shots for *CSI: Crime Scene Investigation,* they are capturing thousands of personal videos. People think they know this town — from film if not firsthand experience — know it from the flashy hotels to the seamy side of the Strip.

And a good number of them know one particular Las Vegas institution.

That would be me.

Oh, I keep a low profile. You do not hear about me on the nightly news. That is the way I like it. That is the way any primo PI would like it. The name is Louie, Midnight Louie. I am a noir kind of guy, inside and out. I like my nightlife shaken, not stirred.

I am not your usual gumshoe, in that my feet do not wear shoes of any stripe, but shivs.

11

Being short, dark, and handsome . . . really short . . . gets me overlooked and underestimated, which is what the savvy operative wants anyway. I am your perfect undercover guy. I also like to hunker down under the covers with my little doll.

Miss Temple Barr and I are perfect roomies. She tolerates my wandering ways. I look after her without letting her know about it. Call me Muscle in Midnight Black. We share a well-honed sense of justice and long, sharp fingernails and have cracked some cases too tough for the local fuzz. She is, after all, a freelance public relations specialist, and Las Vegas is full of public relations of all stripes and legalities.

None can deny that the Las Vegas crime scene is big time, and I have been treading these mean neon streets for twenty-one books now. When I call myself an "alphacat," some think I am merely asserting my natural male and feline dominance, but no. I simply reference the fact that since I debuted in *Catnap* and *Pussyfoot,* I then commenced to a title sequence that is as sweet and simple as B to Z.

That is where I began my alphabet, with the B in *Cat on a Blue Monday.* From then on, the color word in the title is in alphabetical order up to the current volume, *Cat in a Topaz Tango.*

Since Las Vegas is littered with guidebooks as well as bodies, I wish to provide a rundown of the local landmarks on my particular map of the world. A cast of characters, so to speak:

To wit, my lovely roommate and high-heel devotee, Miss Nancy Drew on killer spikes, freelance PR ace Miss Temple Barr, who had reunited with her elusive love . . .

. . . the once again missing-in-action magician Mr. Max Kinsella, who has good reason for invisibility. After his cousin Sean died in a bomb attack during a post-high-school jaunt to Ireland, he went into undercover counter-terrorism work with his mentor, Gandolph the Great.

Meanwhile, Mr. Max is sought by another dame, Las Vegas homicide detective Lieutenant C. R. Molina, mother of teenage Mariah . . .

. . . and the good friend of Miss Temple's recent fiancé, Mr. Matt Devine, a radio talk-show shrink and former Roman Catholic priest who came to Vegas to track down his abusive stepfather, Cliff Effinger.

Speaking of unhappy pasts, Miss Lieutenant Carmen Regina Molina is not thrilled that her former flame, Mr. Rafi Nadir, the unsuspecting father of Mariah, is in Las Vegas after blowing

13

his career at the LAPD. . . .

Meanwhile, Mr. Matt drew a stalker, the local lass that young Max and his cousin Sean boyishly competed for in that long-ago Ireland . . .

. . . one Miss Kathleen O'Connor, deservedly christened Kitty the Cutter by Miss Temple. Finding Mr. Max impossible to trace, Kitty the C settled for harassing with tooth and claw the nearest innocent bystander, Mr. Matt Devine . . .

. . . who tried to recover from the crush he developed on Miss Temple, his neighbor at the Circle Ritz condominiums. He did that by not very boldly seeking new women, all of whom were in danger from said Kitty the Cutter.

Now that Miss Kathleen O'Connor has self-destructed and is dead and buried, things are shaking up at the Circle Ritz. Mr. Max Kinsella is again apparently lost in action. In fact, I saw him hit the wall of the Neon Nightmare club while in the guise of bungee-jumping magician, the Phantom Mage, and neither I nor Las Vegas has seen him since.

That this possible tragedy coincides with my ever-lovin' roommate going over to the Light Side (our handsome blond neighbor and former priest, Mr. Matt Devine) in her romantic life only adds to the confusion.

However, things are not always what they seem. A magician can have as many lives as a cat, in my humble estimation, and events would seem to bear me out. Meanwhile, I am spending more time tracking the doings of Miss Lieutenant C. R. Molina these days, whose various domestic issues past and present are on a collision course. Since she has always considered the Mystifying Max a murder suspect and my beloved roomie his too-loyal accomplice, she may have to eat some humble pie as well as deal with two circling men of her own, Rafi Nadir and Dirty Larry Podesta, an undercover narc who is mysteriously interested in her personal and professional crusades. . . .

I am not surprised by these surprising developments. Everything is always up for grabs in Las Vegas 24/7: guilt, innocence, money, power, love, loss, death, and significant others.

All this human sex and violence makes me glad that I have a simpler social life, such as just trying to get along with my unacknowledged daughter . . .

. . . Miss Midnight Louise, who insinuated herself into my cases until I was forced to set up shop with her as Midnight Inc. Investigations and who, along with her many admirers, will be as mad as hell at her not making an appearance in this adventure, Girrrls always stick together . . .

. . . and still needing to unearth more about the Synth, an ancient cabal of magicians that may be responsible for a lot of cold cases in town and which is of international interest now.

Well, there you have it, the usual human stew, all mixed-up and at odds with one another and within themselves. Obviously, it is up to me to solve all their mysteries and nail a few crooks along the way. Like Las Vegas, the City That Never Sleeps, Midnight Louie, private eye, also has a sobriquet: the Kitty That Never Sleeps.

With this crew, who could?

Chapter 1
Nervous Nuptials

"You're the ex-priest," Temple pointed out. "You must know how we can avoid the wedding from Hell?"

"All weddings, or the preparations at least, are from Hell," Matt said.

He went on, chapter and verse. "I've officiated at enough of them to know that by now. The wedding 'party' always bristles with conflicting, intergenerational agendas. I doubt they're all as highly dramatic as Aldo Fontana's and your aunt Kit's, though."

Temple sighed and stirred on her living-room sofa in the Circle Ritz condominiums and apartment building, where she and Matt had units atop each other on the second and third floors. As, in fact, they were even more closely on top of each other now.

The five-story, round fifties-era building was a whimsical little place even for the city of Las Vegas, which only did whimsical large and on the Strip, but theirs was a whimsical little engagement.

Their lives were Euphemism Central these days. Being "engaged" made "sleeping together" expected, but they were still "living in sin" in the eyes of Matt's Catholic church. In the eyes of Temple's church, Universal Unitarian, she was just a modern woman ready for marital commitment and smart enough to want to know what she was getting into.

At least now that they were "engaged," Temple didn't have to "keep her feet on the floor" when she and Matt shared a sofa. Her feet were on his lap, and he was playing with the ankle ties on the resale-shop designer spike heels she'd worn previously as Kit's maid of honor at the elegant hotel wedding ceremony a couple of days earlier.

Aldo, the groom, had nine brothers, one of whom owned the Crystal Phoenix Hotel and Casino. Hotelier Nicky had been the best man, which left eight brothers to escort Kit's eight bridesmaids. (How a Manhattan resident came up with eight Las Vegas bridesmaids is another story.)

"Only a best man and matron or maid of honor for our wedding, I think," Temple said. "How can we get into trouble with that?"

"You still want the small civil ceremony here at Electra's wedding chapel first?"

"I don't know. We did meet here. Electra's our landlady and would love to marry us in the Circle Ritz's attached chapel. We'd be legal but we'd still be sinful in the eyes of your church. Would legal make you feel any better?"

"The only thing that makes me feel any better is you," he said, his golden-brown eyes darkening.

Temple hiked a shapely but short leg onto his shoulder. "Untie my shoe straps and then we can discuss more important things."

"I don't know how you walk in these things," Matt said, complying.

"Years of being a shrimp and suffering."

He smiled and moved her other foot from his lap to his shoulder. "For a shrimp you have some provocative moves."

"For an ex-priest, you catch on fast."

They grinned at each other. Then yawned.

"That was a rough twenty-four hours in the desert," Matt commented, "then the big wedding ceremony came right after it."

"You were the kidnapping victim," she pointed out. "I was only a member of the rescue party."

"I wasn't the target. I was just along for the ride."

"And what a ride! Murder in a Nevada cathouse. It may not have been in Vegas proper, but it would sure make a great movie. Eight vengeful women, eight captive groomsmen, assorted associates, almost all of the last identifiable mob 'family' in Clark County. Uzis, limos, hookers."

"Not likely for my bachelor party," Matt said, laughing. "I hardly know anybody here."

"You'd be surprised, buddy. I think the Fontana boys plan on doing just that when we finally do get hitched."

"No, a fate worse than a Vegas wedding with Elvis," Matt said, still laughing, and then tickling the bare soles of Temple's feet to make her join in.

She was easy and giggled away on cue. "Stop that! I'm really ticklish!"

He was no fun. He stopped, then frowned. "I really don't know about committing to that charity fund-raiser for all of next week."

"You wouldn't bow out?"

"Ballroom dancing isn't exactly in my résumé."

"Just why you need to brush up before we do the wedding waltz at our reception. Not to mention you're committed to taking Ma-

20

riah Molina to her freshman father-daughter dance in high school this fall."

Matt groaned at the reminder. "I have a lot of sympathy for single working moms rearing a teenage daughter, but who named me proxy daddy of the week? And Mariah's in that embarrassing hero worship of older guys stage."

"Who's more embarrassed, you or her?"

"Me. Teen girls don't get embarrassed, they embarrass everybody else. I'm already freaked. This *Dancing With the Stars* wanna-be show isn't all wedding waltzes and dad-daughter shuffles. Those ballroom routines can be pretty risqué."

"You're out of the priesthood, Matt. You can do risqué. And kids today want dads who can rock out in the school auditorium like cool dudes. Doesn't Ambrosia think it'd be good for your radio career?"

"Ambrosia's in favor of anything that makes me a visual. She believes the world wants a Web presence, a Facebook profile, a YouTube persona, rather than just a voice in the night."

"Let's face it. Ambrosia knows how to market radio today. You make a socko visual. Remember that billboard of you on the red suede couch? I sure do! Blond, handsome, and horizontal."

"Yeah, and all those screaming fan girls." He made a face. It didn't hurt his looks a bit.

"Ambrosia's your producer. Your 'Midnight Hour' is syndicated in a lot of major markets, but there are more to be won over. You can go farther than the usual radio shrink, maybe become the next Dr. Phil."

"Spare me."

"What's wrong with that?"

"That's what I get with an ace PR woman as a fiancée. P.T. *Barr*-num. Dr. Phil's avuncular act is not only bullying, but superficial. I hope my 'Midnight Hour' digs a bit deeper."

"It does." Temple's voice lowered to a dramatic whisper. "You are the most insightful, sincere, and sexy guy on the airwaves. Dr. Phil should be quaking in his Big and Tall Man suits."

"Dr. Phil isn't a dancing bear."

"You *won't* be a dancing bear."

"I've been rehearsing already, so don't bet on that."

"*Ooh.* Who's your teacher?"

Matt hesitated. "No six-feet-tall Strip chorus girls to steer around the floor, thank goodness. Most female pro ballet and ballroom dancers are petite. She's a brunette."

"Should look dramatic with your fair coloring."

"She's the dramatic type, all right, but she's just the instructor. I'll actually perform with the other celebrities."

"Don't glower. Men are so afraid of a little social dancing. Look at all those macho athletes who aced *Dancing With the Stars*. Football players, Olympic skaters."

"Temple, my only 'sport' is swimming. Not exactly a couple's pursuit. Besides. You overlook the sleaze factor. The winning ballroom dancers are all sexy."

"And you're not?" she asked indignantly.

"Not for a mass media audience."

"Nonsense! This will be good for you," she decreed, "and good exposure for your show."

"That's what I'm afraid of."

"You can practice your new steps with me. That'll give you an edge. Extra rehearsal time."

"Sorry. All my free time must be devoted to rehearsal eight to ten hours a day with La Tatyana. Given my night-owl working sched, I'll have no time or energy for fiancées."

"Tatyana?"

"You can talk *Dancing With the Stars*, but you obviously don't watch the show closely enough."

"Guilty," Temple admitted. "I'm too busy to catch a weekly TV show, but I've seen clips."

"Most of the pro dancers are Russian. I guess the baton has passed and the great Russian dancers of today have gone from ballet to samba."

"So what's Tat-y*an*-ah like?" Temple asked, deciding it was time to flex her possessiveness.

Matt winced. "A Gestapo officer in rehearsal and a Lolita on stage."

"Heavily bipolar. Sounds more like a blue movie than a dance contest. I'll have to come to the broadcast every night of the competition to act as bodyguard."

"I'm more worried about missing a step than any domineering sexpot."

" 'Domineering sexpot.' Now there's a role I could aspire to."

"Don't even try." Matt tousled her luxuriant red-gold curls. "Sexy sprite is my speed."

Temple laughed and snuggled into his arms, glad to have Matt in her life and a subdued version of her natural fiery red hair color back after having a blond bleach job foisted on her for an assignment.

Into this premarital merriment a large black shadow descended.

Midnight Louie lofted over the sofa back onto their semitwined laps, earning protests.

"Louie! You weigh a ton," Temple said. "Off!"

Matt hefted the big cat with one hand under his belly and set him on a sofa arm. "He must be protesting being left out of the wedding plans."

"Oh," Temple cooed, "Louie was so cute as the ring bearer wearing that black bow tie collar with the ring box attached."

"You could see he hated the bow tie as much as I would, but he did relish center stage, as usual."

"You'll have to do ring bearer act again for our wedding, Louie," Temple threatened her feline roommate.

He showed his fangs but stifled a hiss of contempt and jumped down to the parquet floor.

"I sometimes think he's trying to come between us," Matt said with a frown Temple found adorable.

Matt must have driven women and girls crazy when he was in the priesthood, Temple thought, enjoying watching her beloved interact with her panther-personality alpha tomcat. He'd kill 'em on *Dancing With the Celebs.* He was classically good-looking in a blond, matinee-idol way. That he never used it made his charm even more devastating.

But looks were deceiving, as usual. Matt's unhappy childhood, first with a beaten-down unwed mother and then with an abusive stepfather, had driven him to become the perfect "Father Matt" he'd never had. He liked the anonymity of radio. She was hoping the dance competition would bring out his extroverted side.

She wriggled her bare toes against his stomach, making him seize her feet to stop the teasing and eye her with unsanctioned intentions. He'd worked hard to overcome his sad early history and was more than ready to start making some promising fresh history with her, except for the occasional qualm about fornication without benefit of matrimony.

She was a lucky girl. Temple sighed again, this time with an odd combination of contentment and excitement. She sure hoped trouble would stay out of their way until they could do something official to end these prenuptial nerves.

Chapter 2
Louie Left Out

Ring bearer.

Who do they think I am?

Frodo?

I *am* short and I *do* have hairy feet, but do I look like I eat seven meals a day?

Well, maybe a wee bit.

Anyway, it was bad enough I was shang-haied into my Miss Temple's maternal aunt's wedding party recently. After all, the event was over the top to begin with, just in having eight legendary Fontana brothers for groomsmen, not counting the eight good-looking brides-maids they squired.

And, granted, I got a little local publicity for being Johnny-on-the-spot, but I got no credit for outsmarting the murderous individual who almost ruined the wedding beforehand by tak-ing out the maid of honor, my very own Miss Temple Barr.

All this wedding talk and reminiscence is making me gloomy. My Miss Temple was "this far" from being the *matron* of honor. The way a maid gets to be a matron is by marrying someone, as she and Mr. Matt Devine are discussing so often these days.

I do so miss my previous rival for turf on the royal bedspread here at the Circle Ritz.

Mr. Max Kinsella was the perfect boyfriend for my Miss Temple.

He lived and slept somewhere secret off the premises.

He customarily arrived discreetly by the patio doors, which is my usual modus operandi.

Although he gave lip service to a future of marital bliss, he led two to three lives and his past career as a magician and undercover counterterrorist kept him on the run and single.

He was so studly he could satisfy with a riveting personal appearance and then stay gone for whole days at a time. There were no nightly assignations to muss the bedspread and my territorial imperatives.

He remained totally protective but at a discreet distance, leaving me to do the daily bodyguard work and also lie guard on said bedspread.

In other words, for a significant other, he did not significantly get in my way. He exemplified the highest ideals of the Alley Cat Code:

friendly, fierce when necessary, and fancy-free.

Mr. Matt Devine, however, is a much more domestically inclined breed of cat. Having no secret missions of an international nature, he lays about the place, especially in *my* spots!

He discusses "their" possible move to his apartment right above us on the third floor, no doubt hoping to erase all bedroom memories of Mr. Max Kinsella. I am not as young as I used to be. A three-story climb is much more demanding than a two-story climb. Show a little consideration for the aging frame.

So move. Fine! I will continue to occupy Miss Temple's rooms all on my lonesome then. I am happy to entertain guests of my ilk in complete privacy. I could use a bachelor pad as much as the next guy. Just because Mr. Matt Devine is from a churchy background and actually considers matrimony holy does not mean those of other denominations, such as myself — I am a devout follower of the Egyptian female cat deity, Bast — must live by his rules.

But this is an empty threat. I have come to appreciate a feminine touch about the place, and also frequent ear stroking. The thought of being edged out of my Miss Temple's bed if not her affections is most distressing.

I fling myself through the flimsy patio doors

that Mr. Max was always urging her to fortify, and scramble down the single old leaning palm tree that is my land bridge to the ground-floor parking lot.

The asphalt is hot on my pads as I skitter across it to the hedge of oleander bushes. They are poisonous eating to critter kind, which is why Ma Barker, my long-lost mama, and her feral gang shelter in here for the time being. No wise street dog will disturb them here. I could use a friendly ear.

Instead, one of my own ears is boxed as soon as I am in the safe shadows within.

"Disappointing boy!" my venerable dam spits in that very now-ringing ear. "This is what you call a safe haven? With gourmet food and distilled water? We have seen nothing but aluminum pie tins full of those awful dried green rabbit droppings."

"I have been busy, Ma. I have not had time to train the human waitstaff on what to serve in which manner. They constantly involve me in the criminal community. And Free-to-Be-Feline is a prime New Age health food."

"Food! It is already in a condition to be eliminated before one can touch fang to its odious smell and texture. When can we expect something juicy and tasty that does not run away on four legs?"

"Soon, Ma! The only crimes transpiring

around the Circle Ritz these days are crimes of passion," I add sourly. "As soon as I can interrupt these proceedings for a few minutes, I will get your needs tended to."

"You had better, son. We might just have to rumble nights in protest if you do not push these people into line. Free-to-Be-Feline! If we were really free to be feline, we would run this town."

You would think I had led them into forty days and forty nights in the desert. Or was it years?

I slink away, caught between the conflicting needs of my kind and my kind of girl.

A Moses of my people I am not.

CHAPTER 3
HOUSE OF MAX

When Matt got back to his empty but beautifully redone apartment — no thanks to himself, who'd lived contentedly for years with rectory furniture donations — his answering machine winked its low-tech red eyelash at him. Message waiting.

Most of the few people he knew in Las Vegas reached him by cell phone. He sat down on his scarlet suede fifties couch, courtesy of Temple's secondhand store expertise, to listen to it.

A good thing he did.

The call from homicide Lieutenant C. R. Molina was a shock. Her rich contralto voice was soft and low and secretive. The formidable policewoman wanted a clandestine rendezvous with him. Pronto.

He was an almost married man, he wanted to protest to the recorded message. Still, romance was the last thing anyone would suspect was on the no-nonsense officer's mind.

And she didn't want him to call her anywhere on any phone. She would meet him at her house at 7:15 P.M. Her house was in Our Lady of Guadalupe parish, near the iffy north Las Vegas neighborhoods. He would stay in the car. She'd come out.

Hey, she didn't want even her thirteen-year-old daughter and the two shelter cats to spot him? What was he, a pariah? Or did she want to avoid "talk" now that he and Temple were engaged?

Oh, and *erase her message* from the answering machine.

Matt did, wondering like crazy what was up.

He looked up the address of the modest Mexican restaurant where she'd wanted to eat in the shiny new Vegas street guide he'd bought after coming to town eighteen months before. The place was in a north-of-downtown area even a Vegas newcomer like him knew was high crime.

So he wasn't about to take his silver Crossfire tonight. Expensive new automotive eye candy was susceptible to theft in that neighborhood. The Hesketh Vampire motorcycle in Electra's back shed was built for fast getaways, but, again, was a vintage collectible with "steal me" written all over it.

Matt had a feeling that the Vampire would have been appropriate for this sudden outing. It had originally belonged to Max Kinsella, as Temple had. Not that she'd ever belong to anyone, including him. Still, she and Max had been serious lovers, with marriage in the wings, even though Max had been absent for almost a year when Matt had first hit the Circle Ritz and met Temple.

Matt, fresh out of the priesthood, had instantly fallen in love with Temple. Like many petite women, she made up for size with energy, spirit, and an Imelda Marcos–size high heel collection. Temple was smart, savvy, funny, and kind. As a freelance public relations person, she had to get along with all types of people to keep major events with casts of thousands running smoothly.

Sometimes that included fending off bad publicity; sometimes that had come to include solving crimes, even murder, if they threatened the event. Temple always put her heart and soul and exotic soles into her work.

Matt was smiling. He always did when he thought of Temple, even when he saw her at a distance, being Temple as only she could. His first flush of infatuation had nearly burned a hole in his soul and newly liberated libido, but he'd had to take cold showers and wait. Max came back.

Max Kinsella.

Molina despised this man without ever having met him. She'd pegged him as a murderer who had gotten away unscathed, thanks to a dead man at the Goliath Hotel and Casino. Temple loved Max with a fortitude Matt had thought would never flag. She *knew* he was innocent. After all, she'd finally learned he'd been an undercover counterterrorist since his teens as well as the world-class magician she'd met in her native Minneapolis and followed to Vegas.

Max was a good guy, but Molina didn't know that and wouldn't believe it, even when Matt told her so. And Max would never deign to defend himself from her false impression. It was *Pride and Prejudice* all over again.

Now Max was gone. Again. Disappeared without warning. Again. For good?

Matt felt guilty about hoping so in his secret soul. He also knew that Temple would be better off knowing how, and why, the ex-magician had vanished, and if Max was alive or dead.

Matt picked up his cell phone and speed-dialed the penthouse number of their land-lady, Electra Lark.

"Hi, Electra, are you recovering okay from being a murder suspect? Who knew attending the big Red Hat Sisterhood convention in town would entangle you with ex-husbands and murdered bodies? All okay now? Good. Say, can I borrow my old Probe back tonight? No, I don't want to be anonymous. I just don't want my Crossfire ripped off. Yeah, it's a pain owning a sexy car. Had I but known, I'd have bought a Prius, which is now an even hotter car. Can't win. I'll be right up for the keys."

Five hours later, Molina darted out of her house and into his idling white Probe like a fugitive.

"Let's get going."

The drive wasn't far. Tio Julio's was a much-added-onto ramshackle wooden building, the kind of restaurant that has served really good food with no fuss and minimal atmosphere for three generations. It was so crowded you couldn't tell waitperson from customer and they were all mostly Hispanic. Vegas ran on chutzpah and illegal aliens well mixed among the legal ones.

Matt felt embarrassed by his Chicago Polish-pale face and blond hair that

36

screamed "gringo" as he waited for Molina just inside the door while she visited the ladies' room, wondering why the homicide lieutenant had picked such a busy venue.

When Molina reclaimed him, it was literal. She slipped an arm through his and pulled him into the restaurant, machine-gunning Spanish at a passing hostess. They followed the young Latina through a noisy mélange of people sipping margaritas and Dos Equis, through a fragrant miasma of picante sauce and sizzling fajitas, into a smaller room as crowded and noisy.

Molina was almost his height. She muscled him into place on a bench against the wall, so they sat side by side, with a 180-degree view of the room and its diners.

Now he could see she was wearing some kind of sequined multicolored shawl. Her usual black bob had been roughened with gel and swept behind her ear on one side. She was sporting huge gold hoop earrings and, when she took off her sunglasses, enough eyeliner and eye shadow to pass as an aging Goth girl, a disguise assumed in the rest room.

"Dios," she said. "Learning undercover makeup tricks from my teen kid; who'd have thought I'd need that at my age? How are

you, Father Matt, the about-to-be-married man?"

"Don't call me that!" he said, though no one could hear. "You need my help, you cut out the harassment."

She made a face. "Just kidding."

Which he knew. He was still sensitive about his ex-profession because it had been a vocation, a sincere one he'd honored to the day he left, and beyond. It was hard to explain to civilians. Maybe police work was too.

"So what's this all about?" he asked.

"Patience. First we order. I highly recommend the enchiladas fiesta. And a pitcher of beer."

The waitress made it to their table in three minutes, the beer in another five, and the food in ten. They'd passed the time with what passed for chitchat with Molina. Was Electra going to come out with any loot from her ex-husband? He looked a bit tired, was being a fiancé all that stressful? No, he told her, rehearsing for a charity dance contest at the Oasis was. Radio guys were always doing bizarre gigs, she said. Did Temple plan to keep taking on big conventions and meddling in murders after they were married? What kind of *hombre* was he, who couldn't keep the little woman at home having *niños* and *niñas?*

He finally broke in. "I get that you think we can't talk about anything relevant until we've got our food and drink and have ditched the waitress, but you don't have to be ridiculous. So, Carmen Miranda, where did you leave your Banana Republic headdress?"

Carmen was C. R. Molina's first name, and she saw to it that damn few people knew it. The only Latina Carmen the public knew was the long-ago goofy movie singer with the fruit basket headdress. Not a positive image. Carmen Electra was more up-to-date, but another stereotyped hot Latin honey.

"It's confession time, *Padre,*" she said, drinking from a frosty mug into which she poured Dos Equis beer. "I want no witnesses, no sound recordings, and no snickering on your part."

Matt was hammered with a bolt of curiosity. Carmen Molina was the most self-controlled person he knew. Now that his profession was radio shrink, he'd put her at the head of his most-intriguing-person-to-psychoanalyze list.

He was getting his chance in the most frantic, frenetic, screeching, and screaming environment on the planet. God surely had a sadistic sense of humor, but then He'd earned it for creating and dealing with Homo sapiens.

Matt was glad he'd ordered enchiladas, which were soft and easy to eat while asking leading questions.

"What hot topic of the month is this about?" he asked.

"The eternal enigma."

"Max."

"Kinsella." She didn't even grant the man the familiarity of a first name.

Was she about to confess what Max had confessed to Matt not too long ago? That she'd caught up with him once in a strip club parking lot and they'd decided whether he'd go with her as an arrestee with a private martial arts session? That the fight had gotten physical and heated in more ways than one? Molina had accused Max of getting sexual with her and had told Temple as well as Matt. Temple hadn't believed it, but Max had told Matt he had . . . a little, as a diversion during the fight. Anything to get an opponent off guard. That was Maxus operandi.

A deliberately single career woman like Carmen would resent that bitterly. And, face it, Matt told himself, strong emotions could turn on a dime. The other side of antagonism between women and men could be attraction denied on one side or the other, or both. Being a celibate observer of the mating game for seventeen years gave him a certain insight.

He found it fascinating that when Molina needed a foolproof disguise, she dolled herself up like an ordinary woman out on a date, but acted like she was going undercover as a hooker.

"He's vanished again, like before." Matt said, getting back to Topic One and Only. "Temple's afraid he's dead."

"Could be." Molina pushed her demolished plate aside and his too, hunkering down with the beer mug. "I don't have the manpower to prove it. I'm not concerned with where Kinsella is, or *if* he is, but *what* he was."

Matt didn't argue. "You finally changing your opinion on that?"

"I still like him for killing that guy at the Goliath Hotel two years ago, when he first disappeared. Still, I'm willing to consider your argument that he was acting as a counterterrorist. That doesn't carry any weight with the police. Killing is killing. It might mean shadowy Homeland Security figures would want to bail his butt out. That's speculation, of course, now."

"*Now?* What's happened now?"

"I found his secret Las Vegas lair. God! That sounds like a line from a hokey old movie serial. I found where he's been living in Las Vegas while eluding me and balling your new fiancée."

"You don't have to be vulgar to get my attention, Carmen. Apparently, he was pretty good at it. Fine by me. Temple's happiness is my greatest pleasure."

He knew his security would eat like acid into her new insecurity.

Molina's beer-pinked cheeks flushed scarlet with anger, and maybe some shame at being called on her harshness. Matt narrowed his eyes. Keeping his cool and rattling hers was working.

Of course Max and Temple had been intimate. Matt was an ex-priest, not an idiot. Yeah, it had driven him crazy when he'd been on the sidelines yearning for her. Now that Temple seemed more than happy with him, his insecurities had mostly evaporated. Clutching onto those suckers was suicide. Letting them go meant Molina couldn't use the usual weapons against him, meant he could control this interview.

"So what's the latest on your eternal pursuit of Max the Elusive?" he followed up.

42

She sighed as if releasing some very old air. "I screwed up. Blew it. When I learned where he lived I went there. The place looked deserted, so I checked it out."

"When was that?"

"Early Sunday morning, like 1:00 A.M."

After Temple had gone to the address the previous Tuesday to find Max and all his magic paraphernalia and possessions gone and some chorus girl in residence.

"Checked it out, as in broke in," Matt prodded.

"Frigging yes," she whispered, leaning intently over the beer mugs between them. "The place had overkill security, but it was in . . . disarray. I got in."

"And?"

"Before I got much of a look at the layout I realized someone else was in there with me."

"Max?"

She frowned. "Why should he be creeping around like a footpad in his own house?"

Maybe because he'd made it look like he and his things had abandoned it completely, Matt thought. He found, with irritation, that the idea of Max Kinsella still being secretly in town stirred the insecurities in his basement after all.

Molina hadn't noticed she'd finally rattled

him. "But then I wasn't surprised that someone outside the law would want to look into him too. Maybe one of those ghostly terrorists you say he was tracking."

"Not so far-fetched. The 9/11 terrorist crew and associates met in Vegas."

"Yeah. Alcohol and hoochie-koochie girls for the last nights of the heaven-bound suicide set. You'd think seventy-two virgins would be enough for them. What were they supposed to do for eternity after using up that bizarre quota?"

Matt shrugged and sipped. Taking his eyes off of her did the trick. She went on.

"Whoever was sneaking around in there had a hate on for Kinsella that makes mine look like a schoolgirl crush. I heard this sound, like a cat in your utility room. Later we found all the clothes in his closet slashed to less than ribbons. Sweaters, blazers, slacks. All cotton, silk, and lightweight wool."

Matt sat stunned. All Max's clothes had been gone when Temple had visited the place with Aldo Fontana. She'd said so, sobbing on his shoulder.

"Anything else disturbed?'

"A knife had been taken from the kitchen block. The biggest one. I spotted that subconsciously, coming in, but never realized . . ."

Her thought drifted off into a swallow of beer.

"Nothing else was taken, his magic cabinets?"

"No. All the furnishings were fine, even that huge, kinky opium bed he had. Your fiancée tell you about that?"

Opium bed? Matt shook his head. He'd want to know about that. Even more, he'd want to know why all the furniture that had been missing when Temple came to check on Max was back in place within four days.

Molina would think mention of the opium bed had him momentarily on the ropes, when it was the clothing and other furniture. Obviously, Temple had been led to believe that Max was utterly gone. Which was a darn good sign that he wasn't. Or wasn't dead, at least. Or were his spy associates just cleaning up after him? Holy moley.

Matt picked up the broken conversation. "So someone else was trespassing on Max's house. Someone who hated him."

"Certainly the clothes slashing was highly personal."

"It wasn't you?" he asked in jest.

"Not a good joke." Molina swallowed another deep draught of beer. "Whoever it was detected my presence. I decided to confront the intruder in the dark hall. I'd taken cover in a closet with those vented folding doors, so had to wrestle them coming out. I was heard. And knifed."

"Knifed?" Matt knew the feeling well. "Bad?"

"A hell of a lot worse than you were."

"God, Carmen. How much worse?"

"I'm not sure I want to describe my battle scars to you."

"Did this someone mean to kill you?"

"Could have, if I hadn't lifted my arm to block the blow I expected. The wound was shallow but long. You'll understand that I couldn't make it public. I've been off work with a 'virus,' 'bird flu,' whatever Detective Alch could think of. I'd get busted if anyone knew I'd done a B and E without a warrant."

"Breaking and entering. And no one knows besides Alch but me? That's okay. You have the seal of the confessional with me, even if I'm an ex-priest."

"Unfortunately, the other guy who knows ain't no saint."

Matt mulled this over. He'd noticed her say "we" had found the slashed clothes. "Not Alch. He's beatified at least for putting up with you."

She wasn't talking.

He drank some beer.

"I can handle this other guy," she finally said. "He's my problem. What I'm having trouble with is how close this incident was to the attack on you several months ago. Both cuttings. You a razor, me a butcher knife. A possible, even probable connection to Max Kinsella, alive or dead. I'm wondering if the attacker is the same party."

"My slasher's dead."

"You sure?"

"Sure. It was this former IRA agent from Max's early years. I mean his *teen* years."

"He was an antiterrorist as a teenager? Antichrist, maybe, I'd believe. Come on!"

Matt nodded, several times. "True. His first cousin was blown up in a pub bombing in Londonderry. The boys had been given a high school graduation trip to their family's native Ireland. Road trip. The damn fools drove up to northern Ireland to eyeball the Troubles."

Molina sat silent.

He figured she was stunned.

"The cousin died?" she asked.

"Presumably, based on the pieces."

"And Kinsella?"

"He was already an amateur magician. Having an Irish temper, teen-boy fury, and survivor's guilt didn't help. He found the bombers and . . . I don't know, ratted on them? Ireland was too hot to hold him; anywhere was. The IRA put a price on his head. That's when he was recruited by this unofficial counterterrorism group, as I understand. They did it to save his life, and I suppose they admired his nerve. As do we all."

"Speak for yourself, Matt," she said with irony, no longer silent with shock. "So the Interpol record was a decoy, full of disinformation for stupid domestic cops like me."

"It meant his life if he was tied to his real past. I'm wondering what this did to the family."

"His cousin's?"

"And his. One lost a son, one didn't. That doesn't go down well even in close families. Maybe especially not in close families."

"That's why he's so fanatical about protecting Temple."

"Probably."

Her palm slammed the rough tabletop. "So Max Kinsella is a misjudged hero and I'm the villainous pursuer of an innocent lamb."

"I'd never call Max 'innocent,' " Matt said dryly.

Molina let herself relax back into her seat, her features wincing. Matt knew that wince.

Knife wounds became inflamed and, he imagined, even healing stitches pulled.

"Kitty the Cutter gave me a four-inch slash, but I saw a shady doctor who managed to tape it shut," he mentioned. "And you?"

"Eighty-six stitches."

"*Whew.* The number sounds oddly appropriate."

To be "eighty-sixed" meant you'd been sunk.

She glared at him, thought about laughing, and then winced instead. "Don't humanize me, Devine. I can't take that right now."

"So what's the deal?"

"Are you right? Kinsella is basically a good guy with a bad boy façade? I've been overreacting and wasting my time?"

He considered it. He was used to weighing right and wrong, good and bad, and giving people a lot of leeway on those black-and-white extremes.

"Yeah. Temple's no victim or dupe. I won't say Kinsella didn't have a big load of guilt to bear, and like all loners he has an arrogant way of thinking he knows what's right for other people."

"Like you and Temple?"

Matt grinned. "Maybe. Still, the fact is he

can't offer any woman a stable domestic life, not that he didn't have hopes."

"Funny." She turned her beer mug around to study the condensation droplets. "I never gave him credit for being human enough to have hopes. Maybe I was judging him by my own yardstick."

"It's a rigorously straight one."

"How the tightly wound have fallen. Okay, Mr. Midnight. Mr. Radio advice man. What do I do now? I may have blown my career chasing a devil who could be a saint in disguise. Three people too many know about my misadventure at the House of Max."

"You including me in that?"

"Yeah. You're young, you're lovely, you're engaged. You'll tell your squeeze. No secrets, right, for love's young dream?"

"No. I won't tell her. I think you should. Someday not too far off"

Molina opened her mouth. Shut it. "You do extract a mighty stiff penance, *Padre.*"

"All in proper measure to the sinner and the sin."

"Pride is the worst of the Seven Deadly, right?"

"Yeah, but the easiest to fix."

She stood up. Threw a couple of twenties on the table. "Dinner's on me. I'll meet you at the rambling wreck in the parking lot. I'm going to the ladies' room to eat crow for dessert."

This time she really needed it. Matt watched her leave, her gait a slightly halting swing, not due to the little beer they'd had, but the hidden stitches.

Would she tell Temple the truth? Give away that Max's place was not really in other hands?

Naw, he thought as he wove through the beery crowds to wait for her by the door. Now that Max was out of the picture, Molina had no reason to hassle Temple about him anymore.

Matt had to wonder on the drive home from Molina's house how he'd been forcibly cast into the role of Hamlet: to tell or not to tell Temple.

Torn between two women, and feeling like a fool. That was a line from an old hit song Ambrosia often played on her radio show. He knew he was on the horns of an ethical dilemma, and they were usually demonic.

Molina had confided in him, and he should honor that. But she wasn't his beloved. Temple was, and she deserved to know that Max was very likely alive, even though missing. Matt couldn't help thinking she — and he — would be better off without the possibility of another Max resurrection out there somewhere.

Not that he wished Max Kinsella any ill. The guy'd led a tough but honorable and likely lonely life. Doing years of penance as a counterterrorism agent to atone for stupid teenage shenanigans turned lethal seemed pretty good payback. Way more than Max owed his cousin Sean. They'd both decided to look in on the Irish troubles in Londonderry. They'd both competed for the favors of Kathleen O'Connor. It wasn't Max's fault that he got the girl and Sean got an IRA pub bombing. The "life narrative," as the politicians called it added up to Max as a hero, though, and Matt was just a midnight talk jockey with a priestly past. He could use a break from rivaling some James Bond with Irish charisma.

To be or not to be: a good friend and an insecure lover, or an honest lover and a Judas friend? He would wait to worry about it until the dang dance competition was over, in a week.

Right now he had to face his nightly radio show, then another daylong dance rehearsal in preparation for the purgatory of a solid week of daily rehearsals and the nightly live telecast of whatever ballroom dance he pulled out of a top hat. Temple had done something like this a couple of months ago to safeguard Molina Jr., Mariah, the would-be media teen queen. If Temple could stomach portraying a Goth teenager, Matt supposed he could cut a rug or two.

Corny. Humiliating. Just like all of national network TV these days. He'd rather go on *Survivor* and eat maggots.

Torn between two left feet, and looking like a fool. . . .

Max would handle it in a cakewalk, Matt thought.

CHAPTER 4
ALPINE DO-SI-DO

"Tall, blonde?"

He nodded anxiously. His name was James McKlosky for the moment, according to the stolen credit card in his back jeans' pocket.

He was on the run from the posh Swiss private clinic just up the Alps where he was registered as Michael Randolph, although he didn't have a scrap of that identity on him. He was secretly known as Max to the older gent who'd paid to have his mangled body and mind admitted and treated there some six weeks ago.

None of this mattered because he didn't remember a thing about himself since he'd awakened in said posh clinic. Just three days ago, he'd fled an attempted assassination with the help of his psychiatrist, his tall, blond, attractive psychiatrist, an intriguing blend of French and German genes called Revienne Schneider.

While she'd delved for his missing memory, he'd found he liked her mind and various French folderols. Too bad something in him didn't trust the luck of the draw. They'd shared a rough road trip for three days, but he still wasn't sure she wasn't a planted assassin. Waking up to find her gone was maybe the gift of the morning. Too bad he didn't buy sudden disappearances, not even his own. He would find her and then find out if she was an enemy, or just a really attractive diversion.

Right now he was pretending she was his missing wife.

"She was wearing a pink suit and boots. The boots aren't pink," he added. "Just black. I missed the bus and she's probably looking for me too."

The quaint upland Swiss town hosted scads of tourists, especially during the spring and summer when the Alps were passable, so the shopkeepers spoke excellent English. This shop had the best view of the plaza. Revienne was handsome enough that she would not escape notice unless she wanted to.

He took a deep breath as the man turned to question his staff in the slightly different German the Swiss people had developed. Scents of chocolate and pipe tobacco soothed his senses, but they weren't succumbing to any of it.

Revienne could have dumped him, been kidnapped, or even be lurking nearby to assassinate him. Maybe he should let her disappearance this morning go, get the hell down off the mountain. The clinic security personnel, as in goons, were bound to be searching for him, for good or bad reasons.

They wouldn't expect a fugitive with casts on his legs to be plaster-free and this mobile already. He owed that to Revienne begging a saw to hack off the casts, and his own pre-injury muscle strength. Six weeks in painkiller and sedative limbo made a lot fuzzy, but he'd lost no muscle tone in his arms, thanks to shower-rod chin-ups on steel fixtures robust enough to hold up a bull.

Why, one had to wonder, was the clinic so industrially tricked out? Simple efficiency, or something more sinister? Torture?

"Sorry, sir." The pleasantly pudgy shopkeeper offered a sheepish smile beneath a down-turned moustache. "None of the staff has seen such a woman this morning."

"She's probably waiting for me at the next bus stop down the mountain." He returned the smile with a rueful grin and was already examining the square for other options before he was quite out the door.

The charming breakfast places with exterior tables under second-story window boxes spilling blossoming flowers had not seen hide nor hair of her. He spotted a huge German bus pulsing in the square, waiting to leave, and started concocting a tale that would get him on the tour without a ticket.

On a whim he stopped at a flower seller's cart that had just set up by the central fountain. The water splashed as vivid gold, purple, and pink flowers scented the clean mountain air. He bought a bunch of fragrant yellow freesias, thinking even as he did that they'd suit a brunette or a redhead more than a blonde. He wondered if he was buying for a woman he'd forgotten, like everything else he'd forgotten since the accident that had brought him here so far so fast from the United States.

Garry, the stranger who called himself his old friend, had said that was the place they called home. The United States. Too bad the guy hadn't left any information on where to reach him in Switzerland.

"For your sweetheart?" the woman asked.

She was an old-country grandmother in an embroidered vest she'd probably stitched herself, dirndl skirt, and peasant blouse. "Sweetheart" was a word out of an operetta, as she was.

He smiled, and poured on the charm he suspected he'd lived off for years. "You might have seen her. You have clever, bright eyes. How could you miss her? Tall, blond, in a chic suit. French."

"Ach, yes. The Frenchwoman never sheds her style. She was with you?" She eyed his new-bought jeans and hiking boots.

His heart had almost stopped to stumble across a lead.

"Can't get her away from the big-time banking position long enough to relax, not even in the mountains," he complained amiably.

She nodded, handing over the simple bouquet in exchange for some coins. He felt awkward as a schoolboy standing there, just holding it. Must not be a hearts and flowers kind of guy.

She smiled at him. "A bank job? No wonder I saw her in the back of that big black Mercedes. I'm sorry, lad, but these flowers come too late. Her driver took her down the mountain when I was coming into the square."

"How long ago?"

"Ten on your watch."

He eyed the cheap tourist model. "How big a Mercedes?"

"A Mercedes 280 SEL."

His surprise at her knowing the model, more than he dared hope for, must have showed.

She smiled and nodded again. "I know that because it was the car Princess Diana was killed in, God rest her soul."

Max frowned, trying to remember Princess Diana as dead. Trying to remember a Princess Diana for a few moments.

The crisp mountain morning air he inhaled froze in his chest. He remembered now.

The chase in Paris, the crash in the underpass. The car. Big, powerful, engineered and customized from the factory, the kind of car driven to ferry the rich, the important, the nefarious. A Mercedes 280 SEL.

This stuff he knew without hesitation.

Not just a Mercedes.

Not just a big black Mercedes.

An armored model built for security purposes, for whisking blond young women away from it all, perhaps to their deaths.

Was Revienne a prisoner, or a lovely lure drawing him farther afield into another booby trap like the one that had broken his legs and clouded his memory?

Only way to know that was to find her.

And Garry, the old man who'd mentored Max and now looked after his semi-self,

Garry must know he'd gone missing by now and be worried.

"You didn't glimpse the license plate?" Max asked.

Her crepe-shuttered eyelids fluttered with surprise.

He said quickly, "I don't know if she's been sent for by the Swiss or the Italian branch of her bank."

"ZH, Zurich, of course. Six, twelve, five-six. My eldest son was born November 6 in 1956."

Confused, he thought: 6/12/56 was June. Wait. No. Europeans put the month before the day: 12/6/56. Her son had been born on that date and year, but in the previous month.

"The Milan branch, then," he said. "The Italians are always unreliable when it comes to money and train schedules, unlike the Swiss."

She nodded, smiling at the compliment.

Max checked his cheap watch again, made not in Switzerland, but — where else? — China. He actually used his wooden cane to propel him faster toward the big bus throbbing in idle before leaving.

The doors whooshed open. He looked up the narrow steep stairs into the cornflower blue eyes of the young brunet driver.

And held out the deceptively purchased bouquet. "*Gruezi, fräulein.* For you."

She took in the flowers, his cane, his face. A tourist bus driver would know English.

"I have a bit of an embarrassing problem —"

She smiled and reached for the bouquet. Not anymore he didn't.

CHAPTER 5
MISSING IN ACTION

Carmen had left her car parked on the street instead of in the driveway or garaging it. Nobody would want to steal her aging Toyota wagon anyway.

She could afford a new family car, but who had time?

Confession was said to be good for the soul, but it just tired her out.

Matt was as easy as they come to confess to. Still, he'd been annoyingly sure that he'd been right all along and she was just now coming over to the side of truth, justice, and the Max American way.

Thinking of sides, her wounded ribs were throbbing. The stitches had dissolved finally, but they still left hot red marks at each insertion point, an irritating, long tattoo of discomfort. Infection loved to feed on shallow wounds.

She faced her own front door. A lot of lies and deception had transpired behind it since she'd been stabbed.

Morrie Alch coming and going like a loyal family friend, covering for her at the office and at home.

Mariah, God bless her heedless, egocentric teenybopper soul, had blithely accepted doing chores for a mother "sick" with a virus that gave the word *virulent* meaning. Even more convenient for her mother's hidden wound from a concealed misadventure outside the law, Mariah had remained on the go, thanks to many nonworking married neighborhood mothers who could chauffeur an extra.

They probably gossiped about her. Not about her and men. Never about men. No cause. Or wait! Was Morrie's attentive presence causing talk? He was sticking his neck out to save her job, not to covet her body, stitched up like a football as it was.

Shoot. Now, she not only had her stalker and Kinsella's stalker and her own iffy actions to worry about, but what the neighbors might think. They'd been deprived of juicy details about her private life for far too long.

Now they had Dirty Larry, too, the undercover cop, who'd paid her a visit or two at home.

Carmen sighed and made herself march up to her front door and unlock it.

A skitter of ratlike nails over kitchen tile and then a pounding on the carpeting made her almost clutch for the paddle holster at her back waistband.

Nothing. Just the two cats going squirrelly from the upset domestic routine here lately.

She turned on the lights in the living room, then in the kitchen before confronting the magnetized message board on the fridge. Right. Thursday. Night. It had been free to meet Matt because her social butterfly daughter had a . . . study date at the Lopez house. Home by — Carmen checked her watch — 8:30 P.M. By an hour ago.

She pulled out her cell phone instead of her holster and speed-dialed Cecilia Lopez.

"Hi. Mariah's mom. Yeah. Fine. Say, wasn't this supposed to break up over an hour ago?" There was a pause while Cecilia spoke. "She didn't. *I* said! No. I didn't. Yeah, I know kids this age. But if she didn't go with your Ashlee after school — yes, please. Check with your daughter."

Carmen started pacing around the end of the eating island, then into the living room. She was almost running by the time she got to Mariah's bedroom and snapped on the overhead light.

Lord, what a mess. You couldn't see a girl in here for the posters and pillows and scattered, rejected outfits. Mariah's Our Lady of Guadalupe uniform was a castaway heap of white blouse and plaid skirt and navy jacket over the desk chair. The laptop computer was open, but off.

Carmen took a deep breath, wincing as her stitches stretched. When would she get over this damn knife wound!

A voice came back on the phone. Carmen repeated each tidbit of information to lock it in her memory.

"Check with Sedona Martinez? Right. And her mother is? Yolanda. Her number is, uh-huh." She'd raced back to the kitchen to scrawl the phone number on a countertop notepad. A 270 exchange. Not this neighborhood. Sedona. Probably bused in from Henderson. Catholic schools were fashionable now. Sedona Martinez? What was next? Paris Solis? Madrid Rodriguez? Barcelona Banderas?

"Thanks," she said. "If you hear anything —"

Cecilia promised to call if she heard where Mariah might be. It was probably just a misunderstanding, she added.

Carmen hung up, thinking about the recent days that Mariah had supervised her, under Morrie's direction, more than she had kept tabs on her daughter.

Ordinarily, a missing person had to be gone twenty-four hours before the police became involved. With a child, if there was evidence of kidnapping, that rule was suspended. With her child, Carmen had to stop running wild scenarios through her head and get practical, fast.

She speed-dialed every family she or Mariah had been in touch with on her cell phone. No one knew anything, and all got those small catches of alarm in their voices. A child being even momentarily unaccounted for was everyone's nightmare.

What about that new friend? she wondered. The transfer student Mariah had taken a sudden liking to? This age fostered intense friendships followed by melodramatic splits. What was that kid's name? They had never done anything organized together, so there was no trail to follow.

She needed to know more before she alerted anybody. The house sounded ominously empty, the only noise the uneasy shift of ice in the refrigerator and any motions Carmen made herself. The cats had curled up to sleep in opposite corners of the living-room sofa, like bookends.

Carmen pushed maternal panic out of her mind and hit one last fast-dial number.

"Morrie? It's Molina. No, the stitches are

fine. It's something else. Something worse, maybe. Yeah. Under wraps for the moment. Can you bear to come over here one more time and maybe save the day? Great. I, ah, didn't ask what you were doing. Oh. This." She tried to find a smile, but couldn't. "Thanks."

"Jesus, Carmen!"

She wouldn't have called Morrie if she'd known he'd go postal.

He was pacing the small living room in the opposite direction she was. He was a Columbo sort of cop, middle-aged, rumpled, nice enough to underestimate. "You can't keep a thing like this under wraps. You think this is the secret service or something?"

"You know no one official will act until tomorrow unless there's evidence of a kidnapping or a runaway kid. And you know I've been down and out lately, with Mariah on her own more than usual."

"So you last saw her — ?"

"This morning before I went to work."

"You've been coming home for lunch for a change. *We* know you were readjusting your Ace bandage. Doesn't she come home from school for lunch?"

"Not as much anymore. We're close to the

school, but she has groups of girlfriends now. They're always working on some project in their spare time." She paused to look him in the eye. "And I skipped lunch because I had an appointment elsewhere earlier today. About Mariah."

"She getting in trouble in school?"

"No. I saw her father."

"Rafi Nadir?"

"There's any other candidate?"

"About what?"

"About his wanting a role in Mariah's life."

"Oh, Lord, you laid down the law according to Molina and he went apeshit and took her anyway."

"I'd love to put an APB out on my ex-boyfriend, Morrie, but I didn't close him down. I told him we'd work something out, as soon as I got a little time."

"And he took it how?"

"Like a lamb. We talked about old assumptions and discovered we'd had a terminal 'failure to communicate,' as the shrinks say." She smiled. "I saw and talked to Matt Devine this evening too, about Kinsella. He'd bought Temple Barr's party line that the magician was innocent of anything but protecting the innocent. After what happened in Kinsella's house five weeks ago, the stalker, I'm beginning to wonder if the people after him aren't worse than he is."

Morrie grinned. "Including you? Sounds like you've been dining on crow, lately."

"Yup. And what's my reward? My kid goes AWOL. Anything about her strike you, Morrie? I've been pretty out of it these last five weeks or so."

"She was a good kid. Did what I asked, right away. Ready to be tearing off back to school, of course."

" 'Tearing off back to school?' Morrie, that's very abnormal behavior."

"I thought kids that age had energy."

"Not for going back to school. Her room's the usual tsunami victim. It doesn't look messed with by more than the resident's usual habits. Yet I don't want to go through things in there in case we need" — her voice got a bit wobbly — "evidence taken, but I think I should check the computer. I haven't since I got 'sick,' and the Internet is the root of all evil these days when it comes to kids getting into trouble."

Molina fetched two sets of latex crime scene gloves from the going-out-the-door supplies in a kitchen drawer.

"You can't think —" Morrie began.

"Anything's possible. One of the mothers I called tonight should have been able to

69

pinpoint Mariah's whereabouts. The kid wrote her destination on the fridge, as we agreed. It's door-to-door pick up and drop off. Even if Mariah fudged things, someone should have a clue."

By then they were stepping over books, and papers, and articles of clothing in Mariah's bedroom.

"I've walked into a nightmare like this before," Morrie said.

"*Blair Witch Project?*"

"My own teen daughter's bedroom, years ago."

The usual cop-shop black humor was rearing its macabre head. They'd both reverted to what gave them the distance that made efficiency possible instead of panic.

"Kids this age do tend to go a little AWOL," he commented. "Testing the limits. They get crazy ideas."

"And I haven't been paying proper attention lately." Molina brushed her thick hair back from her face, but it flopped forward again, thanks to its recent "disguise" as an actual hairdo. "You know teen girls better than I do, Morrie. Keep searching here and I'll check with the next-door neighbors. Maybe they saw something."

When she got outside, the sun was thinking about dropping completely behind the

70

mountains. The streetlights were only faintly lit, also looking like they might change their minds any minute, looking like fancy entry hall lights in better neighborhoods.

The Vargas house on the right wasn't lit inside for the evening yet. She was a nurse's aide and he drove long haul.

Molina tried the doorbell, but heard no faint interior bing or buzz inside. These old fifties' bungalows needed constant updating. So she knocked. Hard. The door cracked open on inner shadow. Slacker youngest son, the only one still at home, looked her over.

"If it ain't the lady lieutenant, all got up to go boogying."

She'd forgotten she wore her Carmen Miranda disguise. "I'll go boogying down to the city jail with you someday, you don't straighten up. Roberto, isn't it?"

He leaned against the door jamb in his low-slung baggies and gang bandana. Almost twenty-one and had never held a job. "What can I do for you?" His smirk answered his question.

"I'm looking for Mariah."

"The kid? She's gettin' kinda cute, lootenant. Still a little porky, though."

Could an adult woman punch out a lippy twenty-year-old man-boy? In her case, yes,

71

but should she?

"You look like you've been hanging at home all day." She sniffed. "Doing weed. You see anyone drive up to my place? Hear anyone, a car or van?"

"Nah. Your place is like a funeral home, usta be you had no traffic nohow. Lately been some dude coming and going at all hours, as they say on TV. Maybe the chickie baby made tracks because your new b-friends were going after her."

He was hard against the doorjamb, her fist twisted in the sleazy fabric of his T-shirt and her knee cocked to ram him in the crotch. The searing pull on her healing cut only made her madder.

"Don't mess with me, punk. I can have you up on all sorts of charges, but most of all I can have a lot more satisfaction leaving a lot of you on this door frame. Did you see or hear any vehicles coming and going at my address today, or not?"

"Not."

She started to relax her grip.

"Bitch."

Before she could ram and slam further, someone pulled her back.

" 'Buzz-E' bad boy Vargas," Dirty Larry said. "The lieutenant doesn't know the half of what you could be put away for, including dustups in Aryan Brotherhood and Crips and Bloods land, but I do. Be a good *niño* and go suck on cannabis until you're in a coma."

"I ain't queer!"

Larry's chuckle was sinister, an older, wiser man's threat. "You don't wanna be, stay out of federal prison and shut up if you don't have any news to offer."

He pushed the punk back into the dark house and slammed the door shut on him.

Molina was fuming. "What are you doing here? I was handling it."

Dirty Larry was chuckling again, this time admiringly. "A bit too much. You can practice your more aggressive moves on me sometime, if you want."

He was called Dirty Larry because he worked undercover. He'd shoved his way into her life on his street cred and a certain sexy interest she didn't trust and wasn't even sure she was interested in.

"Why are you here?" she demanded.

"I was concerned about the LVMPD Iron Maiden being out sick and then sick on the job for so long. You don't look ill, though. You look hot tonight. Now wonder you got scumbag sass."

Walking back to her driveway, where Morrie's hybrid Honda Civic sat uneasily next to Larry's restored gas guzzler, a seventies Chevy Impala, he reached out to snap one of her big gold hoop earrings with his thumb and forefinger.

"You look like a Gypsy queen about to read tarot cards. Been on a date, Carmen?"

"Godammit, Larry! My daughter is missing. I don't give a shit about your issues or inferences."

His mocking attitude dropped like a john's pants in north Las Vegas.

"Mariah gone? That's bad stuff. Sorry. What can I do?"

She looked around, thinking. By then they were at her front door.

"Morrie's going over her room for any clues. Go and hassle my neighbors. You seem to be good at it. Mariah was supposed to be picked up at four for a group study pizza dinner, but the mother-chauffeur says the pick up was called off."

"By Mariah?"

"By her daughter, who said Mariah was going to another girl's house instead. I called there. They had no idea on that end about anything, mother or daughter."

"Hate to say it. Kid pulled a fastie."

"I don't care what she did, I want her found and back."

"Hey." His arm braced her shoulders. "It's

probably a stupid prank. I'll pull fingernails all over the block to see if anybody saw anything."

"They're neighbors. Good people. With the occasional delinquent kid. Just ask."

"Yeah. You go help Alch. He's a thorough guy. I'll cover the waterfront."

She smiled weakly. "Thanks."

"Working undercover, I see a lot of runaways. Your kid is not one of them. Trust me."

She nodded.

No, she didn't trust him. Couldn't. Mariah was gone, and anybody fresh to their lives, Mariah's or her own, was suspect. After all, a stalker had been loose in their house, several times. She'd been so sure who that was. . . .

Suddenly, what she thought or didn't think about Max Kinsella and his disappearing act was irrelevant, immaterial, and a damned, delusive waste of time.

CHAPTER 6
LOST IN CYBERSPACE

Seeing Morris Alch's iron-gray head bent over a laptop computer on a kiddie-size desk while his hands two-fingered their way across the keyboard was an oddly reassuring sight.

He looked up as Molina entered the bedroom, his face craggy in the unflattering light of a small desk lamp.

"Nothing in the room, though your daughter has the drugstore makeup concession knocked."

"I only allow her some lip gloss."

"Yeah, well, that's not hip with the tween set these days. Who knows where those allowances are going, huh? Anything missing from the room besides Mariah?"

"Who could tell in this mess? There's her school backpack, but she wouldn't take that. Cell phone! It'd be on the bed table . . . no. Otherwise, on the desk."

"Pretty soon folks will have their cell

phones implanted. Nope. Not here. Her absence is voluntary, then. You know how to navigate this Web world? Good thing we all have to use computers on the job these days. Keeps our kids from shutting us out as much as they'd like."

"What've you found?"

"Sometimes it's a good thing the Internet is as intrusive as it is. Kids think they know it all but they're no match for Internet crooks and don't know beans about how to erase an Ethernet trail. I'm in the history segment on recent URLs, and your daughter has visited some *veeery interesssting* sites."

She stared at him.

"Sorry. I'm old enough to have seen that *Laugh-In* catchphrase on TV as a kid. I think if Mariah's gone, it's on her own recognizance, Carmen. That's good. Not great, but good."

"What do you mean?" She dropped on her knees beside his chair, eyeballing the computer screen.

"Britney. Miley. She's bookmarked every pop tart teen singer site there is. And *American Idol,* and the site for the Teen Queen reality TV show she competed on. They have mini-movies you can play. Shows her along with all the other contestants. The finals. Her singing that Broadway song. She's good. Better than the winner. She's a mini-star on this thing."

Molina grabbed the keyboard. "I monitor this devil's workshop. I have the V-chip, for God's sake."

"You've been sick, remember?" Morrie said. "Give yourself a break. The sites she went to are just pop culture, entertainment news. The kid's a wanna-be, a groupie. She's probably skipped out to attend some idol's concert."

Molina frowned at the screen. "It's his fault."

"Whose?

"My ex's. Rafi Nadir. He encouraged me in a singing career, but I was an adult. She's just a kid."

"Wait. *You* had a singing career?"

She shook her head. Her usually subdued hair whipped her cheeks. Annoying.

"Amateur night only. I, ah, still sit in at a local club from time to time. Nobody knows my day job. It's a hobby. And it wasn't meant to be a role model thing for my ditsy teen daughter."

Morrie frowned at her. At her hoop earrings and dark forties lipstick, borrowed from her torch singer persona, Carmen. "Is that what the way you look tonight is about?

She echoed his words, "the way you look

78

tonight" in a velvet croon. "Yeah. I moon-light as a chanteuse, but not looking exactly like this. This is a disguise I used to meet with a . . . source."

"A snitch?"

Calling Matt Devine a snitch was hilarious.

"No, Morrie, something more, uh, personal. My life is way more complicated than you think."

"I always thought you were complicated."

"That bad?"

"Bad in a good way. So you think this Nadir guy was going behind your back, encouraging Mariah in her *American Idol* fantasy?"

"He was 'coincidentally' on site at the Teen Queen reality TV show. Yeah, he ran into her. Call it karma. He saw me there with Dirty Larry. That would warn off any guy."

Morrie made a face. "I saw you there with Dirty Larry too. What's that all about?"

"Can't a woman have a social life?"

"Dirty Larry isn't a social life; he's a low-life. You don't need someone like him."

"Maybe not. Maybe he's a suspect too."

Morrie looked at her hard.

"He initiated the contact," she said, "and I needed someone to do some undercover, off-the-meter work for me."

"Chasing poor Miss Temple Barr's magician boyfriend?"

"Kinsella was a prime suspect for the Goliath Hotel murder a couple of years ago."

"Not for the department."

She shrugged. "Larry's canvassing the neighbors, so he might be back any minute."

"Right." Morrie turned back to the screen. "Mariah's got herself posted online too."

"MySpace?"

"Naw, nothing notable. Just this one site you and I never heard of, teenqueendream scream.com."

It came up, featuring primped and posed young girls, made up like movie stars.

"That's *Mariah?*"

Molina stared at the image of a baby-faced young girl in glitter eye shadow and lip gloss.

"The kids post their photos and bios themselves. The site owner is a local DJ. Visitors vote on who's most likely to make it big-time."

"Oh, my God. You see what that bastard Nadir encouraged my kid to do."

"His kid too."

"My kid all along. He was there at the Teen Queen show as security. He didn't know who the hell she was, but he seduced her anyway with the idea of using her voice, like a talent was something the world would welcome. It doesn't. And the path there is ugly. You know that, Morrie."

"I don't think whatever way they connected at the Teen Queen house was enough to send Mariah over the fence. I really don't. Carmen, you don't need villains here. You need to understand that Mariah sees a world where kids her age can live a dream. She has a dream. And talent."

"I know that, Morrie. I fear that. I just hope her dream isn't a nightmare.'

Morrie looked around to see if Dirty Larry had come back yet.

"One more thing, Carmen. Here's the most popular outtake on that Teen Queen Reality TV show site. Six hundred and sixty thousand-some visitors. It's not your daughter who's the pop tart hit of the site. It's this little number."

He'd brought up a small podcast screen and hit the play button.

An animated figure with punk blond hair and a wild outfit was dancing and rapping in the TV show's final competition. She hadn't even placed in the finals, but Molina could place that particular piece of tiny trouble in a Las Vegas minute.

It was Zoe Chloe Ozone, the phony teen

persona Temple Barr had created when a certain homicide lieutenant had pressured her to go undercover to protect her contestant daughter, Mariah, from a possible stalker.

The thirty-year-old PR woman, current Matt Devine fiancée, and ex–Max Kinsella squeeze was an Internet pop tart sensation and didn't even know it.

CHAPTER 7
DUTY CALL

Thanks to modern conveniences, a ringing cell phone had interrupted opera audiences, churchgoers, classrooms, and bedroom intimacies.

"Damn, I should have turned that thing off," Temple complained. At least she had never programmed some dopey ringtone, like the "William Tell Overture," theme song of the *Lone Ranger.*

"*It*'s the turnoff," Matt pointed out as he watched his half-dressed fiancée scramble barefoot across her wooden parquet bedroom floor to the dresser. Coming home to Temple after being in the noisy restaurant with Molina was a nice contrast. He'd promised to keep Molina's problem quiet, even though the restored condition of Max's house was troubling.

Still, Matt could lie back virtuously, knowing he'd thought to turn off *his* cell phone. Of course, almost nobody called him.

Temple's PR job required her being eternally reachable, like a doctor, in case things went wrong. Matt checked his watch: 10:30 P.M. He had to leave for work in an hour, tops.

"Yes?" Temple was saying, looking puzzled. "Gone? Surely you can't think Crawford — Doing? Uh —" She rolled her eyes at Matt. "Nothing. *Now.* Yeah. Right away. I hope it turns out to be a false alarm."

She snapped the tiny slave driver shut. "Molina's kid is missing."

Matt sat up, collecting clothes. "Mariah? No! How long?"

"This evening sometime. Wasn't at the other kid's house where she was supposed to be."

"What have you got to do with this? You and Molina get along like cobra and mongoose."

"Molina wants to talk to Crawford Buchanan ASAP and needs someone who can find the vermin."

"Awful Crawford, the DJ-publicist guy?"

"Yeah, your so-not-serious competition for Las Vegas listeners." Temple was pulling on her knit jogging outfit. "I need to check his show times, and maybe check in with his much-abused insignificant other. Molina said something about the Internet and Mariah and the Crawf's juvenile delinquent stepdaughter, Quincey, being online together. She didn't make a lot of sense for Molina, so I'm guessing the kid is in trouble. I sorta bonded with Mariah at the Teen Queen reality TV house. I'd hop to it for Mariah before I'd toss her mother a stale fortune cookie."

"I know that, next to Molina, he's one of your least favorite people, so what does Crawford Buchanan have to do with Mariah?"

"He was pretending to cover that Teen Queen reality TV show she was competing on."

"Molina roped you into going undercover on that to protect Mariah and you did a great job. Why does she need you so urgently now? That show is old news."

"Maybe not," Temple said. "She said Zoe Chloe Ozone had damn well get her ass in gear and over to her place. You know where it is, Oh Swami of the Desert Nighttime Airwaves? I've never seen her house and she didn't give me a clue."

"Yeah. It's near Our Lady of Guadalupe Church. You've been at the church, at least. To mass. With me." He flashed her a remembering grin. "Whoever thought then we'd be thinking of getting married someday?" Actually, *he* had. "May I add OLG to the possible site list?"

Temple paused in jamming her bare feet into a pair of low platform slides. He could tell she really wanted to stay and finish what they'd started.

"Yeah. Good idea. I guess we should thank Molina for that one." She took a breath. "I know how I'd feel if Louie was missing, so I imagine a kid must be triple that."

"At least. There are so many predators nowadays."

"Why the Crawf?" she fussed. "Oh, well, mine not to question why. Mine to round up the miserable skunk and bring him to —" She snatched the address Matt had just written on a notepad on one bedside table. "Chez Molina, of all places."

"Molina's opening her home to creeps like Buchanan now? I hope it's not serious," he said, sounding exactly that.

"Molina's not usually the panicky type."

"Molina hasn't been too usual lately," Matt noted.

"Aha! You get that feeling too? I can see I'll have to interrogate you further after we do our respective jobs tonight. Wanna bet I'll be ringing your doorbell upstairs around 3:00 A.M. demanding answers?"

"I'll be breathlessly awaiting any and all of your demands," Matt promised with a warm glance.

"Darn right," she said. "Lock my door when you leave."

Temple tuned in the Crawf's local twenty-four-hour talk radio station as soon as she whipped her red Miata out of the Circle Ritz parking lot. Las Vegas was just getting cooking at 10:30 at night, rather like her and Matt.

Somewhere far down on her cell phone call list she had the number of Buchanan's long-suffering girlfriend, Merle. First she'd try the station. Luckily, this was Las Vegas and someone would cover the switchboard 24/7.

"Hi," she said as the phone was answered. "This is Temple Barr. I need to reach Crawford Buchanan —"

"This is not the public call-in line."

Temple could hear the blur of the radio show broadcasting in the background.

"I know that. First off, I'm not the public," she said. "I'm Temple Barr, local PR rep for the Crystal Phoenix, now acting for Lieutenant Molina of the Las Vegas Metropolitan Police Department, aka the LVMPD. She urgently needs to contact Crawford Bu-

chanan. Since I know the media in this city
—"

There was a pause. Then the receptionist's voice blathered excitedly.

"Oh," Temple finally got in. "You read about my aunt's wedding at the Crystal Phoenix. Yes, it was 'some posh do' . . . yes, the Fontana brothers are the most eligible bachelors in town . . . ah, yes, the remaining eight are still 'available.' I'm sure something could be arranged if I can get Buchanan's contact number ASAP. Okay. I'll hang tight."

Temple set the shut phone on the car's central console, shrugging.

It appeared the Fontana brothers were a far more potent force in Las Vegas than a homicide lieutenant. Luckily, Temple was related to them by marriage now. Surely she could con one to help out a good cause by escorting a local lady for an evening. Maybe Ralph, who was girlfriendless at the moment, for rather sad reasons involving the chicken ranch murder case they'd all been roped into recently. If a child's ingratitude was sharper than a serpent's tooth a girlfriend gone bad ranked right up there too.

Temple's cell phone rang seven minutes later. She whipped the steering wheel abruptly right into an empty strip center parking lot. She didn't dare talk to Crawford Buchanan while driving. He made her resort to wild hand gestures at the drop of a consonant.

"You rang, T.B.?" The smarmy radio baritone oozed into her left ear like cold cod liver oil.

Temple again thanked her fates that he'd never learned her middle name was her aunt Kit's given name, and even she never used it: Ursula. That would make Temple's initials T.U.B. and Awful Crawford Buchanan would never let her hear the end of *that!*

"Right here, CB," she shot back.

"And where is that this time of night, *hmm?*"

The next thing he'd be asking was what she was wearing. Kevlar!

"In front of a Dunkin' Donuts store, en route to where you'll be heading."

"We're having a rendezvous?"

"Not my idea. Lieutenant C. R. Molina wants to see you pronto, at her house." She gave the address.

"*Euw.* Not my party hearty part of town."

"Yeah, you're so uptown. I wouldn't dis the neighborhood or irritate Molina in any way. Her teen daughter is missing and she thinks you know something about it."

"Me?" The oily baritone had risen to a squeak. Inside every self-aggrandizing social barracuda is a field mouse.

"You."

"Is this about that reality TV Teen Queen show?"

"I don't know. Mariah did compete in that."

"I remember her. The *Ugly Betty* chub who belted out that song from *Wicked*."

"You'll get a belt from Molina if you refer to her kid like that. And you're just jealous that your stepdaughter, Quincey, didn't even get on that show. What's Quincey doing now, anyway?"

"She's got a waitress job and is a ring girl at the local fights."

"What about college?"

"Her mother goes on about that, but she might as well use her looks while she's got 'em."

"She's what, seventeen, and you think her 'looks' are fading?"

"Face it. The race today is to the super young. There are great opportunities out there for smart kids with ambition. Even Molina, Jr. The younger the better."

"You sound like a pedophile."

"Me? I'm just a promoter."

"Same difference, sometimes, given the

public crashes of all the pop tarts recently. See you at the lieutenant's house."

Temple had to end the conversation to consult the directions to Molina's house and get on the road again. Too freaking bad.

She also had to weave through dark residential streets, vaguely recognizing the modest bungalows that surrounded Our Lady of Guadalupe Church.

Squinting at curbside numbers in the dark, she finally slid the Miata to a stop in front of a house with three cars already parked there, two in the driveway and one in the street, none of them marked police cruisers.

A boxy orange Hummer H3 pulled up behind her. Temple expected the Beach Boys or Leo DiCaprio and posse to pour out of it, but Crawford Buchanan did instead.

"Our cars really clash," he noted, smoothing back his gelled black-and-silver hair as he eyed her red Miata.

"Thank goodness."

"Come on, be a pal." He took her arm, which she jerked away, as they went up the front walk. "You don't want to make me look bad in front of the fuzz, do you?"

Temple was more concerned about her first visit to the Molina home than Crawford's state of comfort.

Matt had been here more than once, she knew. She'd wondered if Molina was as utterly uninterested in men — in Matt — as it appeared. A police lieutenant could afford something more suburban, Temple was sure. Maybe the location was all for Mariah's nearby Catholic school.

Catholics were consistent in their faith and Temple admired that, not that a fallen-away Unitarian would or could convert to a high-maintenance church, whatever the denomination. She mentally slapped herself for relating everything these days to her relationship with Matt.

Better look and think sharp. This was a serious situation, even if she had arrived with the terminally unserious Crawford Buchanan. At least she had stood and delivered him as requested. Molina had to respect that.

Well, no, she didn't.

Morrie Alch opened the door when she knocked. Ringing the bell might have startled the already stressed-out residents. His thick, steel-gray hair looked grayer and so did his face.

"Come in," he said. "This Buchanan?"

The rat in question answered for itself. "Crawford Buchanan, bro, main man about town. You may have heard my On-the-Go radio spots. Everything hip that's happenin'."

Morrie looked at Temple. "Molina wants to see you down the hall, kid's room, right away. "You come talk to me, Mr. Hipster."

"Everybody calls me 'Crawford.' "

Alch made a face, then nodded Temple down the hall.

"Now, Crawford, let's say we have a little talk," Alch said as he gestured the Crawf to a furniture barn sofa occupied by the bony, dirty blond-haired guy Temple had seen with Molina at the teen house. He looked sexy-tough in a military or reform-school way, she couldn't decide which. Is this what Molina was seeing these days? Huh. He was no Matt or Max.

Meanwhile, Alch was whispering sour nothings into her ear. "It's too early to tell if Mariah just stayed late at the mall, but this is serious stuff we've found on her computer."

"Didn't Molina monitor — ?"

"You bet, but she's been real sick lately, and, uh, distracted."

Temple let her face show shock. They didn't call Molina the Iron Maiden of the LVMPD because she took sick days.

"No kidding." Alch stopped in the hall to

address the gravity of the situation. "Real sick. This is coming at a rotten time. Bear that in mind and pretend you're the little drummer girl, ready to march where needed."

"So that's why she didn't show up at the Crystal Phoenix dinner a few weeks ago, other than my crime-solving skills getting public applause."

"I think you won that one. Now, she needs you."

"Me. Again? Aw, shoot, Morrie, my life's a lot more complicated now."

"You have a significant other missing in action?" He sounded vaguely parentally accusing.

He meant, Mariah, of course. A child.

Still, his words slid a hot knife of regret into her gut. *Did* she have a *former* significant other missing in action? Only recently an ex. Funny that the recent past could feel so raw. Max, even missing, could take care of himself, if he wasn't dead. Not knowing why or where he had vanished would always haunt her but she would never regret having opened herself to Matt's love.

Temple nodded at Alch. Now was no time to ramp up the rancor between her and Molina. Mariah was a naïve kid, and her mother must be kicking herself for being sick just when it was most damaging.

Or had Mariah taken advantage of her mother being sick? Kids today could be scary in their media-encouraged ambitions.

CHAPTER 8
POLICE PREMISES

You do not call a roommate of Midnight Louie out in the dark of night without a bodyguard of the feline persuasion walking right in her high-heeled footsteps.

Dirty Larry may take pride in invisibly fitting in with the lowlifes he spies upon, but I can slip invisibly into the dark backseat floors of almost any automotive model made in America and Europe and Asia these days.

Still, I am glad not to be on the move for now.

I am familiar with the environs of Our Lady of Guadalupe Church and School. There is a nearby convent occupied by several elderly nuns and a pair of stray cats named Peter and Paul. They were involved in a very early case of ours, my Miss Temple and me.

I was even present when I saw the striped Molina house cats adopted at the church animal blessing ceremony. That rite must have worked because I have been a blessing to crime-solving ever since.

So I have insinuated myself into the assembly, first outside Miss Mariah Molina's bedroom window, under which I scent enough smells to confuse a bloodhound. Secondly, I slink through the front door when Detective Alch had returned from getting something from his parked car. Nobody much bothers to look from faces to footwear, especially when all and sundry are under stress, so I am usually able to toe-dance inside unnoticed alongside trouser legs and Mr. Morrie is an aficionado of dark suits despite the climate. It helps that there are already cats in the house.

You would think a big, handsome guy like myself would not be so easy to overlook, but everyone's emotions are ratcheted tighter than a tourniquet and we poor domestic slaves are too low on the literal household totem pole to be much noticed at such times.

That is how I am able to pin the tiger-stripe females, Tabitha and Catarina, behind the sofa and wring them out like furry sponges of all the info they have.

It is a good thing I can speak to the animal kingdom. Homo sapiens habitually knows not much to speak of in these cases involving their headstrong young.

With a few well-chosen chirps, hisses, and paw signs, the tiger girls fill me in. This, of course, takes sharp questions on my part to prod a picture of recent events out of them, but I will not bore you with every little chit and chat and physical pantomime.

Here is their story, and I find it as fascinating as Mr. Scott finds a misbehaving *Enterprise* warp drive:

Mama Molina has been laid out with a midnight scrap injury, but this is being kept secret for some reason. Mr. Morrie Alch, one of the visiting toms, has been tending her. The sole surviving kit, Miss Mariah Molina, has been acting strange lately. She has ignored her delightful feline companions to hole up in her hideaway and smear strange-smelling potions on her face. She is also hypnotized by the one-eyed monster screen in her bedroom and spends most of her time in front of the litter-making shiny silver wall on her bedroom closet door . . .

It takes me a while to realize the tiger girls have never heard the word *mirror* and do not understand that their double reflection in same is not a glimpse of lost littermates living in the walls.

These domestic slaves are kept frightfully ignorant of things the lowliest alley cat has figured out by the age of three months. You learn fast to avoid being startled by your own reflection and save the panic and paranoia for encountering a real threat.

The resident Miss has also been cuddling up to her smooth shiny tiny kitten that she coos to and tickles endlessly on the tummy, instead of doing same to her loyal and loving resident felines.

Okay. The tiger girls have never tumbled to the names of such modern inventions and curses as the iPod and cell phone. I enlighten them.

Further, they say, there have been strange comings and goings in the house for several weeks when the occupants are away. They wonder if the lady of the house has hired a cleaning service and know to stay curled up, noses in tails, when these individuals come in.

I do not like this one tiny bit, but what can I do when the resident cats are so naïve and keep their eyes and ears to themselves? There is something to be said for the School of Hard Knocks, of which I am a magna cum laude graduate.

Osama bin Laden could hide out at Chez Molina and go unheralded and unmolested if it were up to these striped feline couch spuds.

CHAPTER 9
TWINKLE, TWINKLE, LITTLE STAR

"Welcome to my little corner of MTV hell," Molina said as Temple stepped into the bedroom. "Is it possible you're still young enough to understand these teenagers nowadays?"

"Not really. I just look like I am. It's one of my greatest crosses to bear."

" 'Crosses to bear'? You get that talk from our favorite radio talk-show host?"

"Guilty."

"Aren't we all? I want you to sit down and look at this Web site I found bookmarked on Mariah's computer."

Temple did as instructed, noting Molina's waxen, taut features under the atypical makeup. That didn't get there in one night of panic about her missing daughter. She had been sick, very sick. And then this. Temple was ambushed by a pang of sympathy.

A click revealed Crawford's smirking face.

His dark hair with the silver froth at the neck had been pompadoured for the photo, giving him a shocking resemblance to Dick Clark, prestroke.

"Euw," Temple couldn't help muttering.

Molina literally hung over her, a hand on the back of her chair and another on the desktop. "My reaction exactly. Tell me he's a harmless little worm."

"Mostly. He's a hustler when it comes to drumming up buzz for his PR business, and an old-style sexist, of course."

"What do you mean by 'old style'?"

"Harmless but annoying. Treating women with a wink and a nod, thinking he's so suave."

"His private life?"

"The usual mousy girlfriend. His step-daughter is a heller, just barely the right side of being a candidate for juvie hall through high school. She has a yen to be a star."

"Don't they all nowadays. Damn *American Idol*!"

"You sing. Wouldn't you have taken a shot if it had been around when you were young?"

"I was never young," Molina said acidly.

Temple believed her, but wondered why that was so.

"What do you think of this 'teen starlet' site he has going?" Molina pushed.

Temple clicked on the interior pages, then checked out the mini-movies and the visitor stats at the bottom of the homepage.

"It's cheesy," she said, "but it's hitting a nerve by tracking all the auditions and contestants for these national reality TV shows. The writers' strike a couple years ago was a bonanza for reality TV shows new and old. Cheap to produce, with free 'talent.' This site is a Dream Machine for every wanna-be kid out there, with Buchanan pretending he can be the wish-granting genie. You think this is what lured Mariah away?"

"If she's been lured, which I hope not, given the alternatives. It's a pedophile's dream site, isn't it?"

"Maybe not. The girls and boys who posted photo bios here seem pretty sophisticated about selling themselves and their talents. Predators like greener pastures, as in naïve, don't you think?"

"What makes you an expert?"

"You asked me here? Look. I have to keep up on pop culture trends in my business. I've got a brain. I used to report for the TV news. Kids, especially girls, are being pushed into premature speculations about their futures, their chances of being something special. I wonder where the kidhood has gone these days when JonBenét Ramsey looks more like a pioneer than a sad miniature imposter of a grown-up girl."

"She was killed more than a decade ago and her murderer was never found."

Temple bit her lip.

"Here." Molina reached past her to click the mouse a couple of times.

Mariah's face gazed up from a homemade glamour photo–style shot that was more laughable than alluring.

Temple sat back. "Ah. Reminds me of the time my best friend Amy and I took our own secret 'portfolio photos.' Nothing digital then. We had to have them developed on the sly and hide the snapshots."

"All girls do this?"

"You didn't? You're a performer, for heaven's sake, and a hell of a good one."

A flush of color made the unheard-of cosmetic blusher on Molina's olive-toned cheeks look downright feverish and her blue eyes absolutely electric. The woman should wear a little cream blush, at least after working hours. Or maybe she didn't have any of those.

"I didn't perform at that young an age, except in the school choir."

"What I'm saying is that Mariah may look a little dopey, but this star thing is nothing any girl her age doesn't dream of, or try nowadays."

"For the big bad world to see?"

"That's a danger. Kids being normal can be used and taken advantage of. Girls just want to have fun, but not every one is as sophisticated as Cyndi Lauper." Temple eyed the site. "You think Mariah is out there chasing these auditions? There's one in Arizona this weekend. Would she really run off and do this?"

"I'd say no, but she wasn't unaccounted for then. There's something else I want to show you."

Molina grimly manipulated the mouse to another site, the Teen Queen house.

"The show Mariah and I crashed," Temple noted. "I didn't know they still had a site up."

"And how."

A few clicks brought up the mini-screen of an online podcast.

After a minute or so, Temple explored the site further, and gasped. A whole three Web pages on little her.

She could watch herself as Zoe Chloe Ozone being interviewed by judges, acting out, rapping out her number, doing the

Gidget-gone-Goth-girl act she'd used to go undercover on the reality TV show.

Molina clicked farther down before Temple had time to enjoy her fifteen minutes of fake fame.

The cursor blinked on the stat logo at the page's bottom.

"Six hundred and sixty-five thousand hits? Since a few weeks ago?"

"You're a star," Molina said, deadpan. "And you're going out into the unreal world again to meet your rabid fans while you look for my daughter in this nutsy subculture before some murderous freak finds her."

"You can't make me."

"Oh, I probably can, but I think you'll want to do it. This is serious. I'll provide protection, you'll get a hell of story out of it for whatever, your PR business, your ego, your eagerness to make the world right for fools and dreamers and thirteen-year-old kids who need a friend."

"Mariah's absence is probably just a kiddish misadventure. You'll find her safe and really sorry at some regional mall where she got brushed off."

"Good. That's the best-case scenario."

"And the worst?"

"That the worst will find her before we do."

We.

Temple got it. Zoe Chloe Ozone, unintended hottie Internet freak, could go anywhere on- and off-line, and snoop.

"The black wig, again?"

"Blond never did it for Zoe. She lost the competition's final performance as a blonde. Black is the best disguise."

Temple absorbed all the bad news. Given the prominence of teen and preteen female pop stars, it was only natural that talented kids like Mariah would want to try it. Back in the film industry's silent days, pretty girls as young as fourteen flocked to Hollywood, snagging adult roles. Many had their mothers, as stage-happy as their daughters, along as managers.

Temple studied Molina, grim, hollow-eyed, strained. She'd obviously been ill, and now this. Of course, a starstruck girl would hardly want even a healthy police lieutenant as an accomplice. Mother and daughter's common singing talent was working to separate, rather than unite, them. That was a pity. Or . . . could it ultimately carve out some common ground?

Would Matt want his fresh new fiancée reviving this oddball persona? Why not? He sympathized with single mother Molina and knew Temple had a nose for the nefarious.

"I'm between freelance assignments," Temple said. "What do Zoe and me do first?"

"First, *I* squeeze Crawford Buchanan of any iota of information the creep might have."

"That sounds . . . rewarding."

"It better be. An interrogation room is the place for it but we have no time. Alch has softened him up by now, so a tough impromptu grilling here should do the job."

"The Crawf and all his works do need explaining." Temple smiled to picture him on the receiving end of a Mad Mama Molina grilling.

Mariah's absence was troubling, but probably a harmless kiddie prank that would resolve quickly. Watching Crawford Buchanan's slimy soles being put to the fire before the happy ending? Priceless.

CHAPTER 10
GRILLED CRAWFISH

"Lieutenant," Buchanan whined, "I'm just a local media personality. Ask anyone around town. I'm a pussycat."

Molina studied the man sitting in Mariah's desk chair. He resembled a pretentiously hip wolverine. He was just this side of greasy, one of those small, dandyish men blessed with huge egos and an old-time radio actor's deep voice.

"Aren't pussycats predators?" she asked.

"Me?" For an instant he became a mouse. "No, sir! I mean, ma'am. I'm an impresario. I give these kids a chance to sing on my radio show. Do a two-minute routine: 'Vegas Voices of Tomorrow.' It's going to lure *American Idol* out here next season. Paula, Simon, Kara, the black guy. Our local talent will be presold."

"You have more than a radio show. You have a Web site." Molina hadn't sat. She liked to loom. She bent to activate the mouse roller ball. Mariah's computer flat-screen flashed open on Buchanan's Teen Queen Dream 'n' Scream site. "Looks a lot like you're selling teen girl pinup photos."

Molina was clicking through photo after photo of kids who'd gotten themselves up to look like Miley Cyrus or Britney Spears before she became Britney Bombed-out. She paused the cursor on one eager young chipmunk face highlighted with glitter makeup.

"This one is my daughter. My way, way underage daughter. How'd she get her photo on your site?"

"Uploaded it. And . . . and lied about her age." He swallowed hard.

"You're saying my daughter is a liar?"

"I'm saying she knows how to spin a ré-sumé. They all do it, add a few years. If you wait until you're eighteen on a singing or acting career nowadays, you're Methuse-lah."

"Why are you running this site?" Molina asked.

"That's the site motto. See? Teen Queen Candy-dates. Tomorrow's Stars Today."

"You do this for free?"

"No, the site costs something. The girls pay a small fee to be featured."

"How small?"

"Uh, just one-fifty."

"One hundred and fifty dollars? Where'd these kids get that kind of money?"

"Usually their parents. Every mom's a stage mother these days."

"Not this mother."

That shut him up for a few precious seconds.

"I'm a DJ," he said. "I also cover Las Vegas attractions, pop culture. I can't help running across new talent. There are reputable agents in L.A., Phoenix, Seattle, Denver, the whole Left Coast, who check with me on fresh talent here in Vegas. In the old days, a young talent had nowhere to go but nowhere."

Molina straightened. Her back ached, as well as her side. Nowadays, at her age, it numbed her rear to perch on a stool at the Blue Dahlia to sing the oldies. She was a never-was who fiddled around sometimes. The creep had a point about ultra-early starts. That didn't mean wanna-be performers weren't targeted by predators.

"The Web is cheap, accessible," Crawford was saying. "These auditions are legitimate. All the major media want fresh talent. Network talent shows, cable TV, the networks, movies. An ordinary person could be king, or queen. The wanna-bes may have more of a chance than ever before but they still need a platform and a facilitator. That's what I do."

"You're the next Dick Clark."

Crawford Buchanan ran a neat manicured hand through the froth of silver curls at his nape. Even wolverines preened. She supposed someone found them cuddly and cute.

"Yeah," he said. "I'm a matchmaker between the average kid with superior talent and the big, bad world out there."

"Then where is my kid?"

His narrow shoulders sagged as he realized that one of his online protégés who was following her star was a police person's missing daughter. "She's a good little trouper with a nice big voice, if I remember rightly."

"You'd better remember damn rightly, Buchanan, because you are going to be my guide into the girls-gone-glitzy world. Where would she have gone to further her so-called career?"

He grimaced. "L.A., maybe? There's an all-talent, mega-audition next weekend. Singing, dance, acting, the whole ball of media stardom. Winners of other regional auditions can pile up points competing with another area's pool of wanna-bes."

"*Next* weekend? What's she going to live on? Who's she going to depend on?"

"They're, uh, real go-getters, these kids. Great at improv. Hang out with each other, get tips."

"So do street kids. Do you have any idea how many parents would like a piece of your smarmy, sorry ass? That's not including the jailhouse rodeo riders you'll be meeting in stir."

His face went as white as the silly froth of curls at his nape. "Oh, Lieutenant, sir, I will do anything I can to cooperate. I have, uh, local references."

"Like, uh, what? Who?"

"Uh. Temple Barr, right here in your house." He nodded to the hall. "Yeah. Lead PR lady around town. She can vouch for me. Knows I've been getting sweet personal appearances for my stepdaughter — well, it's not official with her mother, but kinda stepdaughter — Quincey. She played Priscilla at the Elvis tribute impersonator event at the Kingdome not too long ago. Quincey is a boxing ring girl at Caesar's and getting some real good leads out of that."

"And the original Priscilla was not a rock star's underage child plaything?"

"No, sir. No, ma'am! It was olden days, but the King did it right. Besides, he was from a rural culture, like Jerry Lee Lewis, and they married young girls young then. Not your daughter, of course! She is purely a commercial property at this stage. I mean, too valuable to mess with. These girls get on *Excess Hollywood,* for God's sake. Quincey would give her scheduled boob job for a chance like Mariah's getting. *Ouch!* What the hell was that for?"

Molina had slapped the back of his head in farewell, *NCIS* TV show style, which she hated but which seemed the only appropriate reaction to a cad who would pimp out his teen "sorta" stepdaughter as a boxing ring girl.

She plucked him up by the scruff of his sport coat collar and steered him out of Mariah's room, pleased she hadn't plastered him against one wall and cut off the air to his sleazy wolverine windpipe. But no doubt she was being unfair to wolverines.

CHAPTER 11
WOLVERINE DREAMS

Molina walked Buchanan into the hall, slammed him against the wall, and told him to "Stay."

In the living room, Morrie Alch was waiting with Temple Barr, who'd been disappointed not to sit in on the interrogation. Did that woman have any boundaries? Probably not, which was why she was just the girl for this undercover job.

Molina spoke first. "I'm getting the germ of an idea to go undercover and track Mariah down, but nobody is going to like it, including me.

"Alch, I want your mouth shut on everything for now. Tell command I've had a relapse. Pneumonia, but I refuse to go to a hospital. The Iron Maiden strikes again. Infectious. Home nursing care."

"Can't I help besides a cover story?"

"You've done enough. Keep it shut and I'll be forever grateful, if maybe not useful to your career."

"Barr." She eyed Temple as sternly as an underling, and sighed. "You'll be doing your Zoe Floozy Ozone routine. Get your gear and act together. I'll be at your Circle Ritz place in about four hours and I won't be in a good mood. We may have to drive all over that audition map on the weasel's Web site, L.A., Albuquerque, Flagstaff, so take a week's worth of stuff along, including your cell phone, laptop, and Elvira, Mistress of the Dark, black wig. And the usual chutzpah."

"That's it? That's all I know?"

"You'll be briefed plenty en route."

"What about him?" Alch nodded down the hall to the self-absorbed Buchanan, who was repeatedly roughening his gelled hair so it stood up in porcupine spikes. He looked like a spiny sea urchin rather than a cool dude.

"Let him go," she told Alch, "with the notion that he's under twenty-four-hour observation and needs to be available on an instant's notice, which he will be and does."

"All right, but Lieutenant." Alch eyed Temple uneasily. "What about . . . DL?"

For a moment Molina managed to look utterly blank. As if Temple Barr wouldn't guess Alch was referring to Dirty Larry.

Then she got decisive.

"For now, tell DL I'm on compassionate leave and I'll be in touch."

"But, Carmen!"

She stared him down.

"Right, boss. And someone's been holding on the landline for you. Wouldn't hang up.

"I don't need 'someone' distracting me right now."

Alch shrugged. "You never know. He sounded pretty intense. Might have seen Mariah."

Molina sighed theatrically, winced at what such a deep breath did to her pain threshold, and stomped into the kitchen, Alch trailing her.

She paused to turn that basilisk gaze on Temple.

"Better get going fast. I'll come by the Circle Ritz sooner than you'd like. You don't want to forget a false fingernail that Ms. Ozone requires, so you can mentally pack on the drive home. And tell them at the Ritz, including your light of love, Matt Devine, you're visiting relatives for a few days. We're going on the road."

CHAPTER 12
SHOTGUN REUNION

Carmen Molina was definitely starting to believe in karma.

The "intense" voice Alch had heard on the kitchen phone was indeed known to her.

"What's this about Mariah?" it asked.

Rafi's voice was loud and clear so it would carry over the clink, clang, and conversation of a hotel casino.

"How'd you hear about it at the Oasis?" Molina asked.

"Private cops monitor police radio bands. I heard 'kid.' Alch radioing he was on the way. I heard 'missing.' And I got a chill up my spine."

There was no point in dodging this very unpleasant bullet.

"Your spine is right. Mariah's gone off on some stupid kid quest for 'stardom.' All her own idea from the evidence, but we don't want her preyed upon."

"Preyed upon? She's already missing!

117

Jesus, Carmen, how'd you screw up this badly? I thought at least you were a good mother, that you of all people would know the score when it came to responsibly supervising a teenager."

That "at least" stung more than she should have let it, but she was still hurting from the long slash wound, not to mention her own internal accusing voice.

"What do you mean, a quest for stardom?" he went on.

"You'd better come to my house. It's easier to see than talk about. We've got an informal task force assembled. It's a fine line right now between putting out a wide-enough net for her, and one not so huge it'll spook her to run farther, faster."

"Where is your house?"

"What? You didn't check that out the moment you realized I lived and worked in Vegas?"

"I'm not a stalker, just a damn surprised father despite myself."

She didn't comment, only gave him the street address and directions from his apartment as efficiently as some receptionist.

She shut her eyes momentarily after hanging up the phone.

Morrie Alch was leaning on her breakfast bar, watching her like a loyal Scottish terrier. "That Daddy Dearest?"

"Yup. Private cop at the Oasis. Heard some buzz on the police radio and thought of us."

"He's coming here? That'll be interesting."

"Yeah. Let me put a final scare into this Buchanan creep and get his every contact method before I kick him out."

He eyed Dirty Larry slouched on the living-room sofa. "Mr. Undercover Guy fetched a snitch list from his car and is now calling informants who hang out at the bus station. Good idea."

"His idea. He didn't get any info from the neighbors?" she asked.

"Nada. He know about Nadir?"

She shook her head.

"You want me to clue him in?"

"Thanks, but it's my responsibility."

"You must be beat by now," Alch said.

"Beat up, more like it. By myself. How could I have missed that Mariah was being way too sweet and helpful to her down-for-the-count mama, all the while scheming to make her break for fame and fortune? I should never have let her compete in that goofy reality TV show. Still, she'd showed some initiative in picking a goal and going for it. I thought that would be the end of it.

Where do they get these ideas?"

"It's in the air nowadays. Next thing my married daughter will be racing off to that runway supermodel hunt show, although she doesn't make the age, height, and weight requirement."

Molina managed a weak smile. "I can handle Rafi. He's actually showing paternal inclinations. More than I'd like, especially now."

"You gave him a raw deal." Alch's dark, dog-loyal eyes had gone paternally stern. "Not telling the guy, just running off. Kinda like Mariah here."

"Shut up, Morrie. I'm not in the mood."

"I'm just saying, Lieutenant." He ambled off to give her room and time to stew in her own juices.

She hustled Buchanan to the door, where she pumped all his phone numbers into her cell before shoving him out, while Larry ambled down the hall for another check of Mariah's room.

He returned to join Alch sitting on the couch. The place looked cramped with three adults around, and empty beyond belief with Mariah not about to race down the hall screaming for a missing hair scrunchie or a fresh uniform blouse.

Carmen found her deadliest enemy, emotion on the job, almost strangling her.

She was a cop. A homicide lieutenant, for God's sake! She had to tackle this like any other case or she'd be no good to anyone, most of all Mariah.

She checked her watch: 11:30 P.M. Three hours since she'd discovered Mariah was gone, three hours until Matt Devine was off work and probably on the phone with his fiancée. She'd bet Temple Barr would tell him what she was doing.

Great! Another person to add to the jury of her peers so ready to condemn her.

She checked her watch again. Under the pain of stitches pulled by her tensed stomach muscles and severe stomach acid, she was dreading Rafi coming here, into her life with both feet and a right to be angry.

The knock on her front door made her start. One knock. The minimum.

"I'll get it." Alch was nearest the door and opened it while Rafi still had his back turned to the house, checking out the neighborhood, the parked cars.

He spun around like a wary prizefighter to take in Alch, Larry Podesta, even the two cats weaving around all the alien legs, sniffing. With his swarthy Lebanese-American looks and wearing the plain dark suit of a hotel security supervisor he looked like a sinister FBI man. He spotted her last.

"Carmen." Said with a curt nod. Everyone's eyes snapped to him. Most had never heard anyone call her Carmen.

Now came the ugliest moment. All hers. She turned to the two men in the room.

"This is Mariah's father, Rafi Nadir. He works security at the Oasis Hotel. Alch, take him to Mariah's room and cover the bases."

Dirty Larry had stood, a junkyard dog uneasy about the unexpected stray on his watch.

Rafi sensed the possessiveness immediately. "I know him" — he nodded at Alch — "from the reality TV house." Then he eyed Dirty Larry. "And this is?"

Molina would not have believed she'd ever see two guys getting territorial over her, or, rather, over her house and daughter. She segued into the needed introductions.

"Dirty Larry's usually undercover. That's the name he goes by."

"Wait. You were at the reality TV show finals too," Nadir said. "With Molina" was left unspoken.

Larry nodded. "I saw you there too. You weren't a guest or family member. What for?"

"Freelance security."

"You been a cop?"

"Yeah. L.A."

Larry's head snapped back, impressed. L.A. cops took no guff, though they had a rep for cutting too many corners.

"Cool," he said. "No wonder Mariah's got gumption, however misplaced. Cop kid, one hundred percent." He turned cool gray eyes on Molina and squinted like Clint Eastwood.

Alch and Nadir headed for the bedroom, leaving the two of them alone with the cats.

"You kept this guy tightly under wraps, Carmen," Larry said softly.

"I keep everyone tightly under wraps."

"Including yourself." He grinned. "Don't worry. You got a good team going here. We'll find Mariah. And then you get to decide how long you want to ground her."

"I'd just be happy to have a kid to keep home, Larry."

"I see runaways all the time when I'm undercover. They're nothing like Mariah. She's a runaway *to,* not *from.* Her goal may sound dopey to adults but it all makes sense to her. I bet it's sinking in now, what's she's done. How silly and scary it is. She may even come running back home, or call home."

"I don't think so." Molina shook her head. "She's as stubborn as her mother, and that's a very big, bad overdose."

"You won't be comforted, will you?"

"Not until we have her back."

Dirty Larry produced a crumpled pack of cigarettes and lifted his eyebrows. She nodded. The others were in Mariah's bedroom.

"I didn't know you smoked," she commented.

"Only undercover. It hides any nervousness."

"You're nervous here and now?"

"Yeah. This isn't my scene. Usually the pressure is only on me, all on me. Here, I can't do much but ask questions and wait."

"Me too," Molina snapped impatiently.

Footsteps, two sets, sped down the hallway, sounding like elephants in her small house.

Rafi first, looking sick, Alch second, looking sicker.

Rafi held out something glittery and stiff. It reminded Molina of the reality TV show that sought supermodels, *Runway,* which Alch had just joked about to ease her tension.

"I found this under all the clutter, on the floor near the computer table and the window," Rafi said, hoarse and angry. "Didn't the 'unofficial task force' do a halfway decent search, for Christ's sake?"

She beat Larry to a closer inspection of the stiff, fourteen-inch-long item Rafi clutched like a weapon. She noticed he wore a pair of Alch's latex gloves. Damn, she couldn't fault him on anything.

What he held was . . . a Barbie doll, all done up in an evening dress and . . . all undone, the long plastic hair snarled, red nail polish slashed across the plastic mouth and eyes and throat, an arm and leg dislocated.

"The Barbie Doll Stalker," Larry said like a curse under his breath. "That girl who auditioned for the reality TV show at the local mall, killed and left in the parking lot. You've never solved that case."

"We never found the creep," Molina said in a dead calm voice. "The case is still open. We thought the mutilated dolls looked like a sick, unrelated joke. When did this get here, goddammit! Yes, we searched the room as soon as we knew Mariah was missing, Morrie and I. We wouldn't have missed this."

The silence on Rafi's part implied they obviously had.

"No," Alch said, "it's worse than the notion we missed something."

He eyed her hard, unblinking, so she'd take every word seriously.

"I went over everything near the window, first thing, Lieutenant. That doll wasn't there a few hours ago, but it sure is now. Somebody's shadowing our moves. Unless there's an accomplice, at least it means that Mariah isn't being stalked yet."

"Naw." Larry was talking now. "It means that somebody knows the kid's gone, and is daring us to follow and find her. The creep is probably as much in the dark as we are. I don't get why he'd want to tip us off with a voodoo doll."

Molina took such a deep breath that her hand went to her side as if to hold her stitches shut. To everyone but Alch, it just looked like a frustrated gesture.

"I know why," she said. "I've had a stalker. There've been other tokens left in this house while we were gone, and the last invasion centered on Mariah's room. I thought it all looked intended to shake me up, but maybe it was directed at Mariah more than I realized."

She eyed the three men in the living room.

"Anybody here want to 'fess up?" She was only one-quarter kidding.

"You suspected me of such a stupid, pathetic M.O.?" Rafi asked.

She said nothing.

Larry pulled out another cigarette and

rolled it through his fingers. Nervous? But saying nothing.

"You're still the prime target," Alch said decisively. "Mariah being gone and now threatened is just another way to get at you."

Temple had lingered in her parked car for a few minutes after leaving Molina's house, feeling a bit confused and excited and amazed. "Visiting relatives" wasn't an excuse Matt would swallow, with no relatives in town. She'd have to tell him the truth. Molina was on a mad mama roll to find her errant daughter, and Temple was a critical player.

It both revved and scared Temple that she might be key in finding Molina's missing daughter. The idea of Mariah out on the road, being preyed on by smooth dudes, was deeply upsetting.

She was just a kid! An ambitious kid, but hadn't Temple been writing movie companies with suggestions of books she could star in since the age of eight? True, she'd gotten over that by thirteen, which Mariah was, but in Temple's day there weren't the serious performance opportunities youngsters of today had.

And, face it, Temple had an instant "in" to this online world of would-be young performers.

Zoe Chloe Ozone, her off-the-cuff creation, was an Internet hottie! Was Temple a woman behind her time, or what? She pictured a cable TV show, an interview show — take that, Oprah and Ellen! A sudden guest star career. She envisioned herself as . . . Mariah, swinging out there on a scheme and a prayer.

Grow up, Barr, she told herself.

First she had to help Molina find and recover her daughter.

Then she had to calculate her own star power. Apparently Zoe Chloe Ozone was a wholly Temple-owned entertainment entity that would not die. Oh, mama!

CHAPTER 13
CAR CHASE

Sometimes choosing the right ride is the most crucial decision the private operative will make.

When there is a sudden abandonment of Chez Molina this evening by two parties driving two vehicles, I am confronted by a basic choice: staying at the scene with an unsupervised Rafi Nadir and Dirty Larry, who bear watching, in my humble opinion, or heading out with one of the dear departing; my lovely roomie or the unlovely jerk we both know and loathe.

I have always been a backseat driver and my personal "four on the floor" have massaged dark, discreet interior carpeting from economy cars to limousines. Miss Temple would seem the logical one to stick with, but she will drive alone and this time I will not be entertained by her spiritedly hostile cell phone banter with the Crawfish.

I toy with the notion of riding with Awful

Crawford himself. That orange Hummer tickles my fancy, reminding me of my Halloween birthday. I would enjoy being a surprise passenger in an automotive pumpkin. Has a nursery rhyme and reason to it, like blackbirds baked in a pie.

Besides, just who Crawford will whine to on his cell phone after his interrogation might be very informative.

I do not have long to weigh options as I lurk in the scant exterior shrubbery this clime provides.

A Miata has no backseat at all. Luckily, my Miss Temple, being short, obligingly keeps both seats set forward; the empty passenger seat holds her essential tote bag at the ready. This leaves a dude a smidge of wiggle room to hide behind either seat without being noticed. She is on the cell phone anyway; probably trying to rouse . . . I mean, roust Mr. Matt.

So I decide to indulge my craving for a novel experience and honor Mr. Crawford Buchanan with my guardian angelship for a time. Not that I would lift a split shiv to save him from even a case of dandruff. I hunker under his wheels.

As I suspected, he is on the cell too. Apparently he is alerting his radio station.

"I have an interview with a homicide lieutenant," he boasts, turning an interrogation into a journalistic coup in his own beady little eyes. "Might have a whole new angle on the teen pop tart phenom. Lots of human interest. I am on the trail of the story now. Might be a spectacular linkup to my surprise new gig at the Oasis."

I notice that he does not mention the possibility of needing bail money.

That would be a happy ending, I decide.

Interestingly, the Crawf did put out an All Points Bulletin of his own about the Molina kid to contacts in the teen talent industry at points west, all the way to L.A.

Meanwhile, my Miss Temple has paused to put the Miata's top down for a breezy drive home. So I shelter under the low car. Once the top is down and she's busy starting it up, I loft over the low side into the very mini "rumble seat" behind the front seats. *Oofda!* Squeezes the interior organs like a Swedish masseuse.

What a convoy of two we make. The smooth, small, sassy red Barr Miata, and, bringing up the rear, the hulking, boxy, orange Buchanan Hummer H3 with its shiny chrome grin of a front grille that so sums up the Crawf's sleazy personality.

Miss Temple is in such a grim hurry that I almost lose a tail tip shadowing her into our car. I could just dispense with the secret agent routine, but she seems to have enough on her mind that I do not care to add to it.

Also, once we are a decent distance from Molina's place, she exceeds the legal limit as if we were a squad car in pursuit. Maybe we are. Buchanan's vehicle is soon a gaudy memory in the rearview mirror. We squeal into the Circle Ritz parking lot on a sharp turn, the headlights flashing across the gleaming eyes of a whole startled row of Ma Barker's gang in the bordering bushes.

She runs into the building so fast the big outside door slams shut before I can get through, an unheard of occurrence. No problem. I can take the palm tree trunk up to the secondary bathroom window she keeps open for me.

I know then that something big is up and resolve to be something little but essential in helping her out.

CHAPTER 14
ROAD SCHOLARS

Temple dashed out of the Circle Ritz into the parking lot, hoping not to be spotted by any residents. Leaving in the wee morning hours when it was still dark felt like eloping.

She also felt like Buffy the Vampire Slayer, Sarah Michelle Gellar, in a scene from a summer teen slasher movie. She couldn't believe the sinister, big black SUV, a Tahoe, throbbing in idle near the back door security light was waiting for her. Nor could she believe who sat in the driver's seat.

Rafi Nadir.

What a wild scenario. She felt like the rebellious little Goth girl being picked up by disapproving Mommy and Daddy. At least Molina had phoned to warn her they had a third wheel, a very volatile "third wheel"!

A pregnant Molina had run out on Nadir fourteen years ago, never telling him about

Mariah, but he had ended up here finding out anyway. Temple didn't know why they were so bitter toward each other but she suspected Matt might. If Molina confided in anyone, it was Temple's ex-priest sweetie.

Short form, they'd been rookie cops/ romantic roommates in L.A. Now Molina was a woman homicide lieutenant in a major city and Nadir was making a comeback as assistant security chief at a midtier Vegas hotel-casino. Rafi had met Temple briefly before, but he'd totally bought into her as Zoe Chloe Ozone at the Teen Queen reality TV show house, where she'd been babysitting contestant Mariah for her worried mom. He'd — ironically — taken them both under his wing, realizing something dangerous was up. So Temple didn't feel the hate Molina did for her ex. More important, neither did Mariah.

Big Daddy got out of the driver's side to inspect the huge suitcase and three duffle bags Matt had helped Temple wrestle downstairs.

"You need all this stuff?" Rafi asked, easily slinging the luggage into the cavernous storage space. He was wearing black denim jeans and a muscle T-shirt, looking like the laid-back manager of a Goth girl, who would also be counterculture.

"No, but Zoe Chloe Ozone does. You're driving?"

"My vehicle. Yeah, it's amazing she'd let me take the wheel. Must be because of whatever she's got."

"Flu."

"If you all say so."

"What else would it be?"

"I don't know. You ride in the backseat, kiddo. Don't I wish I could."

He escorted Temple around the SUV and opened the side door. She made a major effort to haul her five-foot frame onto the high step up. Rafi turned it into a giant leap for womankind by boosting her inside with a hand under the elbow.

"They don't make these monsters for shrimps," Temple complained. "Getting in this is like climbing an Alp for me."

"At least you don't have Molina riding shotgun." His quiet tone was glum.

Temple placed herself in the center of the middle bench seat, thinking she was going to be in the middle figuratively for this whole road trip. At least here she could see both of her traveling companions. She'd noticed a couple of backpacks and duffle bags in the rear storage area. Molina and Rafi had a lot less to get together and pack. They weren't the star of this expedition.

But they had a lot more "baggage," nevertheless.

She smiled to remember Matt's wee-hour amazement at this rapid turn of events when she knocked on his door at 3:00 A.M., as predicted. Why had *not* been predicted.

"You're going off to L.A. with Molina and her hated ex-cop boyfriend to audition for a teen talent show? With them posing as your . . . parents?"

"Hey, I can look positively adolescent at times. But, no, nobody got that carried away."

"How can you create a pop tart entity from scratch?"

Temple grinned. "I'm hoping tomorrow you'll talk your agent, Tony Fortunato, into playing along and 'repping' my appearance at the contest finals with those folks. Molina's minions will set up the security end of it. Crawford Buchanan will dutifully pimp the Zoe Chloe mystique on his radio spots. It's not hard to become a full-blown media phenom these Internet days. I'll be working with pros, remember."

"Molina and her ex?" Matt snorted. "I hope you're a good marriage counselor, caught between those two."

"I've been listening religiously to a really

fine radio counselor all my lonely mid-
nights."

"Yeah? I'd kiss you goodbye but you look
so teenage and tasty I don't dare mess with
underage fiancées. Take care, Temple. The
company you're in puts you in a volatile
situation. Think of Molina and Nadir as
furious grizzly bears whose cub is threatened. You don't want to get caught in the
middle of that clawfest."

"They seem strangely subdued. And they
need me to be 'point' girl. A stupid kid with
attitude can ask questions they can't. And
get other kids to confide in her."

"You can do that with more than kids.
From what you tell me, you're the bait on
this fishing expedition. Call me early and
often and let me know what's happening,
even if I'm on the air. I can duck away for a
minute or two. You have my direct line. If
they endanger you —"

"They're more likely to tangle with each
other."

"Keep to the speed limit," Molina said as
soon as Rafi got behind the wheel and
restarted the engine.

"*You* wanta drive, Lieutenant? We're not
even out of town yet, Carmen. Give me a
break."

She stirred uneasily in the passenger captain's seat. "I want to, but it would blow our cover, daddy dearest."

Jeez, Temple thought. They already reminded her of Midnight Louie having a spat with his namesake at the Crystal Phoenix, Midnight Louise. Catfights all the way to L.A. would not be fun.

"Cool it, you two," she said in Zoe Chloe's bored but sassy voice. "I'm the star here, and I gotta plan my audition. Get into character."

"You already *are* a character," Molina grumbled, grabbing her seat belt.

She seemed fidgety, and kept adjusting the plastic strap over her long torso as if it irritated her. Molina was almost six feet tall. Temple would have thought any seat belt would fit her like a dream. They always cut across her own throat like a garrote because she was so short. Even Mariah was taller than she now, which only helped Temple's teen masquerade. Being petite is why her sixty-year-old Aunt Kit looked just right beside her new late-forties' husband, Aldo Fontana.

Gee. Temple got momentarily misty-eyed. Kit and Aldo were on a honeymoon to Lake Como and Florence, Italy. She and Matt would be honeymooners someday soon, but maybe not to Italy. Maybe to . . . Cabo or Monaco. Matt liked to swim. Temple liked to look at him in swim trunks.

Meanwhile, for now, she was off on one of those *National Lampoon* family vacation nightmare movies with a possible teen slasher movie ending ahead of them all.

As the SUV accelerated onto the freeway ramp, Molina cleared her throat.

"As subtle as always," Rafi said, settling himself in the driver's seat. "I won't speed enough to draw any state troopers. Count on it."

Molina lifted a tall Styrofoam cup of Mc-Donald's latte coffee from the central console. "So just what kind of 'interaction' did you and Mariah have at the Teen Queen house?"

"The same kind as me and the little broad in the backseat had. I figured out they were both up to something and kept an eye on them. What with the weird happenings and the place's history as a death house, I figured looking after the competing girls was my beat."

"Some of those 'girls' were of age, in their late teens."

"Yup. And they weren't 'girls,' Carmen. They were manipulative little sexpots."

"Not Mariah."

"No. Not yet. She's gone to Catholic school. That puts off the inevitable some. I know how much you like to put off the inevitable."

"Like you?"

"Like anybody who gets close to you."

"As if you ever did."

"As if you wouldn't have run away if I hadn't."

"Time-out," Temple trilled from the backseat. Zoe Chloe could be an annoying little twit. "Rafi, you're doing more than seven miles over the speed limit. Lieutenant Molina, you're grilling our driver into excess mileage per hour."

"Oh, shut up," they snapped in unison.

Temple beamed.

"Togetherness. That'll get us shinin' through, folks. Just remember that Zoe Chloe Ozone — that's Ozone without an a-pos-tro-phee, Lee — is hanging loose although buckled in. I want to hear you two singing detecting duets, not long-lost lover laments."

Silence held as the SUV hurtled into the dotted-line darkness of the night's open road.

"Zoe Chloe is a brat," Molina said. "Don't overdo it."

"She's a star." Rafi chuckled. "I saw that

Web site. Brats rule, dweebs drool, right, Zoe?"

"Oh, you *so* get us crazy mixed-up Internet kids."

"Yeah, I do." He was looking at Molina. "I 'got' our kid in a few minutes a lot better than you did in thirteen years, Carmen. She's starstruck. She has some good pipes. It was predictable that reality TV thing would fire her up to try for more. You had the hots for performing once. Why weren't you watching better?"

Temple saw Molina literally squirm in her seat, pulling the seat belt away from her body as if it cut her. "Easy for you to say," she hissed, almost with pain.

Something was wrong. Molina was way too subdued. Way too defenseless.

"Kids are tricky these days," Temple found herself saying in Molina's defense. "With cell phones, text messaging, and Internet access their secrets get bigger and go farther. Faster."

"Speaking of secrets" — Rafi put on his blinker to pass a lumbering RV — "what's with the whacked-up Barbie dolls?"

Cop talk Molina could do.

"That showed up just before the Teen Queen reality TV show got going. A girl who was going to a shopping mall audition was strangled in the parking lot. A copier image of a mutilated Barbie doll was found near her. We never tied it into anything, though: the audition, the house, the later murder there. There have been similar incidents nationally since."

"And now a Barbie doll is planted in Mariah's bedroom. I don't like it."

"Neither do I!" Molina sounded furious.

"I meant I don't 'like it' in the sense of it being plausible. It smells. It's too obvious a tie-in, and showing up late too obviously lays a false trail. It reeks of an inside job."

"The incisive instincts of a hotel cop," Molina jeered.

Rafi kept very quiet, while Temple held her breath in the backseat. He was not going to let that pass, was he?

Where Molina was all bark at the moment, though, he kept quiet, like a really big dog that doesn't need to growl.

"So what do you know about this Larry guy you've been nuzzling badges with since before the Teen Queen reality show, Carmen?"

"You're not suspicious of Alch."

"Solid, steady investigator. Your type. This Dirty Larry is not."

Temple tensed in the backseat. Rafi wasn't as volatile as Molina, but he still packed a hard punch.

Molina leaned her elbow on the inside door handle and cradled her cheekbone in her hand as if she had a headache. It was full dark and they were barreling straight into an oncoming stream of headlight meteors in the oncoming lanes.

Molina's tone was brusque, businesslike. "He's the typical uncover type. Loner, a chameleon, craves adrenaline highs, maybe a bit fanatic, or egotistical, but has to be to seriously risk his life for months at a time. He's been rotated to traffic accidents to cool down for a while."

"So how'd he show up in your private life?"

Temple listened with both ears straining. The road sounds made it hard to hear in the empty SUV cabin. She peered over the seat back to see Molina's frowning face.

"Before the Teen Queen show," she said finally.

"Who came on to who?"

"Whom!"

He didn't take the bait, but waited, watching the road, his eyes flicking to the side and rearview mirrors, not on her.

"Nobody came on to anybody. He showed up," she conceded. "I can't remember why."

"Undercover guys are good at that."

"You saying he was *working* me?"

"I'm asking. That Barbie doll in the bedroom makes everyone around Mariah a suspect. And you and Undercover Boy were a couple at the Teen Queen finals. Something new for you."

"I thought you said you didn't check me out when you came to town."

"I didn't look up your home address like some stalker, no. I did check out Our Lady of Guadalupe, chatted up the nuns, got a line on Mariah."

"How the hell did you manage that?"

Rafi finally slid his gaze to her. "I can pass as Latino if I want to."

"I don't believe this." Molina buried her face in her left hand.

"Don't worry. You got all As. Wonderful mother and member of the parish, supportive, on the PTA. Such a delightful daughter, no sleazy men around your house. Guess they didn't consider me sleazy."

"Who did you tell them you were?" Her voice was all steel again.

"Cousin from L.A. Thinking of moving to Vegas. Needed a school for my young son."

Silence and the dark and the meteors of light hurling at them all like lightning bolts of truth. Temple held her breath.

"Little pitcher has big ears," Molina finally

said, nodding behind her.

Rafi glanced over his shoulder at Temple, right eyebrow raised, looking remarkably like Mr. Spock if he'd been played by Enrique Iglesias.

"Good thing they are. Miss Barr is a real asset on this assignment."

Molina finally managed to keep her mouth shut.

Rafi winked at Temple over his shoulder.

CHAPTER 15
EMERALD CITY
EXPRESS

Los Angeles was only three hundred miles away but it seemed as distant as the Emerald City in Oz.

Facing the endless highway in the morning, when you needed mouthwash and had left a trail of gas station rest rooms behind you, the mirage of a huge, phantom city seemed to loom white and gray and glassy green under a haze of predawn heat.

Midnight Louie was sleeping alongside Temple's hip, just as he'd done at the Circle Ritz.

Midnight Louie was sleeping alongside Temple's hip, just as he'd done at the Circle Ritz.

Temple screeched, waking Molina in the front seat. She turned her head to glare around the headrest. Nadir frowned as he looked over his shoulder. "What's the matter?"

Talk about waking up to a pair of grumps!

Temple sighed. "Uh . . . nothing. Zoe Chloe Ozone has just acquired a purse pussycat."

Molina's gel-roughened bob loomed over the front passenger seat's back. She looked as happy as Godzilla on No-Doz. *Eek!*

"Balls!" she said, getting into character.

"He does still have them," Temple admitted, "but they're shooting blanks."

"God!" Molina was violating all of her bad language rules at once. "Can't you go anywhere without that big old alley cat traipsing along? What's your new bridegroom going to say in the honeymoon suite?"

"I don't expect him to be much into conversation," Temple said as Zoe Chloe. "Chill, Cop Chick. This ole boy is a fab undercover op. Paris Hilton and her scrawny Chihuahuas are so over. Louie's got claws and he knows how to use 'em."

Rafi Nadir chose that moment to chuckle.

Molina turned on him like a whipsnake. "Our daughter is truant, missing, in danger . . . and you find a hitch-hiking cat a laughing matter?"

Rafi cocked an eyebrow at Temple. He hadn't missed the "our daughter" either. He wisely didn't draw attention to the phrase. Instead, he went for sweet reason.

"The cat's great cover, Carmen. That Teen Queen Web site had a big mock *Pink Panther* podcast featuring the thing slinking around the competition house."

"The name is Louie, Midnight Louie," Zoe added, pouting. "He is not a 'thing.' I can improvise his travel supplies at the next gas station store. It will only take a few minutes."

Molina glowered at her.

"Come on, us people will have to make comfort stops."

"Just keep him riding shotgun in that big, zebra-striped tote bag of yours," Nadir advised. "Now, where are we shacking up en route?"

"Nowhere," Molina said. "We drive straight through, find and grab the kid, and retreat. The story is she's another of our stars."

"And we're the entourage." Rafi shook his head. "Our IDs?"

Molina tossed him a packet while rolling her eyes. "Phony baloney time."

Rafi riffled through his new ID. "Raphael d'Arc, garage band impresario? Whoever cooked this up must have had archangels on the brain."

Molina frowned, then got the reference. "I called Buchanan and had him dream up these 'hip' fake IDs so I could keep this expedition unofficial."

"And you are?" he asked.

"Carmina Regina," she read reluctantly, as if making a confession. "Ex-singer with the Paper Hangers and PR rep."

"Sure mangled your given and middle names, but we'll respond more readily to identities that sound like our real ones. Smart. Cheer up, Carmina."

"You're betting everything that Mariah will end up down the road at an audition."

"We can't be everywhere."

"I sent out her school photo, but God knows what she looks like after all those 'makeup' parties she claimed to be going to."

"L.A., Phoenix, Denver, 'Frisco," he said. "Those major urban centers have been savvy on runaway kids since the sixties. The cops there will see through any extreme makeup and clothes. They're pros, like us."

Molina didn't have the energy to challenge that "us" any more than she had "our daughter" a few minutes earlier. Instead, she bit her lip.

Temple noticed that she'd been through a makeup session, too, probably from rookie cop days when she'd decoyed johns. The frosted lip gloss she wore made a lot more of her mouth than those dark forties lipsticks "Carmen" wore on the Blue Dahlia club stage. The makeover meant she was pouting almost as much as Zoe Chloe. And Rafi Nadir was noticing.

Interesting.

Temple stroked Louie as she held him close in the big tote bag. She doubted he'd make an easy rider, but he needed to appear docile for the crowds and the cameras.

CHAPTER 16
TEXT FOR TWO

Their triumphal road show journey to the City of the Angels to find the delinquent little angel from the Molina residence was interrupted in the dawn's early light by the unimaginative ring tone of Molina's cell, which sounded just like an ordinary phone. Yawn.

Molina stared at her cell phone screen.

"It's Mariah, thank God!" Jubilation and relief quickly became irritation. "But what is this, Aztec?"

Temple held out a hand. "Let me see."

"You think *you* can read teen text messaging? I hate that! She knows it. Why couldn't she have left a voice mail?"

"Probably didn't want you to hear the fear." Temple frowned at the abbreviated words on the small screen. And here she'd never taken shorthand in high school because she'd thought it was career-limiting.

"Basically, she's saying that something

151

became an 'overniter' and they had to stay in line or lose their place. She's so 'SorE' but will 'xpln' later."

"No hint of where she is?" Molina demanded.

" 'OK n LOFln.' "

"Laughlin?" Rafi repeated. "That's just ninety miles down the highway from Vegas. If we backtrack we can cut off forty-five miles of highway 95. Laughlin's a time capsule of how Vegas used to be in the eighties. What's Mariah doing there?"

" 'AWdishn,' " Temple said. "Who knew phonetic spelling would ever become so hip?"

"It's a way for kids to avoid learning grammar and spelling and parts of speech," Molina said. "Hip-hop rhymes are now 'high' literacy, emphasis on the street meaning of 'high.' "

"Lunacy," Rafi added.

Molina looked up sharply to check if his agreement was sincere.

Temple wondered: if she and Matt had children, what strange symbols would they have to learn to communicate? Aliens R Us. And usually our kids.

Rafi took the phone and, while Temple hung over his shoulder and Molina leaned in to watch, texted: "U sing? Whr R U?" He hesitated and added, "Rafi."

He shrugged at Molina. "I don't know if she remembers me but I might come across less threatening than Ms. Policeman."

New letters appeared on the screen. "Kool, R. Not sing. Dance. Aquarius."

"As in 'the age of'?" Molina asked, mystified.

"Not cool, Mombot," Temple said. "Lyrics from *Hair* date you back to the Stone Age."

"You mean the 'stoned' age."

Temple shrugged. "Well, it *was* the sixties. If I didn't like vintage and theater, even I wouldn't have gotten your reference. I wasn't born yet! It's *High School Musical* today, and maybe a revival of *Grease,* not *Hair.*"

"U momma dont dance," Rafi had texted back. "Me n Zoe meetya ther."

"KOOOL! LOUEE 2?"

"LOUEE 2. Main dsk. 4 hrs OK?"

"OK."

Molina glared at the cell phone screen, but breathed audible relief, then caught her breath and put a hand to her side. "At least she's still a runaway, not a hostage."

"Temple and I will be first contact when we get to the Aquarius," Rafi said. "It's a

153

major Laughlin hotel-casino. You hang back."

"*You* hang back! I'm her mother."

"That's the problem. We don't want her rabbiting. I'm just the security guy from the last place she was a talent contestant, and Temple's an ex-roomie, a pal. We'll find what's going on, and why. Then you can sweep in and put her in cuffs."

"Don't be ridiculous. It takes discipline to rear a kid these days."

"And being in top condition. Come on, Carmen, you've got a major pulled muscle, or worse. This race to the rescue hasn't done you any good physically or mentally. Take some Aleve and make a late entrance as a reasonable woman. We'll clue you in first."

"You are a bastard."

"Yeah, and I'm right."

Temple added, "Why finally find Mariah just to scare her off? You *are* the police. We're not."

Molina's hands scrubbed the expression of uncertainty off her face. "Fine. I agree that you two established a more peer-style rapport with Mariah at the reality TV house." She eyed Rafi. "Keep it that way. You don't tell her who you are unless I say so."

"Aye, aye, Captain."

Silence rode shotgun with them all the way to Laughlin. They retraced their path on Highway 15, then took 164 east to pick up the last forty-five miles on 95 to Laughlin. The highway paralleled the snaking Colorado River as it flowed out of Hoover Dam. They drove until midmorning, when they finally hit a mini-strip of Vegas-style high-rise hotels. The buildings fronted the river, a distinctively non-Vegas look.

This was a movie model Vegas, miniatures so far. Hotel towers loomed only sixteen or so stories high. The skyline looked less pretentious, less expensive, and more fun, like the old style Vegas, as Rafi had said.

Louie had disdained the tote bag to recline on the seat next to Temple for the drive, but now he had his front paws braced beneath the side window, surveying Laughlin with them. He seemed pretty unimpressed.

"Looks like the kid's performing ambitions have gone downscale," Rafi noted.

"Good!" Molina let her anger off the leash. "Upscale is more dangerous."

The hotel was a pipsqueak compared to the behemoths that now ruled Vegas yet the lobby was as swanky, with acres of gleaming marble, blazing crystal light fixtures, and a hubbub of echoing voices and luggage wheels.

Molina paced outside the parked Tahoe under the entry canopy while Rafi and Temple in full Zoe personality bustled up to the desk, eyeing the snaking lines of guests checking in.

Louie in his tote bag bumped Zoe's sixties-patterned hip.

"Jeez, Midnight Louise," she complained under her breath. "It's like dangling Big Ben in a sack from your shoulder."

With that, the tote bag contents shifted and twisted. Louie lofted down to the ritzy floor. In an instant he was a puddle of flowing black India ink, slipping out of sight among the huddled feet and backpacks and wheeled carry-ons, most of them black.

"Oh, shoot!" Zoe cried. "Now we've got two of them missing."

But Rafi was edging expertly through and around the crowds, carving a path for Zoe and in hot pursuit of Louie.

A second later the mobs of people lining the block-long reception desk started rearing back from their prime positions, wailing in dismay. Louie's ears and tail could be glimpsed taking the high road down the marble desk, scattering credit cards, room cards, and pens as he went.

"That cat dude knows how to cut a swath," Rafi said. "Come on! I think he knows where we want to go."

At the end of the reception desk the exclamations and curses stopped abruptly.

Zoe and Rafi broke through the last line, leaving hurt toes and feelings behind them, to see an empty floor. Only a short desk for selling show tickets sat ahead. It took a moment to spot Louie atop it, looking as if he'd just pulled a photo of a magician on a placard out of a hat.

"Louie Too!" Mariah screeched. She shot into view from the right, trying to embrace the big black cat, who ducked expertly behind the placard to avoid having his fur mussed.

Temple stopped dead. "We've found her! And she looks perfectly all right. Perfectly normal."

"Yeah," Rafi said behind her, his tone pleased. "But don't let looks fool you. Kids this age are never perfectly normal."

"Would you want one who was?" Temple asked.

Rafi was regarding his daughter with satisfaction, even a bit of pride. "Nope."

She was wearing orange Capris and a yellow-and-green sixties-print smock top with fluorescent poison-green flip-flops and carried a lavender canvas backpack for a purse. The girl's Dutch bob of highlighted blond over brunet looked hip but wholesome for a soon-to-be high school freshman nowadays. Temple felt a pang that Mariah could accessorize Teen Fashion Queen without even trying, when Zoe Chloe had to really work her look.

"Mom's gonna freak," she muttered to Rafi, "but Mariah looks like she knows what she's doing."

"Terrifying," he muttered back. "Let's find out what that is before Momcat gets here."

Mariah turned to greet them with no guilt, like they were here to join a fun party.

"How'd you guys hear about this?" she asked. "Did the Dance Partee people hire you as security because of the Teen Queen house gig?" she asked Rafi. "And you're a little old to compete," she told Temple-Zoe. "But you look cool, as always."

"Your mom's worried about you," Zoe said with a twinge of Temple disapproval.

Big sigh. "I sent her a text message. She's been too bummed to even notice I'm gone. I hadda do this! Ekaterina heard she could try out and she needs *something* to keep her in this country, or she'll just die! I mean, maybe literally. Could be the publicity will help. And she's just made the finals! Is this

158

a great country or what?"

Mariah was hopping up and down with excitement.

Rafi put a big hand on her hyperactive shoulder. "Your mom's been worried sick about you, and you're right, she's already sick. How could you do this to her? It was really stupid and selfish."

Mariah's glee wilted in the face of adult male disapproval. Her eyelashes batted back regret. She'd thought Rafi had been cool. "Oh, Mom'll be fine. She always is. But EK is a Chechnya refugee and her family's only chance. I had to help her."

"How?" Temple asked.

"I know how these audition things work. I'm . . . I'm her manager."

"Does EK's family know where she is?"

"Not exactly."

" 'Not exactly'?" Rafi repeated.

Temple eyed him. He'd wanted Molina to hold back because she was "too police" and now he was acting like a truant officer.

"No. I guess." Mariah was fidgeting like a preteen. Temple had to give Catholic schools credit for delaying adolescent rebellion and fine-tuning guilt. "We wanted to wait on telling anybody until we knew EK was going to be on the show.' "

"The show?" Temple took over, figuring it

was time for Zoe Chloe to display some camaraderie for *The Young and the Restless.* "What a cool deal! What show is this? Sumthin' I can groove at?"

"My mother got you out of the closet again," Mariah accused. "You're both shills for my mother. Please! I need to help Ekaterina. She wouldn't have made it without me. I did her clothes, her makeup. She can dance but she doesn't know a thing about being with it."

The blind leading the blind, Temple thought.

"Where is your . . . client?" Rafi asked gravely.

"Well, my allowance would only pay for bus fares," Mariah said. "So we're sorta camping out. There was a huge line waiting outside the ballroom anyway, and everyone came early and was sleeping until they opened this morning and let us sign up."

She glanced over his shoulder. "Uh-oh. Mombot heading straight for us. I shoulda known she'd be here too."

Temple glanced back. Molina was grimly advancing on them.

Louie chose that moment to jump down and rub encouragingly back and forth on Mariah's bare calves.

Rafi took Mariah by the shoulders and

turned her to welcome, and face, her mother. Still, she had a wall of defensive male in black denim behind her.

"Mariah!" Molina bent to take custody of her daughter's shoulders. "What possessed you to pull this kind of stunt? We were about ready to put out an Amber Alert for you."

"You can't! I'm not a kid! I'm thirteen."

"You sure are a kid. Amber Alerts can go out on kids up to eighteen."

"No! They're *old*."

"What was so important you had to scare all of us so much? Me, Morrie, Mrs. Alverez across the street?"

"I needed to help somebody."

"Help somebody? Why would you be so foolish to listen to anybody but me and the nuns at school? You're not in a position to help anybody."

"Yes, I am! And she won! Just a couple hours ago. I'm sorry. Really I am. But EK needed a chance."

Molina straightened up, her knees visibly shaky. "What's this about?" she demanded. "Who, or what, is this EK?"

She asked Rafi, Temple noticed, as if he was to blame just for having gotten to Mariah first. As if she'd given up on asking Mariah anything.

Mariah's mouth froze in mid-answer, and

shut as stubbornly as her mother's.

"I don't know," Rafi admitted. "Mariah was just going to show us."

Molina turned to Mariah. "Show me," she ordered.

Subdued, Mariah turned away and led them around the corner to the elevators.

The four joined the people waiting for the cars. Most of them stared at Louie, still playing thread-the-needle with Mariah's calves. She looked down at him and stifled a nervous giggle.

Mama was not happy.

Temple supposed they looked like a normal family to the clustered strangers: mama, papa, kid, and oh-you-kid, one of those awful Goth girl teen delinquents. That would be her. Like any normal family, none of them said anything, except for Louie, who growled occasionally when some stranger bent to pet him. Temple scooped him up and pushed him into the tote bag.

When they finally got an elevator, Mariah only pressed the next floor up. Ballroom level.

"How'd she get here?" Molina asked Rafi.

"Bus."

"And the fare?"

"Allowance."

"Not anymore."

"Not a good idea. Grounding would be better."

"Step two. No allowance will be step one."

Mariah rolled her eyes at Temple.

They were almost the same height, Mariah a little taller. The two adults repeated the similarity at a foot higher: Molina almost six feet in low-heeled moccasins; Rafi a little more than six feet. Temple/Zoe felt like a firstborn daughter. *Ick!*

She hiked the tote bag again bearing the remarkably docile Midnight Louie. He must have realized he was failing to follow the Feline Rule of Domination.

Louie used the opportunity to tangle a forepaw in her hot and itchy black wig.

She was glad this masquerade would soon be over.

CHAPTER 17
LEAVING LAUGHLIN

Twenty minutes later they were all standing in front of a long table with an adamantly bored middle-aged grump behind it.

"But I'm assigned to dance with the cute one of the Los Hermanos brothers," the lanky thirteen-year-old girl known as EK protested, tears in her eyes and voice. "I won."

"I need the signature of a parent or guardian," the guy said. "You're a minor."

"Grandmother Dzhabrailova is in Las Vegas."

"We're signing up the winning girls here and now for tomorrow night's show. Sorry, kid. The cast has gotta be locked in before we shut down the operation and we gotta leave this ballroom in an hour."

Hotel staff were already slamming folding chairs shut and stacking them on dollies. A couple guys had their eyes on the last folding table left standing. This one.

"You can't produce a guardian now, I'll sign up the runner-up." He nodded at a blond girl wearing an expensive highlighted haircut and a bored look that failed to cover hope so intense it seemed to sizzle off her.

Ekaterina's dark brown hair was pulled back in a simple ponytail in a dollar store band. She was a thin, gangly girl, doe-eyed and desperate.

"Mom," Mariah pleaded.

"Mom" stood resolute. "I'm not a relative. I can't sign for her. Besides, I don't know what this is about, who she is, who's responsible for her —"

The blond girl pushed forward into EK. "Can we hurry up? My dad's standing by the door. He can sign right now."

"But I won!" EK wailed.

The blonde couldn't quite disguise a smirk as a sympathetic smile.

"I'll sign."

Temple and Molina, and even Midnight Louie, stared at Rafi Nadir after he spoke.

The man behind the desk frowned. "You're not a relative —"

"Temporary guardian."

"You can't do this," Molina whispered impatiently.

"The girl's grandmother will okay it." Rafi was already pulling the form on bright yellow paper forward and bending over it, ballpoint pen in hand. Mariah grabbed EK's hand and swung it up and down in childish, energetic joy.

"I'll need employment info as well as personal," the guy was saying, still frowning. "If the grandmother takes exception, it's your responsibility." He looked at the sheet Rafi spun to show him the filled out sections. "Oh. Assistant security chief at the Oasis Hotel. I guess that makes you a 'responsible adult.'"

Molina snorted.

"And you're with the exact right hotel, so that's even better. Be at the Oasis in Vegas at 8:00 A.M. tomorrow," he instructed EK, handing her a sheaf of papers.

The infuriated blond girl was about to knock hard into EK's back as she turned away to leave, but Temple jerked the girl's arm and pulled her out of contact.

"Bitch," the girl mouthed, mistaking Temple as Zoe for a peer.

Temple lifted Louie's big black paw and waved goodbye while he added a parting hiss, perhaps resenting his paw being appropriated, but more likely responding to one catty word with another, in actual feline.

They walked away as the sign-up table was turned sideways, folded, and toted away.

EK and Mariah brought up the rear, huddling and giggling like ten-year-olds. Temple had nothing to do but lug Louie and trail the wordless Molina and Rafi to the hotel entrance. Before they left the lobby, Rafi stopped and turned to the girls.

"You two have been sitting in line overnight?"

They nodded. "Everybody did," Mariah said.

"What'd you eat?"

She shrugged. "There are snack dispensers on all the hotel floors. We didn't have a lot of change after bus money, but got a couple candy bars."

Molina sighed heavily.

"EK needed energy for dancing," Mariah said, justifying necessity.

"We want to get something to eat before we leave, or en route?" Rafi asked Molina.

" 'We' want to get the . . . heck back to Vegas and get these children settled at their respective homes."

"EK's grandma doesn't have a car," Mariah said, "and EK has to be at the Oasis by eight tomorrow morning. She'll have roommates there but can stay overnight with me."

"Mariah." Molina's voice was low, logical, and furious. "You ran away from home without leaving word on where you were going and why. You are grounded. You are not entertaining partners in crime overnight."

"But EK has to be —"

"I'm sorry, but EK has to be no such thing. She has to answer to her poor worried grandmother."

"My grandmother knows what I am doing," EK answered, panic rising in her voice. "And I have won —"

"This is a stupid dance contest. That permission this . . . stupid man you don't even know signed is worthless. You can't compete. You two are children, and acted like very irresponsible children, and you'll be treated like children. And that includes not getting what you wanted, or expected. Or even won."

The silence was, well, Temple thought, impressive.

Then EK's thin shoulders started shaking with swallowed sobs.

Molina rolled her eyes and looked around the lobby at the spreading silence as people nearby stopped to watch them. Mariah comforted her friend but still managed to glare at her mother.

"You're such a . . . policeman," Mariah accused.

"Quite a compliment," Rafi said to Molina

with a quiet smile.

To the two girls and the gathering crowd he added, "Let's adjourn to a roadside restaurant down the highway. You girls must be starving. And your mother, Mariah, has been seriously ill while you were busing on down the road without permission or notice. We could all use some peace and quiet and food."

He turned the two girls to the door and guided them out, leaving Temple to deal with Molina. Who was shaking ever so slightly.

"The dude is right, dammit," Zoe Chloe said cheerily. "I hate it when they do that. Men, I mean. We can dis 'em all good on the way back to Vegas, and he'll have to hear every word."

"Can we dis magicians?" Molina's voice was still shaky.

"No," Zoe said seriously. "Never did, never will." Temple met Molina's ice-blue eyes. "Us undercover girls are loyal."

Molina bit her bloodless-looking lip. She *had* been sick.

"Good for you," she said brusquely, sur- prising the heck out of both of Temple's cur- rent personas. "Let's eat."

"Jeez," Zoe Chloe confided to Louie's left ear, which twitched either from her soft caress or her breath. "Nobody's acting in character on this cheesy road trip but us."

Rafi was just slamming the Tahoe's front door shut on Molina in the passenger seat when Temple/Zoe and Louie arrived.

"You girls all sit in back," he said, lifting the tote bag and Louie off Temple's shoulder as he hefted her by the elbow into the high step up. She was pretty sure Molina had received the same gallantry. Interesting.

Rafi to the rescue. How long could that keep up?

"Okay," he said, once again behind the wheel. "I spotted a Wendy's, Denny's, and steakhouse along the highway. What does everybody want?"

What a loaded question, Temple thought. She kept her mouth shut as the girls fought for Wendy's and Denny's and Molina won with the steakhouse. It was time Molina won one, and Temple knew Louie's vote would have been for steak. Very rare.

Molina kept quiet during lunch but EK and Mariah made enough noise for all five of them, leaving Temple and Rafi to play supervising adults. The ravenous girls ordered hamburgers and fries and chattered away, dramatically reliving the highpoints of their adventure. Rafi ordered a big rare steak and devoted himself to hacking it up and eating it. Temple had a Cobb salad while Mama Molina picked at a blander chef's salad.

The girls heedlessly revealed all the details of the long evening bus trip and sleeping in the hotel hallway and interacting with the audition attendees and crew that would turn even a careless parent's hair white. They'd actually been pretty observant and showed some street savvy. Rafi finished his steak and asked EK about her life in Chechnya and as a refugee. That was even more observant and street savvy.

Molina was so self-absorbed she let Rafi pay for the whole party without a peep.

Or maybe she wasn't as absent in mind as she seemed.

"Okay," she said as Rafi was laying down the tip in the middle of the messy fast-food table. "She doesn't deserve it, but Mariah can attend the dance thing with Ekaterina. But not without some kind of chaperone."

Of course Mariah's squeal of joy was followed by an "Oh, Mom, we don't need a babysitter." Temple packed the plain hamburger she'd ordered for Louie and the to-go bottled water for his covered water dish in the truck. She was beat, but at least she and Louie would be enjoying all the comforts — and quiet — of home soon.

North to Las Vegas. Molina leaned against the locked passenger door, as far from Rafi as her body could manage. She had her sunglasses on and was either dozing or fuming.

Mariah and Ekaterina's spirits were rising again. They chattered about the funny people on the bus on the way down (who sounded more creepy than amusing), how Mariah had dug up EK's performing outfit from the school costume cupboard and a vintage shop, about the boy band members who would partner the junior category girls in the dances, and which Los Hermanos Brothers brother was the coolest, the cutest, the hottest. About what kind of dances and costumes EK would get for the show.

After fifteen minutes of this, Molina stirred and shoved her black-framed sunglasses up on her hair like a headband. "Wait a minute. Where is the next stage of this dance contest being held?" She'd been too angry earlier to register the glorious, Rafi-related news.

"At the *Dancing With the Celebs* show at the Oasis," Mariah reported. "EK won a spot in the junior division."

"And I am not even a freshman," EK said, giggling.

"Me, neither," Mariah said, "but the age range is twelve-to-seventeen. We got that right."

They high-fived each other while Molina shuddered slightly. She wasn't thinking of Rafi, but another man of their mutual acquaintance.

"Does that mean," she asked, directing a significant look at Temple, "that EK is appearing in the same dance competition that Matt Devine is in?"

Temple hit Zoe Chloe's forehead with the heel of her hand. With all the fuss and worry over Mariah, she'd forgotten that.

"*Ooh,* Matt Devine," Mariah screamed to EK. "He's gonna take me to the dad-daughter dance next fall. You gotta teach me the waltz or something, EK. He's to-die-for cute, but, you know, old."

The adults in the vehicle, including the host persona of Zoe Chloe Ozone, kept an uneasy silence. Out of the mouths of babes.

Temple had to wonder how Rafi liked hearing about some other guy escorting Mariah to a father-daughter event.

Molina must be cringing about that.

And Temple was not too hot on hearing her fiancé lauded as a teen idol, even though

he was, you know, old.
    Like her.

CHAPTER 18
THE BUS FUME
BOOGIE BLUES

Lord, if they wanted to assassinate him, now would be the time to try. *Please!*

Max had a "seat" on the hard-topped storage box in the tail of the airplane-long bus, where the diesel fumes almost put him under like lethal ether. He needed anesthesia again. His recently abused bones were shuddering with the efforts of the engine beneath him.

As the incredibly long bus zigzagged like a sewing machine through the hairpin turns down the Alps, gorgeous postcards of scenery careened by, making his stomach into a blender for every acid in his system.

A babel of foreign languages simmered like stew from the comfy upholstered reclining seats stretching endlessly toward the front of the bus, and exit, and fresh air.

And Revienne was enjoying the cushy leather comfort of a Mercedes backseat somewhere far ahead. Did he really have to find her?

Yes, dammit.

If she had been kidnapped, he owed her a rescue-for-a-rescue.

If she had been whisked away like a fancy fishing lure he was to be tricked into following, he needed to know that too.

ZH 12656. Tracing a Mercedes license plate in Zurich would be like looking for fleas on a mongrel dog.

He grabbed his duffle bag as a new lurch almost sent it skidding down the long aisle to the pert driver in the front. She shrugged when she'd indicated the far back of the bus: the only spot a hitchhiker could expect. And the price of a bouquet was small admission.

He thought ahead to Zurich. Garry Randolph had said they'd "worked" the Continent together, magicians and spies. Counterterrorists. Switzerland was supposedly neutral ground in the politics of Western Europe, but all the money was here, and there was nothing neutral about money.

Garry must have flown into Zurich. Max would concoct a story: a missed plane connection, a missing uncle. He'd need a new credit card as soon as he left the bus. His long fingers did an arpeggio of anticipation. No dexterity loss there. He could whisper an American Express Platinum from any breast pocket. He needed a better hotel, better wardrobe, some better food, and grooming/disguise time. Might keep the smudge of not-quite-shaved beard. Trendy Eurotrash look. The bus driver had liked it. Maybe not Revienne. She was a silk stocking girl, and they still made those lovely late-lamented articles here, abroad. How did he know that?

Previous life.

Odd, what seemed to be coming back were instincts and memories from the farther past, not the immediate one. Short-term memory was shorted out. He was a man without a country.

Max clutched his elbows to keep them from jolting into seat backs ahead of him and let his disabled mind roam. Maybe it would guide him to a glimmer of Garry Randolph.

Zurich.

They had joked once. He and the older man had joked about the English word *rich* being in the city name. The restaurant had been dark and had served coffee as thick and black as molasses. Max's after-dinner cup had a shot of whiskey in it. He was young and raw-boned, Irish and melancholy, and far from home and could drink under age twenty-one. He was still nervous about it but Garry had chuckled, sounding just like his favorite uncle . . . uncle? Uncle Liam. Sean's father. Sean's sonless father.

"Drink up," Garry's voice came over the grind of the huge engine, as the boozy coffee's aroma erased the diesel fumes. "You've managed to get the one thing most men in the world would give the world for: just revenge. The IRA bastards who blew up your cousin Sean are history. Two shot dead in the raid; three bound for a life sentence. We did it."

So that's what they had done. Acted as an unofficial "equalizing" force against terrorists. Max tried to remember how he'd felt after that belt of Irish whiskey and Turkish coffee. Scared. Just scared. He was too young to be drinking hard liquor. He was too young to be seeing to it that men he didn't know died.

So, had he aged like whiskey, getting stronger, smoother, and mellower? Or had he grown hard and bitter, like coffee? Or was he a combination of dark and light, like most people. No, he'd never been like most people, never would be again, not a teenage virgin who'd graduated from high school to taking lethal revenge on five grown men in a single now-forgotten Irish summer.

■ ■ ■ ■

He must have fallen asleep. The bus was forging through the darkness into fistfuls of glittering lights in a distance that offered little sense of up and down.

People's heads were bobbing on headrests all down the aisles. Asleep, as he had been.

They must be on the outskirts of Zoo-*rich.* Max stretched his long frame, hearing sinews crack. His legs ached like the devil.

And that was appropriate. He had a lot of the Devil's work to do in Zurich if he was to remain free, and remain free to find Revienne Schneider in that mass of people, buildings, cars, and numbered bank accounts.

CHAPTER 19
UNHAPPY HOOFER

Matt walked into the greenroom for the competition, nodding to his new peers. Someone he'd already met was there, the Cloaked Conjuror, the Goliath Hotel's oversize masked magician.

Glory B. was a straw-thin, twitchy teen diva with a bee-stung pout courtesy of collagen injections.

Matt found shaking hands with the handsome José Juarez, an Olympic fencer as lean and limber as a fencing foil, a knuckle-crushing experience.

Keith Salter, a celebrity chef, was as expected — charming, egocentric, and chubby.

The ladies he met were Olivia Phillips, a postmenopausal soap opera star who reminded him of Temple's aunt Kit; Motha Jonz, a hefty black hip-hop diva; and last, but decidedly not least, Wandawoman, a World Wrestling Wrangle Amazon got up like Wonder Woman on steroids.

Matt couldn't help thinking he'd joined some X-manish federation of talented freaks as the token ordinary guy.

Their pro dancing instructors were present, the guys a muscled mystery meat mélange of straight and gay and bi — you figure it out — the women young and sleek and as ambitious as spawning silver salmon leaping upstream.

Matt grinned to think that Temple had pushed him into the heart of this gender-ambiguous, openly sexual world. She must think he was pretty secure. Which he was. Nothing like publicly advising other people about their deepest desires and identity crises to make one blasé.

Matt sat beside the Cloaked Conjuror. He was a Klingon-imposing figure on high platform boots, wearing a completely con-cealing tiger-striped full head mask.

"I, ah, met you at the costume contest you were judging at the TitaniCon science fiction-fantasy convention," Matt said, not sure the man behind the mask would re-member him.

"That's right." He stretched his long legs ending in the Frankenstein boots. "The Mystifying Max's pretty little redheaded girlfriend helped engineer catching a murderer that night. You were there too."

"I'm always surprised when anyone re-members me at such a huge event."

"Not *my* problem." CC chuckled. His mask contained a voice-altering device, so he sounded unnervingly like Darth Vader giggling. "They mentioned you used to be a priest. I bet that and sitting behind an advice-line mike doesn't make you a natural at tiptoeing through the triple-time foxtrot."

"No, it doesn't," Matt conceded, "but you don't seem geared for that either." He nod-ded at the industrial-strength shoes in size fourteen.

"I'll ditch these for the dances."

"Temple said something . . . don't you get death threats from disgruntled magicians because your act is built on exposing the tricks behind their most famous illusions?"

"Temple! That was her name! Max's squeeze."

"Not anymore."

"No? Max dump her?"

"He's missing. And . . . we're engaged."

"*Humph.* So my old compadre bugged out and left you with the girl."

"It didn't exactly happen that way."

"No, I guess not. You look like a nice guy. You'd wait your turn."

Matt held his temper, figuring he'd have

to do it a lot in the next week. This green-room looked like a theatrical variety show and he didn't fit in.

"Aren't you taking a risk?" Matt pushed. "Exposing yourself at a hotel that isn't set up to protect you 24/7?"

"All Vegas hotels are set up for 24/7 surveillance, and I brought my own guys." The massive feline head nodded at two men in wife-beater T-shirts holding up the far wall. Matt had taken them for idle work-men or technicians. Which was the idea.

"Why are you doing this?" Matt asked.

"The charity. I lead a pretty isolated life because of the disguise and the death threats. That makes people even more eager to see me outside of my secure home hotel. Everyone who votes for me during the six days of this competition pledges twenty bucks to cancer research. I figure it's worth the risk. Isn't that why you're here?"

"Yeah. The kids' leukemia fund. And my girlfriend made me."

CC's weird, wheezy, basso laughter some-how conveyed warmth. "I'd do almost anything for a smart girl like her myself. You're a lucky man. I can't afford a roman-tic life."

Matt just nodded. He gazed around the room at the assortment of strangers who'd become friendly rivals very soon. They were sizing one another up as the team of male and female hairstylists, makeup artists, costumers, and pro dancer-choreographers made the round of contestants with the show's director.

"Good," said the head guy when he reached Matt and CC. "You guys are getting acquainted already. Dave Hopper, director. You'll discover a real camaraderie developing between you eight. You'll work harder mentally and physically than you ever have, and cross barriers you never faced before. It takes guts to try something you've never done much of right before live TV cameras."

He sat on an empty folding table as his production team gathered around.

"The Cloaked Conjuror here will be a challenge from start to finish."

"The Penn Jillette of Penn and Teller of our show," a costumer said. "A huge guy, larger than life. I'll have to work around the mask." The tall, blue-jeaned bottle redhead glanced at the lithe blond dancer beside her. "Vivi, you'll need to dream up Beauty and Beast–type routines. The masked man is a romantic image; we'll have to play on it with the costumes and the choreography."

She turned to Matt. "Stand up."

He hesitated. He hadn't been ordered to move since grade school.

"Stand up, cutie. I need to see your build."

He hadn't been called "cutie" ever. But he stood.

"Fit, if not awesome. All-American boy." She sighed and eyed the sinewy brunette who was evidently Matt's choreographer-coach. "Blond and smooth as butterscotch syrup, Tatyana, but that's a handicap in the Latin dances. And those are the audience-pleasers."

"We could cover the hair," the hairstylist suggested. "Zorro scarf and hat. Or go brunet."

Hopper nodded. "Worked for Elvis."

"Could use an Elvis tune," Tatyana suggested.

"Uh, black dye —" Matt began, appalled.

"Just a rinse," the hairdresser said. "Could even spray it in. Look around you. How many of the pro guys and the male contestants are blond? Isn't dramatic enough for guys."

"There's Derek on *Dancing With the Stars*," the costumer noted. "Does work that darling boy thing."

"Not in Latin," Hopper decided. He was middle everything: in age, build, temperament. "We'll go both ways on him. It'll be a real shockeroo when the teen angel boy comes out all dark and devilish for the pasodoble. Audiences adore transformations."

"Plays well against the priest thing," Tatyana suggested. "I can have fun with that: devil or angel."

Matt had a feeling her idea of "fun" wasn't heavy on personal dignity, at least as he knew it.

They moved on, as did CC, linking up with his bodyguards.

And Glory B. moved in on him, taking the adjoining folding chair, then tapping her high and strappy spike heels on the floor so nervously they sounded like castanets. "How'd a priest get talked into doing this?" she asked.

He regarded the notorious oversexed teen idol and decided not to emphasize the "ex" part of his status. "The charity donation."

"Yeah, me too." Her ankles turned out like a kid's wearing white patent leather mary janes for first Communion, skewing the hooker heels to the side. "I want to do something for the kids."

"You were one yourself not too long ago."

"You think so?"

Matt wondered what she wanted from him. Flirting? Nah, she'd mastered that years ago, even though she was probably

186

sixteen, tops. Glory B. He'd seen her name in the newspaper gossip columns, on TV. She'd been in trouble? Drink or drugs? Both, probably.

"I hit someone," she blurted.

With kids her age, it was usually another kid. He frowned, confused. What was so newsy about that? Tantrums must be her middle name.

"With my Beamer," she confessed. "Can't drive it for a while anymore."

"You must have people around who can."

"Yeah." Her nails were painted midnight-blue, but very short. Probably bitten that way. "It hit a kid. You know, a little kid. Broke both legs. So I'm dancing for charity to work off part of my probation."

Matt couldn't help glancing down at her broken-looking ankles. Where does a teenage superstar put guilt? In a tiny purse like the one Glory B. kept beside her on a chain, clearly capable of carrying nothing more than a credit card, and maybe some happy pills.

"Funny," she said. "The kid's in double casts and I gotta dance my ass off for doing it."

"How old is the kid? Girl? Boy?"

"Girl." She stood, wobbling on the four-inch heels. "These shoes cost more than the medical stuff. I was gonna give her a pair when she got better, but they say she might not be able to ever wear pretty shoes. Dancing shoes."

"It's called penance," Matt said.

"Huh?"

"When you do something wrong, you have to pay for it. It's not the probation or what the law says you have to do. It's what you feel inside. It hurts. It's supposed to. You'll remember that the next time you don't think about what you're doing that might hurt someone else. But you can't hurt yourself to make up for it either. That way nobody learns."

She stood there clutching the ridiculous tiny purse, slathered in rhinestones like the cell phone probably inside it, and worth hundreds of dollars. She still looked like a lost seven-year-old and was probably worth millions.

"It's okay," he told her. "Everybody gets a second chance. Maybe this show is yours."

The eyes rimmed in black liner blinked once as she nodded and tottered back to her seat with the soap and wrestling queens. Men, Matt mused, usually got famous for what they did. Women often got famous for being caricatures.

■ ■ ■ ■

"Here come de judges, here come de judges," Motha Jonz announced, springing up from her seat pretty spryly for a woman of size in her forties. Her Afro pompadour had a dazzling *Bride of Frankenstein* silver streak up the front and boobs and booty jiggled with every move she made, like Jell-O on parade.

She certainly diverted every eye in the room from the trio of folks joining them.

Then Matt jumped up to greet — of course! — Danny Dove, Vegas choreographer extraordinaire.

They did the one-armed hug authorized between guys, even when one of them was gay. Danny was compact and wiry, and apparently not considered authoritative because he was blond like Matt, except his hair was even less impressive, being as curly as Shirley Temple's had been.

But his spine of stainless steel put the butch back in blond, and Matt was pleased to see him here.

Knowing a judge couldn't hurt, but mostly it was good to see Danny get back into the Las Vegas event whirl after the trauma of having his partner murdered.

Another blonde, bottle-variety, was on the judge's panel, and Matt knew her by reputation and sight: the endlessly self-resurrecting B-movie ex-actress, Vegas hanger-on, and Temple Barr crown of thorns, Savannah Ashleigh.

She was tall, enhanced by towering platform spikes, and dressed in extreme fashion. A purse pooch, all big black eyes and spidery blond hair, peeked out of a ridiculously expensive-looking bag. Savannah had previously traveled with a pair of glamour pusses, shaded silver and gold Persians named after French starlets, like Yvonne or Yvette. Temple's cat, Midnight Louie, had seemed enamored of the missing pair but they were evidently passé now.

He and Savannah had appeared briefly on a panel together only a couple of weeks ago, but she'd forgotten him already. She proved the makeover crew prophetic by ignoring him to canoodle with the other two male, and brunet, contestants.

"Who's the third judge?" Matt asked Danny.

"Leander Brock, the show's creator and producer. Obviously, I'm the serious credentialed gay one and Miz Ashleigh is the over-the-top female impersonator one. Somebody bi of either gender would have been a nice blend at this point, but we're stuck as a troika."

Matt made a face. "Is it really pre-set up like that?"

"Absolutely. The judges' conflicting personalities drive these reality TV competitions. I was brought on board to be demanding and biting. Any choreographer has to be a bit of that. We're really drill sergeants in tights. Miss Savannah Ashleigh will be ditsy and amusing through no efforts of her own, and Leander will provide the balancing act. Of course, I wouldn't put it past him to cast his votes in such a way as to trigger the most people calling in, but it *is* all for charity. Just don't expect justice. It's all opinion. Mob rule, really, as so much today. Everybody's an expert.

"And so, Mr. Devine, the dancing wanna-be," Danny went on, "what is your better half doing while you're learning the cha-cha?"

"Temple is — I don't exactly know. Between my midnight radio call-in show and this last week of rehearsal for ten hours during daylight hours I haven't had time to think about that."

"And how are you doing in dance class with —" Danny turned to examine the four buff men and women in rehearsal gear stretching and gossiping against the far wall. "Don't tell me! Tatyana is your coach."

"How did you know?" Matt was astounded by Danny's accuracy.

"Temple is the sleuth, but I know dance. Tatyana, though petite, is an iron disciplinarian. I'd pair her with you myself, because you respond to structure and you're attracted to small, feminine women with drive."

Matt raised his eyebrows. "I thought *I* was counseling *you.*"

"That was on your turf; this is mine." Danny's analytical eyes narrowed. "You could learn something from her."

"I am."

"But on your terms so far, I'd bet. Let go, dear boy. Dance is an incomparably liberating art, but only if you sweat like a Clydesdale and aren't afraid to float like a fool."

"Does Muhammad Ali's 'sting like a bee' part come in anywhere there?"

"Only if you become a judge." Danny looked around again. "We need the just-right combo of personalities in the judging or this dance party show dies on its tootsies."

"The whole thing strikes me as a mad tea party."

Danny eyed the contestants. "A rather

lethal tea party. I don't know all these B-, C-, and D-list celebs, but I do know that Motha Jonz was lucky to avoid prison time when she shot a bystander during that limo hit on the hip-hop gangstas a few years back."

Matt whirled to eye the Queen Motha filling out zebra-stripe spandex with proud mounds of cellulite while Danny dished on the woman's history.

"Her 'man' was Mad Motown Guitry, record mogul and mobster. She claimed she was just defending herself with her little pistol when the limo was hit by a rival gang, but the car frame was full of cocaine. Guitry died. No one has ever been indicted, but when she lost his sponsorship her so-called singing career went down the drain."

His eyes returned to Matt's shocked face. "There are a million stories in the naked ambition sweepstakes along the Las Vegas Strip. Yours just happens to be one of the more mild-mannered of them."

Mild-mannered. Matt chewed on that wishy-washy adjective after Danny danced away to pounce on other people he knew there, mostly the pro dancers.

Mild-mannered was good enough for Clark Kent, but not Superman. Mild manners didn't win ballroom dance competitions. Most guys not in the entertainment world would be afraid of looking like a wuss wearing Fancy Dan costumes and waltzing across the polished floor. He got what Danny was saying: do it and do a good job of it, or wimp out and look just like you're afraid of looking.

Kind of what Matt would advise himself. *Admit it, Devine,* he told himself. *You want to perform up to the Max Kinsella standard for Temple.* Play the hero. She was sure to return from her unlikely road trip with Molina's wandering kid in tow. Then she'd get any DVDs of episodes she'd missed. He'd better come out looking like a combo of Gene Kelly and Sylvester Stallone.

Think Michael Flatley. Bring on the slicked-down hair. The high-heeled boots. The attitude. Sword and cape and swash-buckle. It was now or never. Either be a lord of the dance, or a loser. In public.

At least this was just a silly dance competition. Nobody's life or death depended on it. You couldn't get much more trivial than this.

CHAPTER 20
DANCING WITH
DANGER

The two girls were asleep, tangled like gangly kittens next to Temple in the Tahoe's second bench seating row.

Las Vegas's dazzling megawatt halo had been dancing like the aurora borealis on the dark desert horizon when they'd left Vegas many hours before but now both city and surrounding desert were bright and bland.

When Molina's cell phone rang, she sighed heavily and answered it.

"Yeah? Got her in Laughlin. Figured it was too late to call earlier, and then it was too early. Besides, this was a personal crisis." She listened. Neither Temple nor Rafi could figure out who had called. They were trying their mightiest to eavesdrop without looking like it.

"Not her this time. Helping a girlfriend I've never heard of in some crazy scheme to get on a dancing show. *Dancing With the*

Celebs, yeah? How'd you hear about it?" Silence.

Temple eyed Molina pushing herself up straighter in the front passenger captain's chair to listen. Molina swallowed a groan of discomfort. "I'll hold on."

A pause while someone else got on the phone's other end. Molina's tone was crisp, emotionless. "Yes, Captain, I'm glad Alch could reach me. What's up? He told you about my daughter?" Thunder threatened. "That's personal busi— because? At *Dancing With the Celebs*? You're kidding."

Rafi's eyes met Temple's in the rearview mirror.

"Yes, I know you don't kid. The other girl is a babe in the woods but she won . . . and will be on the show.

"Sure, we're set up for undercover, but there's no point now. Mariah's fine. She's sleeping right behind me —

"The same show? That can't be? Yes, I suppose it's 'fortuitous,' but I've got two civilians here — yes, yes he was." Molina glared at Rafi. "Yes, *she*'s along." She twisted her head over her shoulder to glare at Temple. "I know you've seen those Teen Queen house tapes. Yes, it is stupid to argue with success and an easy entrée. Right."

Molina punched off the cell phone.

196

"Great," she whispered under her breath, eyeing the sleeping girls. "I hate it when Mariah comes out smelling like tea roses when she should be grounded for ten weeks."

She eyed Temple. "God, I'm going to hate seeing that black wig of yours."

"And me?" Rafi asked.

"And your new, improved annoying persona. Forget any home runs today. We're going straight to the Oasis to operate our sting at the *Dancing With the Celebs* show that starts a weeklong TV run tomorrow."

"But Matt's on that," Temple objected.

"On it? *He*'s on this case too? *Another* flaming civilian?"

"I meant, he's on the *show*. One of the celebs. Well, he is one. Sort of."

"Perfect," Molina spat, meaning the opposite. She seemed to remember something, looked briefly sheepish, then sighed. "I guess you might want Zoe Chloe to be on site, then. The show's getting death threats, the hotel and sponsors are going ballistic, they're worried the junior performers will attract the Barbie Doll Killer, and the captain is just as happy as heck I can lead my ready-made amateur undercover team right into the killing field. And it will be one, because I'm going to kill Alch for squealing to the captain about who is who and where we were and what we were doing."

"I suppose," Rafi said, "those hokey false identities that Buchanan created for us will work here. What were they again?"

Molina's teeth seemed to be grinding. "You know only too well. It's all set up. We've got access to a high-roller suite at the Oasis. Or, rather, Miss Zoe Chloe Ozone has. Matt Devine's personal appearance agent, Tony Fortunato, did a number on the competition organizers. Apparently even that weasel Crawford Buchanan has some pull. Fortunato negotiated a rock-star package for Our Little Miss Smartmouth. He said if she didn't do the entourage routine she'd look phony."

There was a silence. The backseat girls slept through the verbal fireworks, as fast-growing, sleep-deprived drama queen teens will.

"Death threats, they said?" Temple asked, worried about Matt.

"To the Cloaked Conjuror, mainly, now that he's more accessible," Molina answered, "but that's a given. There's also that national concern that the Barbie Doll Killer has been haunting teen reality TV auditions again. This dance show does have a junior contestant level." She nodded at EK in the backseat.

Rafi frowned as he watched the traffic ahead. "The captain know about the mutilated Barbie doll outside Mariah's window?"

Temple's eyes and ears widened as Molina nodded. "Alch told him. The place will be crawling with undercover and uniformed cops.

"That's awful," Temple said. "Matt really, really didn't want to be one of the adult contestants," she said, "but I encouraged him to do it. I'm the PR expert, after all. I said it would be great exposure for him."

But not to a murderous crackpot after a famous magician or a teenage girl or a dancing celeb.

Nobody had an answer to that . . . or to the stricken tone in her voice, not even Midnight Louie.

Temple stroked Louie as she held him close in the big tote bag.

Now he was part of this rolling thunder bizarre road show too.

She didn't think he'd be an easy rider at this purse pussycat thing, but he needed to appear docile for the crowds and the cameras.

"Louie," she whispered in his perked black

ear with the shell-pink interior, "you are a star, just like Zoe Chloe Ozone. They had footage of you all over that Teen Queen reality TV Web site. This isn't going to be much different than our outing to New York for that cat food commercial assignment, except you're going to have to put up with masquerading as a pet being carted around in a celebrity's tote bag. I know this is a big comedown for you, but please behave. We are getting a free high-roller suite out of the deal and you and I get dibs on the biggest and best bed."

Thinking about the suite's "bedroom assignment" made Temple give a little shudder. Molina had said the captain had assured her Mariah and EK would be safe bunking with the other two junior dancers and their mothers in the heavily protected junior suite.

"Raphael" and "Carmina" would have bedrooms in Zoe Chloe Ozone's fancy high-roller suite too. At least Temple didn't have to worry about hanky-panky in the night.

Domestic violence, maybe, but not illicit sex.

Lions, and tigers, and angry ex-lovers, oh my!

With only one big housecat to monitor them all, one alley cat to do the time and fend off crime.

Midnight Louie.

Chapter 21
Celebrity Is the
Cat's Pajamas

I am not surprised to hear that my svelte ebony image is receiving major online attention.

While I usually shrink from the spotlight during my investigations, I have as much or more star potential than any human around.

Until I was falsely accused of irresponsible littering with the Divine Yvette, I had a nice national TV pitch–cat career going for À La Cat and its healthful food product line, Free-to-Be-Feline.

Those were the days! Being flown to New York City. Roaming the city sidewalks during the well-lit Christmas season.

Getting "well-lit" myself once in the service of busting out of jail. Being the toast of Manhattan. (Well, sometimes that was closer to being toast, period.).

Solving the usual murder. Watching my Miss Temple whisked off by a commanding Mr. Max for a night of sumptuous sin offstage. *Darn!*

(Those intrigued by the above reminis-cences should consult *Cat in a Golden Garland,* my only case occurring outside of Las Vegas. I believe PBS is considering offering it as a perk along with a golden oldie doo-wop promotion, but you will have to check with my agents about the progress on that. I have been completely unable to reach them lately.)

In sum, I do have potent performing genes, even if they are no longer reproducible, and I will do my best to impersonate a big, lazy, cuddly pussycat for the *Excess Hollywood* cameras sure to be at the dance competition finals.

I am also well aware that I am the key undercover operative in this funky little scam. Hotels have been my business since I started out as house detective at the Crystal Phoenix Hotel and Casino when it was being renovated from the old Joshua Tree.

You talk Vegas hotel, and you talk Midnight Louie. I know the layout, the players, the personnel.

If there is anything to these death threats at the dance show, whether against someone as big in this town as the Cloaked Conjuror or as petite as young Ekaterina from Chechnya, I will ferret out the villain and have him or her waltzing right into the Nevada prison system.

Ta-da!

CHAPTER 22
POOL SHARK

After lunch break that day at the huge buffet table the hotel provided in the backstage area, Matt returned to his assigned rehearsal room.

It was empty, but Tatyana had been there. Matt winced at seeing his namesake on the rehearsal-room floor, a padded mat.

The rehearsal mat made an oblong pool of bright blue vinyl on the polished maple boards. This afternoon was "lift" practice. The mat reminded him of high school gym classes. Nobody wanted to be reminded of those days of infamy.

He eyed his reflection in the mirrored wall: army-green T-shirt, khaki pants, black lace-up shoes made from leather soft enough to flex like cloth. Jazz shoes, they'd told him. His hair was still spiky from "product" the show's hairstylists insisted on. It looked a lot blonder because of the portable spray-on-tan booth the contestants had to use religiously every morning.

Its small dark space reminded him of an old-fashioned confessional, if one ever had to take all one's clothes off to go to confession. It gave the stripped-naked soul a whole new look, not to mention the rhythmic sweep of cold dye as one assumed the position and turned.

If the object was to be reborn looking like a Beach Boy, it had worked.

Matt knew he'd hate this celebrity dancing show and all its works, but everyone, including Temple and his boss at WCOO-FM, hadn't wanted him to miss this "opportunity." An opportunity to look like an idiot in front of a local audience. If only the exposure was just local.

Since this was Las Vegas and nothing in Vegas was really "local," the half-hour Hollywood gossip shows were all over the rehearsals. He never knew who would burst through that closed door besides his drill sergeant, ballet master, and dancing partner, Tatyana Tereshchenko, aka Tatyana the Terrible, five-foot-three inches of wiry and wily Russian tsunami.

She burst in now as if summoned by his thought, wearing a wispy tease of skirt over her lime-green leotard and tights, toting a bag for towel and bottled water.

"Matt-*eeeu*, Matt-*eeeu*, Matt-*eeeu*," she mispronounced his name in her heavy Russian accent. "Are you ready to lift Tatyana up to the heavens today?"

"It's just Matt," he said. No point in correcting her. The long form of his given name was Mathias. "And I'm game for lifts if you are."

"Of course you are," she said. Her teaching technique was the whiplash application of carrot-and-stick in rapid alteration. She came close, suddenly kittenish. "Such lovely strong shoulders. Swimming is the most vonderful sport for dancer. Makes long, lovely muscle, all over."

She accompanied this inciting conclusion with strokes and purrs, her position being that his ex-priest status had made him shy.

With her, a Tasmanian devil would be shy.

"But," she added, drawing back and pulling herself up like a ballerina on pointe. "You have *rhythm* and we must *pull* that *out* of you *before* the competition *begins,* or Tatyana will not vin and one thing is sure: Tatyana will vin. *Ca-peach?* As they say on, on . . . *These Three Sopranos!*"

"*Capeach*," Matt repeated dutifully, amused by her slaughtering the language and the TV show name, which he took as a deliberate ploy.

In a week of lessons, he'd learned Tatyana was a force of ego. She was the Yorkshire terrier that lived to boss around Great Danes. And she truly had a passion for dance, and for making him into a dancer.

"Good. You learn. With Tatyana you learn to be dancer and love it. So. Today. Surprise."

He wasn't surprised when the door opened again and a cameraman backed in, filming the incoming newcomers. *Oh, my God!* Surprise was right.

In came Ambrosia, his nightly on-air predecessor host at WCOO and his "Midnight Hour" producer, wearing a leopard-print caftan and singing "Hey, Mr. Tambourine Man" while banging a jangling circle of wood and metal overhead.

The cameraman kept backing up so far he almost tripped on the floor mat, just before Matt himself leaped forward to steer him around the barrier like a balky dance partner. He'd picked up a move or twelve from the driven diva who was his coach.

The cameraman had backed up so far because Ambrosia was three-hundred-pounds-plus of quivering leopard-skin-pattern caftan, and she was followed by a chorus line of women equally larger than life and as exotically clothed as she, or more so.

They were not shy, that was for sure.

Tatyana was grinning like a demon brat.

"So, Matt-*euw.* You say as priest you like to visit these gospel music churches. Miz Ambrosiana has brought whole gospel group to rehearsal. You will no longer hide rhythm from those long, hot shoulder muscles and hips, right, Miz Ambrosiana?"

"Right, girlfriend! We all gonna hip-hop today!"

Ambrosia began by bumping hips with him, but not before he could perform an evasive maneuver that kept him on his feet.

"Show us what you learned at dance school today, Beach Boy," Ambrosia urged.

Matt had heard her selecting songs that soothed and inspired her radio call-in listeners for months now. She was a wonder at massaging sad hearts and sore feelings back into some hope of functioning again. He knew her repertoire, and she knew he'd played the organ a little and liked Bob Dylan.

So they could do a little act for the cameras, which was always what cameras demanded.

"Shall we, Sister Ambrosia?" he said.

"Shall we, Brother Matt?"

"A little Dylan?" he suggested.

"And a lotta rhythm."

After he led on the first line, she joined in singing the rollicking, feel-good anthem of "When the Ship Comes In" as if rehearsed, while the other women clapped their hands and tambourines and shook their booties and joined in.

They formed a line to march around the room New Orleans funeral–style, Matt turning to waltz Ambrosia in a circle, then do-si-do among a few women of the church choir, borrow a tambourine and do a little arms-raised hip-banging with a three-hundred-pound dynamo, then perform a dip with a tall, skinny woman playing the kazoo.

By then the song had segued into "This Little Light of Mine, I'm Gonna Let It Shine" and Matt had circled into the center of the room to sweep Tatyana up into the alternating over-the-hip lifts of the swing dance they'd practiced.

When he let her feet hit floor, she grinned into the camera coming in for a close-up and crowed, "We are gonna be ready to rock with the angels on tonight's show."

Wrap and roll.

The cameraman left, happy not to have been steamrolled under, grinning at the great sound and motion he'd recorded.

The churchwomen filed out laughing and gossiping, Ambrosia last.

"Were you surprised to see me?" she asked Matt after he hugged her goodbye at the door.

"I was floored."

"Did we help?"

He considered. "Sistah, if the church choir can shake it like that, so can I."

"Right on! Don't hold back. That's what you tell our people out there in radioland almost every night, and that's what we do to show 'em the way."

"Amen."

"Now we vork," came a tight, light voice behind him.

Matt turned around to study his tiny but fierce taskmaster. No one who had heard Ambrosia's hypnotically soothing voice for years over the airwaves knew she was a woman of size. Now the world would.

If she was willing to "bare all" on TV for him, he guessed he should be willing to reveal a little "rock and roll and rhythm" for her. Besides, he couldn't let Temple down by looking like a dork.

"Now we work," he agreed.

Danny Dove regularly dropped by all the

rehearsal rooms, being the general overseer as well as chief judge. Matt was glad he came by to help with lifts.

This was Vegas, baby. Dramatic "lifts" might be rarely allowed on *Dancing With the Stars,* but here they were encouraged.

"You two are made for lift training," Danny diagnosed. "You Tarzan, she Jane and weighs a hundred pounds tops. Perfect. And *you,*" he told Matt, "are already at home with slinging a petite woman around."

"He may be able," Tatyana said, "but he is *blushing!* This is the trouble. I need a mate with erotic command."

"A 'partner,' " Danny corrected her quickly, taking pity on Matt after having picked on him himself. "And you need *acrobatic* command."

"Whatever this language means. He must lift me with confidence and skill, and look like he likes it. So far, you would think I was a teacup, when I must be a . . . a kettle."

"A teakettle," Danny corrected her again, "a hot Russian samovar, maybe, about to blow its top."

He turned to Matt. "Once you understand that a female dancer is an athlete who'll be contributing her own strong spring and control to the moves, you won't worry about dropping or hurting her. She's like a cat. If something goes wrong, she can torque her torso to compensate in an instant and make a mistake look like an inspired move. That's what a talented and gutsy partner does."

"Thank you, Mr. Dove." Tatyana folded her arms and regarded Matt with satisfaction.

Matt was unconvinced. "For the show I'll be dancing with the women competitors. Not to be rude, but a couple of them outweigh me considerably."

Danny shook his head with the halo of curly cherubic blond hair, but grinned like the devil.

"It's all in having confidence and learning how to balance the weight. Don't worry about it."

Tatyana nodded forcefully. "You have the easy job, Mr. Man, and the upper body strength for it. Just show a little courage and I will show you how lifts make the dance world go round."

With Danny adjusting their poses, Matt soon realized that his role in lifts was either as stabilizing strongman, turning with Tatyana perched on his shoulders, or human stepladder, providing a steady base while she sprung from the floor into some pose in his arms.

Sweat was streaming off them both, making their handholds slip, when Danny called a break. Matt had actually enjoyed mastering the lifts. He had the strength needed and was quickly developing the balance and skill, even in the turns, which put a lot of pressure on the male partner.

What he couldn't hack was those hokey face-to-face stares and cheekbone-to-hip caresses in the Latin numbers that made him feel like a flea circus Romeo.

"It feels . . . sexist," he complained after they ran through their pasodoble moves for Danny.

"That's because it is," Danny said cheerfully. "It's macho to the max, all male peacock pose and sound and fury. And the woman matches every show-off move with her aloof disdain. It is indeed a love-hate dance, and, sadly, it mirrors a lot of relationships still relevant today."

"So we're miming a mistake."

"It's a cultural thing," Danny said, laughing, as he corrected their pose at the end of a complicated series of turns. "Latin fireworks. But all dance has truth in it and anger is the dark side of love all too often."

"It shouldn't be," Matt said. "It wouldn't be if children were reared without pain and fear."

"True," said Danny, a flicker wincing

across his usually open features. Matt could have kicked himself, pointing that out to a gay. "I always tell myself that in the Latin dances, as often in life, the man may flex and preen, but the woman always wins, and he likes it. Dance as if you know this, and love this, and you will have a Latin soul."

"We Russians understand this," Tatyana interjected. "Soul is always, what's the word? Intense. Extreme. Sexy."

Of course, Matt understood, that's exactly what made him uneasy. He'd just have to overcome his upbringing and find some underground spring of Polish passion. Maybe it was . . . freedom.

Suddenly it all came clear to him. Spain and Mexico were Catholic countries. Sexual repression was a historical given. The dances were little dramas of natural attraction versus social constriction. Even the flashy costumes were constricting, especially over the torso and hips. Okay. Call him a nerd, but once he understood the social underpinnings, he could get the emotional and artistic needs.

He just had to play these Latin numbers like John the Baptist tempted by Salome. But the Baptist had been a saint and resisted all the way. Matt would have to let himself be seduced. Live on television. At least his mother in Chicago and the parishioners of St. Stanislavsky's wouldn't see this regional show.

"Ready to dance again?" Tatyana demanded.

"Olé," he said.

The door slammed open. A stagehand's head frantically eyed all three.

"Anybody here know first aid?"

"Me," Danny called.

The stagehand jerked his head. "Rehearsal room three."

They both followed Danny out, drawn by the sudden burst of urgency, the rehearsal forgotten.

Chapter 23
Shaken, Not
Stirred

A clot of hovering dancers and support staff blocked the door to rehearsal room three.

Whispers rustled the grave, nodding faces like a wisp of wind in a flower bed.

Danny, Matt figured, had seen a lot of rehearsal accidents, but Matt knew about ministering to the distressed.

So he pushed inside behind the choreographer, while Tatyana peeled off to gossip with her fellow and sister pros, who might know exactly what had happened.

The room mirrored his and Tatyana's rehearsal area: portable wood floor laid over impact-absorbing material, wall mirrors, any spare chairs pushed to the perimeter.

But this room also hosted the metal-pipe jigsaw structure of a jungle gym.

That's where Danny joined several people hunching over something on the floor.

The sight had Matt's heart pounding as if he'd just done a six-spin airplane lift with

Ambrosia to hold up.

He rushed over, calming only when he saw a small figure half sitting, answering questions.

"It was scary," she murmured in a daze. "I don't even *know* how I feel. The fall. Everything's tingling, but I can move stuff. My toes. My fingers."

"Stay still," a man in a dark suit carrying a walkie-talkie ordered. "We have a hotel doctor and EMTs on the way. You don't move until someone with medical expertise is here."

Glory B. looked up, wide-eyed. Her left hand was holding her right wrist, but she didn't seem aware of what that might mean.

"It just . . . gave," she said. "When I was on the top rung. Jesse said I needed to work on my agility and balance."

"I'm sorry, B.," said the young male dancer still crouched next to her. "I tested the bars myself after it was erected. Did spins and flips all over them. They were solid. At least for me. I'm sorry. I just don't get it."

Danny knelt to gently test her limbs and rose.

Matt nudged Danny's arm. As he stood again, Matt whispered, "You and I need to take a fresh look at the jungle gym once

Glory is taken away."

Danny mouthed, "Why?"

"Temple Barr disease," Matt whispered back.

Danny got it and nodded, his forehead a broad ladder of worry lines.

Temple Barr disease: never settle for benign equipment failure as an explanation when malign interference might be a cause. And this *was* a highly public, highly charged competition, with a lot at stake for the producers and performers.

If a muscular male dancer bounding all over the device didn't find the weakness, why would a wisp of a girl who was practicing with uncertainty do it?

For now, Glory B., hot up-and-coming teen pop tart with attitude, was just a scared, possibly hurt kid. Matt thought about Temple out there somewhere, on the trail of another lost kid.

Everyone except Danny and Matt followed the ambulance gurney with Glory B. on it out the door. Camera flashes danced like heat lightning in the hall outside. Matt cringed for Glory. No wonder she was a self-involved media brat, with that kind of center-of-the-universe attention 24/7.

Meanwhile, Danny was doing awesome acrobatics on the jungle gym. Matt watched his taut form spin around the high bars and leap down to the balance board. He switched to the high bars again, then suddenly twisted and vaulted to the floor.

"That's it. The right side of the high bar. It's ready to break away."

"Why didn't it come down with Glory B.?"

"She's a lightweight amateur. She stressed and bent the bar, but didn't break it. Her grip broke instead when the horizontal support wavered. You could be right and that bar was rigged to collapse. Luckily for Glory B., she triggered the collapse but didn't fully cause it."

Danny was straddling the bottom horizontal bar — *ouch!* — jiggling the joint where the top bar met the upright supports, using Glory B.'s fallen warm-up jacket as a latex glove.

"Yup. Here it is. Wiggles. Probably sound until the unit was used. I don't know who's going to investigate this equipment, but I bet if you pull the pipes apart, one of them has been cracked mostly through. These things are houses of cards."

Danny thumped down to the floor, eyeing Matt. "I'll have hotel security witness me taking it apart."

"Photograph and save the pieces," Matt

suggested. "Are you sure we shouldn't call the police?" he asked doubtfully.

"Overkill. There's no concrete evidence here. It could be metal fatigue. Setting up equipment in non-normal dance venues makes for shoddy assembly. Accidents happen in rehearsal. And . . . these amateur dance contests get heated. Might be some overeager fans around. I'm thinking I need to keep an eye out for sabotage as much as good form and talent. So, just in case . . . watch yourself."

Matt nodded. Who would have thought ballroom dancing could be so dangerous?

CHAPTER 24
EN SWEET

An Oasis hotel flunky met our party at the double doors opening onto the "Mata Hari Suite," aka the Zoe Chloe Ozone suite for the duration. All right. A high-roller suite, free! Obviously, Midnight Louie has finally *arrived!* Sweet.

As soon as our party enters, I am decanted like a fine bottle of French wine from Miss Temple's tote bag onto the plush carpet of the suite that will be our joint base of operations.

Both my Miss Temple and Miss Lieutenant C. R. Molina immediately massage their ears with cell phones, checking with their outside connections.

I rub on Mr. Rafi Nadir's black denim calves just to let him know who has more hair to lose and who is boss in other departments too.

He is watching Miss LCRM with a frown I recognize. He does not like being outside the loop, or the phone link, in this case. His hands are pushed into his jean pockets as if he is keeping them from grabbing the cell phone away from his former lady friend.

She takes the cell phone from her ear and clicks it off. "Mariah says Ekaterina has connected with her cocontestants. Mariah will be allowed to bunk with the whole crew, contestants and moms, since EK has no adult chaperone. I think —"

Then Miss Temple shrieks from the adjoining room.

Rafi and Carmen dig in heels to wheel like paired Dobermans, charging across the expansive living room and past its six-foot plasma TV screen.

My Miss Temple is standing in the center of a huge bedroom looking ultra Zoe Chloe and teensy teen, her hands splayed out. "I cannot believe it! All the M&Ms have my *name* on them! How cool is that?"

I leap atop the console table to inspect the huge Easter basket of goodies. I know that it is past Easter, but the bunny appears to have passed through here on its way out of town and laid a whole lotta sweets and treats down in farewell.

"Look!" she is crooning, holding up one colored candy shell after another. "Zoe. Chloe. Ozone. Is not that sweet?"

Only I notice that both Rafi and Carmen are pushing discreet semiautomatics into paddle holsters concealed by their denim jackets. One wears black and one wears blue. Naturally, Miss Carmen's is law-enforcement blue. Naturally, when one thinks of this long-estranged couple, it is in terms of black and blue, not that I am saying anyone whomped on anyone other than emotionally.

"Get a grip," Carmen spits at my roommate.

I am forced to growl, low and long like a dog. I hate resorting to shallow canine tricks, but sometimes humans only heed the overobvious.

"And you shut up, you mobile dust bunny!" Molina rants on. "I am about to call off this whole silly charade. I am out of here if nothing breaks in the next couple of hours."

Nobody says anything, including me. Without the lieutenant's cooperation, we are all off duty faster than a dropped and smashed M&M.

Where would the Miss Lieutenant go? we are all thinking. Mariah will not forsake her little friend who is in the finals of this contest. EK is her new "cause." And the contest itself helps seriously ill kids. Even a hard-nosed police lieutenant cannot bow out of that, despite having to play a personally repugnant undercover role with her ex-boyfriend, least favorite female amateur detective, and her own kid, who has gone star-mad.

I count myself blessed to have evaded this horrible, hormone-hyped state called teenagery. My kind goes from litter to littering in a heartbeat, with no awkward in-between stages but hunting homes or eking out sheer survival.

Maybe human kits would be better off if they did not believe that life offers more than constant struggle, danger, deception, and death, as those of my ilk have long known.

I have just returned from a leisurely inspection of the suite's three bedrooms, deciding on my lodging for the night, to find that my Miss Temple has claimed the big central chamber with the black marble bathroom.

She says it will "look odd" if the celebrity did not take the biggest bedroom. Not that anybody is going to come in here and ruminate on who is in what bedroom. Still, right on! So Baby Bear gets the biggest bed. I do find the black-and-gold brocade coverlet a bit overdone, but a suitably splendid backdrop for one of my coloring.

Miss Carmina Carmen strides into the bedroom to my Miss Temple's left without inspecting it first. "The usual tawdry high-roller taste," she declares.

That leaves Mr. Rafi Raphael to shrug and take the bedroom on Miss Temple's other side.

"Ah," I hear him say, "a really big plasma screen."

I pad in after him. The décor here is royal blue and gold, a bit downscale from the central bed-and-bath combo, but cushy nevertheless. I frown at the wall-mounted screen, already on some sports channel. I prefer House and Garden, being the domestic sort when I am not trodding mean streets. Bye, bye, Papa Bear. I whisk around the corner and sneak up on Miss Carmina Carmen.

She has slung her hobo bag atop the black-glass-topped dresser and is examining the assorted luxuries with hands on hips. She is still frowning. The mounted plasma TV screen is black and shiny like my coat. It will be quiet in Mama Bear's retreat tonight. The coverlet is ruby velvet. In fact, this is the royal red room.

She spots me and holds out a pointing finger. It is not tilted upwards at least. I take the hint and leave. Despite the striped pair among her household, I can see that Mama Bear is no mammal to cuddle up to.

It looks like I will have to fight my Miss Temple tonight for the primo square footage of bedspread, as usual.

Rafi is in the living room, roaming the vast space as he talks on his cell phone.

"Mariah is safely settled in," he announces

loudly, nodding at whoever is talking to him.

The two women hustle out from their respective retreats.

Rafi-Raphael gives them the "okay" sign of circled thumb and forefinger.

Manx, once again I wish for an opposable thumb! There is not much I can signal with a dewclaw and four shivs except a desire to rip and roll.

He clicks the cell phone dark. "That was my head of operations, Hank Buck. He reports that Mariah has been registered as EK's roommate, but all four competing girls and their mothers — or mini-manager in EK's case — are sharing a suite with multiple bedrooms, like this one."

"Why did you hang up?" Miss Carmina Carmen demands. "I want a full report on Mariah's setup in the contest. Where she will be when."

"I will get you a schedule, but she is completely safe with the teen contenders, Carmen," Rafi, aka Raphael, says. "The hotel has provided high security for all of the girls. Trust me."

Miss Lieutenant C. R. Molina, now back in action, does not think so, and says exactly what she does think, which resembles the third degree.

"Just who is chaperoning the contenders? What is the security level? Mariah should be up here with us for complete safety."

Mr. Rafi is staring at Miss Carmen with blank disbelief. "Did you not hear me? She is folded in with the junior competitors. You would jerk her away from her new friends and the excitement and responsibility of helping EK through the competition?"

"Mariah ran away. She took a terrible risk. She deceived her custodial parent and took advantage of —"

"Took advantage of what?" Rafi asked, as quick as I to notice that Miss Lieutenant C. R. Molina has suddenly gone quiet and pale, as if remembering something she should not say.

"Took, um, ad-advantage of my being distracted by a very de-demanding job," she finished.

By now my Miss Temple is also staring at the stuttering lieutenant, and frowning.

"You really want to do that?" Rafi asks. "Take away what she has helped someone else earn, another kid's dream? Right on the brink of it maybe coming true?"

"The odds against EK winning are huge."

"But they are the odds Mariah helped her earn."

"She took a horrible risk and needs to pay a major price."

"Yes, but I am sure you can think up a big-time one after the competition is over. Today is Saturday and the competition only runs through the end of the week, Carmen. We are assigned this duty, and Temple and her cat are on their own time."

"But this charade we have set up —"

"Will allow us to see our daughter in action without inhibiting her."

"She has been a willful, foolish child. She should not be rewarded."

"You can ground her for six months."

Miss Temple piped up, "And keep her from going to the fall father-daughter dance she was so hot on attending."

My Miss Temple does not often "innocently" lob verbal hand grenades into a situation, but she did just then. I sit back with her to watch the fireworks coming up.

Rafi caught it on the first toss. "Father-daughter dance? That's right. Let us discuss this. Mariah is eager to go?"

"Sure. It would be her first dress-up formal event. She is all hot to have Matt Devine do the honors."

"He is hardly a friend of the family, is he?"

"He *is* friendly to us."

"And," Temple put in helpfully, "Mariah thinks that he is hot."

Rafi tossed the figurative hand grenade to the ceiling. "An ex-priest? A childless, never-married ex-priest? Escorting my daughter to a father-daughter dance? What is wrong with someone really paternal, like Detective Alch?"

"I suggested that from the first," Miss Carmen says nervously.

Between them, Miss Temple and Mr. Rafi have her squirming, and both are enjoying it for what I assume are vastly different reasons.

Miss Carmina Carmen goes on. "Mariah rejected Alch. She does not have a truly grounded idea of what a father figure is. She can be amazingly mature one moment and hopelessly shallow the next. As for the father-daughter dance, it is not some major emotional crisis for her. She just wants to wow the other girls with an older more glamorous escort."

Rafi shrugs and folds his arms across his chest. "You are not canceling this event on her. She will just have to wow them with me."

"I had said I *might* be ready to broach Mariah with the subject of you in good time. Not now!"

"This dance is not for a few months. Time enough to 'broach' a lot of things. I may not be Golden Boy, but I am her real father and I could 'wow' the other girls better than Uncle Morrie."

I eye Mr. Rafi Nadir. This guy has nerve. Miss Lieutenant C. R. Molina is all bristling officer again, her own arms folded tight across

229

her stomach, but also under her breasts, which is a somewhat inflammatory posture to take with exes.

Thing is, for whatever reason, Mr. Rafi Nadir has tightened and tautened and taken the upper hand since slinking into Vegas a loser a few months ago, and his dark looks might indeed cause a feminine heart to flutter, not that Miss Lieutenant C. R. Molina has either of those two attributes in high supply, femininity or heart.

But something is making her face flush a deep, carmine-red, fury or fever.

My Miss Temple has dropped her Zoe Chloe posture to stand there gracelessly gaping, which is so unlike her.

"This is *not,*" the policewoman declares, "the place or the time to discuss Mariah's parental custody arrangements."

"This is the exact right time," Rafi pushes. "You can discipline Mariah however you think is necessary, but it should not affect what she does next fall, or my right to continue building rapport with her. I get what she wants, even if you have forgotten what it ever was to want anything."

The silence in the room is long and deep enough to keep a tiger litter sleeping peacefully. I eye my Miss Temple, who is biting her lip and holding her breath and crossing her fingers, all at once.

Our not-so-favorite favorite homicide lieutenant takes a deep, shocked breath, which suddenly doubles her over. Rafi reaches a hand out to her upper arm to steady her, but she twists violently away, her next breath ending like a bellows with a little puff of shock. Her face is clown-white pale.

Rafi Nadir is pretty shocked too. "You are not just being the usual hard-ass," he says as if he is just working this out while we eavesdrop. "You are . . . in physical pain. You are hurt."

"Nonsense," she says so emphatically that we all know it is not nonsense.

"You have been wounded," Rafi diagnoses with narrowed eyes. "A triplicate form desk jockey. How? Why?"

"None of your business," she tells him, letting her fierce gaze pass over him to freeze Miss Temple in a burgeoning comment she swallows like a double wad of bubble gum.

"I am not the focus of this insane rescue effort," Molina spits out. "Mariah is. As you say, she is safe now. And we are stuck in these loony undercover personas babysitting a two-bit dance competition getting flaky death threats to see that she stays that way. I'm not crazy about her rooming elsewhere, but you proved that cutting a kid from the herd in a situation like this would be considered cruel and unusual punishment by said kid. Your people had better keep a damn serious eye on them all."

She turns and vanishes behind the double doors to her bedroom suite, leaving us three twitching whiskers and blinking eyes. At least I am the only one able to whisker-twitch.

"Wow," Miss Temple says to Mr. Rafi. "You pushed more buttons than I knew she had."

"Right now," he answers, "if I had any stake in anything, I would be more worried about her than her daughter."

His cell phone rings and he claps it to an ear as hard as a sparring partner might hit it. *Ouch!*

I cannot tell you how sick, ticked, and piqued I am about cell phones. These miserable little devices are like a medieval infestation of rats. They breed everywhere. People are entirely at their beck and call, and run shrieking to cuddle them every time they squeal. And they have a thousand annoying voices, some famous. This fad to have unique "ring tones" is a plague on humanity. Anyone with sensitive hearing is assaulted daily, and also left out of the loop watching folks speak loudly as they wander down the street. Time was, people behaved that way, they were put in custody "for observation."

Now, if you are not mumbling or screaming meaningless phrases when you front down the street, you are not hip. You are the new "boom boxes."

I must say that my kind has admirably resisted the trend to constant and showy communication. We still say more with the blink of an eye or the twitch of a back or the flick of a shiv.

Still, such are these times that my Miss Temple and I are forced to tear our attention from Miss Carmen's most satisfying meltdown to regard Mr. Rafi's one-sided monologue.

"The Barbie memo? Sure, anything on that would be good." He paces, nodding and listening. "No kidding. Just today. Missing? Search the mall, and do not forget to comb between every row of the parking lot. Especially the parking lot. There is precedent. Get back to me as soon as. The lieutenant? On the other phone. I will make sure she gets the message."

Miss Temple and I have edged nearer on one very provocative sentence.

"Another Barbie doll has shown up at the Albuquerque audition site," he reports grimly, "and a female competitor is missing. I had better tell 'Carmina.' Unless you —"

"No," my Miss Temple says wisely. "She is all yours. I will check the Internet for fresh

Barbie doll atrocities."

So there we are again, torn between a cell phone and the Internet. I tell you, the art of investigation is not the same old gray mare it used to be.

CHAPTER 25
EVERYBODY
UNDERCOVER, QUICK!

Temple figured she was playing a pretty good Mariah substitute at the moment.

She even had the typical teenager's quarreling parents. There was no doubt that Lieutenant Molina and Rafi Nadir made volatile partners. After they'd made it to the high-roller suite, Raphael and Carmina made sure to get as far as possible from each other in their bedroom assignments. Lions, and tigers, and angry ex-lovers, oh my!

As soon as Temple could relax in the presumed privacy of her star bedroom, she phoned Matt on her cell.

"Where are you and what are you wearing?" she said when he answered.

"Who *are* you?"

"Your light of love in a kickier, bolder persona. Enjoy."

"Temple, where are you?"

"Don't you want to know what I'm wearing?"

"If it's the usual Zoe Chloe Ozone Goth issue, no. *Ish,* for sure. Can I make it any plainer, because I certainly can't make her any plainer."

Temple was not about to relinquish making a provocative call from a high-roller suite.

"You are about to lose a date," she told him.

"Our wedding date?"

"No, sweetums. We haven't even set that yet. I'm referring to your dinner-dance date with a star, Mariah Molina."

"Huh?"

"Surely you haven't forgotten *the* glamour event of the fall, the father-daughter dance at Our Lady of Guadalupe High School?"

"Shoot. I had. Your crazy new assignment has my mind going to mush. I'm supposed to squire Molina Jr."

"Yes, you are, and we've found the little footloose and fancy-free rascal. She's managing a hot newcomer in the junior division of this very hot *Dancing With the Celebs* gig you'll be dazzling with your fancy footwork."

"Good for her."

"Not good for Mama Bear's composure and now Papa Bear has ID'd her as a walking wounded policewoman, which makes her twice as dangerous a bear. Did you know anything about that? Molina getting hurt?"

"Uh, maybe."

"Oh, no! Matt, you haven't been playing Wailing Wall for the enemy? What's this all about?"

"It's hardly relevant to what's going on now."

"The heck it isn't. You've got a rival for Perfect Dream Dad. Rafi wants to escort Mariah to that dance."

"His world and welcome to it. Her mother sort of railroaded me for the job anyway."

"Her mother railroads us all, but right now she looks like she's been working on the railroad, rode hard, and put up wet. What is going on with her?"

"She's been . . . wounded. That's all I can say without violating —"

"The sanctity of the confessional."

"In a way. I swore."

"*Humph.* The only way you *would* swear. Fiancés shouldn't keep secrets from fiancées."

"I know. I'm between a frying pan and the steel wool here."

"What a labored metaphor," Temple hooted. "Who's the steel wool, me or Molina?"

"Okay, that was a bad figure of speech. Say, if Mariah has been found and is back in Vegas, your charade is over and you can go home, right?"

"Wrong." Temple lowered her voice. "There was another mutilated Barbie doll outside a mall audition in Albuquerque. One of the teen wanna-be competitions. Molina's boss has decided they have a decent team undercover here and wants our show to go on."

"Mariah will see through you all in a millisecond."

"She did, but she likes it. Drama queen. We're all going to share the multibedroom Zoe Chloe Ozone comped high-roller suite, except Mariah, who'll bunk with the junior division competitors. So far Mama Bear has given her holy hell for taking off and Papa Bear has been introduced as an investigator from hotel security, which he is. We'll all keep an eye on her, and she'll keep her mouth shut because she badly wants her little friend to compete. Ekaterina is a Chechen refugee and a world-class dancer, apparently. What I've gotten out of the kids is that, caught between Russian troops and Chechen security forces, a new wave of Chechens have been immigrating since 2003, mostly to European Union countries and a few to the United States. EK could qualify as a cultural refugee with the right creds. Like winning this contest."

"If this Barbie Doll Killer is branching out to auditions in New Mexico, the finals here would be a free-for-all for him and you are masquerading as a teenager, Temple. Now that I'm a fiancé, I'm saying you should forget it and go home for your own safety."

"I've got two police types living with me, practically, and you're booked into a room here, too, for contest week. And I'm key to the undercover operation. Or Zoe Chloe is."

"You make this zany character sound almost real."

"It's scary how real she is to these teen fans. I needed a phalanx of hotel security getting to the private elevators. They were screaming and shooting photos. I felt like Marilyn Monroe come back from the dead. And Zoe Chloe doesn't *do* anything, except broadcast attitude."

"All this is supposed to reassure me?"

"My job is to stick with Mariah, and we'll have Mama and Papa Bear all over us, believe it. It's like they're in a competition to safeguard Mariah."

"Guilt." Matt's tone was grim. "They each need to prove they're the perfect parent. I really hate you being caught in the middle there, Temple, whether it's between dueling parents or a serial killer and his prey."

"Is it because we're engaged now?"

"It's because you're a target two ways: as part of an undercover police team with a known stalker on the loose, and as the crazy pop persona, Zoe Chloe, who attracts maniac fans. Max isn't here anymore to play guardian angel. He did, you know, and he was darn good at it."

Temple was stunned into silence. Matt was right. She'd always had her secret "shadow," had unconsciously taken it for granted. Even now.

"I'm sorry," he said finally. "It's the truth."

"I know. But I committed to this. Mariah's a neat kid. Maybe her yen to perform is really an unconscious hope of pleasing an absent father. She did this not for herself, but to help another kid who could really use a boost. I don't know what Molina told her daughter about her parentage, but I'm seeing something happening with Molina and Rafi. A coming to terms. Mariah, too. This enforced mission might even settle things with all three of them. I can't bail."

"And you don't want to. You've always been hooked on investigating things, and now you're hooked on being a teenybopper star."

"I am not!" But the suite was cool and the masquerade got her old drama queen juices going. Besides . . .

"Don't worry, Matt," she said confidently. "I'm not only the apple of the LVMPD's many eyes but Midnight Louie hitched a ride with us. The Hooded Claw is my bodyguard."

"Ever since that debacle at the chicken ranch, I must admit Louie has a lot more street cred with me."

"He saved me from a mob hit man."

"I don't give him *that* much cred. He was just acting out in the manner of his breed. He went a little crazy in a speeding vehicle, is all. Cats hate riding in cars."

Sure. Temple eyed Louie, sprawled dead center of her huge, round, gold-satin-covered bed like a big, black, hairy, giant tarantula. His absinthe-green eyes squinted with mobster relish. He'd loved lolling in the big black SUV on the ride to Laughlin and back.

Yeah, baby, yeah.

Midnight Louie must have been exhausted by the roundabout trip to the hotel.

He didn't budge for an instant from lying

dead center of the mattress.

Since it was a round bed, Temple had to curl around him like a worm. So much for Internet stardom.

She had trouble sleeping, which might have been the position, or her, um, position.

She was now officially a fiancée acting against her intended's better judgment. She hadn't had to answer for her own safety to anyone since leaving her Minneapolis home almost three years before. True, she'd been living on her own since she was twenty-three, and she was pushing thirty-one now.

Temple tossed and turned, trying to track down the gnawing feeling of guilt taking nibbles out of her innards. She'd left Minneapolis with Max, which was hardly a huge independent step, although leaving her smother-loving family was a hard break to make.

Max had been concerned about her safety — he'd left her without a word for almost a year to lead some nasty hoodlums away from their love nest. Love nest. Temple smiled. Max was hardly the nest type. They'd lived together, but Max had always had a secret life she finally found out about. So he'd never moved back into their Circle Ritz condominium once he was back in

Vegas and her life. They were both free to come and go.

Matt was a lot more conservative than Max. He worried about her unleashing Zoe Chloe Ozone again, even though the police were unofficially encouraging her to do it. Temple supposed a suspect nicknamed the Barbie Doll Killer might be a tad unsettling to a fiancé who wasn't a secret agent on the side, like Max.

But she'd gotten attached to Mariah when she and Zoe had been roommates for the Teen Queen competition. Temple had only had older brothers in her family, always bigger, stronger, surer, "righter." Mariah was like a little sister who needed advice on being girly, being a performer, being a snoop.

Temple grinned. How could she and Zoe be any safer? She had two relentless protectors in the form of feuding bodyguards, each competing to be the more perfect parent and police officer.

Chapter 26
Insecure Security

The ballroom where the show would be held seemed football field huge, with electricians and stagehands running around it like fire ants.

Temple eased her candy-apple red patent leather platform shoes over the snakes' nests of black cables crisscrossing the carpeted floor.

"Watch your step, little lady." Rafi took her elbow and almost hoisted her above the entangling cables.

On her other side, Molina frowned. "You two are on cozy terms."

Rafi gave Temple a Cheshire cat smirk. "It's all about working together on that reality TV show. Bonds form fast."

"You and a bunch of teenage girls. I may heave."

"Not on the cables. That could be dangerous."

She looked mad enough to spit on both of

them, but shrugged and stalked ahead, her tailored loafers missing every sheaf of cable.

"Man, she is wired," Rafi said.

When Temple laughed, he caught her eye.

"Appropriate choice of words, right here," he said. "I don't know whether her problem is concealed pain or . . . concealed something else."

Temple was not an ex–marital counselor, like Matt, so she let that lie. "How do we go about investigating in this massive place? A determined killer could be running around in one of these workman's overalls."

"I'm sure that's where Carmen's gone. She's got undercover cops here. They'll have checked lists of workmen, program personnel, waitstaff, anyone with business in the area. And they'll continue checking. You think you could find an outfit more likely to scream, 'Here I am, mob me or kill me'?"

Temple looked down at her black-lace leggings, racy red shoes, and short, full skirt. She waggled her fingers in the long spiderweb-pattern Goth gloves and hefted the orange patent leather tote bag holding Louie and little else higher on her shoulder.

"I have to be fashion-forward. The world expects that of Zoe Chloe. Golly, Rafi, how long do I have to lug Louie around as a purse pussycat? He weighs a ton!"

Louie's large, cheeky tomcat face looked very Halloweenish peering over the pumpkin-colored tote bag.

"Cats aren't supposed to like being carried around," Temple complained further.

"He's a good prop," Rafi said, lifting the double tote straps off her right shoulder.

Before Temple could sigh her relief, Louie hissed at his new custodian and wriggled out of the bag onto the floor. In a few smooth darts, he threaded the workmen's legs before they even noticed his presence and, like Molina before him, disappeared.

"That cat has a nose for trouble," Rafi commented. "If Carmen wouldn't have my head for leaving you, I'd follow him."

"Let's both do it. Louie thinks best on his feet."

So they tripped the cables fantastic until they arrived at the backstage area where floor directors, the producer, the music director, and press agents were milling around.

"Miss Ozone!" exclaimed a jovial man shaped like a bottom-heavy wine bottle that comes in a basket wrap. He waddled over, operating a cell phone camera. "Fab to have you here. You look fab. The show will be fab with you emceeing our junior division and bringing all your online fans along for the ride, not to mention making new fans through your appearances here. And this gentlemen is?"

"Mr. Raphael d'Arc, my manager and occasional personal security agent."

"Hmm." The officious fellow looked Rafi over and decided he looked both secure and personable. "Not the usual mindless muscle in hip-hop bling. Quite refreshing, Miss Ozone."

"I aim to refresh," Temple said. "So tell me what's all happenin' so I can jive with the jukebox in perfect one-and-ah-two-and-ah-three-and-ah-*bam* git-down, tank-up, thank you, ladies and gentlemen time."

"She is a pistol, isn't she, man?" the guy asked Rafi as if they were secret frat brothers, with a wink and a would-be jab in the ribs.

Rafi easily evaded any contact and drew his black denim jacket back to reveal a tan leather holster. "*This* is a pistol, man. Who are you and why are you accosting Miss Ozone?"

"Hey, chill, dude! I'm the DJ for breaks on this show. Gotta keep the live audience mellow yellow between segments. I'm just a fan of Miss Ozone. She is one scintillating little mama."

"You're on the set the day before the

actual broadcasts?"

"Yes, sir!" The DJ was getting very Private Gomer Pyle after seeing the iron Rafi was pumping. "I need to watch the rehearsals, get the rhythm and the routines down. Just like Miss Ozone here. That's why you're here early, isn't it? A real hip little pro. Always a 110 percent for the gig. These teen pop tarts are all energy and nerve and flash edges, even if they burn out fast."

Temple thought that was pretty true, but coming from this oil-slick guy it made her sick to the stomach.

Rafi had the same reaction and he had a wanna-be pop tart daughter who was still as naïve as cornflakes. "Maybe. But Miss Ozone is only paid to perform on stage. You keep your distance and do your job, and your lame little soul patch will not be torn right off your chinny-chin-chin."

Temple shivered as the guy shimmied away like a bowlful of lard. "That was mean."

"He's a creep. This is what Mariah wants to run deadhead into. Today's entertainment industry is run by gangsters and creeps on the make and slimy celebrity 'judges' who make dough from ridiculing people, some of them pathetically hungry for approval, on live TV."

"Wasn't it always that way?"

"No. Talent used to matter and bullying wasn't entertainment."

Temple blinked.

Rafi shrugged. "You discover you have a kid you never knew about, you start to worry about the world. It's nuts, I know."

"I think it's kinda sweet."

Rafi's fist took a mock swing at her upper arm. "Cut out that kinda talk. You don't mess with my rep as the Big Bad Wolf That Ate L.A., Red."

"I'm closer to a lively strawberry blond these days."

"And a tasty little fruit tart you're playing. But don't underestimate the fruit flies."

Temple nodded. She was liking Rafi Nadir more and more.

Would that frost Molina.

Maybe she did have a guardian angel, Mr. Raphael d'Arc, even though Max was gone. Temple wondered where his wings were in residence now, and hoped it wasn't heaven.

CHAPTER 27
REINVENTION WALTZ

Fiery leg aches sent shooting pains through his entire frame, but for the first time since his escape, sitting in the elegant Hummer-bar drinking an aquavit, he felt he lived up to his real name, "Max."

Maximilian Fleming was registered at the Hotel St. Gotthard on Zurich's main shopping, eating, banking street — the Bahnhofstrasse.

Five new stolen credit cards reposed in the eel skin vertical wallet in the breast pocket of his new leather blazer. His magician's fingers were still matchless at the Misdemeanor Waltz. The five cards had been extracted from obvious American tourists, all the better to remain undiscovered for longer. Tourists moved on fast these days, and, in patchwork Europe, could scoot two countries over in a day.

His slacks and silk turtleneck were Ralph Lauren, his shoes Bruno Magli. He'd also bought an electric razor that would beat back his black beard (with a slight gray sheen — when had that happened? Or was it new? Just how old was he?) to a disguising, yet film-star-hip smudge of three days' growth. The way the bristles had annoyed him on the road, he figured he'd been smooth-shaven previously. His hair had been expensively barbered into the miserable spiky male coxcomb in vogue nowadays that made guys look like the village idiot, or worse, Clay Aiken. Everything elegant and costly was available within walking distance on the Bahnhofstrasse, despite the current economic swoon, a key advantage. Conspicuous consumption never died.

He figured bold was the best disguise. A rich Irishman would not be out of place here. The once-impoverished island nation where his forebears had starved for want of potatoes was having an Irish Spring of high-tech industrialization.

Yes, he'd donned a faint mist of brogue. It came as easy to him as German, even the Swiss variation. As had the facts of recent Irish economic upswing before the recent global recession. That he knew these geopolitical facts and other languages made Garry Randolph's story about their being partners in counterterrorism for years ring ominously true.

The only things he didn't know about was *his* childhood, boyhood, and personal, educational, professional, and romantic history. Details.

He'd shopped before he approached the Gotthard's front desk, where he'd muttered in broken German about a skiing accident in the Alps having delayed his getting to a banking appointment in Zurich. He was rather embarrassingly marooned at the moment but had a crucial appointment at Adler and Company, Privatbank, in the morning. Was any sort of suite or even a single room available?

His illness-drawn face and the hokey carved cane, which he regarded with rueful disdain and reluctant dependence, had convinced the hotel manager. That and his Gucci bag. Snooty service staff assessed women first by their handbags, then their shoes, and finally their jewelry. For men, the order was watch, luggage, wallet, shoes.

That's why a shiny new Patek Philippe high-dollar watch weighed down Max's bony wrist, courtesy of an oil company executive from Texas. Max didn't like the piece's looks and overhyped luxury, but wore it proudly in the name of Enron ripped-off ex-employees everywhere. Corporate greed deserved a comeuppance.

See? It was all coming back. The nightly news. The exhausted American economy, the Irish renaissance. Brand names. Foreign words. But . . . nothing Personal. He felt like a data-gorged robot.

Maybe that was why he was chasing Revienne and her Mercedes chariot when he ought to let her go her own way, villain or victim, true purpose unknown.

But he couldn't. She'd laughed over dinner in the mountain village, and wolfed down her meal like a real girl. She'd scavenged for him in the mountain meadow farmholds, finding a saw to cut through his imprisoning casts, begging food and clothing. She'd massaged his mending legs until he'd fallen asleep, as trusting as an infant.

If she'd been kidnapped because of him . . .

If she'd been leading him on . . .

Who was Max? Hero or killer? Or just Garry Randolph's protégé, long past the age of needing mentors?

After this drink, and a dinner of the restaurant's famed seafood, Max would be whisked five stories high in this 1889-vintage building to an arty suite with an Internet connection.

Did he even know how to connect to the Internet, much less real people, including Revienne? Had to. If the languages had come back to him, so would the technology. Just . . . nothing Personal.

His mind did another of its disconcerting flashbacks: to bright alpine wildflowers, a bouquet of fragrant yellow freesias, a pretty brunet bus driver who wrangled a major German bus and had granted him passage, and . . . a redheaded woman with gray-blue eyes. Revienne was blond.

Max lurched up. The "lurch" was partly his legs and partly his aquavit. Time for dinner and then a tour of the world by Internet. He'd punch in the words "Garry Randolph," "Revienne," "Schneider," and "Max."

As Edward R. Murrow, the pioneer TV broadcaster, used to say in closing his TV news program, "Good night and good luck."

See! He remembered vintage catchphrases from before he was born.

Why not his own damned history?

CHAPTER 28
PRECIOUS TOPAZ

While my human posse is introducing itself to our new venue, concentrating on the *Dancing With the Celebs* set and environs, I figure I better get my black velvet pads pussyfooting over the Oasis Hotel's entire layout.

One never knows when the big picture will come in handy.

The Oasis is one of those midlevel Las Vegas people palaces, like the Luxor, and the remaining grand old dames of the Strip like the Riviera.

This does not mean that the Oasis is not the usual wild and crazy theme park of an attraction. Where the Luxor exploits the archeological fascination of ancient Egypt, the Oasis concentrates on eastern mysticism in general. Which is a nice way of saying that architecturally and thematically it is a hash of pop culture: ancient hidden treasure, camel trains of stolen jewels, Marco Polo, a little Sinbad and the 1001 Nights, harems, gypsy fortune-tellers, belly dancers, you get the Kodak. It has grabbed the lost Aladdin Hotel's marketing spot with a more multicultural air.

An undercover operative like myself often ends up spending the most time on the shady and elite sides of the Strip. Crime tends to erupt at the extremes of the social scale. The happy middle is where passion and money tend to be on the mild and cheap scale. It is not surprising that Mr. Rafi Nadir could quickly rise to a second-in-command security position here, not to take anything away from his admirable reformation.

Apparently, discovering an unknown out-of-wedlock child can stabilize a man.

I cannot say that the discovery of my *reputed* offspring, Miss Midnight Louise, provided me with any impetus other than to run the other way. My impulse was intense, I will give the situation that. Miss Midnight Louise would be cranky that I am operating solo now, but purse pussies do not come in pairs, unlike shoes, or even gumshoes.

So I prowl the busy-patterned carpet underfoot, a mere shadow in the corner of everyone's eye, busy educating myself to the scene of any crimes to come. For there will be at least one, with so much ill will already expressed in terms of death threats and the repeat appearance of the Barbie Doll Killer's calling cards.

A Vegas hotel floor plan is like a small city to a guy my size. My walking tour would be hard on my pins were it not that I have discovered that this place houses something of deep personal interest, namely a dame.

She first appears to me on the back of a playing card that has fallen to the carpet. Now, this is a mortal sin, or at least a killing offense in Vegas, where every card being accounted for is a matter of life and death.

Loose cards imply dirty tricks, fixing, or worse.

So I nudge my find farther under the black-jack table, braving overexcited and milling human feet. The light is not so good here but I can still make out the lithe photographic form: sleek, asphalt-dark curves fast enough to derail a Porsche, legs that never end in black silk stockings, a flexible rear appendage long enough to derail a train, and the most unearthly, twenty-four-karat golden eyes I have ever seen.

These orbs — and, yes, that expression is okay, folks, because they are as round and brilliant as harvest moons — would hypnotize a Svengali.

Phew. I can hardly tear my gaze away already. I am so smitten I risk exposure to scale the table and eye the dealer's shoe, which is not footwear, but a device for holding several decks of cards. Oh, my yes. Bingo! Every card slipped out of the shoe is a graphic tribute to this most sublime feline form.

"Hey!" some twenty-one happy gambler carps at my sudden presence. "I was just about to double down."

I spit out the card I found on the floor so it falls to the green felt.

"Uh," the loudmouth grunts. I found the card under his chair.

The dealer is frowning. "Stay right there, sir."

"Damn cat!" the guy spits at me.

I snatch up the card and jump down.

"Damn cat!" the dealer yells in parting. I can hear the crooked player chuckling to see the evidence vanishing with me.

I am not about to give up my card until I can find the model and have her personalize it.

There are two things I now need to locate: a pedigree pin-up book to pin down what breed of cat she is, and info around the hotel to find out who and where she is.

First I stash the card under a roulette table.

I cannot go wandering around a casino with a loose playing card clenched in my hot little black lips and sharp white teeth. Being an ace investigator, I know it is no coincidence that this hot, hairy little honey is backing every last darn Oasis playing card.

Pretty soon I am seeing those opulent gold eyes gazing soulfully down at me from posters and signs all over the hotel.

There she is, Miss American Beauty, curling into the Big O of Oasis over the show ticket booth, atop the registration desk on giveaway cards in Lucite boxes, six-feet-long lounging over the word "Theater" in the marquee to the nightly show.

Oh, no. I hope she is not literally a Big Cat. (There are some limits to even one of Midnight Louie's romantic prowess.)

By now I am frantic.

I cannot believe that a dude of my discrimination and wide-ranging territory and nose for news all over Las Vegas has failed to notice the hot new girl in town! I must lay eyes on her, if nothing else.

It is while crossing the casino carpet, ignoring the hustle and bustle and jostle, that I at last catch her scent. It is sweet, earthy, musky, like expensive perfume. I immediately think of rare ambergris. It may or may not be based in that treasured effusion of the sperm whale that the ancient Egyptians burned as incense — they worshiped cats, if you recall, so they were the smart sort — but it is music to my nose. It means that she is not "fixed," that abomination of birth control perpetrated on my kind for its own good, but also for a major reduction in fun for me.

Now that I have a scent to follow, it is nose to the nap around the casino. In fact, I am so much the bloodhound on a trail that I bump into a table leg, face-to-face.

No! Not a table leg, but the leggy object of my search.

She is sitting there like a statue of regal Bast, the Egyptian cat goddess, only she is not eight feet tall, or even three feet tall like a Big Cat, but only a foot or so high and warm and satin-furred and I am lost.

I can see why I mistook her for Bast. She wears a collar and from it dangle glittering amber crystal teardrops. She looks like a billion bucks and I am just a two-dollar bill. I am always falling for dames beyond my station.

"My apologies, miss. I was so hot on the trail I missed your presence."

"What trail are you on, sir?"

Well, I cannot come right out and say it. That would be crass.

"Allow me to introduce myself," I say, bowing so my luxurious black vibrissae blend tips with hers. (Vibrissae are known as whiskers to the commoner sort, such as humans.) "I am working undercover in this hotel. You may have heard of the *Dancing With the Celebs* event."

"Then you are masquerading as a dancer?"

"No, I am masquerading as a celebrity mascot."

"Oh! I am a mascot too!"

"What a coincidence. What are you a mascot of, or for?"

"This whole hotel. And your mascotery is —"

I am not about to identify myself as a "purse pussy."

"I am a private detective by profession, Midnight Inc. Investigations, assigned to one of those currently popular teen pop tarts in the dance show, one Miss Zoe Chloe Ozone, as a personal pet. Only for appearances, I assure you. I am no one's personal pet, although there are occasions when I would make an exception for the right little doll who could wrap me around her long supple tail."

"You look like you have quite a long supple . . . tail yourself, Mr. Midnight."

I am about ready to belie my words and do the happy dance.

"And how did you become a hotel mascot, may I ask?" I go on. "Other than sublime good looks, of course."

She tilts her head adorably to the side and runs her little red tongue over her vibrissae, making them tremble, and me too.

"My mistress is a public events coordinator for this hotel."

"What a coincidence! Miss Temple Barr, my

current roommate, is a freelance version of same. She is a clever and comely and petite little doll to whom I am devoted."

"How amazing. My Miss Tuesday Weldon answers to the same description and is devoted to me. I inspired her theme for the entire hotel."

"What a coup for catkind. You are truly a pioneer."

"I only assist my mistress. You are the first feline PI I have heard of. You must have carved a trail too."

"This is top secret. I assist my roommate too. We are both undercover."

"This is my hotel, Mr. Midnight. I deserve to know what danger assaults it."

"The usual death threats so far."

"Yes, that is quite usual these days. Well, Mr. Midnight —"

"I do not stand on formalities. Call me Louie."

"Very well, Louie. I am working right now and must be on my appointed rounds."

" 'Appointed rounds'? Surely you are not delivering mail?"

Her laugh is an entrancing burst of soft purrs. "No, no. Nothing so mundane. I am to cover the floor and show myself."

"You are not being put on parade like a showgirl!"

"I *am* a showgirl, Louie," she responds, patting my cheek with velvet paw. "I appear nightly at the Sandbox Lounge in the hotel, with the house magician."

I stiffen. (Not that way!) The evil Hyacinth, the late Shangri-La's feline assistant, had hitched her star to the only Asian female magician in Vegas.

"My main job," she goes on, "is to stroll around with my necklace of amber-colored jewels. I am a walking special offer. The hotel's guests can earn free chips, a dinner, a lodgings discount or other prizes by spotting me on my rounds and unfastening a pendant jewel from my collar."

I would like to unfasten her collar! "So your work is promotional?"

"Purely."

"I see your mistress is clever indeed and that I must not detain you longer, no matter how much I might wish to, as your job is to be mobile."

"You are so . . . intuitive, Louie. I do like a sensitive male. I hope our paths cross again."

"I am sure they will. And if a feline chap were to snag one of your valuable dangles — ?"

"He would return it. For, alas, only humans can redeem the pendants for rewards."

"Oh, I think there would rewards aplenty for an enterprising feline PI."

"Just between you and I —"

I lean inward, not about to correct the grammar wafting from that honeyed breath.

"One of the faux pendants they place on my collar each morning is not just crystal, but a precious jewel. And the reward for finding that is major."

I think for a moment, which is a considerable challenge, under the circumstances, as you may imagine.

" 'A precious jewel.' Perhaps a jewel as precious as your name?"

"And what would that be, Louie?"

I am about to display my precious deductive gift.

"It is a gemstone," I say, watching the flash of an appreciative gleam in her glorious golden eyes, "often having others substituted for itself: plain citrine, even lowly smoky quartz. But the true stone is worth a thousand times the lesser stones' value, and ranges through a divine rainbow of warm gilt colors, from faintest dawn gold to the warm, ruddy sherry of sunset, and it is called 'precious topaz,' as are you.

"It has been a pleasure to meet you, Miss Topaz. I trust it will not be the last occasion."

I am rewarded by the sight of her almost invisible airy black eyebrow vibrissae lilting high in shock and pleasure at my correct prediction of her name. I bow and back away.

Midnight Louie knows when to leave them
laughing, and, more important, when to leave
them swooning.

CHAPTER 29
BROTHERS, WHERE
ART THOU?

It nearly killed Temple to wake up early the next morning. This was Sunday, the day of the first live evening show but she doubted Matt would miss mass.

She ached to trail the cop side of the undercover team, but she knew Zoe Chloe Ozone needed to hang with her "peeps," the four teen girls dancing with the barely older singing sensations, Los Hermanos Brothers.

The boy band's name was redundant, *hermanos* being the Spanish word for brothers, but Temple supposed record and TV moguls liked the spin of a bilingual name.

The brothers themselves, ranging from twelve to sixteen, were reassuring both to their adoring fans and their mothers, and even to Temple.

Early showbiz exposure and training had made them smooth and creamy tween idols. They all had the cheeky, choirboy innocence of the young Bobby Dylan, not that it meant that they were. Nowadays, though, looks were everything.

Each girl had her soundproof mini-rehearsal "room." Ekaterina was unique in having her own "manager," Mariah.

Temple imagined Mama Molina was as thrilled as she was that Mariah and EK were joined at the hip for this competition. Official nerves were as tight-strung as the high E-string on a guitar about the junior competition members' safety with reports of the Barbie Doll Killer elsewhere as well as the usual Cloaked Conjuror worries.

Los Hermanos Brothers made millions and the girl contestants were invaluable as the ordinary members of the community who were getting a gazillion-dollar chance to turn pro. Anything bad happening in this neighborhood was a disaster.

Temple donned Zoe Chloe makeup and clothes, which took an hour over a room service tray, and headed for the theater area. Things were getting serious. Maybe that's why Midnight Louie had donned his best ears-perked attitude and came along like a lamb in his tote-bag transport.

He even proudly wore the silver collar trailing a bib of rainbow-colored heart-shaped beads Temple had made from an overdone ankle bracelet she found at the nearest dollar store. Well, he wore it without bucking out from under it and scratching it with the massive scimitars of his hind claws once Temple had explained that they all had to suffer through abominable articles of clothing to make this undercover operation work.

Louie's aloof green eyes had then surveyed Molina's Woodstock tie-dyed headband, Rafi's leather vest and Navajo shirt, Temple's Goth fingerless spiderweb gloves, navy-blue-painted finger and toenails, and skunk-striped pantyhose, then leaped for cover in the depths of her zebra tote bag, his collar strands clicking like mini-castanets or Chihuahua toenails on a kitchen floor.

All four girl contestants were in EK's and Mariah's "rehearsal room," sitting on the wooden portable dancing floor in frog posture with their ankles together and their knees splayed flat as if they didn't have a joint or sinew or protesting muscle in their bodies.

Louie jumped down to join them, getting copious *oohs* and *aahs* and pettings.

Zoe Chloe elected to perch pixielike on a nearby ladder, so as not to overstress her knees. Jumping down would be so much more graceful than jumping up from the cold, hard floor.

"That José Juarez is hot!" the black girl named Patrisha opined.

"So is Captain Jack!" a blond girl breathed.

It took Temple a millisecond to realize they were referencing the metrosexual Jack Sparrow from *Pirates of the Caribbean*. She blinked at the advanced level of sophistication of young girls today. She'd never dreamed she'd be behind the curve ball at thirty.

For a moment, she ardently sympathized with Molina, who must be at least seven years older than she, and only a decade away from being able to sit on the floor. At all.

Watching the four competitors sink bonelessly to the floor and let their hair down was amazing. They chattered away, ignoring her now that Zoe Chloe was just another semi-adult supervisor.

EK's doe-eyed, sallow look made her seem as wary as a starving alley cat. Skateboarder Patrisha's elongated ebony frame was pertly elegant. She seemed a likelier candidate for a supermodel contest than this gig. Meg-Ann was a soccer star, big-boned, strong, and determined. Her long brown ponytail and sunshine-spawned freckles gave her tomboy appeal. And, of course, there was the perfect, cool, spoiled blond girl wearing the latest fads and destined to be prom queen, if nothing else: Sou-Sou Smith.

"What we really need to decide," Sou-Sou said with a toss of her highlighted hair, "is who has the hottest Hermanos brother. I vote for my partner, Dustin. His sideburns just radiate sex."

Sideburns on teen boys? Temple wondered. When did the world turn back to the seventies when she was born?

"You're just pimping your dance partner," Patrisha said with a, well, patrician sneer. "I got Brandon, babe. He has that delicious name and that open shirt and tie bit going. Speaking of bite — I may go gaga vampire on stage."

Temple blushed at this open teen lust.

"Chris is cool," tomboy Meg-Ann added matter-of-factly. "That back flip he did on the last tour was awesome. He'll win this thing hands down, literally." She glanced politely at the tongue-tied Russian girl. "You like your guy, EK?"

"Adam has very nice curly hair."

"Wuss!" Sou-Sou hooted.

"And he has much better rhythm and tempo than the other boys." EK sounded positively assertive for a change. "We will

270

do very well together."

A silence prevailed. Girly had gone gritty. Each one of these girls was highly competitive, far more than the already famous boys, probably.

Mariah, on the sidelines with Temple, leaned against the ladder.

"EK's right. Adam is the youngest, but he's the least anxious to impress the girls, rather than the judges. The older brothers think they're so big boy and hot! They're such a pain." She rolled her eyes.

Mama Molina would be happy to hear her only daughter dissing smooth older boys.

Temple wasn't.

There was as much rivalry, gender maneuvering, and naked ambition among the junior dancers as among their supposedly wiser and older counterparts.

Musing about naked ambition, Temple escaped the adjoining rehearsal rooms for the ballroom performance area and looked up her most likely source for an inside view on the show personnel.

Unfortunately, that was her least favorite person, Crawford Buchanan.

She cornered him in the backstage area, already preening in penguin evening dress.

"How did *you* get the emcee gig for this

event?" she demanded.

It took him a moment to recognize her previous disguise from the Teen Queen house.

"Well, if it isn't the one-girl brat pack. How'd *you* arrange to emcee the junior division?" he shot back. "I guess you go where your Teen Queen little buddy girl goes, the cop's daughter who got me into so much trouble. Guess she didn't run away after all."

"Mariah was never lost," Temple lied. "And Zoe Chloe Ozone is an online diva in high personal demand."

"So am I."

"You?"

"Check it out. I'm the Dick Clark of the West Coast."

Dick Clark had founded the teen music TV show, *American Bandstand,* in the fifties, and, forever young, had been a major figure in TV and pop music until his stroke a few years ago. To imagine Crawford Buchanan enduring another forty years like his on-air idol was revolting.

" 'Dick' is so right," Temple retorted. "I need a quick rundown of who's who and what's what. How long does this show run?"

"It runs all the lighter attendance nights in Vegas, starting Sunday to finish with a flourish on Thursday, when all the weekend crowds come in. We introduce the contenders tonight with a dance de jour, then they have the next day to rehearse a new dance with their pro teacher and present it that night, and so on until the Friday grand awards ceremony."

"Who's all participating?"

Crawford finally had a chance to show true form and leer at her. "Checking up on the competition your sweetie is facing, huh? I see you and Matt 'Mr. Sob Story Radio' Devine hanging together. José 'Hot Hips' Juarez, the Olympic fencer, will samba him off the stage."

"Blimey, Crawf 'the Barf Bag' Buchanan! Are you going to introduce every contestant with those 'quotes included' nicknames? Pretty lame emceeing. Come on, tell me who's in the whole cast, besides Mr. Olympic Olé."

"I'm sworn to secrecy," Buchanan said. "So hold your horses, honey, and weep."

Temple wanted to say she was a designated police snitch, but she was sworn to secrecy on that. She stomped her foot so hard he jumped to save his patent leather slip-on shoes from danger of smudging.

"My horses say your hide is history," she said.

At that instant the tons of teenyboppers in

line recognized their fave YouTube Girl.

With a screech, a wave of them surrounded Zoe Chloe, pushing Crawford Buchanan out of the bright lights of the roving videographers.

He turned away, hunching against the sound and fury. If this were a Victorian melodrama, he'd be muttering, "Curses, foiled again!" into his mustache.

Temple was only able to ditch Zoe Chloe's fans by signing about a hundred autographs and escaping into the maze of rehearsal, makeup, and wardrobe rooms. Major hotels could tailor-make spaces with portable walls to fit any event.

While she shook her aching right hand and wrist, she quickly toured the facilities.

Separate dressing and makeup rooms were assigned the male and female adult and junior dancers. She encountered Mariah outside the female junior rooms, along with Rafi Nadir. Temple thought Molina would cringe to see the pair camped out on metal folding chairs, chatting like buddies.

"Where's our Glorious Leader?" Temple asked.

"Liaising between the hotel and competition and media and the police people," Rafi told her seriously. "Rotten job. And all the while playing in character as *your* obnoxious agent. The police are in on the joke, but they'll never let her forget it at work later."

"It's so totally cool that I have an obnoxious agent," Zoe Chloe trilled. "Mariah here can learn how to rep her 'talent.' "

"Have you seen your boyfriend yet?" he asked.

"My boyfriend is in a boy band," Zoe announced as some tech workers passed by. She lowered her voice. "I clued Matt in, but maybe Mariah's mom will do more of it. It was a fast phone call. Zoe Chloe would *sooo* not hang with an older guy unless he was Ashton Kutcher."

Rafi chuckled.

"You see something funny in this situation, dude?" Zoe asked.

"Yeah. I see the new, New Age Molina telling your straight-arrow boyfriend that we are all here on police business and he needs to play along. Exasperation becomes her."

Temple glanced at Mariah, who was watching Rafi with a certain hero worship of his obvious disregard for her mother's authority, if not the outright adoration she rained on Matt. Temple couldn't say what she wanted to in front of the kid but realized she wouldn't have traded places with

Molina for all the cool jazz arrangements in ASCAP.

CHAPTER 30
UNDRESSED
REHEARSAL

Just like on *Dancing With the Stars,* Temple discovered, the local *Celebs* stars got only one dress rehearsal, two hours before the live show.

Four couples doing a minute-and-a-half routine didn't seem like it would be a big production, but they had to rehearse the opening intro, coordinating with the live band and backup singers, and wrestling the buttons, bows, and spangles on the elaborate costuming that had been cooked up literally overnight.

(This was Vegas, baby! Costumes were the equivalent of street clothes here on the Strip.)

Zoe Chloe settled down in the front center row of audience seats, her bodyguards-cum-posse at her side. Louie prowled the area, his favorite perch being the empty judges' table, where he sprawled finally to yawn, scratch, and lick his privates throughout all the rehearsed numbers, greatly amusing the crew.

"Two hours wasted," Rafi groaned, "to watch amateur twinkletoes. Private cop work is worse than public cop work."

"Anything might happen," Molina snapped. "A life may be at stake, given the threats, and it's on your turf and your watch."

"I get it, Carmen. Too bad Mariah's whole life wasn't on my watch."

"And what would you have had to offer? Child support? Please."

Zoe Chloe leaned forward between them, effectively becoming a Goth girl wall.

"Peeps! You're forgetting you work for me now. Cut the personal crap. I need to watch this to learn how Crawford Buchanan emcees the big boys and girls so I have a role model for my star turn with the little girls and boys."

"Yeah." Rafi snorted. "You learning from Buchanan. That'd be like the lieutenant here learning from Deputy Barney Fife. Call this what it is, babysitting."

He nodded at Mariah and the junior dancers huddling in the front row of the side section, looking rapt and a little scared by the bored Los Hermanos Brothers sitting on their spines behind them.

"It's not natural," Rafi rumbled. "Real guys don't dance."

Molina kept silent on the subject.

"That is sooo a middle-aged 'tude, dude," Zoe Chloe said after a three-beat pause. "If anyone here says Matt is not a real man, I will hit them with my designer tote bag, with Louie in it!"

"Present company's fiancé excluded," Molina said quickly. She eyed Rafi. "*Some* men have out-of-date macho issues."

"Max danced," Temple said suddenly, in her own persona. "Like a dream."

Rafi shrugged. "From what I hear, he was all balls, so I stand corrected."

Molina fumed visibly as her face turned a dull beet-red, but she literally bit her lip.

Temple had the funny feeling Molina had known Max danced.

Or was the Iron Maiden of the LVMPD recalling when she and Max had done the martial arts tango in the strip club parking lot several months ago? Good ole Carmen the Cop had told Matt that Max had gotten sexual with her then, but she was always ready to blacken Max's motives. Temple had never confronted Molina about that. Maybe she should.

Luckily, right then Crawford Buchanan oiled on stage and crooned into his MC's handheld mike.

"Welcome to *Dancing With the Celebs,* Las Vegas's answer to presenting new terpsichorean stars of the entertainment firmament." Every eye was on the top of each side staircase, where the first couples would pose and descend. Temple knew that walking head up and smiling down steps without looking at your feet was a demanding art.

She was also as rapt and eager as the junior girls to ogle the lavish costumes, makeup, and hairstyles. Stagecraft always delighted her. She figured Zoe Chloe was a glamour groupie too.

Temple had wedding bell stars in her eyes when his name was announced and Matt came out with a fragile-looking Glory B. on his arm.

"The first dance is a waltz," she whispered to no one in particular, eyeing the women's full, floating skirts and the guys' formal evening getups. On either side, her undercover escorts tried to blink their eyes wider open to stay attentive. Obviously Molina and Rafi had never treasured wedding day dreams even when they first met years ago.

A full, formal wedding, yes! In Chicago and maybe *again* in Minneapolis. She was Glory B.'s size. Those yards of white organdy and trailing chiffon and pearls and rhinestones, a bride on a cloud with Matt glitteringly blond — what had they done to him? Oh, the spray tan, spray-in platinum highlights, then black-and-white formal dress. Matt would seethe about the artifice, but Zoe Chloe would have to beat them off with a baseball bat.

Ooh! The first threat of brutal violence at this competition and it was in Temple's head.

"Prince Charming," Rafi conceded, reading her besotted reaction and realizing he had just dissed her fiancé. "I guess a father-of-the-bride would put up with that if the guy could play pool."

Temple felt ridiculously pleased, as if her father were sitting there okaying Matt.

Molina kept silent.

Did the woman have no hormones? Temple wondered, gazing happily on her beloved. The other couples weren't tacky, either. She sighed as she absorbed the romantic costumes. And here Zoe Chloe was exiled to the lost-and-found department of teen angst: painted-on Goth tears and bedhead hair, long waif legs in funky hose under ultrashort skirts. Schoolgirl decadence.

Then she pulled herself out of the pack of overwhelmed audience and back into the persona of eagle-eyed observer. This dress rehearsal was the first time anyone had seen the contestants perform and could evaluate them. Even the judges would not arrive until the actual performances to give their thumbs-up and thumbs-down.

Temple's innards were fluttering, hoping she hadn't led Matt astray. Hoping he would perform as well as he looked. Hoping she got a hell of a wedding reception waltz with the groom out of this stunt.

Molina was looking more forbidding than ever, keeping a keen eye on Mariah and her giggling young cohorts and the smooth boy-band stars sitting behind the girls. The four junior couples would perform one to a show the four days before the finale.

What was different about this program was that the celebrities would take turns dancing with each other, after being coached by their pro partners.

So, trailing down the treacherous stairs after Matt and Glory B., came the Cloaked Conjuror in stunning Phantom of the Opera mask and costume with a red-silk-lined cloak that preserved his anonymity even as it glamorized it. He had drawn escorting the ripe (firmly past fifty but sucked and tucked to make a TV living) Olivia Phillips as the Lady in scarlet satin and tulle.

Next came the lean and darkly handsome Olympic fencer, José Juarez, escorting the Amazonian wrestler Wandawoman, clad in off-the-shoulder jonquil satin that displayed her pumped up shoulders and arms, yet made power look feminine.

Last came celebrity chef Keith Salter, whose Three Tenor physique had somehow been jammed into a suave formal dress profile. His partner was the self-described "Hip-Hop Ho," Motha Jonz, who had been corseted up and toned down into a jazz age queen in mocha chiffon and sequins.

Temple loved these onstage transformations. That was what made *Dancing With the Stars* a hit. Sure they were B- or C-level celebrities on the brink of has-beenship. It was never too late. Anyone could apply themselves to a new discipline, work hard, and come out fresh and even svelte from the chrysalis. It was Cinderella and the American dream all over again. Over and over. Makeovers were ratings kings.

Why anyone would want to taint such a glorious American showbiz tradition with sabotage and death threats was puzzling.

What with Awful Crawford botching his intros, backstage costume problems, and ladies' high heels catching in trailing, floor-length skirts, it took the entire two hours for each couple and the first junior contestant to get their full moment in the sun of the spotlights.

Matt's waltz was smooth and sweeping. He was a dream prom date. Mariah's compadres were giggling and whistling and clapping up a storm for him.

Temple relaxed, well pleased.

The Cloaked Conjuror already had a dramatic stage presence, and if he was heavy on his feet, he had an operatic majesty that made a stately frame for Olivia's seasoned charms.

José Juarez executed a number of swoon-inducing masculine flourishes that made light of the task of steering the statuesque Wandawoman smoothly around the floor.

Weakest was the Keith Slater–Motha Jonz combo. Both were portly, and neither cooking nor hip-hop seemed professions that lent themselves to the froth of performing an elegant waltz. Both seemed embarrassed by everything: dance, costume, music, each other.

No one would be booted off until the end of the week, but judges would score everyone each night. Viewers would call in their votes daily, each call contributing twenty dollars to the cancer fund. In a reverse of the usual order, the judges' scores would remain secret while the viewers would dominate the scoreboard. The kicker was that the judges could overturn a ranking.

Because both dancing partners were being scored separately, it would be hard to tell the leaders from the losers until the very end. And the viewers would become more frantic to visibly boost their favorites as the scoreboard player favorites.

"Care to make a bet?" Rafi asked Temple, leaning in to whisper.

"My money is on blond over black," she said. "Our boy is looking good, but I admit José has the edge on the Latin dances. Polish is not the Latin type or temperament. I'm sure they started with the waltz to put everybody on an even basis to begin with."

Molina leaned in on Temple's other side, as if competing with Rafi. "This is all hopeless hoopla. If Ekaterina didn't look like a lost sheep, I'd jerk Mariah out of here in half a heartbeat. Rafi, you're backup. Watch her!"

He nodded. "I'm glad she's not competing. That's where all the attention is focused."

"My point exactly. We've got to focus on Mariah *because* she's in the background."

"So far this has been pretty tame," he said.

Molina eyed her large, serviceable watch.

"Everyone gets a dinner break before the show. Zoe-ee can take her cat and hang in the junior girl's dressing rooms. You and I can split," she told Rafi, "to cover the men's and women's dressing rooms."

"Uh," said Temple, "I might want to buzz by the men's dressing room for some hit-and-run secs."

Both stared at her. She realized what "secs" sounded like.

Molina frowned. She might not rock 'n' roll, but she was becoming a champion Botox candidate overnight. "You don't want to blow your cover as a ditsy Goth girl."

"*Pish!* Zoe Chloe is a total man groupie. She just wants to google-oogle the guys in the changing room and report back breathlessly to all the junior girls. It's part of her *job* building rapport with her peeps!"

"Will you *stop* using that asinine expression? No one is . . . are . . . your 'peeps.' " Molina eyed them both, then made an executive decision. "You," she told Rafi, "will watch this loose cannon and make sure she doesn't roll right over all our efforts to lock down the danger quotient at this contest. And you," she told Temple, "will keep your contact with your fiancé to the bare minimum."

Zoe Chloe smiled like a cherub. "I wish I

could make certain that those female contestants did that too."

"Molina sure has a burr up her nose,"
Temple said as she hustled alongside of Rafi
Nadir through the mazelike backstage area
to the dressing rooms.

"This is one of those thankless stakeout
jobs you can't ignore, but won't get anything
but grief from," he answered. "Look at it
from her perspective. She's having to go
back to undercover, like she hasn't since
they made her do john stings in L.A. Her
daughter's on the premises, and she's got to
put up with you and me."

"Oh, yeah. But look at the bright side. She
gets to support her daughter in something
that's very important to her. She gets to
know what a stand-up guy you are."

Rafi snorted.

Temple went on. "She gets to see Matt
transformed into a hoofin' hottie."

Rafi snorted again. "You think she hasn't
noticed your boyfriend? Even I can see they
have a history, and I'm brand-new on the
scene."

"Nothing . . . sexual."

"Chickie baby, your guy may be an ex-
priest, but that would be right up her alley
at the corner of Guilt and Common Ground

Streets. Those Catholics stick together."

"Max was brought up Catholic too."

"I rest my case. Carmen wouldn't have such a hard-on to accuse your ex-boyfriend, Max, of something if he didn't have something she doesn't know she wants."

Temple couldn't keep bouncing along like Zoe Chloe on bubble gum any longer. She stopped and confronted Rafi. He eyed her seriously. Almost sympathetically.

Rafi might be right, but that road ran both ways, so Temple had the last word, and took it.

"By your logic, Molina wouldn't be as hard on you as she is if *you* didn't have something she didn't know she wanted either."

CHAPTER 31
HOT STUFF

Zoe Chloe was one subdued little Goth girl by the time they arrived at the men's dressing room door.

Rafi Nadir wasn't the dumb, disgruntled ex-cop Molina acted like he was. Maybe he'd been bitter and angry when he'd first discovered his ex-roommate was alive and well with his unsuspected child in Las Vegas. That was then. He'd pulled it together since, as far as Temple could tell, maybe *because* his ex-roommate was alive and well with his unsuspected child in Las Vegas.

And maybe he was just a tad jealous of any man Molina knew in this town, which included two of Temple's.

Rafi knocked on the open dressing room door. "Femme coming through." He must have done touring show security work to know the backstage routines.

A leg trousered in black kicked the ajar door wide. "We're loaded with femmes.

Bring her on in."

José Juarez was lounging in a metal folding chair, his dress shirt open to the navel. He eyed her. "You one of the kiddie dancers? Sure you're old enough to be here?"

Rafi was there like a bodyguard. "Ms. Ozone is the celebrity emcee for the junior competition. She wanted to acquaint herself with the adult division competitors."

José spread his arms to display his pecs and washboard stomach, reassured she was of age. "Acquaint yourself."

Obviously God's gift to the female gender. Temple eyed the women costumers who were still fussing around with final touches.

Three of the four men contestants were stationed at mirrors framed with lightbulbs as thick as dotted Swiss. Tasty snack food on hotel ware lay amid the scattered hair products and makeup, a buffet for the harried hoofer.

At Keith Slater's station, a full dinner filled a room service tray accessorized with linen, sterling silver, and a single rose in a vase. Too bad Keith was standing, with a weird air of satisfaction and embarrassment, as a female costumer knelt before him to repair an entire seam on the fly of his pants that had ripped out during the rehearsal.

His food was getting cold, but he must be

so severely corseted for the dance that the trousers couldn't be removed for repair. Backstage mishaps broke down the usual modesty bounds, and at least Salter's corset ensured he'd have good posture during the waltz.

Matt was at the other end, wolfing down a ham sandwich while being admonished by Tatyana.

"Shoulders back and you will be perfect," she was saying.

His grooming remained perfect, except for his tucked front white shirt, open at the neck for breathing and eating room, and revealing a bit of tan rub-off inside the collar.

"You were awesome in rehearsal," Zoe Chloe cooed. (When you had a name like Zoe Chloe, you could coo.)

Tatyana rolled her hazel eyes. "When he has shoulders back properly, he will be this 'awesome.' Do not swell his head too much, little Miss Muffet, or his collar will not close for the actual performance. A good rehearsal can jinx the real thing."

She huffed away to pick at another of her pupils, the Cloaked Conjuror, whose costume and full-face mask forced him to stand and watch the others eat while he killed time. He was just visiting, as Zoe and Rafi were. Because of constant threats on his life, he'd been given a separate dressing room, with his own bodyguards on duty as well as hotel security.

Matt sighed relief to see Temple and Rafi.

"You are looking at an airbrushed portrait of a person," he said. "Was the waltz all right? I felt like a badly soldered tin soldier on parade."

"First-rate," Temple whispered in her own voice. "Right, Rafi?"

"Jumping around in that monkey suit must be worse than having shingles," Rafi said, "but even Molina shut up to watch you. You must be doing something right."

Matt momentarily shut the unexpectedly brown eyes that made his enhanced blond hair look so electric. "That's right. This is not radio anymore, Dorothy. Everybody will be watching me. I just ask that my performance be passable, and the kids' leukemia fund gets lots and lots of money."

"Don't let that dance machine hear you say 'passable,' " Temple warned, eyeing Tatyana. "She is a Russian bear down to her size-five jackboots. Besides, you were great! Unbiased reaction from a Goth brat totally unimpressed by anyone and anything. All right?"

"All right," Matt answered. "You better

spread your unbiased sunshine elsewhere for a while, but not on Mr. Leer near the door."

"He is so lame," Zoe Chloe said. "Hitting on a teen babe like me. I mean, I go for *younger* guys, like those Los Hermanos hotties. Speaking of which, I gotta peel to see what the deal is with my crew in the junior division."

"Mariah okay?" Matt asked, his eyes darting from Temple to Rafi.

"Super," Zoe answered. "I'm leavin' my man Raf here to watch all you big, bad boys, and will be hangin' with my homeys down dressing-room row. Mariah is in her girlie element, *believe.* I will have her running off with a Hermanos brother before Mama Molina can say 'Amber Alert.' "

"Poor Molina," Matt said.

"You *watch* the kid," Rafi ordered Temple. "This isn't all fun and games."

She left them, Rafi standing uneasily by Matt, eyeing the guys being fed and primped down the mirrored line, looking like a visitor from another planet who'd like to level this one.

Temple was beginning to understand how proud mothers felt as she sat beside Rafi and Molina on her left and Mariah on her right. This was the real, live show. They'd been asked to view the show on the huge greenroom monitor.

Temple was near the door, so Zoe Chloe could anticipate her entrance and hop up discreetly to take the mike and do emcee duty.

Matt and Glory B. had glided through their opening waltz like a couple atop a wedding cake. Glory B. looked gorgeous in her wedding white gown but Temple wasn't jealous. Poor Glory B. was too obviously one crazy mixed-up kid to regard as a rival.

In a way, this swaying, smooth, adult dance with Matt was reinventing her before Las Vegas eyes. She clearly adored him, and Temple guessed it was more than his Prince Charming looks, it was the Prince Kind personal attention he gave everyone on his radio call-in show and everyone, period.

He made "nice" seem necessary, as it was in this cold, anxious, raw-edged world. Young women who acted out needed a steadying hand, and Matt was a master at that. *Shoot!* Zoe Chloe was tearing up; couldn't have that.

The applause was thunderous, so the judges couldn't give their opinions for a few moments. Never mind. Danny Dove was beaming like a middle-aged cherub. When he could speak, he was almost giddy with praise, obviously relieved that his personal friend and counselor had acquitted himself well.

"Perfecto. Both of you. Glory be!" he added with a grinning play on the girl's name. "Discipline becomes you, young lady. You floated like a butterfly, and better yet, like a beautiful, graceful bride. The Viennese waltz should be supernaturally smooth. It was for both of you. And, Matt, you were the perfect partner. The set of the man's arms and shoulders in formal routines like this is critical and very unnatural to the untrained. Tatyana gave you the ideal frame."

"Splendid," said Leander Brock in his turn. "An excellent start to the evening and the show. Matt, your lead was impeccable, but, of course, Glory B. is a bewitching wisp of a thing to steer around. My dear, you were glorious! I expect great things from both of you as the competition continues."

Glory B. was blushing like the bride she reminded everyone of as she and Matt hugged with relief and glee.

Then it was Savannah Ashleigh's turn. Temple held her own and Zoe Chloe's breath. Temple had recently inveigled Matt to moderate a panel Savannah thought she should have had the spotlight on. Would she bear a grudge?

"Well, I don't usually like waltzes too much," Savannah began, fanning herself with the judge's scoring card. "It's too easy for the girl to get away with sloppy footwork under all those swaying skirts, so I kept my eye exclusively on our friend, Mr. Midnight there, because men can't get away with anything in pants, if you know what I mean."

Everyone onstage kept a smile pasted to their faces at the syntax verging on the risqué.

"But his shoulders and his feet were right where they should be every step of the way, and Glory B. did keep up with him well. Nice job."

Mariah was nudging Temple with excitement, even at the last, lukewarm review. Zoe Chloe, though, had to appear neutral, so she just smiled and nodded.

After the pair tripped hand in hand up the steps — Glory B. was wearing the usual high heels and Temple figured all the men would try to assist their high-heeled partners on the treacherous stairs — the judges flipped up their rating cards. A nine from Danny, an eight from Leander, and a seven from Savannah. Temple guessed she was still a bit miffed, and hoped she'd mellow by routine two tomorrow night, especially if Matt looked like a winner.

Crawford darted forward, mike at his lips.

"Matt Devine and Glory B. waltzed down the aisle into the judges' and audience's hearts. Now we'll see what our second couple, Olivia Phillips and the Cloaked Conjuror, can do."

The Cloaked Conjuror and Olivia Phillips made a dramatic entrance down the curved staircase in their black and scarlet costumes, and swept into a less agile but still stately waltz.

Only thirty seconds into the routine, crisis struck when Olivia's red-satin spike heel snarled in the yards of her tulle skirt, almost jerking her backwards off her feet as if she'd been garroted.

The crowd *oohed* with horror at the impending crisis.

Molina and Rafi leaped to their feet.

Midnight Louie rolled out from Zoe Chloe's tote bag. He raced out of the greenroom and around the corner to go skating and skidding onto the adjacent dance floor.

Then came one of those amazing, almost Maxlike "saves."

The Cloaked Conjuror bent at the knees and swept the falling Olivia into his arms, turning with her in a circle, her gown trailing them both like a spectacular comet.

No one had expected the graceful gesture from this huge man in his cumbersome disguise. Everyone in the audience stood then, and whistled and shouted and applauded the potential disaster turned into a magical moment as he set her gently down and they resumed their dance.

That was why these dance competition shows were so popular, Temple mused as she sat again to watch a disgruntled Louie trot back to her. She was sure he had already plotted some dramatic move to save the day . . . and make him the hairy black hero of the hour.

A Maxlike move to save the day and the dance.

And hadn't that been a Max "save"? Disaster magically changed at the last moment into triumph? Could it be a *real* Max moment? Both CC and Max at six-foot-four were tall and virtually interchangeable, and magicians. Anybody could hide under the Cloaked Conjuror costuming — any body — and CC's separate dressing room to conceal his identity and increase his security could also cover a switch.

Max had always said naked was the best disguise. The Cloaked Conjuror was a friend of his. A switch would be easy, and Max could move faster and dance better than CC any day.

Temple forced her attention back on the competition. How pathetic! Did she have to see Max under every disguise in Vegas? Maybe she would, for longer than she'd like.

"Wonderful," Danny told the Cloaked Conjurer. "Your persona and costume would seem to keep you heavy on your feet and your side vision obscured, but you reacted swiftly and sharply when your partner had a wardrobe malfunction. And Olivia, the moment you touched toe to dance floor again, you were right on time. Your heel caught in your skirts, is that it?"

"No," she answered. "It almost broke all the way off. Just folded out from under me." She bent to gather up her voluminous skirts and reveal her left foot. The red satin heel swung from the last like a pendulum, affixed only by the cloth covering. "Since the women all have to dance on their toes anyway I just continued, arching that foot a little more so the heel wouldn't drag."

"A championship effort," Danny decreed. "The mishap recovery was so smooth that although we'll have to dock you for it, it'll be much less than a fall would have been."

The audience protested that, but Leander Brock patted his palms downward for their silence. "The judges have no other choice, but the viewing audience can call and e-mail in to support their favorites no matter what happens, and every vote will add to our callboard of success."

He pointed to the large glitter-decorated LED board that would record the votes for each contestant by name and the cancer fund amount.

"I, too, applaud our sorely tried dancers, and especially Miss Phillips, who is very game to try this at an age, not that she looks it, when many women would be afraid of serious trouble from a fall. You remember the Frank and Ernest cartoon. It's one of my favorites for the distaff dancers: 'Ginger Rogers did everything Fred Astaire did, only she did it backwards in high heels.' "

The quote got the expected laugh.

"Right on, Leander," Savannah Ashleigh said, waving her placard and displaying her score, eight, ahead of time. "I don't dock a performer for a wardrobe malfunction."

Danny revealed his grade, a seven. Leander also flashed a seven. The crimson couple left the stage for the greenroom to wild applause.

For the first time Temple considered the sympathy vote. Matt might be a little too perfect for the viewing audience. He'd striven all his life to meet high ideals and had made it look easy to be smart, polite, and caring. Good looks on top of his natural charm and civility could spur jealousy.

At least no matter how the votes went, the children's cancer fund came out a winner.

"And now," Crawford trumpeted at the mike, "Olympic fencer José Juarez exchanges foil for a female partner, the awesome Wandawoman, queen of the wrestling arena. Be interesting to see who leads here, folks."

José Juarez brought on the Hispanic drama as he led Wandawoman down the stairs and then around the floor at a gallop, like Mad Max wooing a human jonquil. Wandawoman had moves, but not for the waltz. She looked clumsy.

"Again," Danny raved, "a male partner with impeccable posture. Your sport requires it, so it's not quite as remarkable as it was for Matt, but bravo! Wandawoman, you are a wonder on the wrestling mat, but I'd never give you a waltz to dance. Decent job, under the circumstances, but not designed to showcase your literal strengths."

Leander was in accord. "The amazing Danny Dove nailed it. Here's hoping, Wandawoman, you fare better with tomorrow's dance. Everybody is learning as they go."

"José," Savannah enthused. "How can one go wrong with a sexy Latin fencer? Looks, charisma, flexibility, yet really a great upright profile. Wandawoman was just too big to float in a waltz and all that yellow . . . my dear, you should shoot the costume department."

The scores, from Danny down, were seven, seven, six.

The last couple was the unluckiest.

Motha Jonz did her best, but floating like a butterfly was not her shtick either. Although her sophisticated café-au-lait gown with trailing scarves hid her stocky figure, she resembled a dancing cocoa bean. Keith

Salter's dance for the show was worse than his dress rehearsal. His spine looked like it had been sewn to his stomach to the disservice of both. He was far too stiff.

The judges gave them sixes across. Even allowing for lower scores to start with, it was a glum couple that thumped up the four steps together to return to the greenroom backstage.

Temple scored Matt and Glory B. tops for a flawless waltz, with CC and Olivia the crowd-pleasers for sudden drama. The other two were ill-matched, but that would all change tomorrow.

She was so busy analyzing Matt's chances of partner she only realized it was her turn in the spotlight as she heard Crawford's oily baritone summoning Zoe Chloe Ozone.

She quickly joined him at the sidelines near the judges' table.

"Here she is, folks, the dainty darling of the YouTube set, our *junior* emcee, the petite pint of dye-no-mite, the little girl who puts the Goth in 'Goth, she's good,' Miss Zoe Chloe Ozone."

Temple grabbed the mike and put several steps between her and the self-proclaimed "emcee of excellence."

"Ladies and gentlemen," Zoe Chloe riffed, "it is time to sit up and stand up for the next generation of dancing dervishes. The jazzy *junior* division debuts its first A-list couple, dreamy Dustin of Los Hermanos Brothers and Sou-Sou Smith, putting all the sass in the mambo that the older folks do."

Out they pranced, miniature versions of the adult dancers. Sou-Sou wore a short, tight spangled costume as cute as a pink rhinestone butterfly pin. Cuban-heeled black Mary Janes encased her tiny, flashing feet. Her nonexistent hips flounced to the rhythm as the older boy managed the odd hips-back moves of the adult male dancers, which was as if an invisible string from their butts went straight up to the flies above.

The junior pair was impressive, and too cute to believe, until Sou-Sou suddenly stepped away in a series of turns from her partner . . . and kept on turning, her rouged little face screwing up in an agonized cry, her feet prancing high off the floor as if she were tap dancing on a red-hot stovetop, or doing the tarantella, not a slick, hip-slinging samba.

For endless, awful seconds she was like the girl in the Red Shoes fairy tale, dancing and spinning endlessly, unable to stop. She twirled finally to her hands and knees, and her slim body kept on rolling as she scrabbled as wildly as a water bug across the polished floor. Her appalled partner followed, stunned, his hands reaching out to stop her.

She ended sitting on her sequined rear, kicking her heels on the floor and bawling like a three-year-old, her red face making the hot pink of her costume pale by comparison.

Onlookers rushed toward her.

Her mother, obviously, was the larger version of blond and rouge and glitter that swooped to her side first. The thump of six twelve-size shoes on hardwood came hard on her heels as three Oasis security guards arrived to hold back concerned onlookers.

Oasis security uniforms were unisex and more discreet than at most Vegas hotels: khaki cargo pants and short-sleeved safari jackets. Even the essential duty belts were low-profile, which was both good and bad.

Molina and Rafi and Zoe Chloe's disguises kept them held back among the concerned onlookers being pushed away, but Midnight Louie slipped and slid between the gathered forest of legs, which included the spindly shanks of Sou-Sou's three rival junior dancers, Mariah, and the three other Los Hermanos brothers.

Then something dark and huge swooped

down to pick her up. Sou-Sou left the stage in the strong arms of the Cloaked Conjuror, whose persona awed her long enough to forget the cause of her distress for a few key moments. She was swept behind the rear velvet curtains, her mother and the security forces trailing them, the rest of the cast and crew and audience held back.

"Rats," hissed Molina as her group retreated as ordered by Crawford Buchanan's deep bass over the microphone. "No badge, no gun, no authority. Undercover sucks."

"No kidding," said a retreating videographer who overheard her, lowering the camera to reveal his face.

Dirty Larry.

"Welcome to my world," he said.

"Did you film anything important?" Rafi demanded.

"Kid squalling. Couldn't tell why. We'll go over all the footage with a magic-tech program later."

"Who'd sabotage the *junior* contestants?" Temple wondered.

"Some one wanting to raise a ruckus," Dirty Larry said promptly.

"To create a distraction." Rafi turned away, lifting a cell phone to his ear to warn his security forces to watch the adult competitors.

"Take Mariah to the suite where she's staying with the rest of the junior dancers," Molina ordered Temple. "I'll be along as soon as I can check on the injured girl backstage."

Zoe Chloe Ozone could have pointed out that she didn't babysit, but at least Molina wasn't ordering her daughter home, which would have produced a tantrum that would have made Sou-Sou's distress look like an attack of the sniffles.

"Bring Louie along when you come back," Temple told Molina.

"I'm not toting your alley cat anywhere."

"I'm not babysitting your daughter unless I have a bone fide feline icebreaker present. Louie will distract those girls into speaking truth."

"I'm not hunting all over for a cat." A smug light dawned. "Maybe I'll call Rafi to bring him to me backstage."

"Whatever floats your barge. Just trust me. Bring him." Temple turned to Mariah, who'd watched their battle of wills with sharp eyes and ears. She was getting a whole new take on her mother.

"Come on, big-time manager," Zoe Chloe told Mariah, who sat beside a dazed EK, "we gotta get tight with our homegirls before any more of them end up dancing on hot coals."

"She's a little bitch," Mariah said as they left, trailing the mothers shepherding their dancing daughters. EK, her eyes bigger than dinner plates, trailed them. Mariah was her ersatz mother. "Isn't she, EK?"

The girl nodded, and from her wince at the phrase, Temple guessed Sou-Sou had been meanest to the most defenseless of her competitors. And maybe the most talented. EK had a quiet intensity and intelligence that was almost disturbing in a girl so young, if you didn't know she'd escaped a terrible political situation.

Who knew what EK had already needed to do to survive? Maybe a bit of sabotage was child's play compared to what she'd already faced — loss of home and family, starvation, and death. Who could guess how badly she wanted, needed, to win to ensure a scholarship to guarantee staying in this country?

"Wow!" When the party arrived at the elevator to the suite, one of the girls ahead turned back to regard the trio taking up the rear. It was skateboarder Patrisha. "Zoe Chloe is hanging wi' us, sistahs! Kewl."

The mothers frowned and blinked at the gaudy Zoe Chloe persona, mystified.

"For sure," ZC answered, moving forward

to high-five her fans. "I'm gonna see you girls and mamas get safe home to your hotel suite, so these hunky boys in uniform can guard your door."

One of the two security guys who'd joined the party, probably on Rafi's orders, was under thirty, but one was fat, bald, and on social security.

He was the one who chuckled and said, "You betcha, ladies. We'll keep the big, bad bedbugs from your door. You can count on Roy."

The three girls collapsed in giggles at the idea of this old guy being hunky.

"I'm Hank. Hank Buck," the younger, buff one said. "I'm in charge of operations for this jamboree, so you'll be seeing me around. You'll never know when and hopefully anybody bad won't know when either. I'll be looking out for you girls, trust me."

"We are getting more security than Los Hermanos Brothers," Meg-Ann boasted to her friends as they rode up in the elevator.

"That rocks!" Patrisha agreed.

Zoe Chloe stood outside the suite's double doors as mothers and daughters and mini-manager filed in, the girls still giggling, as they passed the guards, eyeing the younger one.

"Don't you belong in there, miss?" Roy,

the older guard, asked. "It ain't very safe out here."

"No, sir," Zoe said, all pretend pouty. "I guess media stars like Los Hermanos Brothers and me don't rate attempts on our performances and sanity. *Pooh!* We'll never make *Excess Hollywood* that way."

The senior citizen guard glowered at her irresponsible attitude, but the young one eyed her overexposed fishnet-clad gams. He was only, like, twenty-nine and had no idea she was an older woman.

Kewl.

Temple bopped Zoe Chloe Ozone outa there into the hall before she triggered a response from some lethally jealous tweeny-bopper. Girls just want to compete.

Maybe to the death.

CHAPTER 33
HOTFOOTING IT

If there is anyone in this entire place who is fully qualified to smell a rat, it is I.

I mean this quite literally.

A lot of scents assail my highly developed sniffer during these recent, critical moments since I pushed my way past a phalanx of human legs to the side of the little doll who was most cruelly afflicted.

First, human foot odor. *Arghh!*

This alone is enough to knock a sensitive dude — a *short,* sensitive dude — off his four pins. Why will they insist on confining and cooking the unhappy aroma of their pathetically unclawed feet inside these thick leather and canvas boxes?

Air, my fellow Americans! Please! We four-footed citizens only ask that you aerate your tootsies as fully and often as we do ours. You will notice that we are not subject to such ills as bunions, corns, hammertoes, and athlete's foot, although we are better natural-born athletes than the whole kit and caboodle of you put together.

Having fought my way through this chemical hazard of foot odor, I am able to insinuate myself next to the maternal unit, which is swamped in a chemical cosmetic haze of other, supposedly pleasant odors.

A word to the wise: cover-ups never work.

In the confusion, and under the cover of this one large, hysterical lady who goes by the appellation "Mama," I am able to thrust myself into the heart of the problem: the tiny dancer's still twitching feet.

Whew! I will give credit to the heat of the dance. This little doll's feet are sniffing up a storm. It is not the unnatural natural odor I am accustomed to.

It is rank, but artificial. In fact, it makes me draw back and box my snout to stifle a sneeze. Itching powder? I have heard of such an item being used for practical jokes, but this is no joke.

The first solo dance in the junior division has turned into a debacle. Although Miss Sou-Sou is something of a snot deserving of a comeuppance, I cannot endorse dirty tricks among the young teen set.

As the fascinating feet in my purview are lifted aloft by the awesome CC, I resolve to do what my human associates cannot do in their present guises. I will accompany the victim until I learn what is going on, and who and what might be behind it.

Ouch! Of course some careless foot has kicked me in the puss.

Dodging these ticky-tacky boxes of milling footwear, I manage to maintain a low profile by stifling any indignant meows.

At last I insinuate myself into the junior girls' dressing room, although I am by no means either a junior or a girl, and join the privileged circle surrounding the now crying child, who alone of her group is still in the set area. For a thirteen-year-old human kit in pain is just that, no matter how many slinky costumes she wears.

In a moment or two, it is as if I am back in my checkered past, fence-sitting at midnight and yowling some selected riffs guaranteed to attract any nubile females in the vicinity. Only I do not attract nubile females of any species, just the usual hurled footwear reeking of abysmal pedal swamps . . .

These are a pair of petite Mary Jane–style shoes ripped off the feet of the suffering little doll. I dodge the Cuban heels, which could make a nasty dent in my cranium, and put my nose to work. You may notice I understand the fine points of female footwear, thanks to my roomie's formidable shoe collection.

The whines of the victim and coos of the comforters vanish from my consciousness as my nose for trouble inhales a big gulp of the hot and bothered linings of the shoes in question.

Yeow!!! I leap back, forced to swallow my natural vocalizations. My pea-green peepers beloved of females of all species tear over and cry crocodile tears onto my jet-black bib. My sensitive, exposed nose skin burns like the very devil was exhaling the breath of Hell itself on it.

I know what has happened, if not why yet.

What a despicable plan, a dirty trick of the first water, and I do mean watering eyes! I backpedal out of the room as fast as I can, my mitts eager to box the obnoxious, polluting fumes from brutalized nostrils.

No wonder the poor girl was screeching.

Who would commit such a nefarious act?

It is clever and underhanded and mean, and thus totally and utterly human in its conception and execution from first to last. I cannot wait for my humans to find out what has gone wrong.

CHAPTER 34
MAMA'S GIRLS

Molina came charging down the hall outside the junior girls' hotel suite so fast the two hotel security guards at the door put their palms on their gun butts.

"Chill," she said, "LVMPD shield."

She produced it after transferring the tote bag containing Midnight Louie to Temple's custody.

"He was in the dressing-room area already. Pesky cat," she growled at Temple. "And he weighs the advertised ton."

The guards glanced from the tote bag cat to Molina's retro-sixties headband and love beads to her jeans and moccasins.

"We've been told there were undercover city cops on the premises," the old guy said.

"The little girl will be all right," Molina said. "It was a nasty prank. I want to interrogate the other girls and their mothers without it looking like it, so Ms. Ozone here and I will be doing that. And I'll probably take a couple of the girls back to our high-roller suite, where your assistant security chief is . . . on duty 24/7. Of course no one is to know who I am or any of this, right?"

"Got it, Lieutenant," the young guy, Hank, said. "Rafi Nadir made me floor boss on this detail. You can count on me."

The older one just gawked. Lieutenants weren't usually out in the field. Then he eyed Zoe Chloe and Midnight Louie and swallowed.

"I'll be ordering a couple of room service pizzas," Molina added. "Check 'em and the waiter out, even though I said they're coming. You know the room service waitstaff, right?"

"There are an awful lot of 'em in a place this size," Roy said.

"I know the equipment and the drill, Lieutenant," Hank assured her. "I'll call human resources on them if there's anything suspicious."

"I got a granddaughter these girls' age," Roy added as further reassurance.

"Okay." Molina knocked at the door and nodded at Temple to go in first. "Tell 'em the Goth fairy is bringing cat hair and pizza."

Molina might be a security fanatic, but did she know kids.

Everybody in the room squealed when Zoe Chloe fronted in. She was the next best thing to a Los Hermanos brother.

An announcement of pizza for all was the third best thing.

And Louie to coo over was a solid fourth.

Molina dutifully called room service like the Zoe Chloe Ozone middle-aged flunky she was portraying while the girls shouted out their druthers for toppings. Like most hotel order-in pizzas these days, an outside franchise handled the calls, so the menu was pretty standard.

Except when Zoe Chloe Ozone ordered a custom shrimp, artichoke heart, and jalapeño one for her star-self alone.

"Any news on Sou-Sou?" the question came from kids and mothers alike.

Neither Temple nor Molina had gotten a good group look at the mothers. The over-blown Smith woman was with her absent daughter, leaving only the two others present, since Mariah was serving as EK's "manager."

Patrisha Peters, the only African-American contestant, was a lean, leggy skateboarder, but her mother was a pleasantly plump, attractive woman with a calm manner. She introduced herself as Frances Peters. Meg-Ann's mother wasn't anything like her hard-driving soccer-athlete daughter. Angie Peyton was unpleasantly plump, her clothing straining at all the most unfortunate places, her hair showing dark roots, and her manner both harried and disinterested. In a sense she was the sloppy side of Yvonne Smith. Temple guessed she was underemployed and financially stressed, probably through no fault of her own but divorce and bad luck.

Snap judgments were often all wrong. Now was the time to ask the women to reveal themselves.

Zoe Chloe plopped down cross-legged (all the better to show off her skull-head white-on-black tights) on a sofa.

"This is my personal assistant, Vicki," she said, waving at Molina. "I had her check with the staff backstage. What'd they say, Vick?"

As she'd hoped, Zoe Chloe had invented a name for Molina that the policewoman hated, from the expression on her face.

"Sou-Sou got a literal hotfoot from a substance put into her shoes," Molina said, sounding way too copish with that "substance" talk.

"Then it was deliberate?" Frances Peters asked. "Sabotage? None of us here would do that."

"That's the thing," Zoe Chloe said. "It doesn't look good for any of the other contestants. So we gotta find out who and what everybody is, so we're ready when the police get involved, if they do."

"The police?" Angie Peyton asked, alarmed. "God, that's just what our girls don't need right now. They have enough stress."

"Hotel security was talking about calling them in," Molina, aka "Vicki," put in virtuously, as if she wasn't one. "Ms. Ozone is right. The more we know about the junior group, the more everybody will be off the hook."

"What about that soap star whose heel broke?" Angie asked. "That was just an accident. Why isn't this?" She seemed a woman born to be in denial.

"It could be," Molina answered. "We've got to be ready if it isn't. You know tabloid TV will be all over this."

The girls remained listening, bright-eyed with curiosity and excitement at the mention of national TV exposure. The mothers' brows were wrinkling with a realization of what bad press could do. Mariah was watching them all, not obviously. Even Ekaterina was serious and alert, trying to figure out what this meant.

Would a girl like EK, with so much riding on winning this contest, be the one to stoop to sabotage? Temple wondered.

"I suppose," Frances Peters said slowly, "it'd be hard to say whether the girls or us mothers are the bigger suspects?"

Molina jumped in. "Everybody is suspect. I've spent years trying to spin good publicity from bad, and it can't be done. Even Ms. Ozone is suspect. You moms are here to protect your daughters, but I'm here to make sure Ms. Ozone's career isn't damaged."

Temple had to admire Molina's gift for throwing a scare into people.

Meg-Ann and Patrisha exchanged the uneasy looks of kids who might know more than their mothers did, and Ekaterina's waif-wide eyes expanded to pizza pan size.

Only Mariah remained unworried. She knew she was an undercover kid.

"So, anyway, peeps," Zoe Chloe summed up, "things could get pretty unpleasant for all of us until someone finds out who put the hot sauce to Sou-Sou's shoes. Hey, sounds like a funky song title. I say we can turn this into a fun gig and find out about each other and chill with some hot pizza and Dr Pepper." She turned to her personal assistant. "You did remember to order Dr

Pepper, didn't you? That's all I drink."

Molina set her teeth and picked up the phone to order from room service, asking the other girls if they had any preferences. Awestruck by the Zoe Chloe Ozone presence, they only wanted what their idol ordered.

Man, Temple could dig being a pop tart . . .

Forty minutes later, everyone was sitting on the carpet, dozens of cheap paper napkins unfolded, smearing a gloss of red pizza sauce over lipstick. A lot of chitchat and chatter had gone down with the pepperoni slices and melted cheese, but no clues that stood out.

Midnight Louie stole the show by darting out a black paw to snag yet another circle of sausage on the now-cold pizza remains. Everybody laughed. They hadn't laughed earlier when he'd knocked a plastic shaker of red pepper flakes over on the carpet.

"If we don't know *what,*" Mariah opined between chews on the best-tasting generic pizza in the world, because tension had everyone feeling starved, "how can we begin to know *who?*"

"Sounds like sound police procedure to me," Molina put in, earning a glancing flash of gratitude from her daughter. "The police won't know *what* until tomorrow morning. Tell you what. Since Ekaterina has no responsible adult present to look after her, Ms. Ozone and I will take her and her friend Mariah up to our suite, so you two mothers only have your own daughters to watch over."

Two maternal brows frowned at the idea. "Separate the girls?" Angie objected. "They were just bonding."

Mariah rolled her eyes, indicating the opposite, so Temple jumped in.

"It'll be easier to alibi the kids if anyone gets carried away and starts tossing out accusations."

A long silence indicated they all knew who might be slinging accusations around: Yvonne Smith.

"That's very generous of Ms. Ozone," Frances Peters said. "And it might be best for EK." Her glance at the girl also indicated just who'd been the butt of Sou-Sou's snobbery.

Molina nodded, well satisfied with the new arrangement in all of her identities: cop, mother, and undercover teen star flunky.

Chapter 35
Purse Pussycat Prowl

It is not like me to be so clumsy but it is like me to be so nosy.

Of course I did not "accidentally" overturn the red pepper shaker. That was just an excuse so that I could sniff around on all the shoeless feet and unguarded purses on the floor as children and mothers eat like starving lions and chatter like parrots.

Oh, that silly fellow. He just has to have his nose into everything.

Of course what I get for my sleuthing efforts is a flake up my left nostril and a sneezing fit. For this reason I doubt that actual pepper flakes were used in the incident.

It is not easy to conduct discreet investigations while sneezing up a storm. So I hunker under a chair to smother my nasal paroxysms and wait for the fit to subside. It is actually a clever way to get all present to totally forget about literally little me.

And *that* gives me plenty of time to overhear

this and that, especially when Yvonne Smith comes in breathless about the vicious attack on her daughter and with a long report on Sou-Sou's poor feet being tended by the hotel doctor in a security-guarded location. She is urged to sit down, relax, eat, and drink.

Thus, everyone has been lulled into forgetting my presence and I have reduced my aversion to red pepper flakes to the occasional sniffle. Floor-sitting ladies tend to forget against which object of furniture they have laid their precious purses. I slink out from concealment and sniff my way to each in turn.

Unfortunately, my clever red pepper exposure has served to blunt my usually sharp sniffer.

Miss Frances Peters's bag is a large leather Stein Mart affair decorated with safari pockets and lots of metal hardware. You would not want to take it through an airport security line.

I detect a few ancient flecks of tobacco in the very bottom. Since I detected no such scent on the owner, I make the deduction that she purchased the bag from a resale establishment.

Nothing wrong with that! My Miss Temple does that all the time, especially in regard to high-end high heels, an item the original owners of which turn over almost daily, like Band-Aids for bunions.

This purse was never high-end, though, so I am guessing the Widow Peters is putting a lot of her money into survival. Patrisha's win in this contest would get the kid opportunities her mother could never afford. Something to bear in mind.

Next I snuggle up to the bright yellow ruched leather bag favored by Angie Peyton, mother of the innovatively named Meg-Ann. You would never know her daughter was an athlete, but maybe Meg-Ann needed to overcome that first name.

Parents are even worse at naming offspring than they are at naming animal companions. I cannot complain about "Midnight Louie," though. It is my street name, bestowed on me in my first neighborhood before I moved uptown. It is a moniker used by the street people who shared their humble meals with me when I was a kit, and I wear it proudly. My magnificent mature physique is a tribute to the less fortunate and their care and consideration for the even less fortunate.

If my Miss Temple does not have me down to a wraith again with her slavish devotion to feline health food! But I am not here to criticize anyone's home cooking, and Angie Peyton's bag is sweet rather than hot, holding loose chocolate-covered raisins and Oreo cookie four-packs.

Next I push my schnozz into the late-arriving Smith purse. This is a scarlet patent leather hobo bag, within which I pick up the scent of a woman: peppermint — *achoo!* — candies from restaurants. *Aha!* A careful woman. Burt's Bees lip balm, which indicates a nervous woman; and . . . *aha!* . . . a not tightly capped can of pepper spray!

Granted it is not unusual for women to carry such self-defense items in their purses, but the scent is dead-on exact to the smell inside Sou-Sou Smith's dainty little Mary Jane dancing shoes.

Should I sound the alarm on Mama Smith?

If I can so easily find this incriminating item in her purse so could anyone who hangs out in the junior suite. In addition, these tween girls all carry fashionable little purses, except for Mariah, who totes one of those sensible, small oblong wallets.

I see I have a long night of purse snatching, unlatching, and searching ahead of me while others eat, drink, and make merry.

After many wearying attempts to break unnoticed into everything that could be construed as a purse, including a Hello Kitty one that belongs to EK, I return to the scarlet Smith one. It is large enough and an excellent color. I curl up on it and pretend to sleep so well that I actually do.

The next thing I know, I am being shaken awake by my dear little doll. I remain limp and "sleepy."

"Louie! We have to leave. Come on."

She bends to heave me up. I have cleverly stuck my paw into the ajar frame and as she pulls me up the purse opens wide, like for a dentist. Oh, look what the purse fairy has left! A nice big can of pepper spray.

Of course my brilliant associate immediately gets the message. She looks over her shoulder at Yvonne Smith, who is busy yakking with Mrs. Peters. She reaches for the spray, hesitates, and appropriately purses her lips.

I can guess what she will do: alert those who need to know that Sou-Sou's mother probably sprayed her own daughter's dancing shoes to up the sympathy vote. It can't be proven and I doubt Miss Temple would blow the whistle unless Sou-Sou wins.

"What a good boy, Louie," she tells me as she lifts me up to her face for a mushy cuddle. "You always get into mischief in just the right way."

That is ever the lot of the undercover operative, and he is glad to be of service even if he does not get full credit.

Especially if he can also snatch one last slice of free-range pepperoni after he is put

down and before he leaves the scene of investigation.

CHAPTER 36
RED HOT CHILI
PEPPERS

"Capsaicin in her shoes? That's red pepper, isn't it?"

Temple pretended to be stunned by this news, despite relaxing with a glass of sangria in Zoe Chloe's suite. Rafi had used his position as assistant security chief to order up a pitcher.

Molina, looking more in the mood for a whiskey sour, had even permitted him to pour her a glass.

"It was a prank!" Temple didn't so much ask, as exclaim. She couldn't pin the prank on Mrs. Smith for sure, despite Louie's valiant detecting efforts. Lots of women carry pepper spray.

"A nastily effective prank," Molina said. "The hotel doctor said the girl's feet are swollen and tender, but guarantees they'll be normal by morning."

"What's the treatment?" Rafi asked.

"Think you'll have another case of capsaicin poisoning at the Oasis soon?" Molina jeered.

"I can ask the doctor."

Molina swallowed the sangria as if it were hemlock. "Don't bother. I got the routine. They try shampoo or other soaps first, then oils or creams. This was an extreme enough case that he ordered milk-soaked rags from room service, as well as ice to relieve the burning symptoms. Poor little kid was severely unnerved and in real pain."

"Still, I think what hurt her most was that her dance number was ruined."

"They'll let her repeat it another night," Temple said. "Mariah thought so, anyway. If she recovered."

"The Smith girl is moving to another hotel room with her mother. Now that we know how competitive they are, not a bad idea. I wish Mariah hadn't ever bunked with those other girls." Molina eyed Rafi as if the show rules were his fault.

"I pulled in more female security guards from off duty," he said. "One will be in the hotel suite with the two remaining mothers and daughters at all times. And the costumes are now under guard."

"Mariah said," Temple put in, "that Sou-Sou was 'a little bitch.' "

"She didn't learn that word at home,"

Molina assured, bristling.

"This smacks of a malicious trick," Rafi said. His dark eyes seemed ringed in charcoal. It wasn't just his daughter's safety involved, it was his ex sitting here on his recently acquired turf, judging every move he made. Or didn't make.

So far, he'd maintained his cool better than she had.

"How does this tie in with the death threats?" Molina mused out loud. "With the seriously homicidal kooks the Caped Conjuror always attracts? With the threat of the Barbie Doll Killer? With the tension and jealousy of the adult competition?"

"I don't know," Temple said. "It could be the junior rivalry is hotter than the senior."

"You're putting your own true love in the 'senior' category?" Molina asked acidly.

"Relatively speaking. Actually, there's more rapport building among the adult contenders than the teens."

"Adults know how to lose gracefully, or at least to pretend to," Rafi put in.

Molina shot him a sharp look.

Temple shivered internally. Everything exchanged between these two had an unspoken double edge. Being with them was like acting as the net during a killer championship tennis match. Something had to give, eventually. Hopefully, it was not her, the separating agent.

Volleys of unspoken recriminations were bouncing over her head.

And yet she detected a certain heat.

It was hard to think of Molina having a sexy bone in her body, but the lieutenant's iron professional control was probably a challenge to certain overly macho men.

Not Max. He was too smart to act macho. Rafi came by his Mideastern macho culturally and was trying to overcome it. Dirty Larry was another case entirely. She didn't think she *or* Molina quite knew what he was about. Temple guessed that Molina unwittingly posed a challenge to these men that she really didn't want or need.

Life was funny. People often attracted the people who were worst for them. She herself was a case study in attracting a daring lone ranger like Max and a supportive sweetie like Matt. If only she could compress them into one delicious totally perfect boyfriend.

Eek! Zoe Chloe Ozone stomped a black lace-up oxford worn over fishnet hose down hard on Temple's ruminations. Was she even s*peculating* that women didn't really know what they wanted? Or needed? And men too?

Her head hurt, and her feet ached in

sympathy with Sou-Sou's. The girl was obnoxious, but young girls often got confused about which way to go, *Wicked,* as in the Broadway play, or nauseatingly "good." Either extreme was an overdose.

Witch way would this crazy dance competition go now?

CHAPTER 37
THE SHOE MUST GO ON

Rehearsals for Monday night's dance began at 8:00 A.M. the next morning.

Temple and Louie padded down the hall leading to the junior rehearsal rooms. The big black cat was terminally tired of the tote bag and had adopted dog behavior, heeling alongside Temple like a well-trained spaniel.

They had barely turned down the hall before they had to stop. People were crowding wall to wall, and a constant murmur of voices echoed off them.

"Excuse me," Zoe Chloe said, trying to elbow her way forward. "I'm in the cast. I have to get through."

People gave way, barely sparing her a glance, which was saying something. She wore a black derby hat, blue lipstick, an orange-striped leotard, hot pink tights, and chartreuse Minnie Mouse platform shoes.

The bulk of TV station cameras loomed over the crowd ahead.

By the time Zoe Chloe and Louie reached the door to the first rehearsal room, it was obvious a media feeding frenzy was underway.

"Oooh," Zoe Chloe trilled. *"Hellooo* remote feed. Pardon me while I boogie my Cheshire cat and me into the dancing party. I'm the emcee-ess of this little super circus and I need to see my dear little emcee-*ee*s."

That got the lights and cameras turned her way.

Temple knew they expected the third of the usual trilogy — *Action!* — so she danced sideways through the small tunnel they made singing, "Cockles and mussels, alive-a-live-oh."

Zoe Chloe inhabited Alice in Wonderland territory as Temple saw it, and the more nonsensical she could be, the better. *American Idol* proved eccentric sold.

Rafi's hotel troops kept the room uninvaded and Hank Buck saw that they let her through with a recognizing grimace while Roy stood by shaking his head.

The major media reporters and videographers were already inside, clustered around Sou-Sou and her feet. They were bare and normal this morning, but her mother was busy describing them as swollen as if a thousand bees had been at them the previous evening.

A series of foot-soothing devices were lined up for the famous feet: bubbling foot-baths, soaking salts, blowing air dryers, ice baths and steam aerators. Sou-Sou was poking her hot pink footsies in them, as instructed by various media folks, as though they were exotic shrimp in need of many exotic sauces.

A second wardrobe malfunction had become a major media opportunity.

"Glorious, isn't it?" a deep voice thrummed at the exact level of her ear, which was about four inches higher than usual, thanks to the chartreuse platform shoes.

Zoe Chloe eyed Crawford Buchanan and his glistening gaze agog at the publicity.

"Gross," she responded. "Like cannibalism on *Survivor.*"

"*Exactly!*" he crowed. "You can't arrange another interesting mishap, can you? That'd really raise ratings."

"Someone sabotaged her Mary Janes," Zoe Chloe pointed out. "That is *baaad* behavior, even on a reality TV show."

"Hey! No permanent damage, just maximum media. That is *goood* showbiz. You're just jealous, ZC."

"Like her!" a woman yelled.

Zoe Chloe looked up to see Mrs. Sou-Sou pointing at her hot pink tights. "That's how bright my poor Sou-Sou's feet were last night. Like a boiled lobster's."

"Would you mind losing the shoes for us, Ms. Ozone?" a bold cameraman asked.

Crawford nudged her in the side. "Your big moment."

She stepped out of the platform shoes and went flat-footed, herded by the reporters next to the preening Sou-Sou so they could pose with tiny feet together. Cameras crowded in to fixate on Zoe's hot pink socks next to Sou-Sou's hot pink bare feet. Flashes winked.

Then everybody laughed.

A large black paw was dipping in the foot-bath as if trolling for colorful koi.

When it came to scene-stealing, Midnight Louie was a master.

But his interference also gave the avid media maggots the money shot they craved. They faded away into the hall, leaving Zoe to mount her platforms again and assess the situation.

"So Sou-Sou can dance tonight?" she asked Yvonne Smith and her "Proud Parent" name tag.

No wonder the daughter had an exotic first name.

Mrs. Smith honored Zoe Chloe with a displeased once-over, but bowed to her on-line notoriety.

"Oh, yes. Doctor said a night's elevation of her feet, along with ice packs and soothing ointment would have her in top tiptoe condition, and she is. Doctor said she just needs to keep her feet soothed between learning the new dance's steps. She'll trip the light fantastic like Tinker Bell by tonight."

The woman smiled happily, basking with her daughter in the afterglow of media attention. Nobody would even wonder if mom had planned the shocking, attention-getting mishap.

Only Zoe Chloe had such a nasty, suspicious mind. And Midnight Louie.

Speaking of which, Temple decided to search out her light of love and see what insight he had into the goings-on.

The adult rehearsal rooms were down a whole different hall, one that Midnight Louie did not choose to explore. Maybe he guessed things could turn mushy if she could get Matt alone. Nothing hated mush more than a tomcat.

The Terrible Tatyana was in full cry.

"You are the perfect pupil but you have

not a drop of Latin in your soul!" she was keening in despair when Temple teased open the door to Matt's rehearsal room.

"That's not true," Matt answered reasonably. "I have spoken it, sung it. The old Polish neighborhoods in Chicago still have one Latin mass a Sunday."

"Not this church Latin of the priests! I speak of the Latin of the bullfight and the sword and the cape, of the hot intemperate zone. Spain! Portugal and the prado singers. Of passion that is known only in the shadowy taverns of the Old World or the tangos that inflame the South American countries of the New World. This is not to be found in Chicago churches," she finished, her words and voice and posture saturated in scorn. "This is to be found in the dancer's *soul*."

"There's a lot of soul in churches," Matt said, unperturbed.

Temple saw precisely what drove Tatyana crazy, the laid-back sweet reason that made Matt a master of the late-night airwaves. Also, he was too sophisticated to buy into the Old World domination mode of the battle of the sexes.

The Russian spitfire was right. This was a severe handicap in the current situation.

Tatyana turned her temper on the intruder.

"Who are you?" she demanded, whirling around in her tight spandex dance clothes as if wearing a ruffled skirt and castanets on her imperious fingers. She absorbed Zoe Chloe Ozone's kooky façade and dripped more disrespect.

"Oh. This silly Internet clown-girl. You deal with the children division. You have no right here. We rehearse."

"No." Zoe Chloe swaggered onto the wooden dance floor. "You badger. And I deal with *him.*"

"Ladies," Matt began, so not getting it.

There were no ladies here.

"I would like a word," Zoe Chloe said, "with my fiancé."

Tatyana's eyebrows snapped up toward her hairline. "This is true?" she demanded of Matt. "This ridiculous circus girl is your lover?"

"Fiancée," he said quickly. "And there's nothing ridiculous about her." He eyed Zoe Chloe. "This is a performing persona."

"Ah." Tatyana eyed Zoe Chloe with more respect. "She is 'playing' the zany gamine."

The last three words came out: *ze zanee gah-meen.*

The French pronunciation made Zoe

Chloe sound like an exotic animal. So she stamped one thick-hooved platform sandal.

"Darn right, toots. Now take a sweat break and let me deal with the dude."

Zoe Chloe's American slang had Tatyana blinking in confusion. She threw up her hands. "He is impossible. I need break. Tell him if he does not do sexy it will not sell and Tatyana will be fool of the entire competition."

She exited with a final slam of the door.

"She's temperamental," Matt explained after a long silence.

"She's exasperated," Temple said, turning back to him, "because you do not do sexy."

"I didn't sign up for sexy. And she's right. I don't have that Old World Spanish temperament. I don't preen at killing tormented bulls. I don't want to sling women around the floor. I don't get it. At best, it's hokey. At worst, it's abuse."

"Sure. It's all those things. It's theater. Look at me! Zoe Chloe is theater. It's hokey, but Zoe Chloe thinks she's sexy. I don't need to be her but something out there in Internet land needs to think she's special, that she is what they could be if they had the nerve.

"Sexy is in the mind of the beholder, Matt. You spent half your life not allowing anyone to see you that way. It worked great while it lasted, and that you still don't need to strut makes you sexy in a whole new way to all those dear hearts and lost souls on late-night radio.

"But to me" — Zoe Chloe slid nearer on her ridiculous shoes — "you are ultrasexy because you love me, because you dare to feel. And that's what the dances demand. Feelings you can show. These Spanish dances ought to be a cakewalk for you."

"No way on earth! Why?"

"Because . . . they are all about control. Self-control. And self-control is very sexy, because it can be lost."

"You're talking about virtue lost."

"Or love found."

"In the tango, the couple barely look at each other through most of the dance. It's sublimated violence."

"Yeah. You do get it. But she's as powerful as he is. She can reject. We are twelve millennia from the cave days when a guy in an animal skin could drag a woman by the hair into his bachelor pad. These ritual Spanish dances explore the power of 'no.' The man can be gloriously egotistical and commanding, and still get shut down. It was a great leap forward for the species."

"So . . . you're saying?"

"Passion makes life earnest and real, the arts revealing, spiritual, affecting. I know you've got it. In what you believe in, in other people, in what you feel for me. I ask you. In your place. Here. Now. What would Max do?"

His head reared back as if slapped. "Temple —"

"And you think Tatyana is a demanding taskmaster." She kissed her forefinger and pressed it to his lips to shut him up. "You've got the same smoldering dark brown Latin eyes José Juarez does, and a swimmer is as supple and strong as a fencer. You can out-tango him any day. The pasodoble is yours if you want it. You got me away from Max, didn't you?"

Talk about pressing someone's buttons. Talk about motivation.

He looked shocked, angry, turned-on.

He looked ready for the pasodoble.

Hell, he looked ready for Max.

But all he had at hand was her.

Matt seized Temple and pasted her to him like a paper doll, his long gliding strides propelling her backwards while he stared into her eyes as intently as a cobra practicing hypnosis. He spun her left and then right, ending each dizzying twirl with a full frontal embrace that hot-glued them together from neck to knee. This dance should be banned in Boston.

Temple wasn't aware of her feet touching the ground and they didn't need to. Matt flung her around with such skill and authority that she couldn't think of anything other than being caught in a sensual eddy of motion that had her stomach lurching like she was plummeting over the scary top of a Ferris wheel or experiencing sudden serial stabs of pure lust, pardon the oxymoron. . . .

He dipped her parallel to the floor, leaning closely over her, never breaking their gaze, and let her settle there gently, only his braced arms on either side of her shoulders keeping him from pinning her to the hardwood in an R-rated hip-lock.

Temple, as breathless as a Victorian virgin, felt her bosom heaving in and out in the prescribed manner. They were alone. They were engaged. There was no reason this dance shouldn't have a very personal climax.

Matt's face with its seriously hot expression drew near to hers. Surrender was the only reasonable option.

He kissed her lightly on the lips, grinned, and pushed himself up to extend a hand and pull her upright again.

"And?" he asked.

"I want a really private rematch later, Valentino."

Temple patted her hair and heartbeat into place again.

José Juarez was chopped pico de gallo.

Chapter 38
Mercedes
Pasodoble

The Internet had been as unrevealing as his memory.

He'd visited the Hummerbar again for a nightcap. He was revved. Revienned. Couldn't sleep. An Internet search for the Mercedes license plate had gotten him nowhere. A Bailey's Irish Cream and coffee in the bar only deepened his phony Celtic accent. He was a faker without a memory.

He limped out of the hotel onto the Bahnhofstrasse, still teaming with foot traffic a lot more sound than his three-way thump of cane and then two footsteps.

He's paced this expansive, expensive tourist trap avenue for a day and a night. Was he grinding his legs to permanent disability? He sensed he never knew when to give up.

And then, there it was, a gift of the teeming night.

Black car. Zurich license plate, pulled up to the curb, pulsing there with a muted

Mercedes purr. A blond woman in a pink wool suit was pushing out of the open back door as if her skirt was too tight (it was), her boot heels too high (they were) . . . and the pale pink leather was shriveled up the heels as if they had been thrust repeatedly down into resisting dirt. (They had been.)

Revienne! Trap or lucky break? That was the price of amnesia, constant second-guessing.

She struggled upright, glancing around wildly, staggering away from the car.

He bounded forward (*ouch!*) to grab her elbow in a gentlemanly way.

"Need help, miss?"

Her stricken eyes met his without recognition, only panic.

He pulled her away from the car and behind him. Right. Like he and his game legs were any kind of wall. But this street was Tourist Central.

Two beefy men poured from the car, one from the front seat, the other from the opposite back door. He felt Revienne shrink against his back.

He lifted the cane.

"Hey!" An American GI on leave, probably from some hellhole, was making this his fight. "This guy is handicapped and this woman wants out. What's going on, buddy?"

Now three American Army buddies gathered around, the word *buddy* needing no translation.

"Michael! Is it you?" Revienne breathed in his ear like an answered prayer.

So just right. So suspicious. But the cards were all falling his way. Play them.

She eyed the instant rescue party and spoke in English. "I don't want to go with these men. They separated me from my husband. Call the police!"

The three GIs had brawny bodies and three months of boot camp behind them, marine-tough expressions and, if you looked very, very close, far too young eyes. He knew their breed well. *They* form a wall much better than he can.

"Until the police come, we'll do the policing," one announced.

By now a crowd had clotted around them, a cross of casual tourist class and well-heeled Swiss natives enjoying an expensive night out on the town.

American soldiers on leave weren't necessarily a rooting-for entity in Europe these days, but attractive women fleeing obvious muscle had propelled many a movie plot and was always box office magic.

One thug reached for a firearm against the eager young soldiers.

Max used the cane like a sword to ram him in the stomach just before the trio swarmed him. Whirling, he used its length to trip the other man as Max spun Revienne hard into the custody of his free arm. Backstepping with long strides abetted by using the cane for leverage, he saved Revienne from tripping on the cobblestones and clasped her close to his hip while he watched the incident's last act.

The firearm never appeared because its owner was clasping his cane-punched gut as the two middle-aged thugs retreated before three young jaws jutting outward, fists leading, and witnesses well able to testify. They vanished back into the car as quickly as they'd appeared and it glided away into the teeming traffic.

Revienne had arranged herself artfully against Max's side but stopped leaning on him and pulled herself upright, for which he was grateful. He wasn't quite ready for dance partners, not even in a sexy pasodoble.

"Thanks, mates," he told the three American soldiers.

"Aussie?" they asked.

"Irish," he answered.

"Same diff."

What did they know, at this age? Maybe

more than he did.

The men from the Mercedes had vanished like all bad guys do when foiled. Max didn't believe in happy endings but Revienne was clinging to him, smelling like freesias, keeping him upright in more ways than one, and he didn't want to argue right now with fate or connivance. He could learn from both of them.

"Thanks, fellas," he said with a grin.

They grinned back and swaggered away. He led the prize, Revienne, back to the Hotel California, where you can never leave. Or never want to. *Revien.*

It means, in French, "I return."

Revienne.

It means, in English, "I'm an idiot, but I wonder, and I burn to know more."

CHAPTER 39
CHEF DU JOUR

Instead of urging her fiancé to find his inner Zorro for Tuesday's pasodoble, Zoe Chloe should have been worried about her upcoming patter as emcee tonight, when the quickstep ruled.

Instead she was watching the huge flatscreen TV in the greenroom. It was nervewracking for the kids of the cast to have to sit here nightly watching the adults flash their footwork while they had all evening to get nervous before their own big moments. So Zoe Chloe had come in to keep them company.

Each dance lasted less than two minutes, but the hour show was expertly managed to reap the most major commercials and milk Crawford Buchanan's oily chitchat over the mike and with the judges.

Meanwhile, the young performers' nerves felt no mercy.

Sou-Sou's mother had her off to the side

under her literally protective wing: a filmy bat-wing tunic. The girl's foot injury seemed to have subdued her adult-encouraged air of superiority. She looked smaller, more human now. Humbled.

Temple couldn't help wondering if that had been the point of the nasty prank. It was hard to imagine a child coming up with that subtle a form of harassment. Yet for an adult to stoop to hurting and scaring a child was chillingly sick.

She eyed the other contestants' mothers. Frances was relaxed but alert. Angie looked the usual distracted. Temple recalled the Texas cheerleader mother who paid a man to kill the mother of her daughter's rival, feeling a dead mother would take the girl out of the running for a cheerleader spot.

Pinning adult ambitions on a child would curdle the blood.

None of these moms looked that loony, not even Yvonne Smith with her overdone, aging beauty queen look.

Meanwhile, Temple tried to weigh the performances of Matt's rivals between watching her possibly lethal brood of mothers and daughters.

Sou-Sou would repeat her sabotaged dance on the third night. Ekaterina would be tonight's featured junior dancer. Her thin limbs were drowning in a ruffled ball gown for the lighthearted foxtrot. She nervously eyed her dancing Hermanos brother, Adam, while watching the performing adults with intensity.

Matt had drawn the right to squire the lean and glamorous Olivia through the quickstep. The aging actress had played a heavy for decades on the soaps, so she grabbed at the chance to unveil a lighthearted, flirtatious flair that took decades off her face and figure.

Matt had responded to her theatrical lead by morphing into a twenties playboy, the Great Gatsby on speed, as they smiled and flirted and flounced all over the stage. How amazingly the costumers and makeup artists could remake their contestants completely to match each dance. Matt and Olivia were delightful together. They had this dance knocked!

The judges thought so too. Danny's enthusiasm for them both was champagne-bubbly. Leander, himself past sixty, was clearly smitten with Olivia Phillips. Savannah was now fully into Matt, and babbling about them starring together in a revival of *The Boyfriend.* Nine, eight, eight.

The Cloaked Conjuror had drawn Wandawoman, and they were two people never destined to quickstep anywhere for any reason. Here the costumes went wrong. The decision to "lighten" CC's look with a diaphanous black cloak only made him look like a large gray moth.

Wandawoman, stuffed into billowing, knife-pleated pink chiffon studded with black sequins, resembled an overblown rose about to wilt from black spot. Her muscular power would shine in the ponderously sensuous Latin dances but now CC could barely steer her to keep up with him, nor did her moves evoke any sprightliness.

Even Danny Dove became acid in evaluating the dance: "Too slow, the steps were more galumphs out of Lewis Carroll. I thought your costumes were competing for an Oscar for 'most sickening sunset clouds in collision.' "

Leander tsked. "I can't say either of you were convincing. This is one case where lightness of being is a prerequisite and you two are not angel food, but pound cake."

Savannah was, predictably, on a different page. "I thought it was magnificent. The metaphor of the large gay . . . I mean, gray . . . moth flitting about the sparkling rose in the garden to sip its essence is so profound."

"That's *butterfly* and rose," Danny put in,

teeth gritted as tight as Molina's had been earlier this week.

Savannah babbled on. "One would expect the courting gray moth to be awkward and heavy . . . er, winged. And the rose is full-blown, fat and fluffy as a dandelion head just when the wind shatters it and blows it away." She sighed deeply. "Touching beyond words."

Six, six, ten.

"The first ten of the competition," Crawford crowed, caressing the mike.

Ick.

José's lean and lethal fencer's frame looked sexy in formal evening wear. He had the speed and the lilting moves down, but Motha Jonz, wearing white full-length feather streamers, looked like a poorly plucked chicken. It was the aristocratic fencing foil engaged with the street switchblade or, worse analogy, the kitchen shears.

Seven, seven, seven.

Temple watched the others follow Matt and Olivia and fail to better them. She cheered inside, mostly for Matt, but also for the token older woman in the lineup, who wasn't expected to win.

Last came the celebrity chef and the troubled pop tart teen, another match *not* made in Bob Fosse heaven.

Keith Salter was too rotund to do anything quicker than shortbread, even though Glory B. was giving the dance her all, looking as adorable as a butterfly flitting over a hot stovetop. She'd have scored big if she'd been partnered with Matt instead.

But it was Olivia who'd been as flushed and happy as a bride when she and Matt had taken bows for their standing ovation. He'd stood aside to give her the center stage, kissing her hand with European flair when she turned to give him the applause. It wasn't his nature to take the spotlight, but in partners dancing a gracious man looked like a prince for deferring so effortlessly to the woman.

And Matt had that part knocked before he'd ever touched sole on a dance floor.

Temple was ready to burst with pride and declare him the winner in her head, when the last couple galloping around the floor took a sudden tight spin and broke apart.

Everyone in the greenroom took in a deep breath.

The camera closed in on Keith Slater, flabby white face studded with rhinestones of sweat. He broke contact with Glory B., then spun away. She automatically tried to resume a partner position, but he sank out of her grasp, writhing to the floor.

All the kids and adults in the junior greenroom were on their feet.

The camera drew back on the main stage. It showed a fallen Salter twitching horribly before Matt and the Cloaked Conjuror ran to him. The burly magician's beastlike masked face glowered at the camera, then CC swept his ludicrous diaphanous cloak over the scene, obscuring the fallen man.

The camera panned in tight on the judges' shocked faces . . . well, the shock showed only on Danny and Leander's faces. Savannah Ashleigh looked merely stupefied, emphasis on stupid, and the camera caught Danny Dove in the act of vaulting over the judges' table to get to the fallen dancer.

The producer sat as if cast in stone, in place and silent.

Crawford Buchanan, however, was stalking forward into the camera's face, achieving a tight close-up, gloating with phony horror and all too real zest to be the center of attention.

"Oh, my gosh, ladies and gentlemen. We have *another* mishap. Keith Salter, celebrity chef known *the world over* has fallen *unconscious to the floor.* It is *another* Marie Osmond *dive.* Let us *hope* that *Keith Salter* has only *fainted like a girl,* folks. He was a bit chubby and these dances take *a lot of starch* out of the *old pancake gut.*"

Danny Dove appeared to wrest the hand mike from Crawford's death grip.

"Mr. Salter is being attended to by medical personnel the show has standing by at all times. Break. We're going to break," he ordered the camera operator, "and will be back as soon as we can."

The door to the junior greenroom burst open as a harried floor director burst in.

"Quick! We need to get back to the live broadcast with the baby dance. Who's up tonight?"

EK stood, looking grim and fragile, as usual. Adam rose behind her, shaken.

"You two, into the wings, ready to foxtrot this crowd's anxiety away. *You.* Introduce them."

Temple recognized her outer Zoe Chloe being called to man the ramparts.

Okay. She couldn't be any more upset and scared than her young introducees.

"Snap to it, Broadway babies," she ordered her petrified dancing troupe of two. "We're gonna save the show and you're gonna foxtrot the audience to distraction."

CHAPTER 40
RAPID RECOVERY

Luckily, there was no time to think.

Temple was on camera clutching a mike before you could say "Midnight Louie."

The two kids were standing behind each other in the wings off-camera.

The floor director hissed a last instruction to her, and then backed away, holding onto his headphones and pointing a silent, demanding finger at . . . Temple. Counting down with his four fingers.

Oops.

Zoe Chloe was *on!*

She strutted over so the camera could pan on the judges behind her.

"Here we are all in our places wearing shiny dance-mad faces. Keith Salter is doing well backstage. It looks like a touch of stomach flu for the famous chef, folks. All that hip-hopping about is hard on the duodenum.

"Meanwhile, we have to ask . . . just what

can a pair of these *junior* dancers do with that most fabulous, flying squirrel of a dance called the foxtrot? So here we have the youngest and, oh my, cutest — an eleven on the Zoe Chloe one-to-ten hot guy meter — Los Hermanos Brother, Adam. We have the lightest-on-her-feet girl squirrel and you have a heap of hype and entertainment comin' your way . . . Miss Ekaterina and the Sole Brother Hipster on the q.t. doing the quickest hot crossed biscuit step you ever saw. Gentlemen, waggle your Adam's apples, and ladies, put your hands together for Adam and EK!"

Temple breathed her relief to see the red light of the active camera wink out, taking her out of the picture.

Crawford sidled up. "That bastard judge stole my thunder, but I see that you still have a little lightning left, ZC. Now give me that mike."

"Not until somebody else tells me to," ZC gritted between smiling teeth.

You never knew what camera might be on, and on you, on a panic-stricken set.

Behind the curtained area, she heard the flurry of Keith Salter being loaded onto a gurney and rolled out by EMTs. Not a good sign.

Who would have it in for a chef, for

heaven's sake? Crawford Buchanan she could get. *Uh,* get that someone might have it in for him. Not "get" personally, as take revenge on.

Although . . .

Meanwhile, Adam and EK were tripping the foxtrot fantastic, as only lightweight teens could, with dazzling, show-must-go-on desperation. Wispy Ekaterina had pulled out a bundle of endless energy. The pair mimicked their elders' skill and sophistication so perfectly that the crowd was standing and applauding them even before their dance was over.

Talk about the perfect distraction!

Temple heard the music peak triumphantly, then end as the pair stood holding hands, panting and grinning and bowing. Innocent youth was sure the ideal distraction.

EK was radiant, a performer whose charisma couldn't be measured until the dance began. Adam made an ideal partner. They both seemed stunned by their own success.

Temple didn't even notice when the mike was gently pulled through her hands.

"A truly rare performance," Danny Dove told the audience, who knew it, with a calm smile. "I'm sure everyone is also eager to know that Mr. Salter is fine and being attended to. Check www.dancingwiththe celebs.com for a progress report on his condition. Of course, the judges must score only on what they saw of the full dance, and so must the audience."

Behind them, Crawford was leaping and capering, trying to regain center stage.

Zoe Chloe let Danny Dove pull her close, like a coconspirator, like a cohost.

"Meanwhile, this is Danny Dove and the effervescent Zoe Chloe Ozone pulling the curtain closed on another episode of *Dancing With the Celebs.* And wasn't that Matt Devine and Olivia Phillips quickstep, well, divine?" he finished with a totally inappropriate plug.

Temple could only nod and grin.

The camera's bleary red eye winked out as the floor director pantomimed brushing a hand over a sweaty brow.

Staff and judges, and the other adult and child dancers, came pouring from the backstage area to gather around, congratulating the shell-shocked kid dancers, chattering, and asking how Keith Salter *really* was.

Danny called for quiet.

"He'll be all right, we think, but for now we don't know what hit him, possibly . . . food poisoning."

The buzz all around them only heated up.

"Yes," Danny said. "The hotel contracted to keep a buffet going for our performers and staff, and everybody used it. If any of you feel the least bit queasy, call the hotel doctor immediately. The Oasis has three more on call now, in case we're dealing with something more than a quirk here. Meanwhile, I'd suggest you patronize the hotel restaurants from now on."

Temple spied Mama Molina with Mariah in tow and Rafi Nadir on the fringes.

Having the whole ruptured family Molina-Nadir together was awkward with a capital AWK. Not to mention EK as a fourth wheel.

Temple frowned, mind back on the poisoning problem.

It was possible that Keith Salter had eaten something too exotic or heavy for bouncing over the dance floor. He was built like an opera singer, as in a sack of cement.

Who would poison the food of a cook? Okay, a chef, not just a common cook. A celebrity chef with the airs and chutzpah and tummy roll to prove it.

A chef who'd made a media name for himself by descending on unalerted restaurants and totally trashing their food, their preparation, their reputation, and their house chefs.

There was a whole country full of suspects primed to slip some E. coli in Keith Salter's personal appetizers. Especially before he made a public appearance on TV.

It couldn't have been in the buffet food, or several people would be tossing their cookies by now.

Then she remembered glimpsing Salter in the men's dressing room with his own special tray.

He was too snobbish to eat hotel food from a buffet.

And in a dressing room, his tray could be quickly doctored by almost anybody.

It was time Zoe Chloe had another tête-à-tête with her new hottie hero, Matt Devine.

Chapter 41
Too Dead to Dance?

She reached him on her cell phone and answered his "Hello?" with a breathy . . .

"*Ooh,* Mr. Devine. I do so want a private quickstep with you. This miserable, unpaid show did give you a private room, didn't it? If not *the* private star dressing room you so richly deserve."

"Listen," he answered sharply. "I don't know how you people get my cell phone number, but I'm here to perform for charity, not crazed fans. I can guarantee I'll have a different cell phone number faster than you can quickstep off this line."

"Matt, no! Don't hang up. It's just me being silly."

"Temple! I thought they'd be keeping you on the set to figure out tomorrow's show if Keith is too ill to dance."

"Or too dead to dance."

"He was in bad shape, and you can't tell in these cases until the stomach's pumped,"

Matt said grimly.

"*Ah,* gross as that news is, I'm still waiting with bated breath to hear whether you bunk alone. We can't do much confidential public consulting in our current personas."

"You're the only one with a persona. You mean you'd desert your happy, high-square-footage home in a high-roller heaven with Molina and surprise family to visit my lowly plain hotel room?"

"Oh, yes. It's like rooming with Mothra and Godzilla up here, and Spawn and Friend have joined Mother Mothra."

"I bet Molina is a joy to associate with right now."

"You know what's going on, don't you, Matt?"

"Some of it, maybe."

"That I'll have to torture it out of you after this road show is over. So, do you want to meet Zoe Chloe in your room or not? And just how many fans have managed to snag your cell phone number?"

"Zoe Chloe, no. Temple Barr would be welcome, but I've got to wash off my makeup and peel off my costume and shower first."

"First? Sounds like you could use a dresser. Or an undresser, rather."

"You want to talk, or something else?"

"I'll take both when I can get it."

"Room twelve thirty-four. I do have to leave for the radio station by eleven thirty."

"Don't worry, Cinderfella. I'll be through with you by then."

Temple snapped her cell phone shut. She wasn't kidding about the undressing part. Zoe Chloe was such an impetuous little gangsta girl. They'd have plenty of time to talk after.

There was something about being naked in bed in a hotel room that was sinfully stimulating.

Temple and Matt each leaned against their two fat piled-up pillows, the heavy hotel bedspread tucked discreetly under their armpits.

"You have to slip my costume back onto the dressing-room rack tonight," he said. "Show rule. I really shouldn't have worn it up here to my room."

"You can always plead being rattled by the emergency situation, although you never are," Temple said, studying the formal white tie tossed on an armchair, the satin-striped black trousers draping the desk chair, the white tucked-front shirt sprawled like a ghost over the ottoman. "So why didn't you change first before I came up? Or down in

367

my case."

"You were in a hurry to meet. And . . . you kinda seemed genuinely interested in acting as my undresser."

"That was Zoe Chloe talking. She is such a sexpot."

Matt eyed Zoe Chloe's scattered accoutrements, from striped thigh-high stockings to miniskirt to puffed-sleeved Victorian jacket to sequined tube bustier.

"She has the fashion sense of a yard sale after a tornado," he said, "but she's pretty adorable anyway."

"And that spray-on tan really looks good on you. And it stays on really well too. Passes the taste test."

She'd finally pushed him out of his comfort zone and he looked uneasy. Matt hated the artificial, and now he was one.

"Leticia is having a hoot giving me a hard time about this at work," he admitted. "Says I'll be her color by the time the dance show ends and we can go on the road with a soft-shoe act."

Temple laughed. "She's a grand lady. That filmed segment of her church choir coming in to lead you in the rhythm chorus was just . . . wonderful. She's never come out from behind her radio persona as Ambrosia before, has she?"

He shook his head. "That took guts."

"What you're doing takes guts."

"What you're doing takes even more guts. I can't believe this Zoe Chloe persona. She's a pistol. I can see why the Internet dweebs adore her even though I feel a little predatory when she wants my spray-tan body. Where'd that come from? Seriously, Temple."

"Maybe we all need an outrageous alter ego. I don't think *I* would have pursued coming up to your room tonight. At least not all the way." She wiggled her toes under the bedspread. "But it was hot, wasn't it?"

"Oh, yeah. But now's the talking part. Keith may be seriously, even mortally ill."

Temple nodded, sober and her full self again. "I'm trying to put this together. Hot pepper in Sou-Sou's dancing shoes. A chef stricken by gastronomical problems. There's an odd foodie element here. I don't like that the mishaps bridge the adult and junior casts."

"Glory B. fell from a defectively assembled jungle gym in a rehearsal room even before these incidents," Matt told her. "Danny and I were there but he thought it was just a rehearsal glitch. Now it could look deliberate."

"Sure could."

"The dancing shoes had to be sabotaged by someone deliberately," he pointed out. "Keith's condition could be accidental."

"What'd you think of him?"

Matt clasped his hands behind his neck to consider while Temple gaped appreciatively. That spray tan went on everywhere. She used spray sunscreen, but maybe she should try a tan. Looking different in someplace different was a total turn-on. And if she got a teeny-weeny yellow bikini. . . .

"Chefs are a breed of their own," Matt mused. "Culinary prima donnas. The kind of grown men who have tantrums. He insisted on his own chair before his own spot along the makeup mirrors, his costumes always at the right end of the rack. His meals had to be absolutely prepared to his specifications, fresh from the kitchen, brought and served by an under-chef. He'd never touch the common buffet table for cast and crew we all ate from."

"Was he a tyrant, or was he afraid of something?"

Matt sat up, rethinking the man's eccentricities. "Was he persnickety, or was he *paranoid,* you're thinking. And rightfully so. Could be."

"Who would hate a chef?" she mused. "Other than his kitchen staff?"

"Keith Salter? Plenty. He had that reality TV show, *Butcher's Holler,* where he anonymously ate at restaurants all over the country and then tore the menu, food, and service apart."

"Could Keith Salter be why *Dancing With the Celebs* had death threats before it even aired? Everybody in Vegas would figure the Cloaked Conjuror for the target. He's had local death threats since he opened his Goliath show exposing the other magicians' stage tricks. That might have led the authorities astray. It could be someone from out of town, following Keith to kill him."

"You think like Agatha Christie," Matt said. "Now that I rethink it, Keith could have been scared, not just a snob. He didn't have much to do with the rest of us."

"What are 'the rest of you' like?"

"José has the drive and dedication of an Olympic athlete. If I've got a rival in this thing, it's him. But he's fanatic about winning, and I'm not. I lack his Latin fire, but I have a certain ease of self and lightness of heart he could never master. I mystify him. I suppose I'm the most laid-back of all the contestants. I don't have anything to prove. Keith must, or he'd have never made a career out of exposing and disparaging his peers. The Cloaked Conjuror has given up fellowship with *his* peers for immense amounts of money, but has to endure anonymity and hatred, the worst of both worlds."

"*Hmm.* Incisively put. I think I'll keep you. What about the male and female dance pros who train you?"

"They're doing this because all dancers wear out their bodies in a few years. Founding a studio and teaching and doing choreography is the next stage in their impassioned careers. And they *are* impassioned about their art form. I get that. I get the dedication of a true vocation. That's why the kids' competition is important. Start young, make hay while your legs last, or forget it. Olympic performers have that same pressure. Chefs and ex-priest radio shrinks, not so much."

Matt finished with a self-deprecating grin.

"And the women?" she asked, astonished by his insights.

"I don't share a dressing room with them. Only you." His voice had lowered on the last two words, and an intimacy break was definitely in order.

"I'm glad you came," Matt whispered as they took a breather.

She decided not to comment on the double entrendre. Zoe Chloe Ozone had been hired to be a G-rated act.

"The women," Matt said, now fully cerebral, lying back again and staring at the white ceiling. "I really enjoy dancing with Olivia. She feels she has a lot to prove, works hard, and I like helping her look good. Neat lady. Dotes on her grandchildren. Pretty amazing for an aging femme fatale on the soaps. She knows she's an anachronism, but loves her work. Maybe it's just a job for her now, but she has her pride and she needs the income. The soaps are dying. Not Olivia."

"You made her look twenty-eight tonight."

"She made *me* dance like *I* was still twenty-eight. Olivia made Olivia happen. She's a pro."

"Glory B."

"Makes you want to hug her sane. So much talent. So much pain. She knows she's almost totally blown her career, and is so scared she rushes to the one real worst thing to do like a lemming to a cliff. I'd like sixty counseling hours with her, but I only get a few hours of rehearsals."

"She was the first one hurt in rehearsal."

"Maybe a real accident? She's accident-prone. Look at her driving. I honestly think she's been driven so hard since her TV commercial days at ages six and seven that her body and mind haven't kept up with the career push. She works harder than Olivia, and it's harder on her. And she's only sixteen."

"Motha Jonz?"

"I haven't worked with her yet."

"Not a clue?"

He shook his head. "That hip-hop, gangsta, drug and glitz world is so alien to me. The materialism outdoes the greedy corporate executives. I don't see where women fit there, except as victims. Motha Jonz's 'man' was gunned down in Vegas by any of a dozen so-called record executives, rappers, media 'starz.' It's its own little gold-weighed-down, diamond-ear-studded, fancy-ride-driven alternative universe."

"She was literally caught in the crossfire when D'mond J supposedly offed QuE2 here in Vegas a couple years ago."

"I looked it up before I came to this competition. She was riding on the passenger side in the back of D'mond's limo. She was found to be carrying a pearl-and-diamond-handled .22 pistol, like something out of the musical *Chicago*. A messenger boy, just a teen, white, was shot and killed in the exchange of bullets. The bullet went right through and was never found. She might be a murderer. She certainly was hooked on drugs then."

"The authorities didn't settle this case?"

"It was one of those guns and drug cases where everybody was so guilty it was hard to pin anything on anyone. The men are still fighting legal battles. Motha Jonz has been out on her own as a performer ever since, but she's not making it. That's why she's on this show."

"Someone helped fill you in on all this."

"Leticia keeps her ear to the hip-hop underground."

"And she told you all this?"

"She told me to watch my back around Motha Jonz. Maybe not so much because of her pearl-handled piece, but because of her former associates. If she wasn't a perp, she was a witness."

"God, Matt! She could have a hit out on her. You could be dancing the jive with her and playing a target at the same time. In a crowd like the audience for this, it'd be easy to take out any one of you."

"Right. Thanks, coach, for the career advice in getting me here."

Temple clapped both hands over her mouth.

"Lordy. I had no idea what I was sending you into gang warfare *and* spray tans. I'm going to have to solve this thing for Molina just to get you off the hook."

"You need to watch your own back."

"Zoe Chloe doesn't have an enemy in the world, except Crawford Buchanan."

"She's lucky," Matt said sourly. "That doesn't seem to be the pattern around here."

CHAPTER 42
PASODOBLE DOUBLE CROSS

Sometimes the show seemed like a guided trip to Europe. If it was Tuesday, it was Spain and pasodoble night.

Temple had to choose a new Zoe Chloe wardrobe fit for an emcee role, which was getting tedious. It was hard to be a clothes-horse. Who knew how much effort pop stars must put into looking outrageous? Luckily, the show costumers were into the ZC look and welcomed her to their rack of castaways and boxes of accessories and trims.

"Red, black, and purple tonight," Temple told them when they had attired their charges and were relaxing with sodas and cigarettes.

"Kinda Red Hat Lady-delinquent-Goth?" asked Brandi, a gamine-haired sprite who looked much younger than she was thanks to a hip wardrobe.

"Got it."

"You seem edgy tonight, Zee," Manda

mentioned after Temple had rejected three choice looks.

"Yeah. The improvisation when things go wrong is getting to me."

"We're glad our deadlines are backstage."

"How'd it go?" innocent Zee asked. "Who are your odds on tonight?"

"The pasodoble always makes or breaks the guy," Brandi declared. "I mean, you either break hearts or break wind out there."

While everyone giggled, Tee in Zee guise probed further.

"Which guy, then, will win?"

"José is in the zone, and the ethnic bull-ring," said Yolanda. *"Olé!"*

"The Cloaked Conjuror will comport himself well, as usual," the older Manda said.

"Salter is gone! History in haut cuisine." Brandi was the group's talker. "And wait'll you see what we did to the blond. He is locked and loaded. All he has to do is deliver." Her eyes rolled with wicked anticipation.

"Really?" Zee Tee squealed, hoping for more racy girly tidbits.

She was disappointed. They returned to critically eying her getup, adding a large scarlet silk rose here, pinning up her full skirt with one, judiciously ripping her fishnet hose, adding temporary tattoos and a red feather boa. One thing about Zoe Chloe Ozone. She could *never* be overdressed or overexposed.

Well, Zoe Chloe Ozone would certainly get a breathless play-by-play from the dancing tweens, if not the jaded young Los Hermanos Brothers who'd mastered their own dance routines. She left the costume room to hang with her crew in the greenroom.

There she found that Zoe Chloe's "posse," Rafi and Molina, had joined the group, next to Mariah and EK. A little parental rivalry there? She sat on the long couch between the exes, on principle, and to make someone else as uneasy as she was tonight. Rafi and Molina scooted over to avoid crowding, but wanted some whispered guidance on the night's program.

"What's the dance?" Rafi asked Temple.

"Pasodoble."

"Paso what?"

"Spanish for 'double step.' Inspired by the bullring. Matador, cape, bull."

"So what's a girl doing in that dance?"

"She's either the cape or the bull. Gets tossed around a bit. It's a sexy, intense confrontation."

" 'Tossed around,' " Rafi repeated, looking at Molina. "Sounds like someone could get hurt."

"Nobody's gone after Motha Jonz yet," Molina speculated.

"Or Wandawoman." Rafi rolled his eyes, as if he doubted anyone would.

"Or Matt," Temple finished up.

She was still alone with her secret Temple Barr anxieties.

No way would Zoe Chloe Ozone be able to hold a mike tonight to introduce this day's junior performer and her partner at the end of the four adult dances. Her Kool Kid palms were oil-slick before even the first adult performer had been introduced in the overdone fashion of Crawford Buchanan.

"Ladies and gentlemen," Crawford's deep baritone oozed into the mike, amplified all through the set and the live audience and the greenroom.

"Crawford Buchanan is da bomb!" Meg-Ann declared.

"Da stink bomb!" Sou-Sou trilled, trying to ditch her prima donna image.

How sweet it was to hear a new generation dissing Vegas's answer to a walking, talking oil slick.

ZC sat back to watch and shutter her ears against screeching teen fans. At least she could "hang" with her adult "posse." Mariah and EK next to them were fairly mature and quiet, allowing Temple to indulge a long internal arpeggio of anxiety and regret.

This evening's dance was true adult entertainment. The pasodoble. "Double step" was the literal translation.

This was where the rubber met the road in the ballroom dance world.

Along with the tango that ended this competition Thursday, the pasodoble was the most demanding and dramatic dance. It didn't call for lifts, but it required slides and drags. The woman was the slidee and the dragee.

So it was Latin to the core.

The man was the matador, macho and lethal.

The woman with her elaborate Spanish skirts was both the scarlet cape the matador wielded with swashbuckling dash and the wild creature, the bull to be conquered. Or not.

Temple was always pro-bull whether it came to the ring or the rodeo, but this time she wanted the matador to win. Well, she wanted Matt to come off acceptably. To master his inner sexist and slayer. To out-Max Max.

This was terrible! How could she be so shallow? What was best about Matt was that he didn't have any of that macho baggage. Oh, heck, like any other red-blooded American girl, she just wanted her sweetie to come off hot and sexy.

Max could do this number. A given. He'd been a performer forever and knew how to turn sexy on and turn it off like a switch. Rafi could do this dance. He had that smoldering Latin love-hate attitude toward women, twice removed, culturally and personally.

José would do it, exquisitely. He was from the culture.

Crawford Buchanan couldn't.

Was she so wrong for hoping that Matt could?

Yes, because she'd coaxed him into doing this gig, taking this chance, putting him out of his element. It *was* a good career move. It just might not be a good move, period.

Temple swallowed. Her throat felt like a wad of gum had stuck in it.

Everything that was good about Matt would not work in this dance. It would have to be a total acting job. He was cast utterly against type and could be exposed as a wimp in front of the whole world, although he was anything but.

What had she been thinking?

Crawford's bass voice was issuing a dark

challenge. "Tonight we separate the men from the boys. Tonight the matador rules the dance floor in the sexy pasodoble. Who of our quartet of competitors is man enough to command the cape and the bull and the killing ground?

"Who will deliver the final thrust to his partner and competitors?"

Temple was slinking down in her seat, Zoe Chloe Ozone curling up in anxiety within her.

Mistake.

She couldn't watch.

The order of performance and pairing of the partners was never announced beforehand, or known to anyone on the show but Leander Brock, the producer and judge, who gave Crawford his notes at the last minute. The dancers rehearsed in secrecy.

Crawford was back, crooning verbally into the mike.

"Ladies and gentlemen, we have our first pasodoble couple, and they go together like Salt and Peppah."

Temple cringed at Crawford's attempt at being hip-hop.

"I give you . . . Keith Salter and Motha Jonz! Together again! Without interruption, we hope. Live and in passion" — Zoe Chloe almost hurled — "on the *Dancing With the Celebs* stage."

The audience *ooohs* celebrated the fact that Salter was upright, and back dancing. Scattered clapping audience members stood in tribute to the stricken celebrity chef's grit in going on with the dance.

He wore a gaudy black-and-white, embroidery-scrolled Cisco Kid outfit, if anyone remembered the early TV series that featured Latino stars seven years before Lucille Ball forced studio execs to accept her Cuban husband, Desi Arnaz, as a costar.

The embroidery was the pattern you'd see on the huge sombreros of mariachi bands at Tex-Mex restaurants. On Keith it looked like a drizzle of angel hair pasta over a burnt potato pancake. Cheesy in a Velveeta way, not flattering. More nacho than macho.

Motha Jonz was a tasty Latin sausage in ruffled scarlet satin stolen off of José Juarez's back. They glared at each other in that fiery manner across the raised stage, then stomped down the stairs to the dance floor a fourth-beat off rhythm.

"Lame," a watching Mariah leaned across her mother to rasp in Temple's ear. "Even EK could be sexier than Motha Jonz and she hasn't the boobs to go with the costume."

The music was heavy on trumpets and castanets, but no amount of will could make the pair look sexier than an animated set of red pepper flake shakers maneuvering on a border diner's Formica tabletop.

Temple cringed, but Zoe Chloe nodded with sage teenage disdain. "Lame lamé mama!"

Alas, Salter and Jonz were game but just as lame as she'd anticipated. The food poisoning incident had taken the starch out of the chef's onstage presence, and Motha Jonz was just too hefty for him to dominate.

Temple spent a full minute stifling giggles imagining this odd couple in each other's dress. That would be a more believable scenario.

The rest of the dance was plain painful, but the audience gave Salter a few, fevered huzzahs.

"Undercooked," Danny decreed. Keith Salter, he declared, "was the Taco Bell version of a matador, heavy on the stuffed enchiladas and light on hot sauce. Not your dance, either of you. The attitudes are stiff but the moves must be as supple as a fencing foil. You both got 'stiff.' Alas, supple eluded you. Six."

"Passive," Leander echoed. "A pair of dancing bears lumbering about a bullring, a pair of dolorous bullfrogs courting on a lily pad, two dinosaurs sinking with their great weight into a tar pit, that would best describe your pathetic attempt at a pasodoble. Five."

Temple cringed for the winded and unhappy couple in the camera's eyes, got up in froufrou like figures on a Weight Watchers midway point cake.

"Well," said Savannah importantly. "I . . . just . . . *lurved* . . . it."

The silence made its own impact but the panting couple looked toward her hopefully.

"*Wonderbar!*" Savannah said in German, puzzlingly. "You were cooking, Chef Salter, and, Motha Jonz, you were the peppa to his salt. Oh, yes, you were! You are on my choo-choo train from Savannah to Havana heaven, honeys. Hot Cuban crimes of passion. W*hoo-whoo!*

"You are *perfectly* matched. So cuddly and cute! I like fluffy things with coot, chubby, widdle cheeks, top and bottom." She winked, broadly and commended Motha Jonz's commanding pacing and strong turns.

Six, five, nine!

"Ladies and gentlemen," Crawford's booming bass trumpeted, "our next performers are that gay blade" — Temple cringed. Surely even Crawford . . . — "of the Olympic fencing team, José Juarez, and the queen mother of the P.M. suds, Miss Olivia Phillips."

Temple cringed again. *Gay blade?* Sure, point out Olivia was pushing sixty. *Clod!*

After Crawford's overhyped intro, the audience sat back.

They were waiting.

The lights dimmed, the music paused, and the spotlights showed two silhouettes at each side of the wings. A cigarette spark flared at each etched facial profile, then went out. The pair stalked toward each other.

Another thrill of guitar music, two lean bodies profiled against the stage far pillar. A high Spanish comb and mantilla making the woman looked horned. A flat-brimmed hat, cape, and sword etched the man's silhouette against a drawn red velvet curtain.

José and Olivia were perfectly matched figures, like mobile wrought-iron images: tall, thin, dark, intense.

Even everybody in the greenroom caught their breaths.

This was a contender couple.

A whip uncoiled from the man's side to snap once. The woman fled down the four steps in a trail of trembling lace ruffles. The whip snapped and followed.

When they reached the dance floor, she turned to confront him, haughty profile defiant, hands upraised to twine around each other like sinuous serpents. The whip cracked one last time and was flung aside as the dancers circled each other like courting scorpions.

The man flourished a sword, then wrapped his scarlet-lined cape around it and wafted it to and fro, frowning at the circling woman, who seemed to spit disdain and seduction at him in equal measure.

Her skirts swirled to match the cape as he advanced threateningly. With a grand gesture, he flung sword and cape to the floor, and seized her to flourish instead. He swung her from side to side like a ship's sail in a storm, took her from standing to skating across the floor, a fallen heap of limp skirts and suddenly — she was an uprising figure of spine and spitfire, challenging him again.

José and Olivia made the perfect paso-doble couple, as lean and wired as whips, gliding in a lethal mating dance that picked up pace and tempo until they were coming together like lightning even as the moves of the dance had them spinning apart; she was thrown down and sliding across the floor like a fan of limp lace, only to rise when he drew her up for an anguished embrace.

Their pasodoble was a dramatic battle of the sexes, their fingers flaring as they caressed each other's faces, looking as if they'd like to scratch each other's eyes out after a passionate kiss.

The live audience was already standing and hooting and applauding before they took the final pose, him bent over her like a conqueror, but she rising up from her prone position, a serpent ready to strike.

"That was awesome," Mariah shouted, hardly able to be heard over the enthusiastic hooting of Los Hermanos boys and screams of junior dancers. Even Rafi and Molina applauded.

Zoe Chloe Ozone kept strangely silent among the whistling, hooting, and screaming teens.

What had she got Matt into? They didn't teach that in seminary, for sure.

Olivia was so winded it looked like she'd do a Marie Osmond dive before the judges let her vanish backstage to the greenroom cameras for a postmortem on their scores and the dance. José managed to uphold her and swoop up his abandoned cape and sword en route to the judges' table.

The judges rained praise down on the

couple, Danny incisive and urbane, Savannah Ashleigh making a total fool of herself rhapsodizing over José, who offered a deep bow and sword salute to the only female judge.

What a showboater!

"Fabulous," Danny (the traitor) said. "Perfect tempo, perfect intensity, a thorny rose of a pasodoble, totally flammable."

Leander was already nodding. "What can I add to that? I was utterly absorbed in the dance and the emotions. You both have outdone yourselves. The ideal partnership and you two are the ones to beat in this competition."

"Well," Savannah said, and then paused. Of course everyone held their breath. She was always contrary. "You two were shocking . . . shockingly good. Olivia, you are my 'vamp of Savannah,' and you make the real one look like an ice cube, if I say so myself."

The results: nine, nine, nine.

Temple calculated. Matt had drawn either Glory B. or Wandawoman as a partner. She prayed it was Glory B. As Matt had reported that Danny had noted so naughtily, Matt was used to slinging a petite woman around and this was what the pasodoble asked of the man.

The seriously muscular Wandawoman? She'd been a rhythmless lump in her dances so far. Given the small number of contestants, it was too likely they'd draw each other again.

So, fingers crossed: Matt and Glory B. And then . . . *Dancing With the Celebs* glory. It would take a lot to overtake José and Olivia, but Matt and Glory B. could do it. Maybe.

"Now, ladies and gentlemen, our third scintillating couple," Crawford announced. "The Cloaked Conjuror and Glory B."

No! Matt had drawn Wandawoman.

A hand pushed down on Temple's shoulder. "Take it easy, Ms. Ozone," Molina's husky voice whispered in her ear. "You're hyperventilating."

In the greenroom, the clustered Los Hermanos Brothers rooted for CC, liking his massive masculine presence. None of them looked en route to massive. They were clean-cut teenage boys who could attract tween-age girls' ecstatic devotion, with the only sexual pressure being in everybody's heads.

Temple remembered that stage of girly development well.

So she would have to sit there, subdued, and watch CC flourish his usual cloak and toss Glory B. around like a graceful hand-kerchief. It would be his best dance, because his partner was so easy to handle.

The Cloaked Conjuror's usual cloak lined in crimson satin was now the toreador's cape. Glory B., a tumbling leaf of scarlet burnt black around the edges came hurtling and spinning and sliding into the center spotlight. Her blond hair had morphed into a dead-black, high-piled wig edging her face with a wrought-ironlike mask of brunet spit-curls. She looked small and poisonous, like a teen pop tart Medusa, with a long-stemmed rose in her small white teeth.

A mere webbing of black laces held her costume to her torso and the skirt was a peacock-tail grand swoop of scarlet ruffles overcast with spiderweb black lace.

The routine began slow and sultry, CC's bulky masked persona more suited to the role of bull, but making a commanding toreador.

CC and Glory B. did not fight the battle of the sexes, but rather went through the motions with intensity, if not passion. The audience's applause announced that they were pleased but not bowled over.

"This dance," Danny told the couple before the judges' table, "is a paean to power. There is a ritual stalking element, which you both captured well, but beneath the controlled moves lies guts and glory, a life-and-death drama, and you danced right over the top of it."

Savannah jumped in out of turn. "Well, I thought the rose in the teeth thing was just too 'cute.' And when he tore it away and stomped on it, all I could think was those thorns must be hell on lip gloss."

"The thorns had been stripped off," Glory B. interjected.

"No pain, no gain, honey." Savannah shrugged to display her ruffled off-the-shoulder neckline of scarlet silk roses, in case anybody viewing the show didn't know who *really* ought to be out there shaking her flounces and stomping her high-heeled jackboots, so to speak.

In the greenroom the girls giggled nervously.

"She is so lame," Mariah said.

"So *old* for that dress," Sou-Sou added. "Her shoulders look fat."

"And her mouth is just a funny blob," Patrisha pointed out.

Zoe Chloe resisted making a crack that obviously Savannah's collagen had shifted to her collarbones. After all, she was the "older" woman in this youthful bunch and didn't need to pile on here.

Leander Brock shifted magisterially in his seat when he commented.

"Of course I favor our masked friend the Cloaked Conjuror. He has deliberately handicapped himself by wearing disguises that limit his vision, and I do understand that problem. A stirring rendering, sir, but unfortunately the pasodoble is a stern, fast, sharp, stiletto-lethal dance, and you are a broadsword. Your partner couldn't match your onstage strength."

Still, the pair walked off the set with two eights and a seven (from Danny), a respectable score.

"Booring," was the chorus from the greenroom kibitzers, boys and girls together.

At least, Temple thought, CC wore a mask and any criticism that stung wouldn't show.

Temple was almost in cardiac arrest. Why had she encouraged Matt to enlist for this crazy, accident-haunted competition? Nothing had jinxed any contestants yet tonight. Matt was on last. He had Wandawoman to squire around in the most demandingly macho male role in all the dances, except for the final tango.

Temple cringed inside Zoe Chloe. No one was going to outmacho José Juarez tonight. Matt was toast.

CHAPTER 43
STOMP 'EM IF YOU GOT 'EM

"Matt's next," Mariah breathed reverentially in her ear, all hero worship and teen crush.

Zoe Chloe managed to growl a sour *"Olé,"* but Temple stuck a fist in her big mouth.

Take the shot. It'll be good exposure for your career.

Publicly humiliating your intended was so *not* a good move. She'd just never thought about this whole Latin dance thing. Matt came from northeastern European stock, Polish stock. They fought for centuries for freedom from foreign rule, not to kill cattle.

But it was too late. Matt's hat had been thrown into the ring.

By her.

And Crawford was already gloating at the mike.

"Well, well, well. Our first three contestants have surprised the audience and the judges by turning in their finest performances of the competition so far. The pasodoble seems to be the make-or-break dance. What will our mild-mannered radio guy do partnered with the formidable wrestler babe, Wandawoman? Methinks he's outclassed in the weight department. In the center ring, ladies and gentlemen, gentleman Matt Devine and the lady who's not for burning, but who could start a few conflagrations, Wandawoman!"

Temple closed her eyes. And couldn't keep them that way. She split her mascaraed lashes just a little.

"Ai carumba," Rafi muttered on her left. "Wandawoman is a heavy-metal load."

"Ouch," Molina murmured on her right.

"Don't watch," Mariah urged from her mother's other side.

The music again deepened into the Latin chords of big-bodied acoustic guitar, piercing trumpets, and shaken, not stirred Mexican maracas.

Temple understood this dance celebrated the moves of teasing a bull to madness and then striking it dead of a sword stroke in the ring. She always rooted for the bull. Now she was obligated to cheer — symbolically — for the bull-slayer.

José had copped the whip, sword, and mask of a Zorro costume. Chef Salter owned the plain black pants and shirt concession. The Cloaked Conjuror had captured the massive cape and boot approach.

What could the exhausted costumers have left to do with poor Matt, who danced last?

"Locked and loaded," Manda had said.

The stage was dark, one spotlight on the center.

The guitar strings trembled.

A man stepped from the dark pillar of the wings, caught in silhouette.

His head bristled with stiff projections like a metal crown. Temple recognized the miniature projectiles. She'd signed some online petitions against the ignoble sport of bullfighting.

Before the toreador even enters the ring, the bull is tormented by three banderilleros on horseback each sticking a pair of lances called banderillas into the charging bull's neck and back. Six wounds tormented by the very act of moving, forcing the bull to run around the ring trying to escape the agony.

The pain-maddened creature charges the cape-flourishing toreador on foot, distracted by the moving cape, not the human pole around which it flutters, until he's drawn close enough for the bullfighter to drive his sword into the killing point, the neck aorta.

At least José's sword was no longer on stage.

As Matt leaped over the four steps onto the dance floor, Temple levied Zoe Chloe to her feet in the greenroom. This dance celebrated killer moves. This dance contest was haunted by could-be lethal incidents.

Wandawoman, slathered in black lace that disguised her less-than-hourglass bulk, a black widow spider corseted in a lacy web, lifted her head to eye her partner.

Well, he sure wasn't one bit blond, Temple thought.

A skull-clinging scarlet scarf covered his forehead above a wig of dangling black dreadlocks twisted with bits of gold chain and stiff quills reminiscent of the crown of lances on a bull's high humped back. He had a black mustache and the requisite Hollywood fringe of beard along his jawline, emphasizing its strength. His eyes were contact-lens jet-black and surrounded by smoky liner, à la the sexy sheik of silent 1920s films, Rudolph Valentino, or that latter-day reincarnation and sterling metrosexual sex symbol, Captain Jack Sparrow, courtesy of Johnny Depp. Mediawise, it didn't get much better than this. Olé to the costume and makeup folks.

His boot-cut trousers, tight as black molasses above the knee and flaring dramatically below, had side seams of gold coins that clicked like a rattler's tail at every dramatic stomp of the Cuban-heeled boots.

The audience leaped to their feet, cheering just the transformation already.

CHAPTER 44
TOO HOT TO HANDLE

Poor, poor Mr. Matt Devine.

I understand why my Miss Temple has a hard time concealing her anxiety for the end of this pasodoble episode of *Dancing With the Celebs.*

I have drawn midnight dance duty myself, and well remember having to deal with honeys in heat who outweighed me by a third. Females of my species can be quite a handful any day of the month. When they are in heat, they literally can be too hot to handle.

These celebrity human females have already demonstrated their flair for temperament in the tabloids. I would hate to have to lead them around the floor, gazing hotly into their eyes and bumping intimate body parts right and left.

But this does not matter. I am too short for the job anyway. The job I am not too short for is keeping an eagle eye on the dance floor. If the judges really wanted to know the scoop on fancy footwork, I could consult on this in a heart beat. In fact, my four-on-the-floor pick up the vibrations of a whole lot of stomping going on, particularly in this fiery Spanish dance with Cuban heels on the guys and the usual spike heels on the gals.

I almost do not recognize Mr. Matt. The wizards of the dressing rooms have even further darkened any of his skin that shows: face, hands, and the deep open-front V of his white, long-sleeved, clinging, semitransparent shirt. I do not understand the need or purpose of a semitransparent shirt. Apparently the females in the audience do, for they had become quite rowdy just on his entrance on stage.

The theme du dance here is Spanish gypsy. Mr. Matt's golden hair is hidden by a gaudy scarf from forehead to nape of neck, where it is tied, and from which a brunet ponytail hangs. He now has black eyebrows and (ghastly vintage fashion!) long sideburns. He looks quite the different fellow.

Nor is Miss Wandawoman recognizable. Her dishwater blond hair is now a tangled mass of raven-black. I cannot fault this judgment call to multiply her locks: when it comes to hair color, black is beautiful. Miss Wandawoman wears much gold dangly jewelry. I much prefer the simple large hoop Mr. Matt sports in one ear.

Her gown is backless and hipless on one side, held up only by flesh-colored elastics my sharp eyes detect. A wide black satin ruffle runs from one shoulder across her body, back and front to the opposite hip. It would resemble the sashes that beauty queens wear, except there is almost no gown under hers, and the sash is ruffled, like her full skirts.

All and all, I must admit they look the parts.

When the music starts, they assume the taut upright poses, one arm flung high, heads haughtily erect, as if sniffing skunk.

Stomp! They are stalking across the floor eyeing each other like mortal enemies, he down on one knee to swirl her around him like a ruffled cape. He rises to seize her for a pair of matched close steps, then swings her aside, thrown away. She circles around to cling as their profiles nearly touch while they glare fiercely.

And so it goes. The audience is whistling and stomping and clapping and hooting, so I suppose this folderol is passing as pasodoble mastery. Much ado about nothing much, think I.

He twirls her tight to one side, spinning her away and then close again. She is leaning hard into him, and when he steps away to give her his back (this is not a polite dance), she slides slowly down his leg.

The audience is shrieking with delight. People here have very high auditory pain thresholds.

He reaches down, twirls her on the floor in a spectacular spin as she executes a full split, and then pulls her prone body through his wide-legged stance to slide halfway across the stage.

The audience is on its feet at this spectacular move, drowning out the sound of the music's final flourish as Mr. Matt strikes a victorious pose beside his partner and then bends to mime one of those frozen passionate lip locks that end dances around here, despite seeming to be a serious contradiction in impulses. Passion is not usually a freezing and posing matter, I would think.

Her supposed-to-be-proud neck bobbles onto her shoulder. Her legs remain splayed and inert, not moving to assist gracefully in her own resurrection for a bow.

While everyone there on two legs freezes in position, possibly passionate, I am there like a bullwhip on a horsefly, sniffing at her mouth and nose. I smell scented lipstick, metal and sweat, and nothing telltale. I *think* I feel the slightest stir of breath.

And then I am near trampled as the tardy

security detail surrounds Mr. Matt and his partner, who will be taking no bows and getting no judges' ratings tonight.

CHAPTER 45
POSTMORTEM ON A PASODOBLE

Temple raced from the greenroom to the stage, only to have Crawford slap the mike in her hand as she headed for the clot of security uniforms that surrounded Matt.

"We're off-air for two minutes, ZC," he said. "Get ready to bring on the kids waiting in the wings. I'm out of here. I'm going on my radio station live on the latest *Dancing With the Celebs* mishap. This has become the most suspenseful reality TV nightly gig in history. Audience numbers are skyrocketing. I'm off to do a national pickup on the 'cursed celebrity hoofers' story. See you tomorrow night. Ta-ta."

Temple stopped on a dime, not willing to be Zoe Chloe to the rescue again.

Then she spotted Rafi directing his troops and Matt carting an unconscious Wandawoman offstage amid a circle of security uniforms. Not to mention Dirty Larry following them with a video camera in hand.

She was stuck announcing the final acts: Sou-Sou's "special, secret" makeup solo dance and Patrisha and Brandon's jive. It meant the world to these kids.

So she heard her amplified Zoe Chloe voice tap dancing through some nonsense patter. What caught her attention was Sou-Sou's costume for her jazz ballet solo.

She came out as "Baby Phat" Barbie, all in hot pink with spandex thigh-high spike-heeled boots, skimpy miniskirt and halter top, with flowing hair and chunky earrings, slinging around a stuffed purse pooch on a leash as she pranced and posed.

Temple could only gape in horror. Sou-Sou's "secret" routine was as a Barbie doll, with the possibility that the Barbie Doll Killer was in town?

The ninety-second routine seemed to take a year, as did the judges' warm comments to the little girl.

Only the sight of Patrisha beaming hopefully from the wings with Brandon right behind her wound Zoe Chloe up again. She was beginning to feel like a Barbie doll herself and was relieved to see Molina waiting to pounce on Sou-Sou as soon as she left the stage, the girl's mother in tow with Dirty Larry behind her. Temple would love to eavesdrop on that quartet, but couldn't desert her post.

The judges looked dazed too, but Patrisha and her Hermanos brother gamely poured their energy into the lively jive dance, distracting the audience with their show-must-go-on verve.

Lousy Crawford didn't bother to show up again for the closing, as advertised, so Zoe Chloe winged that one, so torn between concern for Wandawoman, Matt, and Sou-Sou that the usual spirited ZC babble must have been incoherent.

As the cameras blinked off and drew back, people pounded her on the shoulders as if thinking she needed to start breathing again, saying what a "fab" job she'd done. One of them was Danny Dove, who extracted her from the judges and the scrambling tech people and guided her through the noise and lights to a relatively quiet hallway.

"Matt's fine," he said. "He handed Wandawoman over to security and the EMTs. She was breathing and en route to the hospital. They're getting tape of the routine from all the covering media as soon as possible and want to go over it with Matt. Apparently the costume young Sou-Sou wore has really riled up the undercover police people. You okay?"

"Incoherence never killed anyone. Wanda-woman?"

"The theory is drugs. Probably not voluntary. We've got two dance nights to go. We need to stop this dirty trick stuff, but the producer's in love with the numbers and the police are even more gung ho about using the competition to nail the trickster and they're particularly revved by Sou-Sou's nauseously Barbie outfit." Danny's worry-wrinkled face softened. "The judges have decided to view their pasodoble again privately, if Wandawoman recovers, and rate it uninterrupted. It was killer, Temple. Matt was out-Joséing José."

"I think winning this thing is the last of his worries."

"Maybe. But he was in it to win it, and he still could. And he knows it." Danny grinned at her. "I admit his paso knocked me out. I'm damn impressed. Heart is always the key to dance."

"And everything."

"And everything." Danny hugged her. "I think that interesting two-person 'posse' of Zoe Chloe's wants to see her ASAP."

"Danny, they're —"

"Enough already." His voice went Humphrey Bogart. "I recognized the dame the minute I saw her." He knew Carmina was Molina.

"I want to see Matt."

"The security people are having him go over all the recordings of the routine. I'd save the best till last."

CHAPTER 46
A PERFECT BARBIE
DOLL

Molina watched the walking Barbie doll bounce offstage toward the wings, not at all subdued by the anxious ending to the final adult dance, the egocentric glee of youth personified. She needed to get back to deal with the major mishap situation, but knew Rafi would be on it, a surprisingly soothing idea.

Meanwhile, she had to find out how a living Barbie doll had ended up center stage at the kind of event that drew a stalker who was leaving a wide swath.

"That went over great," Sou-Sou bubbled at her, jiggling with teen hyperactivity. "My makeup number and costume was even cooler than the first one. Did you see it? Did you?"

Molina nodded, not to Sou-Sou but to Dirty Larry, whose firm grip held Sou-Sou's mother in check from the same theatrics as her daughter.

Scattered metal folding chairs for waiting performers caught Molina's eye.

"Let's all sit a bit and talk," she suggested.

Dirty Larry started rounding up chairs and seating Smiths on them.

"You're with Ms. Ozone's manager," Mrs. Smith realized. "Oh, my Sou-Sou is an up-and-coming client for you. That Ozone girl is getting too old."

"I'm her manager's assistant, but this is Officer Podesta of the Las Vegas police. I'm helping ask some questions. How did Sou-Sou happen to wear a Barbie doll getup?"

"Well," Mrs. Smith seesawed her ample behind into place on the skimpy metal seat. "That was my idea. I act as her manager. Glad you liked it. Barbie is an icon, and that's what I want Sou-Sou to become. I even had some Polaroids taken before her entrance, if you want to see them —" She reached into her garish yellow purse.

"That won't be necessary, Mrs. Smith," Larry said. "What I need to know is why you dressed Sou-Sou that way? Anything trigger the idea?"

"Nooo." She set her purse on the floor. "I'm just creative. Maybe I saw something in the paper about Barbie dolls being found at shopping malls, but it doesn't take much to stimulate my brain."

411

"Those Barbie dolls found that way might be calling cards for a predatory killer of young girls, ma'am," Larry said. "You couldn't have done a better job than we would in setting your daughter up as a decoy."

"Oh. Oh!"

Sou-Sou's eyes were pie-plate round.

"Better get that outfit off of her pretty quick," Molina told the mother. "These dirty tricks are no joke, and your daughter is already the victim of one."

"You mean," Mrs. Smith asked, "a killer could be loose?"

Before either Molina or Larry could answer, a strange metal trolling sound came into their midst.

Everyone glanced at the black-painted stage floor. A small metal canister with a red cap was wobbling among their circled feet. A large black cat had joined their circle, one paw still lifted like a golfer holding up his club while waiting to see his shot land on the distant green.

The cat was positioned next to an open scarlet purse that now lay on its side, the contents spilling out, Polaroid photos, lipstick tube, nail file.

Larry bent to bag the rolling tube. "Pepper spray, Mrs. Smith? From your purse? We think that was used to doctor Sou-Sou's shoes the other night. Another creative idea?"

"Oh."

"Moth-er!" her daughter accused with a screech. "That *hurt!*"

"Lots of women carry pepper spray," Mrs. Smith insisted, bending to stuff the items back into her purse. She held out an imperious hand to Larry, open. Her fingers were trembling and Sou-Sou was standing, pouting rebelliously.

Molina nodded.

He slapped it into her waiting hand. "That was child endangerment, ma'am. I've got bigger game to track here but you try anything further like this and your daughter will be blackballed on the dance circuit. Now get her out of that Barbie outfit and burn it."

The pair scuttled away, sounds of shrill recrimination echoing from the hall outside.

Molina looked around for the cat. It was gone. Of course.

"I've got to get back to the main event," she told Larry. "Looks like this Barbie connection was just a coincidence."

He nodded.

"I'm not certain your being here is one, though."

"You mean where? Near the stage?" She was silent. "In the hotel, on this case? Yeah, I sorta assigned myself. I'm not useful?"

"Yes, you make yourself useful. Too useful. I'm not sure why and I'm thinking you don't want me to know why."

"You really don't think a man would simply be attracted to you? You *have* lost yourself in your job, Carmen."

"And you haven't, undercover man?"

"I'm on leave from that."

"Don't fool me and you won't fool yourself. You're still working undercover and you're using me to do it. I'm seeing things a lot more clearly now. Sometimes friends look like enemies and enemies like friends. Which one are you?"

He stepped close, his voice low and intense. "I'm your friend. Really I am. You don't know how much."

Was it a promise, or a threat? She didn't know but she would, eventually.

"You showed up on the scene of the local Barbie doll killing, and here you are still today, pushing your way into my investigations. What? You want to make me or to make detective? Or something else?"

"You are so wrong."

"Again? Is that the unsaid ending? I have been wrong and I may be wrong again, but right now I have a choice of dumping you or watching you, and I prefer the latter."

CHAPTER 47
MADNESS IN HIS
METHOD DANCING

Twenty minutes later, Temple returned to the empty greenroom and picked up her tote bag, digging out her cell phone and dialing. Where was Louie, anyway? Not playing a purse pussy anymore, that's for sure.

"Yes?" Molina barked into her ear.

"Ah, Zoe here."

"If you've quieted the natives, get up here. Your M&Ms are missing you."

Click. Gone.

She hefted the tote bag over her shoulder. It suddenly felt very heavy, even without Louie, and she headed, not for the high-roller suite, but into the deserted rehearsal areas. The backstage dressing and rehearsal rooms were eerily empty, but muffled voices had her heading for the men's dressing room.

Sure enough, some light spilled into the dim hall and a group of men sat hovering around a camcorder, looking and listening.

She recognized Rafi Nadir and one of his uniformed security lieutenants, Hank Buck. Dirty Larry held the camcorder while Matt told him when to pause. A couple more security guys stood by, arms folded.

"She seemed fine here," Matt was saying. "Only at the end did she falter, and then it was like she went out cold in two seconds. I was already holding her up for the leg slide, still trying to save the routine, not realizing anything more than a misstep was wrong."

He'd swept off the head scarf and false black lovelocks. With his highlighted blond hair showing against the intensified spray tan, he now resembled a surfer dude instead of a matador. Not a bad look, either.

"Are they going to alert you on her condition soon?" Matt asked.

"Soon," Rafi said, "but the EMTs reported from the ambulance that it looks like a common sedative OD. Could be something she took for nerves."

"A pro wrestler at a dance contest?" Matt asked incredulously.

"Not likely," Rafi admitted with a smile. "Police procedure avoids jumping to any conclusions. Given the other incidents on stage here, it'd be safe to guess it's not voluntary. You all drink water?"

Matt looked around at the empty plastic water and energy drink bottles on the long makeup dresser tops. "Constantly. Even the makeup lights are hot, and we rehearse until we sweat like overhydrated pigs. Then there's the stress of waiting for your performance results."

"The police will test all the empties they find. Okay," Rafi said, glancing at Temple in the mirror. "That crazy mixed-up kid you want to marry has come calling. I think you two can have some face-to-face time in the hall."

Matt's warm brown eyes seemed black in this artificial light as they met hers. He stood, knocking his chair back a little. After all the complicated dance-floor moves, he suddenly seemed awkward.

Having your partner pass out in your arms on live TV might be a bit disorienting, Temple thought, not to mention the uncertainty about Wandawoman's condition.

They went down the hall far enough so they couldn't hear the murmur of investigators, and the investigators probably couldn't hear them.

"You all right?" she asked.

"I'm fine, and you heard Nadir say Wandawoman will be too. This competition is looking more 'killer' by the moment. What did you get me into?" he added mock rue-fully.

"This major sexy costume," she said, past-ing herself against it and running her fingers down the deep front V of the transparent mesh shirt. "Pardon my pawing, but I'm standing in for all the women in the audi-ence."

"Yeah?" He smiled down at her. "You're the only one I care about."

"And aren't I lucky? Matt, how did you manage that amazing transformation? Danny said you outmachoed José. It can't be just Tatyana's whip hand."

"You know, this 'acting' stuff that you talk about, and that Tatyana is trying to drag out of me by hook or by crook, has given me some new insights. Is it supposed to work like that?"

"*Ye-es.* Acting forces you to inhabit other people's skins and that's very enlightening. Sooo?"

Their embrace stayed close as he com-bined almost kissing her with a dutiful recital of his recent epiphany.

"I knew I had to commit totally to this competition, even the parts of it that made me uncomfortable. Tatyana loved my swim-ming physique, but, unlike fencing, it's not a very passionate or romanticized sport and you don't learn drama doing it. So I thought about the dance, the pasodoble. The love-hate aspects. Didn't help me much. I'd been working on the 'love thy fellow human' part for years and even purged my hatred of my rotten stepfather once I found him here and saw what a pathetic weasel the bane of my childhood was."

Temple cuddled closer, needing a romantic interlude after the anxiety and hurly-burly all around them.

"You're gonna laugh," he warned. "I knew I had to take charge and sling Wandawoman around like a seventeen-pound matador's cape, all the while feigning passion. So . . . I imagined I was dancing with Kitty the Cutter."

"What brilliant Method acting, Matt! No wonder you were so relentless, so powerful, so passionate. You were dancing with the Devil. The classic attraction-rejection dance with evil incarnate. Kathleen O'Connor was a perfect embodiment of that."

"When I let out my anger at Kathleen O'Connor for cutting me, in a way I *became* her. I *felt* the pent-up rage that makes a person so destructive. And, thinking about her attack, I realized for the first time, maybe because I'm different from then, because of, you know, us."

Temple nodded. "Us" was a first and only sexual commitment for Matt, and it had been hard-won.

"This may sound sick."

"The truth often can."

"I sensed for the first time, thinking back as I had to, something sexual about her rage and her attack. I don't think of women as sexual predators, but I believe she was."

Temple nodded again, solemnly. "You were fresh out of the priesthood when you encountered her, so you didn't get her underlying motives. I think you're right. You remember the story of Max and his cousin Sean visiting Ireland as a high school graduation present?"

"Yeah. Sad story. Could make a modern opera out of it. I get Max's guilt. I've always understood that about him, even when he was being his most caustic. It must have been hard on you."

"Only when he was in those Irish melancholy moods, and that was seldom. Max helped nail the bombers. He got revenge, for what it was worth, and went on to prevent a lot of awful acts of terrorism from happening. Sean's loss was there, but it was old news. But I don't think you understand just how innocent they were, those boys."

"Catholic high schoolers? Back then?

Sure. Trust me."

"And eager. This was their first time unsupervised, in a foreign country during perilous times, and yet it all looked so cheery and all pub songs and ale and no one carding them. Kathleen O'Conner was older, in her early twenties. She was a woman, and the game the boys played competing for her was semiserious. They were virgins and here was a free woman who seemed to want to change that, and they'd be scot-free, never likely to see her again. No risk, all gain."

Max won, he thought. He didn't have to be embarrassed about being a seventeen-year-old virgin ever again and his cousin Sean wouldn't hold it against him that he'd gotten there first. That apparently literal roll in the hay saved Max's life but cost him his peace of mind.

"I know he came to believe that Kathleen was allied with the IRA and *knew* the pub would be bombed. What a sad, sick woman," Matt said.

"He also came to believe that Kathleen *knew* Max would meet his cousin at that pub, afterwards. To brag a little, and celebrate. He believed that she *picked* him, and so *picked him to live,* so that his first act of love turned an act of trifling boyish betrayal into a mortal personal loss. That's why I call her 'Kitty the Cutter.' She existed to mess up other people's lives with whatever it took on her part, sex or violence."

"You're describing a psychopath."

Temple nodded. "She tainted the lives of the only men I've ever loved."

Matt was silent, accepting the simple truth of Temple's love for both of them.

Then he sighed. "My God, I never thought I'd be glad someone was dead. Or that someone deserved to die, or to be stopped, anyway. Max was there? He was sure?"

"She was still chasing him, chasing his car on that demon's motorcycle of hers. After all these years, she was furious that he was alive and happy and free of her. It was a single-vehicle accident. She gunned that motorcycle off the road into a fiery crash. He stayed around long enough to search for a pulse in her broken neck. There was none."

They kept silent, their close embrace and mutual mood completely turned from triumph to a sober clinging.

Matt pulled Temple away to see her face finally, looking roguish, deliberately lightening the mood.

"Tragic story. Like I said. I got off lucky," he commented.

"You mean the wound she gave you was only physical?" she asked.

"I mean I got away from that homicidal man-eater still a virgin."

Temple laughed through the unacknowledged sheen of sorrow in her eyes.

She let herself be swept back into the arms of the sexiest pasodoble dude on the planet. Well, in Las Vegas, anyway.

CHAPTER 48
PASO DE DEUX

In the Hummerbar, all heads turned as she entered, as if a prima ballerina had just spun onto the stage.

Disheveled, distracted, Revienne remained a femme fatale.

Max, meanwhile, calculated all the amazing coincidences that could have led so quickly and incredibly to their reunion. And if he could get her into bed tonight. He's the knight-errant, after all, the guy left behind who soldiered on and caught up with the girl. He's had a lot of pain, no gain, and he so needs a lay.

Does it always come down to this? Naked need? Probably.

In a vague sense, he understood what he needed more: Garry Randolph is the man who knows who Max is and why he ended up here in this condition, and what he really needs. But Garry is a figment now. Revienne is real, and she needs a martini.

"*Mein Gott*, Michael! Those . . . monsters. They grabbed me off the street in Alteberg, held me overnight in a filthy, dark warehouse. Why? What have I done?"

Her gray eyes narrowed over her Gray Goose vodka gimlet. Nice combo. "What have *you* done?"

Not enough with you, lady.

That was the trouble with lust. It was utterly unreliable. Secret agents like himself must deal daily with the unreliable, yet must crave the reliable. That was a delusion. God, his left knee ached. The left knee of God. God must have had them, because so many of His devotees kneeled. . . .

Max didn't believe in luck, in kneeling, in Gods who demanded both, or in good women who turned up fortuitously in bad places. Maybe he didn't need to get laid that bad.

"Was that the village's name, Alteberg?" he asked.

"Yes." She gazed at him over the glittering rolled rim of her martini glass. "I'd gone out for breakfast. You were comatose."

"Not like in the clinic." He had dropped the Irish accent. Sounded like himself, whoever that self was.

"No, just from food and wine and . . . overstimulation."

Her massage.

"You were dead to the world."

All too much so.

She shrugged. She had wide shoulders for a woman. He didn't find that unattractive. She must work out hard on her upper body strength. Why?

"That's when you were kidnapped," he prodded. "Do you know who? Why?"

"No more than you do." She waited.

He waited.

She ran the tip of her tongue over the cocktail glass rim.

The muscle in his right calf jerked. Over-stimulated. The more seductive she was, the less his mind wanted her.

This was a game of cat and mouse. The roles hadn't been assigned yet. He'd thought he'd needed to find her, to make sure she was safe. He'd thought he'd needed to find her, to prove he could. And he thought he'd needed to find her to seek shelter, to find out for sure if she wasn't to be trusted.

Now it was all too easy. You'd think a man with a short-term memory loss and two bum legs would want it easy. But he didn't. Hell, he was Irish. He knew that much. Some people thrive on adversity, and he was one.

He rose from the dim table in the storied

bar. Tossed a ten-euro tip on the varnished surface.

"I've reserved a room in your name. You should be able to rest and freshen up there. I doubt those men will bother you further."

Her gray eyes flashed fury.

"I'll be gone before you are in the morning," he said. Threatened. "Thanks for your help."

"That's it?" she said before he could take up his cane and walk. "I nearly break my own ankles walking down half an Alp and I get a drink and a . . . what is it called in the American movies? A kiss-off? You don't even want to know what happened to me, what those men wanted?"

"Do you know what they wanted?"

Her anger ebbed as she sat farther back into the leather club chair, reassured that he wasn't leaving quite yet.

"They took *me,* but they wanted you. It seemed they were sure you would follow. They drove down the mountain slowly. Stopped for lunch! All the while holding a pistol on me."

"What kind?"

"Black, sleek, how do I know what kind? I am a psychiatrist, not a policeman."

"And they came straight to Zurich?"

"It's the biggest city at the bottom of the

northern Alps. Anyone leaving the clinic would have to go through Zurich."

"How did they come across you? Know you? Know you were with me?"

"From the clinic."

"And they didn't force you to take them to me in the village?"

Her eyes grew evasive. "They didn't want to cause a fuss in that little town. They said they'd make their move in Zurich."

"In what language?"

"English," she said, surprisingly. "But not American, as you speak. It had a more musical sound."

"An accent?"

"I suppose so." She frowned as she sipped again, more deeply. "It wasn't British English. I've heard that on the BBC. Maybe English wasn't their native tongue. Maybe they were Latvian. I don't know!"

"Maybe what you don't know is a safeguard." He'd slipped back into a soft, nonstagy Irish brogue.

Her eyes widened like a child's. "Yes! They spoke exactly like that."

Max smiled, although he didn't feel like it. The IRA was defanged these days, of its own volition. Why would Irish muscle still be after him? Unless it was the rogue branch, and even then, such a connection was ridiculous. Yet, the accent had enveloped him like a second skin when he'd wanted one to cloud his identity.

"What is it?" she asked.

"You haven't heard a Celtic accent before?"

"Celtic? You mean Scottish?"

He didn't correct her because she seemed sincerely puzzled.

European countries could be insular, despite being closer cheek by jowl than most American states. She'd probably heard a bit of a brogue in passing, but had never bothered to assign it to any particular foreign country. The French were almost fanatical about preserving their language from creeping Americanisms. Her ignorance of other accents seemed reasonable.

"You have come up in the world, Mr. Randolph, since we parted."

He mentally shook himself to attention again. She meant his upscale new clothes.

"Same method of shopping?" she said.

"I haven't won the lottery in the past twenty-eight hours."

"Only twenty-eight hours? You counted. Is that all it's been?" Her sleek features sagged momentarily.

"I take it you prefer my company to your friends in the Mercedes."

"They are not my friends! Oh, they didn't hurt me beyond worrying me to death, and you were as much responsible for that as they were."

"I was?"

"You are my patient, infuriating and uncooperative as you are! I am responsible for you."

"For my mind and emotions, maybe, but this is no longer a therapeutic situation."

"Actually, it is." She was all business now, as when she had first visited him in the clinic room, but she didn't stop sipping the cocktail. Emotion and alcohol were warming her cool blond cheeks, and him by proxy.

"You have made an impossible physical recovery in the past few days. I daresay running for one's life could now be recommended as excellent physical therapy. You laugh? I'm dead serious."

"But you were being sarcastic, even funny. You've never been funny before."

"I am not amusing. I am angry, rightly so. It's clear that you have also recalled some survival strategies that indicate you have a most interesting history, professional or personal, I am not sure which yet, but I mean to find out."

"And if I don't mean you to?"

"Given the progress you have made in

these last few days, if we had a few solid hours of consultation, you might make a real leap. Then you would know who these men are who tried to use a hypodermic to silence you, and who kidnapped me off the cobblestones of innocent Alteberg to use me as a hostage and lure. Why did they think I would be valuable to you? Why did they even bother with me?"

If she truly was the innocent bystander she claimed, that was an interesting question.

He felt his face flush. Going after her when she'd vanished, in his condition, with the distrust he harbored, was idiotic. Apparently, someone who wanted to kill him — or maybe someone else who wanted to use him — knew that he would be just that idiotic. Was he a fall guy for a pretty face? Or someone with an overactive sense of responsibility?

In a way, only time and maybe Revienne would tell. She was the sole link he had now to his past, both for what she might be able to do for him as a psychiatrist and how useful she might be as an ally, or a secret enemy.

Either way, having taken all this trouble to find her, it was even more idiotic to let her go.

"We can discuss this in your room," he said.

Her pale eyebrows raised as she lifted her martini glass to finish it off.

"I ordered a bottle of champagne," he added.

She lowered the wide-mouthed glass without drinking, eyeing him with approval. "A nice thought, but that is too . . . sleepy-making for the work we have ahead of us tonight. This is an occasion for unconventional methods. Martinis would be better to loosen up the unconscious."

"Mine, or yours?"

"Let's try it and see what happens."

"You said a 'room.' "

Revienne's tone was accusing.

It would be called a junior suite in the United States. It had a small refrigerator, nice postmodern furnishings, a hair dryer and jetted tub in the bathroom for rich Americans used to excess.

"Ah, divine."

She sat to yank off her boots and the nylons inside, now pocked with holes. She snapped them free at the thighs of a garter belt he'd never suspected she wore.

His pulse jumped. In America, garter belts were cheap or expensive sex accessories.

Bought sex. From somewhere, he remembered that European women were different. They might not shave their legs or underarms, but they might just shave a more intimate area. They might just wear garter belts and hose daily, but skip panties.

My God, he'd been on the run for several days, around the clock, with a woman who wore no underwear and he hadn't known it. Luckily, she hadn't noticed his juvenile curiosity and even more infantile excitement.

"First, I bathe," she decided. "You order me another martini and appetizers." She unbuttoned her jacket to reveal a black lace camisole under it and threw it on a chair, disappearing into the bathroom, drawing the door shut behind her.

He heard the lock turn and smiled. She had her suspicions too.

The boots had been ruined; the hose too. He picked up her jacket. It was a light wool-silk weave, lined in silk crepe, hand-sewn with silken tape covering the seams. It would feel smooth as a cloud on, as his new designer clothes did.

He sniffed under the arms, smelling no deodorant, a faint perfume, and also a strong acrid waft of dried sweat. So she may have been terrified in the Mercedes, or may just have worked up that sweat during their hike down the mountain.

Max did as she said, calling room service, not sure whether his psyche or his suspicions or his sex drive was most in need of stimulation and therapy at the moment.

CHAPTER 49
ANOTHER OPENING,
ANOTHER BLOW

Temple had never felt a worse case of stage fright.

Wednesday night. Cha-cha cha.

She was stationed in the wings, pleased to be going on second, long after her bête noire, Crawford Buchanan.

For a "black beast," as the French phrase put it, his face looked as white as a ghost, but then he'd always been pasty-faced. The undertaker-severe black suit he wore tonight didn't help.

But Temple's stage fright wasn't for Zoe Chloe Ozone, who was wearing a spiderweb body stocking under a purple tutu with pink ballet flats and a pink marabou feather-covered top that made it look like she actually had a bosom.

It was for Matt Divine and his fourth-night debut as a master of the hip-slinging cha-cha. He was again partnering with the overbuilt Wandawoman, probably to reassure the audience that the reputed "killer" slinger of the wrestling ring wasn't down and out for the count.

Temple spotted Molina in watchdog disguise in the opposite wing, fairly drooling to find Wandawoman guilty of Latin loitering or dancing without a license.

Temple just hoped Matt didn't suffer any more dance-floor hit and runs involving the hefty wrestlin' mama who was his partner.

His "costume" was black and white: black slacks and white shirt, the long sleeves rolled up to the elbow and the first four buttons undone to display the spray-on tan gilding all the men, even the pretanned José Juarez.

Call it clean-cut sexy. The simple clothes suited him. Although there was a lot of hip-swinging and over-the-shoulder partner smiling, the pairing came off amazingly well. There was a minimum of close contact, which kept Wandawoman from looking like an overdressed gravel truck dancing with a Maserati sports car.

Her legs on high heels looked sleek and strong and Matt managed to make the moments when he supported her in a dip or a pose look effortless.

All in all, a surprisingly respectable performance. Wandawoman came back strong from last night's fainting spell, and got a standing ovation when she finished.

The complimentary judges gave them eights.

Glory B. and José Juarez were agile and athletic together, but somehow uninspired. Maybe it was the vast height distance, at least a foot. They never seemed "together."

They racked up two eights and a seven.

Temple held her breath when Keith Salter stood back-to-back with Olivia before they began for their version of the cha-cha. After ten days of rehearsal and performance his abdominal profile was notably shrinking, especially following Monday night's stomach pump. He almost looked sleek next to the elegantly gaunt Olivia.

The cha-cha was a busy little number, but not the most demanding. If Keith could hold it together, he'd be over the hump. His shirt and pants were slimming black. He and Olivia didn't generate any onstage heat, but they managed their steps and took a very spectacular bow.

Two sevens and an eight.

That left only the Cloaked Conjuror and Motha Jonz, a partnership made in media Hell.

Temple could think of no disguise for CC that would fit the fast and lighthearted cha-

cha. And Motha Jonz, well, she was criminally hot in law enforcement circles as well as on the *Dancing With the Celebs* stage, but how would the choreographers and costumers turn her into fun and fluffy instead of fat and puffy?

The band struck up some familiar chords from oldies radio.

Oh, it was crooner Barry Manilow's old eighties' standard "Copacabana."

This was one of those funky Frankie and Johnny "story" songs about Lola, a dancer at the famous Copacabana night club, "where music and passion were always the fashion," her lover Tony, and Enrico the new guy in town.

The first shock was the initial pose of the dancers, also back-to-back. Motha Jonz had a real man as a partner. No mask, no bulky fake head for a face. The Cloaked Conjuror was going barefaced! This was big news! Also a big risk, given the disasters that had dogged the show so far.

Without his full coverage head disguise, CC was a tall man with a dark pompadour and sideburns, and a pencil-thin mustache.

He wore a glitzy red satin shirt with sleeve and chest ruffles edged in black thread. Black skintight trousers and Spanish boots of black Spanish leather made his usual bulky figure seem to tower sleekly.

The audience was still audibly gasping at the Cloaked Conjuror revealed . . . until they saw what Temple had just realized as she began laughing with knowing surprise.

CC was *still* wearing a mask! A celebrity one. He was the spitting image of that *Dancing With the Stars* Las Vegas favorite: Wayne Newton. He had revealed nothing but another entertainer's iconic persona.

Applause broke out for the clever conceit and the costumers who'd accomplished it.

Which meant that many had missed Motha Jonz's equally inspired transformation. Until now Motha Jonz had most resembled a dreadlocked punching bag attired in overdone and glitzy flour sacks. Not anymore.

Temple was clapping for that transformation from the wings.

Someone had turned Motha *Jonz* into a sleek cross between Queen Latifah and Catherine Zeta-*Jones* in the musical, *Chicago.* Her hip-hugging costume billowed out into salsa-hot orange ruffles at her thighs below and her shoulders above, giving the impression of a waist. Her dreadlocks were swirled into an updo that sported chrome yellow feathers and a rhinestone Spanish comb a foot high.

Her sleek lower legs and arched foot ended in four-inch platform spikes.

All of this made her look as tall and almost as thin as her partner.

The song said the Copacabana nightclub was the "hottest spot" north of Havana. As the impudent rhythmic lines of the song were sung by the show vocalists, CC and MJ circled and strutted, enacting their on-stage love affair . . .

Lola had "yellow feathers in her hair."

CC was her waiter-lover Tony, who moved from the "bar" — the beaming judges' table . . . well, except for producer Leander Brock — to join Lola on the dance floor to court her.

The audience gasped as a third figure in black appeared at the fringes of the dance floor.

José Juarez posed there in his Zorro outfit, sans mask, cape, and sword, with a four-carat diamond ear stud. He cut in on Tony and Lola, and wrested her away in a twirl of ruffles, dragging her across the floor paso-doble style before Tony dashed in to draw her upright again.

The song lyrics said there was "blood and a single gunshot," but only red spotlights smeared the dance floor.

The gunshot, though, was real: a sharp

bark that pierced the amiable Latin beat.

The music and dance reached a crescendo.

Music and passion is always in fashion.

"But who shot who?" the lyrics asked as audience members started standing up one by one to see. The dancers froze in place.

"Lola" Motha Jonz was posed with her ruffled skirt pulled up to one hip, a tiny pearl-handled pistol lifted from a red satin garter on her fishnet-hosed thigh. Smoke wafted from the tiny silver barrel as a spotlight caught it dead-on.

Music and passion were always the fashion.

And "Rico" José lay still on the dance floor. . . .

Music and passion were always the fashion.

At the Copa, Copacabana.

Wait a minute!

Rico hadn't fallen, as in the song. That was what was so confusing. Both men wore black, but one was bulkier.

"Tony" CC had fallen. Hard. Gracelessly. His limbs were splayed in ugly disarray.

Music and passion were always the fashion.

The audience giggled at the awkward staging.

The music stopped.

The cast froze in place.

Music and passion were always the fashion.

Lola's shot had gone wild, which wouldn't

have mattered if she had been firing blanks as planned. If not . . .

Someone breathed "Oh, my God" over a microphone in a deep, dramatic voice, Crawford Buchanan finally getting to use his most sepulchral tone.

A man from the sidelines executed an emergency knee slide toward the fallen fencer. Rafi Nadir of all people, also all in black.

The audience actually broke into scattered, spontaneous applause.

This was all part of the show. "Wasn't it?" they were asking each other.

For a moment Temple recalled Max's identical knee-slide entrance on the stage of the Elvis impersonator competition at the Kingdome.

But the next onstage speedster was Danny Dove, the choreographer-judge used to handling dance floor injuries. He joined Rafi in gauging the fallen man's condition.

Molina didn't slide on her knees but she was there almost as fast as Danny. Her hands, gloved in latex, which went oddly with her hippie garb, snatched the toy gun from Motha Jonz's hand.

"He's been shot," Rafi announced softly, pressing hard on the downed man's upper arm. "We need a doctor!"

"Oh, my God," Crawford Buchanan intoned again. "Commercial break, goddammit! Commercial break. What the hell?"

José and Motha Jonz, after freezing with disbelief, had edged over to the fallen man.

Temple's close observation of the scene was rudely interrupted.

Crawford grabbed her arm and twisted her to face away from the crime scene. "Thirty seconds to the Brat Brigade. Thirty seconds until you're on."

Temple opened her mouth like a fish told it was headed to a sushi bar.

He shook her a little. "*You* are the distraction, ZC. Get yourself and your junior hoofers onstage. Now!"

Yeah, right.

Temple wanted to know what Danny and Rafi were doing, how CC was. Instead, she had to amp up the annoying Zoe Chloe Ozone. What would even she say in the face of televised mayhem?

Something snappy and ad-libbed.

The cameraman was pointing to her. The red light on his camera flashed as if a train were coming right at her. Five, four, three, two . . . live!

"Ladies and gentlemen, boys and girls. And dance freaks everywhere. This is your instigative reporter, Zoe Chloe Ozone, on site and on — ah, none-of-your-business-unless-you're-a-narc — here at *Dancing With the Celebs,* said celebs taking a well-deserved break as all old folks should.

"Do not worry. We are going to shake and shiver and quiver your YouTubes. I am here to hype those two teenage masters of the samba, Meg-Ann and Chris.

"Now, Chris you know as the senior, sexiest, and most-likely-to-be-mobbed Los Hermanos Brother. Meg-Ann you don't know as the girl most likely to kick a soccer ball to kingdom come.

"They are here up close and personal to kick assumptions about young dancers to bits and bytes. Get your home videos rolling; let's give it up for a couple of young up-and-comers who never give up, Chris and Meg-Ann, dancing the samba!"

Zoe Chloe clasped her fingerless gloves together in a gesture as much prayer as goad.

The young couple galloped into camera range on cue, heads level, feet flashing, and butts bouncing like Meg-Ann's carroty curls.

Girls in the audience started screeching like banshees to see a nobody like themselves primped up and polishing the hardwood with the oldest Los Hermanos hot-

445

shot. To Temple he looked like a full-cheeked choirboy with unfortunate sideburns. To teen girls everywhere, he was the hottest thing on Clearasil.

Temple watched her kids with an almost maternal pride. Much as she was invested in EK and her booster, Mariah, athletic Meg-Ann was displaying lots of pizzazz and personality as she moved from intense sport to hard-driving dance.

Their energy and enthusiasm were banishing the image of the Cloaked Conjuror being wheeled away on an emergency gurney like a downed football player, surrounded by people never introduced from the stage, except for Danny Dove, who got a round of applause when he vaulted the judges' table again to take his seat at the far right.

Savannah Ashleigh was looking around as if still not sure what had happened, her mini-Chihuahua purse pooch scrabbling its claws in tune with its owner's panic and scattering judging papers to the floor. Producer Leander Brock was still frozen in disbelief.

Zoe Chloe's emergency stint as emcee ended with the wild applause for the junior dance routine.

Unfortunately, nothing about tonight's show had been routine, except for yet another onstage mishap.

Temple was mobbed by young autograph seekers as she tried to escape along the hallway to the back elevators.

"You were sooo coool," her girly admirers cooed.

"We wanta see *you* dance!"

"What did it feel like to be *right next to Chris* after they left the stage?"

"Is he hot or what?"

"Meg-Ann is kinda butch for a hot guy like that."

"Patrisha would rock his world."

"Dustin is hotter, don't you think?"

"Brandon is, you dork!"

"Adam!"

"Where do they hide out before and after the dances? We can't find them *anywhere!*"

Zoe Chloe retreated, disappearing into the service elevator finally. "Forget about Adam and Chris and Brandon and Dustin. Where's Waldo!" she asked as the doors closed, citing a kids' picture book from before when these ardent fans were born.

That oughta confuse them long enough to make a getaway.

CHAPTER 50
ONE-ARMED BANDIT

"How bad is CC's arm wound?" Rafi wanted to know.

They'd all been waiting in the suite for Molina to return.

"Nasty," she said, collapsing into an armchair. "But everyone's happy, including the Cloaked Conjuror, because they can put him on pain pills, wrap up the arm, and he can still dance the tango for the final round tomorrow. The mishaps just up the ratings. Showbiz!"

She laughed, adding, "Look at you all! I've never seen a sadder set of glum clowns, including me. The show will go on, but I'm not sure the junior division will be onstage for the awards shows."

"Mo-*ther*, no!" Mariah wailed from the huge ottoman she shared with EK.

"There's been gunplay on the stage, sweetie. No way am I going to risk any minors."

"Did Motha Jonz fire the shot?" Matt asked. He'd returned to the suite and shared one of the living-room love seats with a sober-faced Zoe Chloe Ozone.

Molina raised an eyebrow. "You supposed to sling an arm around that underage professional brat?"

"I'm eighteen, copper," Zoe crowed, sticking out her tongue, much to Mariah's giggly approval.

"Forget staying in character," Molina said. "It's wearing; on us, if not you. We all have some serious thinking to do. I haven't given the producer the go-ahead on the show. They're continuing rehearsals for now."

"You can shut this whole thing down?" Matt asked.

"You betcha, chorus boy."

"Mo-*ther!*"

Molina glanced sourly from Matt to her daughter and back. "And you've all got dance fever."

"You don't want to shut down the show," Rafi said.

"And you have a say in this, because — ?"

"I don't have a say in it, but I am involved, Carmen, and you know why."

During the ensuing silence, Mariah glanced from Rafi to her mother, sensing the unspoken tension and wondering how a security guy could call a police lieutenant by her first name that almost nobody used, even her mother. Except when she sang.

Molina's jawline grew tighter than a drum skin in the show band. "I would think the *assistant* director of security at this hotel would want to avoid further disruptive . . . violence."

She left it unclear just what kind of violence she was referring to.

Rafi remained unruffled. "These are acts of sabotage so far. You didn't answer the question. Did the shot that hit the Cloaked Conjuror come from Motha Jonz's gun?"

"Yes."

Matt got it. "So . . . a prop gun was loaded, instead of just having a dummy smoke-generating shell in it. Nobody off-stage was shooting."

"And this is better, how?" Molina asked Rafi.

"It's criminal endangerment so far. Nothing lethal. You shut down the show, we'll never catch who's doing this."

"Sometimes avoiding violence is better police work than catching perps and risking lives."

Rafi shook his head.

"It's always better to *catch* a *stalker* than let him disappear back into the woodwork to crawl out again. I think that's what we're dealing with here, and what you've dealt with before. I wouldn't want *my* teen daughter on the loose without it being settled. I'm sure if you ask the other junior moms, they'll go along. Me and my staff will cover those girls like a blanket. I have a lot of good female staff. They're bunking together, easy to supervise. Your people can handle the adult cast."

Molina's sallow cheeks flared with color at his reference to a stalker. "If anything happens to those kids, I'll have your job and your head."

"Nothing new, Carmen."

Again, one of those loaded silences. Temple snuggled into Matt's shoulder, glad it was unwounded. "I wish you didn't have to go back and forth to the radio station nights," she whispered.

Molina must have had ears in the back of her head.

She hiked her neck around to stare at them. "I am not in the mood for eavesdropping on Love's Young Dream. You don't want to follow through as Zoe Chloe, Barr, so much the better for me and my nerves."

She snapped her head back to face Rafi. "Okay, Nadir. You've got the whole world in your hands. Don't freaking drop it." Only

451

she didn't say "freaking."

Mariah's gasp was audible, but she managed to ask, "Does that mean EK and the other guys can still finish out the show?" "Guys" stood for the teen girls and their pop star partners.

Molina nodded, once. "And then there are those Hermanos brothers to guard like British royals. *Aii, carumba.*"

"Tango's the last dance," Matt put in.

Molina's glare was so toxic that he rose right away. "I'd better get along to the radio station." He eyed Rafi. "Zoe Chloe is one of the 'juniors' you've sworn to protect, right?"

Rafi rose to shake Matt's hand before he left. "Absolutely. Although I'll probably need to protect Crawford Buchanan from her more than her from anybody else."

"Crawford!" Zoe spat. "I can outemcee that dude in a New York, New York hotel minute. Talk about useless. I don't even know why he's here."

"That's a very good point," Molina said after Matt left, staring at Temple. "He has a stake in the show attracting media." She turned to her daughter and little pal. "Okay, kidlets. Time to hit the hay. Into your trundle beds and no whispering, giggling, or eavesdropping."

The pair, ecstatic about the reprieve,

hustled away, eager to engage in all specifically forbidden activities.

Temple and Zoe Chloe were a pretty tickled pair too. The so-called "trundle beds" were a pair of imported cots, and the staff had been disdainful to the max to import such homely items to a high-roller suite.

As the door shut on the kids, sounds of two forbidden activities trickled under the door, whispering and giggling.

"Mama" Molina did sorta know how to handle tweens.

At that very moment Mama Molina sat heavily and lifted a curled hand. "Some of that fancy freebie wine," she ordered Rafi.

Amazingly, he complied, and poured glasses for Temple and himself. He delivered Temple's next, with a wink.

It was just the three of them again, and that felt scarily right, Temple thought.

After all, they'd been in on this almost from the beginning.

"How many have access to Ma Jonz's prop gun?" Rafi asked.

Molina said, "Anyone backstage, and anyone who wanted to wander backstage. You've got to plug those holes."

"It's a typical showbiz operation," Temple said. "Even at a major regional repertory theater that I PRed, like the Guthrie in Minneapolis, putting on shows is chaos."

"I know," Rafi agreed. "Vegas is no exception, but 'typical showbiz' will kill us. Or someone else."

Temple sighed heavily. "We've all got someone at stake here. We better solve this thing."

"What if it's more than one thing?" Molina asked.

Rafi turned a desk chair around to straddle it. "What have we got for incidents so far? Motives? Suspects?"

"You always wanted to make detective," Molina charged. Remembered. Her tone had been dangerously . . . personal.

Rafi winced. Temple read his reaction. He was so far from that lost uniformed officer position. Molina was a lieutenant of detectives. He looked at Temple to escape staring the implications in the eyes.

"You have any ideas, Ms. Ozone?"

"Ah . . . yes."

CHAPTER 51
CRIME SEEN

"Something about these incidents is bothering me," Temple said.

Rafi regarded her raptly, but only because he wanted to shut Molina out at the moment. Molina was frowning at her hotel notepad, doodling.

"Matt's getting to be the only one who hasn't had a personal mishap," Temple noted.

"Other than getting engaged to you," Molina put in without even looking up.

"Yet," Rafi said.

"He's the only celebrity who doesn't have a visual presence in the media," Temple went on.

"You mean he's the most obscure and least celebrated," Molina suggested.

Temple went speechless. Molina was in a major down-on-men mood.

"And the best-looking," Rafi put in, "as if you hadn't noticed." He turned back to

Temple. "You're right. We've had enough 'incidents' to look for similarities and differences."

"Unfortunately," Temple said, "the contestants were chosen for their variety. Entertainers, athletes, and quasi-glamorous careers like chef and radio show host."

"Except they are all celebrities of one sort of another," Rafi added. "They have fans, and fans can get obsessed."

Molina turned in her chair to face them fully again. "That's what I meant. You're assuming that one mischief-maker is at the root of every troubling incident. What if more than one motive and one person were behind these 'accidents' that are coming too fast to be accidental?"

"It would have to be somebody involved in the show, near it every day," Temple mused. "Or who could seem to be legitimately near it. You're saying there are several freaked-out fans here all at once?"

Molina was unshaken. "This is a variety show as far as the competitors go. Why not a surfeit of suspects all working separately?"

"That's an Agatha Christie novel," Rafi said sourly. "*Murder on the Orient Express.* It narrows down nothing."

"You read Christie?" Molina pounced.

"They make movies," he retorted. "Look.

The Oasis Hotel is one huge interior metropolis of support staff and the public milling around together. Temple is right. Looking for suspects starting from the outside in is futile. We've got to work from the victims out. There are five of them."

"And only three who haven't been victims," Molina pointed out, "which may be more telling."

"Let's go through the possible attacks," Temple suggested. "First would be Glory B.'s jungle gym fall."

"Pure accident," Molina said. "She's a kid practicing new tricks."

Temple disagreed. "Danny Dove tested that equipment and took it apart. He said it *could* have been rigged and if anyone in Vegas knows stage equipment and rigging, it's Danny Dove."

"The second was Olivia Phillips," Molina said.

"Nothing suspicious there," Rafi said. "How do you figure that?"

"You're the assistant security chief here. Guess, or figure it out yourself."

"He's a guy," Temple told Molina. "He's handicapped." She eyed Rafi, who was starting to look steamed. "Olivia Phillips's wardrobe malfunction, when the heel of her pump collapsed. It could have been rigged too."

"Was rigged," Molina corrected.

"A guess?" Rafi jeered.

"I checked it after the show, and bagged the shoe for evidence. They were faint, but forensics found half-moon imprints in the red satin: a small hammerhead hitting the inside of the spike heel. The nails holding it on were weakened, and it snapped. Next?" she suggested, consulting Rafi.

"The most blatant case of tampering so far involves the chef, Salter," he said. "Appropriate name for a cook, huh? Poisoning is the easiest method to pass off as an accident unless you can identify the toxic substance, and the toughest to bring home to any one suspect."

"You *do* read Christie," Molina pounced again.

He shrugged. "Had to do something on all those sit-down security jobs after I left the L.A. Police Department."

She was smiling like the cat who'd nailed the Camembert.

"Okay," said Temple. "Agatha Christie is not going to solve this thing for us, no matter who reads her, including me. It's interesting that Salter is such a persnickety chef he didn't eat from the buffet the hotel provided the cast. He would be easy to poison without hurting anyone else."

"A suspect with a conscience?" Molina asked. "No collateral damage."

"Or," Rafi said, "a suspect who wanted to make dead sure he or she got the intended victim. Any diagnosis yet on the cause of Salter's tummy upset?"

"The forensic staff is overworked, as usual here."

"L.A. East?" Rafi suggested, almost sympathetically.

Molina sighed, and nodded.

Hmm, Temple thought. "Okay," she said. "The first two cases are iffy as official 'incidents,' but Salter did collapse of food poisoning, Wandawoman did pass out from drugs, and someone substituted real ammo for the blanks in Motha Jonz's garter gun."

" 'Ammo'?" Rafi echoed her with amusement. "Sounding real cop shop there, kid."

"Zoe Chloe gets around."

"Can we keep on track?" Molina said. Ordered.

That was the real Molina, too. All work and no idle talk. No wonder she didn't get along with anyone.

Temple shrugged. "All the dancers are responsible for keeping track of their costume pieces, but the costume and prop people are all over the dressing rooms. It would be easy to do the switch. I could have done it."

"It was a revolver," Molina said. "Only three of the bullets were live."

"That conscience again," Rafi noted.

"One could kill." Molina was adamant.

"But Motha Jonz wasn't aiming for a vital organ," he said.

"Could have hit one so easily."

"Didn't," he said.

"Doesn't prove anything," she said.

Temple inserted herself into the verbal Ping-Pong match. "This is an odd incident. Was it aimed against José or CC or Motha Jonz?" she asked.

Rafi leaned back, arms folded as if Temple had just gotten off a killing salvo for him.

"Temple's really hit the bull's-eye, Carmen. The loaded stage gun hurt both of them, the Cloaked Conjuror physically, but Jonz . . . I guess in reputation and morally, you'd say. This incident will bring up her sordid past, and she easily could have been made into a killer."

"Nothing new for her," Molina said, "she hung out with enough of them."

"The only criminally involved celebrity dancer," Rafi pointed out, "involved with the most potentially lethal 'prank,' if you want to call it that."

"She'd gotten away from all that," Temple objected.

"But had 'all that' gotten away from her?" Rafi shot back.

Molina sat up, her vivid blue eyes flashing with speculation. She caught her breath as if she had a sudden stitch in her side as well as an inspiration.

Rafi's eyes narrowed. "What the hell is really wrong with you, Carmen?"

"Shut up. I'm thinking." She glanced feverishly from him to Temple, and back again, her tone rising as she began speaking. "That may very well be it. I don't keep up with tabloid papers or TV gossip shows or online rumor. *Barr!* Just what all was Glory B. put into jail and rehab for?"

"Uh, I don't exactly —"

"Think!"

"I don't have to," Temple said, turning to flip open her laptop. "I can do a search for it."

She keyed in some words and then clicked through various sites. "I know Glory B. was DWI in her new Porsche and rowdy when arrested. She hit another car . . . here it is! Last year. Just had her license for four months. Leaving a nightclub. God, she not only let down her hair but the whole top of

461

her dress and it didn't have much to begin with. Anyway, the text says the car she hit was occupied by a mother and nine-year-old daughter . . . mother's face hit by the air bag, daughter on passenger side had intrusion from the collision. *Ooh.* Both legs broken. Lawsuit. Hush-hush settlement. Glory B. did ten days in jail and three months public service, volunteering at an animal shelter, and required time in AA."

Temple looked up. "And Glory B. could have broken both legs or her back if that jungle gym failure had been more . . . effective."

Molina looked both grim and triumphant. "That is a triple-A class motive."

Rafi wasn't so sure. "That 'dirty trick,' if it was that, was lame. Glory B. was fine."

"It was the first attempt," Molina said. "Practice makes perfect."

"There's an escalating element to the incidents," Temple said. "Glory B. just had a minor fall. Chef Salter got really sick, and the Cloaked Conjuror could have been killed. That could show a variety of amateurs, some good, and some bad. At being bad, I mean. Nobody is good."

"Or one person learning?" Rafi asked.

"Damn, we are good!"

Temple and Rafi turned to Molina to see

a glitter in her eyes and fever spots on her dusky cheeks. Stick an orchid behind one ear and she'd look like Carmen the lounge singer.

"I mean," Molina said . . . modified, "there might be some good ideas floating around there. Number one is we raise security on the show tomorrow night ten notches. Done deal?" she asked Rafi.

"Signed, sealed, and delivered," he agreed.

Temple was just glad he hadn't made it "delivered with a kiss."

That would have been just too icky even for a post-tween like her.

CHAPTER 52
REHEARSED TO
DEATH

"You sure this daily dance gig ain't burnin' out your baby browns, boy wonder?" Ambrosia asked Matt as they shut down their mics and she became just plain Leticia again.

He nodded as he yawned.

His "Midnight Hour" stint at WCOO-AM was over. Rehearsing dance numbers days to perform them live on TV evenings, then doing a two-hour live radio show at midnight was getting to him.

Leticia also passed him a yellow message form as soon as he had hung up his headphones for the morning. "Two A.M. and all is well, or not well?" she pressed.

"No rest for the wicked," he muttered, reading the name and phone number, then the message scrawled beneath them, and groaning. "So my *Dancing With the Celebs* taskmistress is insisting I need an after-hours, early-morning rehearsal to 'brush up' my tango footwork. I'm glad this is the last dance. You remember the formidable Tatyana?"

"You sure that's all she wants?"

"Sure. This woman is all business."

"All business shaking her jiggle parts."

"You seemed to have that routine down too, when you visited me at the rehearsal," he reminded her with a laugh. "No, life is all work and no play with Tatyana. The other pro dance instructors lighten up a little, but never her. You'd think she wanted to rehearse me to death."

"Then don't go. You're the 'celeb,' sweet boy. Show a little temperament yourself. You're too easygoing, Matt. Always accommodating other people. I like that when *I'm* the 'other people,' but you need to put your foot down more."

"Believe me," he said, rising, "I'm putting my foot down plenty these days. Especially in those Spanish dances. It's okay, Leticia," he said. "You know it's always hard to settle down after two hours live on the air anyway."

"Yeah, you and Wayne Newton. Or should I say Elvis?"

"Haven't heard from his ghost lately, thank goodness. No, I could use some exercise after hunching over a hot mike for two hours."

He didn't add that his fiancée was bunking in an alternate persona at the dance competition hotel and he had no one to go home to at the Circle Ritz. Odd how having that option had made relaxing after a show no issue at all. That's why he'd taken the comped room at the Oasis all the celebs got.

In the mellow hot-fudge night outside, he smiled ruefully as he clicked his silver Crossfire unlocked under the lone blazing parking lot light, waiting to see Leticia's silver Beetle pull safely out of the driveway before he left.

In an hour he'd be drilling with Tatyana in the empty rehearsal room far below Temple and Louie sleeping above in a giant suite with two tweens, Molina and her ex.

Politics wasn't the only thing that made strange bedfellows.

Passing through the lights, noise, and action of the Oasis's casino area a half hour later reminded him that Max Kinsella had played his last stint as the Mystifying Max at another Vegas hotel, the Goliath, and had lived up to his magician's moniker by disappearing after a dead body had been found in the overhead spy spaces above the gaming tables.

Now Max was out of the picture again and Matt had performed here nightly — for almost a week. Life was crammed with ironies.

Coming here to rehearse at this god-awful hour actually kept Matt's energy high and hyped. He relished burning off his frustration. He'd gotten used to living with and loving Temple, used to the summaries of their days, the companionship of their nights.

He was starting to think he needed a day job so they'd be in better sync. People would think him crazy to quit "The Midnight Hour" and its syndicated success, but relationships were more important.

This mini-separation had him thinking a lot of things. Like it was also crazy to delay marriage. The only reason he had was wanting Temple to be sure she wasn't in love with Max anymore, wanting to be sure he was a good enough substitute, but nothing in life was sure.

All he knew was that he'd never been happier.

Maybe he could convert to a daytime show, television, or Web-based even. Talk shows were myriad and female-hosted these days, so maybe the field could use a new guy. Maybe Oprah could make him the way she'd made Dr. Phil.

He laughed out loud at his mental maunderings and ducked through the door leading to the maze of rehearsal halls ringing the ballroom set for *Dancing With the Celebs.* Just the word "celebs" was a clue to the essential sleaziness of the concept. Cheerfully admitted sleaziness.

Guess that made the world go 'round.

Matt moved down the dim hall and barged into "his" rehearsal room without thinking about it.

The place was as black as King Tut's tomb.

He backed out, surprised, wondering if the message had been garbled. "See Tatyana at 3:00 A.M. to rehearse." *After work.* Underlined. "Your tango footwork stinks," had been added.

The insanely early hour was no surprise. She knew he worked nights. The bluntness was all Tatyana. Her sentences came as short and sharp as bullets.

He guessed he'd be entitled to hand her some bluntness for being late to a wee-hour meeting *she*'d called for. Guess that was what Leticia meant about him being too easygoing.

He reached in and patted the wall until he found the light plate.

He pushed down the plastic switch.

Nothing.

No light.

Matt sighed loudly. The station receptionist must have written the information down
wrong. It wouldn't be the first time.

He stood on the dark threshold to this
room so familiar to him, now just a black
hole, and started tapping his foot on the
durable vinyl tile meant to survive the
constant scrape of folding chairs and spilled
water, coffee, tea, and stronger stuff.

The sound echoed like bullets in the
empty darkness. One hand clapping. One
foot tapping.

Clap!

The real sound of cupped palms meeting.
A call to the dance. Sharp. Summoning. Arrogant. Spanish. Then the drum of distant
boot heels pounded an echoing wooden
floor like an indoor hailstorm. Not this floor.

He knew where the sound came from.
Tatyana must be playing one of her dramatic
games. She liked to put her students on new
ground, in "unsafe" dance situations. He
left the rehearsal room and followed the
maze around in the dark until he felt the
brush of velvet curtains backing the show's
set.

The Spanish boot heels throbbed on wood

flooring like a joke set of chattering false teeth. Machine-gun fast. Automated, almost. Endless.

Matt brushed through the curtains into more darkness, feeling around the bulk of the big light and sound console onto the actual stage. Everything was black except the well-lit image of the now-familiar space in his mind.

The flamenco beat of steel nail heads covering leather soles kept up the frenzied chatter. Matt stepped farther into the darkness, toward the sound as it clattered toward him, then stopped.

All he could hear now was his heart pattering like a hard rain in reaction to that visceral vibration in the floor beneath him.

A ripping sound jagged by his left ear.

He couldn't help putting out a hand to sense *something* in this dark carnival of sound.

His left palm touched passing fire and separating velvet.

The solid curtain behind him was now torn in two and his palm was creased with a line of fire that had thickened like lava and turned sticky.

He recognized that moment of stunned sensation taking fresh shape as pain.

He'd been cut across the hand, across the

palm's head and heart lines. Blood was flowing and running down his bare forearm.

He made a fist to stop the flow and pain. Useless.

Boot heels retreated in the dark, sharp and fast as the angry, mocking laughter that accompanied it.

"Die, bastard, die!"

Matt wheeled and turned back.

Not to run.

He bumped into the big sound console and, dripping blood from his closed fist, ran his uninjured right hand over all the many levers, releasing demon voices of sound bytes, prerecorded snatches of mambo and waltz and samba music, sprightly and stately and frantic in turn.

His hand reversed the buttons as fast as his fingers found them until a light blossomed on the opposite side of the backstage area. There was the single backstage "ghost light" that should be on at all times. He flipped more metal switches along that row, illuminating a random patchwork of high and low spotlights until a dark, grotesque figure became visible in the shadows thirty feet away.

Jesus, Mary, Joseph, his mind breathed in long-accustomed prayer.

He faced Lucifer out of an operetta,

poised for battle in shiny black satin cape and mask.

Matt itched to swipe his burning and throbbing wounded left hand down his outside pants leg, clear off the blood, but he knew he needed to keep the arm upraised to slow the flow. Up high. Like a dancer. Like a fencer.

He turned sideways to face the figure posed the same narrow way as a duelist to avoid exposing his vulnerable trunk full on. The scanty lights showed the straight, thin line of a rapier raised from its hidden position along the man's leg high into the air above his right shoulder.

Matt recognized the clothing now. José Juarez's Zorro getup, complete with mask and flat-brimmed hat, with gloves and sword, boots and spurs.

His thoughts were still shocked, sluggish. Zorro ready to cut him into mincemeat, and he in his knit shirt, khakis, and lace-up suede shoes.

Not a lot of stomping going on his way.

Going My Way. Major forties movie with Bing Crosby playing a priest. Crosby and Hope on the *Road to Sliced Liver,* or Bali or Mandalay, bungling and making comedy villains trip over their own feet.

Okay. Not a lot of role models out there

in the collective unconscious for dueling demonic Zorros. He felt a cool, clammy sweat break out on his face. The blood was coming mostly from his wrist, below the hand slash. From the cut vein. It was already getting hard to organize his thoughts and he couldn't tell whether the symptoms were of fear or blood loss.

Matt ran through his memorized impression of the set. Easy. Cut-rate *Dancing With the Stars* rip-off. Four steps up center stage with winding staircases at each side. Dance floor. Judges' table and chairs at his right, backup singers and live octet setups at the left. Audience chairs on three sides of the dance floor.

And now this out-of-time addition, the heart of darkness poised on the dance floor with a blade that had already tasted innocent blood.

Shoot. Didn't he wish he had a semi-automatic, or even a vintage dueling pistol? But all he had was a sense of self-preservation, some martial arts and dance moves, and a pure heart that had been a little bruised lately.

"José?" he asked, not really believing this costumed figure was the Olympic fencer, even though he flourished the blade as if he knew how. Or that he would admit it if he was.

The ersatz Zorro simply shouted, *"Ha!"* and advanced sideways toward Matt, each step magnified into a sharp, drumming dance.

Maybe this was Michael Flatley, the lord of the dance himself?

No. This was someone else who knew the steps. Matt himself had practiced them, and could produce this same sinister, stuttering advance if he wore the same heeled leather boots and cared more about prancing than survival right now.

He needed to hoard his energy, wear out his adversary. Playing this extravagant role would tire someone not accustomed to it.

Matt sprung up the four steps to the stage. "Zorro" leapt over them.

Impressive. Also wearing.

Matt ran up the curving staircase he'd glide down at the moment of introduction every night. Zorro stomped up behind him, then began slicing the sword back and forth in *S*-shaped swathes.

Grace took time and energy, and Matt was more interested in saving his hide from more bloody creases than looking good. His heart in his throat, he sat on the slick brass railing and slid down it, an unrehearsed move he'd only seen Wandawoman use.

His weight teetered left and right, but he slid off the end and hit with both feet flat-footed at the end. *Ugh.* The friction put his rear on fire. Wandawoman must have worn asbestos shorts during her seated railing run.

The *thump* of his rubber-soled shoes sounded like the battle cry of a rabbit rather than a steel-hooved steed.

Of course he had his cell phone in his pants pocket, and could use it to summon help.

Except . . . Zorro was swooshing down the railing with a lot more swashbuckle than he had and Matt needed twenty seconds in good light to punch in even an auto-dial number, probably Temple's, wake her up, and remain still enough long enough to say where and what.

If he could manage all this while dodging the lethal tap dance spitting sound at him like Uzi bullets and sword thrusts as fast as heat lightning, he'd probably get Rafi Nadir to the rescue on the run, with Oasis security behind him.

By then he'd be a bled-out shish kebab. One dead bastard.

His mind wanted to stop and figure out who'd want to damage or kill him. Disable him for the stupid contest? His reflexes wanted to maintain a sword blade's distance between him and the Zorro gone amok.

Matt stumble-ran across the dance floor to the judges' skirted table and dove over and behind it, reversing Danny's recent emergency moves in the other direction.

Nail-studded boot heels and toes clattered after, his enemy's body knocking the table askew.

Matt was already dashing for the velvet curtains the dancing couples retreated behind after their numbers. His discreet Hush Puppy soles obscured his exact route.

Thank God! He'd said that vocally and mentally thousands of times in his life and had never meant it more.

Here, in the less open spaces, martial arts moves had a chance against the thirty inches of steel death in a darting rapier.

He crashed into the velvet curtains, making them sway and disguise his position.

The dark was almost total again behind the curtains, just a halo of light visible from the few illuminated spotlights on the dance floor. It would hide Zorro's approach.

Matt danced with the dark, twirled himself into the velvet curtains' embrace, felt them twitch and shake as the sword pierced them with quick, blind thrusts. He stepped away in one bound, then jerked them back against the way he'd come.

The boot soles stilled. He wrapped the curtains around and around the dark in his wake, hearing the rent of heavy fabric muffling, and then stopping.

He'd hoped to wrap up his attacker and his flashing rapier like a mummy in the heavy theatrical velvet. He finished his reverse spin with a killer kick, feeling the side of his foot impact a barrier of bone and muscle.

Zorro's breath escaped on a belly-deep *oooph!*

Matt's bleeding left fist still held a world of burning pain, but he punched it full strength into the slowly twisting bundle. He felt a body sag. His own energy flagged.

So.

The sword was wound and bound along with the mystery man who wielded it.

He could stay here on guard, letting his wrist bleed until he passed out — and a lot of blood had streamed out already — waiting until a technician came along in five hours just before rehearsals began, or. . . .

Now that he was still again, he felt dizzy. Was he getting woozy already from blood loss? He'd have to get to someplace with more light to use the cell phone. The lit number pad seemed to flare and blur.

Holding his left arm high, elbow doubled back to apply at least some pressure higher up the arm, he turned and stumbled farther into the backstage dark. The light board's high-intensity bulb that illuminated the controls should overcome the fuzzy glare of his double vision.

Leaning against the console, he was dismayed by how slowly he moved now, by how close the attempted murderer still was, a sagging lump in the curtains. He saw enough to use the menu to auto-dial Temple's cell phone, but what chance was there that she'd hear it at three in the morning? It was probably tucked away in a purse outside the bedroom suite. She'd said the place was palatial. He doubt he'd remain conscious long enough to tell 911 the complex details of where he was and what had happened.

Her cell phone rang and rang, and there was no answer.

He punched the number again. He was feeling drained. No kidding.

The phone rang and rang and there was no answer.

Again.

Again.

Matt's head was throbbing. Adrenaline, blood loss. He'd seen a finger cut sop an entire terry cloth bath sheet with blood. This was way more serious.

Then a faint voice, as if from heaven.

"Louie! Where are you?"

Temple's voice. She wasn't talking to Matt, though, but to the cat in the room.

"You must be really hard up, cozying up to a cell phone I left on vibrate. It's not a purring pussycat in heat. It's just a damn midnight solicitation —"

"Temple!" Matt called into his phone. His voice was half the usual loudness. "Temple, it's Matt."

"Matt? I thought you were going to get all the sleep you could after your radio show, given the early-morning rehearsals."

"I'm here already."

"Here?"

"The dance set. 'Zorro' just tried to slice me to ribbons."

"Oh, my God. Matt!'

She was moving. Her voice stuttered like a strobe light. He could hear her pounding on a door.

"Rafi! Matt's in the hotel. He's been attacked on the dance set. He's bleeding. Call your guys pronto!"

The phone sounded as if it was being dropped.

"Yeah, Lieutenant. I *know* your daughter

is *sleeping.* Matt's been attacked on the dance show set. Rafi's gone to — God, that's a big gun! Do you sleep with that thing? Yeah, I'll watch Mariah. But —"

Matt was surprised to find himself sliding slowly over a metal landscape of toggle switches on a tide of slippery syrup. Couldn't pass out. His tormenter was probably coming to by now, and velvet curtains weren't iron manacles. . . .

Lights blazed on in the audience area. Houselights.

Footsteps came pounding. Someone grabbed Matt and propped him up against the light board console.

"God, look at the blood. Looks like the left arm."

"Tourniquet, quick. Belt will do."

"We found him, sir," a youthful tenor male voice crowed from what seemed like a half-block away.

"Get the hotel doctor immediately," Sir ordered in an urgent basso Matt didn't recognize.

"Matt!" Temple cried, her slightly raspy alto voice soprano with anxiety, her warm palm soothing the side of his face. And then, said to someone behind him, "I'm *watching* her! She's with me, all right? I wasn't staying behind to babysit."

"I don't need babysitting." He recognized Mariah's light soprano, scared and defiant. "Is he all right? Mom? He's supposed to take me to the school dance."

Ah, Matt thought, feeling oddly buoyed by the young's assumptions. The thoughtless egotism of the tweenager . . . he'd be happy to go to that dance now.

"Attacker's gone, but the sword isn't." A male voice from a distance. "Skewered in the curtain. Maybe we'll get fingerprints."

"Wearing gloves," Matt croaked.

"Damn!" The dark mezzo of Carmen Molina had the last word, as always, and sang the same old song.

"Rafi, get your guys locking down this whole area pronto while I call forensics. Everybody else in this damn-fool party — you know who you are — get up to the" — a very pregnant pause — "Zoe Chloe Ozone suite. *Now!* Mariah Molina and EK, your shadow, that means you."

CHAPTER 53
FIGHTING FORM

Of course no one recognizes that were it not for my extreme sensitivity to vibes of both a physical and psychic nature, no one would know Mr. Matt Devine was suffering from duel fatigue and blood loss deep in the deserted part of the hotel.

Even my Miss Temple did not suspect I was fresh from clawing my way up the silent butler shaft from the high-roller suite service area two floors below, which includes a fully staffed kitchen as well as twenty-four-hour maid, bar, and concierge services. It pays to be rich in Vegas.

So it just looks like I was idly sleeping on her vibrating cell phone when in fact I had just arrived there, panting and not much better off than Mr. Matt Devine himself at the moment. But I knew he would be phoning her if he could manage it, and I had to make sure our joint Sleeping Beauty would hear it.

This may seem a desperate and frantic ploy,

but I am not Lassie. I could run howling through the casino and no one would heed and follow me, except to boot me out onto the Strip.

I have done what I could through this whole awful nightmare of lethal surprise attack.

I have no doubt that both the masked attempted murderer and our own Mr. Matt have the impression that they were dueling mano a mano all over the *Dancing With the Celebs* set. And quite a thrilling, but lamentably unfilmed, contest that was.

But no, the contention was mano a gato in some respects. ("Gato" is the Spanish word for cat.)

I keep a keen eye on all the Circle Ritz folks at this shindig and happened to be sniffing around the company buffet table backstage during the very wee morning hours, hunting clues about the mishap involving Mr. Keith Salter. Okay, he ate separately, but you never know. Not that I was copping a free meal, although I was not loath to lap up any unclaimed crumbs from said spread for a Midnight mid-night nosh.

Be that as it may, or may not, my sharp olfactory senses can pick up what humans overlook even without a supersensitive canine nose. I did find crumbs of things I would rather die than eat, such as cranberry muffins, but nothing that I could die from if I ate it.

So it is the wee-est hours on the deserted set when I hear footsteps and decide to widen my area of inquiry.

I am there when Mr. Matt blunders in, searching for Miss Tatyana.

Any other investigative dude would suspect him of making an unlawful romantic rendez-vous. I, however, know Mr. Matt is already uneasy enough about his unsanctified hanky-panky with his own fiancée and my dear sweet roommate, so I doubt he would be canoodling with a hot-tempered Russian fireball.

At that point, I am as innocent of suspecting lurking menace as he is and am merely curi-ous about this after-hours rehearsal. Perhaps Miss Tatyana thinks she can draw out more of his secret Latin soul with late-night sessions. He was not Antonio Banderas material until he did that righteous paso doble the other night.

I myself, on the other hand, was born with dark, Latin good looks, masculine grace, and *cojones* (and I kept them despite now being politically correct for my species in the repro-duction department).

As I was saying, I was born with the brunet swagger to stomp and slither about the stage intimidating the ladies into swooning at my feet. All four of them. Feet, I mean, not ladies.

Though I am not averse to social quintets.

I expected to have some merriment watching Mr. Matt trying to go Latin lover again in the tango, and then Zorro shows up.

I see instantly that Mr. Matt is outmatched.

I see instantly that the only dude here who can fight Hispanic fire with Hispanic fire is a longtime alley shivmeister.

So while Mr. Matt does his best to sidestep the unexpected weapon, I am playing the cape in this lethal pasodoble for dudes.

This means I must hurl my much outweighed self into the fray.

Alas, the cameras are not rolling.

They would see my agile, unbooted toes doing a fierce flamenco with the unnamed dude in black's high-heeled boots. Any stomp that I failed to elude would break all my shivs, not to mention my toes.

It is very close. Only my lithe full-body twists keep me from death by stomping.

The dark dude is as fast as his rapier work. I dodge both boots and sword-point, seeking two vital goals. One is keeping Mr. Zorro from spearing my roommate's current beloved (okay, I cannot yet forget Mr. Max, who is a dude after my own parts). The other is attempting to mark the masked man's hide with my four-on-the-floor: the wide track of my shivs that will identify him later if I can but manage to install a full house of claws to the epidermis.

I must say that Mr. Matt is surprising both the attacker and myself. He is faster on the draw — and the withdraw — than I expected. And what is any dance but drawing closer and retreating farther, much like human relationships.

In fact, I must admit that my own amatory adventures are a continual process of advance and retreat.

Perhaps this attack is a far, far better dancing lesson than Miss Tatyana could administer, if she had truly been hoping a late-night challenge would unleash Mr. Matt's deepest emotions. Which at this point would be to live, now that he has finally attained the hand of my lovely roommate in marriage.

Recognizing what is at stake for me and mine, I hurl myself at our opponent without regard to life or limb. I am an unseen shadow tripping his every step, leaping to catch and capture his sword arm on every blow.

At times the flurry of steps catches me in the staccato enemy fire of his boot heels and I go rolling over the darkened dance floor, my torso caught in the crossfire and beaten and bruised.

I have not been in such a rumble since I was a young blade. So it is Zorro versus gato.

Fox against cat. We are both sly and agile creatures, which is not exactly how I would describe Mr. Matt, splendid fellow that he is.

He needs his shadow ally and I rise to the occasion, literally leaping into the billows of Zorro's cloak, rending as I fall, ripping it to shreds. But I am outweighed.

My ribs are bruised, and my breath heaves in and out like a bellows.

A random kick sends me spinning like a Frisbee to the edge of the dance floor. I heave myself upright, cheered to see that Mr. Matt has backed our adversary into the heavy velvet stage curtains and smartly rolled him up like a fried rice and bean enchilada.

Revived, I push myself to my feet and rush forward, slipping under the heavy curtains, risking the flamenco stamp of our contained enemy to leap high one last, desperate time. My shivs flare out, curved scimitars seeking purchase. Both my sword arms sink like pitons into the man's rear face (except it is hardly his face, *heh-heh*) as I slide down the mountain of human flesh, leaving a grooved bloody trail of skid marks.

His screams of frustration are satisfying. This dude will be ID'd by his ass for the next six weeks . . . if anyone can find out who he is and order a strip search.

Parting is such sweet sorrow, as one far

more famed than I has noted.

The dude's parting scream is muffled by the thick velvet curtains Mr. Matt is using for an impromptu winding sheet.

Dude! I would slap pads and palms with Mr. Matt if I did not have only ragged shivs to offer.

We did it!

Oh, wait. I will get no credit.

I am so bummed out. You did not notice my baaad, baad moves, my self-sacrificing footwork, my killer rock, rhythm, and rakes? I am to the dance floor born. I should *win* this thing.

What is new? My kind is always underestimated.

All I can do is race to the nearest elevator, eel into a car crowded with people too drunk to notice an unauthorized passenger, sneak onto the all-night celebrity-catering floor, operate a silent butler, silently, with my snagged nails, crawl back into the suite my roommate occupies, and cuddle up to her cell phone so she can get *your* call for help, Mr. Matt Devine.

Who should win this competition, paws down?

The dude in black who is not carrying a grudge and a sword, only shivs and street soul.

Me and the ghost of Johnny Cash.

Okay, we fade to black. Together.

So.

Were it not for me, Mr. Matt would not be sitting here now an hour later in the vast living room we all share, having his slashed wrist and hand repaired by the hotel doctor.

This involves a process called "stitches" that Miss EK, Miss Mariah Molina, and I gather 'round to watch with equal curiosity. Only a child can rival a cat for a certain carnivorous attraction to blood and gore. Of course, we cats cannot coo, "*Ooh,* gross."

Not that Miss Mariah Molina would care to be characterized as a "child," but she still is one, as are various kits I know, like Gimpy.

Mr. Matt is pale under his spray tan, but then he always was. It comes with that yellow hair of his.

Mr. Rafi Nadir has ordered from room service a gleaming topaz liquid called Scotch despite Miss Lieutenant C. R. Molina's disapproving scowl. In fact, he has ordered an entire bottle of this Caledonian beverage on the tab of the LVMPD and is imbibing himself, as is Miss Temple.

"The cuts are not very deep and will heal well," Dr. Cuthbert is saying to Mr. Matt. "With rest you can perform this evening, although I recommend against it. With the palm slash, you can expect tingling and loss of feeling for some weeks. Blood loss is never as flagrant as it looks, and you did an excellent job of keeping the artery compressed by elevating your cocked elbow. Smart. I understand you are committed to this dance contest. A pressure wrapping should be fine for now, and can be disguised by the show's clever costumers. I suggest a Michael Jackson–glove approach. I will stand by during the show to ensure we have no unseemly bloodshed."

"From a *preexisting* wound," Miss Lieutenant C. R. Molina adds sardonically.

This "sardonically" is a lovely word that means she is being sarcastic and is in no way convinced that this contest will not produce future bloodshed.

She is a woman after my own heart in this respect. It is obvious that some bloodthirsty souls have been drawn to this display of the terpsichorean arts. That is an ancient Greek term for their goddess of dance, and we all know how good the ancient Greeks were at war, gore, and dark tragic family secrets.

Luckily, cats were not the factor in that culture that they were in the Egyptian, or the body count would have been much higher.

I must admit I am feeling particularly bloody-minded at the moment and take the first opportunity to slink out of the suite (with the doctor) to consort and consult with the cat known as Topaz.

As a famous mascot she will have lots of first-whisker lickings when it comes to gossip about the celebrities to whom we are accessories both before and after the fact.

(Besides, I know who will be sleeping in my bed the rest of the night. Mr. Matt will recuperate under my roomie's fond care in Miss Temple's bedroom here.)

No room on the bed for Midnight Louie.

As soon as I enter the casino area, I am ambushed and spurred by a single scimitar claw to dodge under a twenty-one table.

Rich eyes of pure gold with the pupils a pair of dagger-thin slits interrogate me.

"I heard the security staff abuzz over the attack in the dance set area, Louie," says the sublimely slinky Topaz. "Am I wrong to think that you know all about it? This is my hotel and I am not going to take some cheesy dance show making itself the subject of tabloid TV headlines. I want this out of the news pronto. What are we going to do about it?"

"We?" I ask, afraid for the first time this perilous morning.

Manx! The last thing I need is another female partner in Midnight Inc. Investigations. Still, I can hardly wait to do the noir tango around the Oasis with this toothsome bit of decidedly unfluffy feline.

CHAPTER 54
REST AND
RECREATION

Matt was beginning to know what a sultan would feel like.

He'd been established naked on his back in the thousand-thread-count sheets on the huge double king-size bed in Temple's bedroom. (Getting him pajamas at this wee hour hadn't exactly been a priority.)

His left arm was positioned on a feather pillow beside him to feel the least stress. Another feather pillow supported his head and a satin soft cotton sheet covered him to the shoulders. On his right side, a satiny soft Temple, clothed in some skimpy slip thing, cuddled against him.

The lights were all on rheostats and dialed down to a peaceful glow. On one of the elaborate bedside tables rested a room service tray of sirloin tips. Temple would feed him one bite-sized piece from time to time. The doctor had recommended eating protein, but had not prescribed the soft kisses that bracketed its administration.

How wonderfully decadent, Matt thought, to lie here while Temple doted on him, unable to keep her hands and lips from constant caresses. It wasn't passion; it was an expression of love and fear.

The danger had drawn them closer.

"You don't really know," she whispered, "how much you love a person until you realize you're in danger of losing him."

"I couldn't stand to think of dying without seeing you again, saying how much I love you. The thought of you kept me alive, Temple."

Their mutual smiles of complete understanding felt like a soul kiss. This seemed like a honeymoon.

Matt closed his eyes and drifted into sleep for a while.

He opened them a few minutes later to find her still there, right there for him. "It might not have been a man," he said.

"Zorro, you mean?"

"Wandawoman is about that size, and strong."

"And trained to fight. But why her?"

"José is too obvious a suspect. Still, neither one of them have motives."

"You forget José's your closest rival for the men's championship, and you beat him at his own game, the pasodoble. It may not seem like a big deal to you, but he's an Olympic champion already. They live to win."

"*Hmm.* For a small-time dance contest? I don't think this has anything to with that. Whoever it was bellowed, 'Die, bastard, die!' in such visceral hoarse tones it didn't sound human, the rage was so intense."

"How could *you* evoke that emotion in anyone, Matt?"

"Maybe it's not me personally. Maybe it's what I represent."

"An ex-priest? A radio shrink. That's pretty far-fetched. Still, you really shouldn't perform the tango tonight," she said. "It's only twelve hours away, and it makes you a target again."

"The police and hotel security are determined to end this tonight. As for the dance, we all rehearsed steps from all the dances the previous week before the competition. Each number is just ninety seconds. Tatyana will figure out a way to help me memorize the steps without walking through them full tilt over and over."

"I know you *can* do it, but should you? Other performers have been attacked, maybe not as obviously, and they're real celebrities. In fact, if you think of it, several of them have been celebrities behaving badly. I wonder —"

He was following his own new line of thought.

"The loaded prop pistol incident was just before me, and that was the most serious so far. Until now. Olivia's broken heel could have been a repaired shoe that malfunctioned, or minor sabotage, and Keith Salter's illness could have been ordinary food poisoning."

"It's escalated from a sabotaged dancing slipper to a sickened performer to a drugged one, to a shot one, all onstage during the dances. You were lured here to your attack, alone, at night. That was one-on-one with a deadly weapon. You must have done a heroic job of fighting off a surprise assault like that."

"Amazing how the life force kicks in. Whoever it was should have some pretty good body bruises. Once I had the . . . person — can't say 'bastard' back, could have conceivably been a woman — temporarily disarmed by rolling 'Zorro' up in that curtain, I did my best to disable the attacker with martial arts blows. But I was already weakening."

"So if it's another dancer, he or she might move a bit stiffly."

"Wandawoman was a victim herself," he objected, going back to the earlier suggestion.

"Self-administering too many antianxiety meds would put her out cold *and* remove suspicion. And she could control the timing."

"I suppose you're going to suggest the Cloaked Conjuror as a suspect too."

"Good idea. Just because we know him a little . . . who can tell what size and build he is under that costuming?"

"He doesn't need a mask for something like this, though. Going maskless would be a better disguise."

"True. Brilliant, in fact," she said. "Apparently you have plenty of blood to the brain despite it all."

"Yeah. Other places too."

"Oh?" Temple looked deliciously wicked at the moment. "Maybe I'm as good as Tatyana at figuring out a way to help you go through the steps without having to go over and over it again. But I'm aiming at a bit more than ninety seconds."

CHAPTER 55
LAST TANGO IN ZURICH

Humid warmth wafted from the small-by-American-standards bathroom when Revienne opened the door thirty-five minutes later, her pink skirt and the suspected black garter belt over one arm.

Max's automatic inventory was part investigation, part self-indulgence.

The black camisole was really a thigh-brushing teddy. If she'd ever worn a bra in this escape escapade, it wasn't on her now. Not that she needed one. Probably never had worn one. She was French. *Whew.*

"I can't stand another moment in that suit! Okay with you?" she asked.

"I'm sometimes an idiot, but not now."

"You Americans. All for sex but so ignorant of sensuality. I suppose you will stay fully dressed, wearing that tight belt, although it is Versace, those nice new shoes, that silk tie with the subtle but expensive tack."

"Good tailoring is as comfortable as pajamas."

"Well said. I know you are rich, but rich Americans usually go for the obvious. How did you escape that?"

She settled in the other upholstered chair, like Venus curling into her clamshell, her bare legs tucked under. They were shaved, but a slight stubble caught the light. Whether there was anything under that slip of a skirt was up to the imagination of the beholder.

"Is seduction a part of your therapeutic technique?" he asked.

"Not usually, but thank you for noticing. I have been through hell for you, Mr. Randolph. I am going to enjoy the first few decent hours I've had in days. I am clean, I am not wearing the same clothing, I have a cool drink coming and a handsome man hanging on my every . . . word. I plan to enjoy it. I also plan to strip your psyche down to the bare neuroses, whether you intend to let me or not."

"Fair enough."

He settled into his chair, enjoying sinking his bone-tired frame into a cradle of goosedown upholstery. This psychic striptease was not going to be a one-way street. His chair was placed to observe both the door and the windows. And even if there was any "consummation devoutly to be wished" tonight, he'd be fully clothed and ready to fight, flee, or some other appropriate f word.

"I'll buy you some new clothes in the morning and a ticket to wherever you need to go," he told her. "I owe you much more, but that'll have to wait until I'm far away from your friends in the Mercedes and their ilk."

"They weren't very friendly."

As she lifted a hand to push back her dampened hair he saw the bracelet of bruises on her pale wrist.

"I see that."

"What?" Her eyes followed his gaze. "Oh." She turned the wrist and looked at the other one, also marked. "Didn't know that showed. I didn't just hitch a ride, as you put it, with them. Although, once they produced their firearms I admit I co-operated. I wouldn't make a good Bond girl, would I?"

"In that outfit, maybe. But you're too cerebral."

"Cerebral?" English wasn't her first language and some words weren't in most textbooks.

"Smart."

She raised an eyebrow. "You like that in a

woman?"

"No." He'd surprised her, as he'd meant to. "I require that in a woman."

" 'Require.' That is a demanding word. Are you demanding, Mr. Randolph?"

"Of myself." He stirred uneasily.

"I see you don't like that in yourself."

"What? Why? How?"

"Your restless body language."

He laughed. "My 'restless body language' isn't giving away my inner state. It's because my 'banged-up' body can't stand any position for too long at the moment, no matter how cushy."

"You can't stand?" She sat forward, alarmed. "Just a few minutes ago you did, and walked quite well."

" 'Stand' is an expression. It means I can't tolerate" — she still looked blank — "endure" — she nodded — "the same position long."

A soft knock came on the door. "Room service," he said, starting to struggle out of the chair softer than quicksand.

She leapt up to anticipate him.

"You can't answer the door in that," he said. "That's why I stayed fully dressed."

"I can, but I've a feeling you wouldn't . . . stand . . . for it."

He threw her a grin. By then he had used

the cane to get him to the door. He nodded to the bathroom, and she ducked inside.

He used the peephole, then opened the door to admit a waiter rolling in a room service cart. He laid the cane atop the cart as he signed the bill and indicated the tip. His curled left hand concealed a roll of coins from a money exchange kiosk in the street, his only weapon besides the cane.

The balding waiter murmured *"Danke sheine"* and left.

Max double-bolted the door and swept the cane under the cart's tablecloth, ensuring no assassin lurked beneath the snowy linens.

"You *are* suspicious." Revienne spoke from the open bathroom door.

"And you're not, after what you went through?"

"Of course. But I'm also suspicious of you."

"Me?"

"Obviously, you are a tough guy. Who knows what you're capable of?"

"Why don't you see what goodies are on the table here, before turning it on me."

"Sometimes you speak nonsense."

"English idioms. Figures of speech. I can use German. Or French, if you prefer."

"In bed, yes. Both."

"I don't think either of us is ready for bed yet," he said dryly. *"Regardez."*

"Mon Dieu!"

She picked up the champagne in its silver bucket to read the label, then the bottles of red and white wines. She eyed him, mischievous.

"You must surely bear a platinum card from a titan of industry." Under the silver domes she lifted in turn lay croissants, a huge salad for two, salmon and *pommes frites* — the original French fried potatoes, as thin as angel-hair pasta — fruit and cheese and small candied sweets.

"This is a feast," she said.

She looked at him leaning on his cane, slipping his homemade set of brass knuckles into his pants pockets, not that she knew what he was doing.

"Now *you* do as *I* say. Sit. On that hard chair, where you will not sink like a stone."

She was right that he needed support now, not wallowing comfort. He couldn't assume they wouldn't be traced here and attacked in the night.

"I will serve you," she decided, rolling the table to his chair and handing him an elaborately folded serviette.

He took it, watching as she lifted the cart's side extensions, pulled a chair to her side of the table, selected the red wine for the salad, poured it. He watched her bare arm muscles shift with purpose under her creamy skin, her breasts ebb and flow against the thin silk netting them, tender and pink as the salmon.

She understood the show she was putting on, of course, but that only made him feel free to enjoy it.

When she sat and pushed the salad plate toward him so they could eat off both sides, she suddenly gasped in surprise. Her white linen napkin was in the shape of a graceful swan, not the formal roll that had come with the service.

"You do napkin origami!"

Surprising her in this small way gave him an unexpected bolt of pleasure, completely nonsexual. She quickly turned the moment to the more adult.

"I'd noticed what long, agile fingers you have."

She gave him a Princess Diana smile, head cast down, eyes cast up, shy and seductive at the same time. Now he remembered her very well, the late, unhappy royal wife. He washed some of the exquisite wine over his tongue and resolved to enjoy every nuance of both the drink and the woman.

Was she seducing him for some undercover purpose? Or was she just a woman who'd survived an arduous mountain trek that had stripped every scintilla of womanliness from her?

They began forking pieces of romaine lettuce, walnuts, blue cheese, and caramelized pear slices into their mouths, not speaking, just savoring the enjoyment of a leisurely fine meal, sipping wine between every bite.

If he knew the French, this dinner would take at least an hour. No bolting the food American-style. He supposed his butt might go numb on this hard chair by then, but numbing the nether regions was probably a good idea right now. He didn't want to be swept away before he knew more about her than she knew about him.

"Why did you become a psychiatrist?"

She looked up, surprised. "It's a good profession. I meet interesting people." She tossed him a smile and a bow of her head. "I help them."

"And you make a lot of money."

She shook her head as she sipped wine, not quite able to answer. "I do now. That wasn't my motive. Actually, your generous contribution for my services here in Switzerland will help me meet with my Algerian patients in Paris."

"You're an altruist."

"Pardone-moi?"

"You try to help mankind, not just . . . man." He returned her smile with the bow of his head as he sipped wine. Great stuff! Great verbal fencing too.

"I believe everyone who is blessed has an obligation to serve those unlucky enough to have been unblessed."

"So amnesiac millionaires who fall off mountains are just a charity case for you?"

Her gray eyes warmed with appreciation. "So you have . . . turned the tables on me now?"

"You catch on fast."

"You didn't fall off a mountain, Mr. Randolph. You are not the type to climb cold, hard Old World mountains."

"Then how did I fall?"

She sipped wine, shut her eyes, tilted her head. "I see you climbing . . . a skyscraper."

He raised an eyebrow.

"You are one of these urban daredevils. You are in New York City. You reach the eightieth floor before the police can arrive and you snap a line to an opposite building. You will wire-walk over the urban chasm while everyone below gets stiff necks watching and waiting for you to fall. You won't fall, but you will get arrested at the end of your stunt, and a great deal of publicity.

When you have your press conference, you will present the lovely lady from Channel Five with a flower shaped like a dove, and take her to bed later."

He laughed, longer and harder than he thought he was capable of.

"Will the lovely French psychiatrist the court orders me to see take me to bed also?"

"That depends how much she likes her swan-shaped flower."

Revienne daubed her lips with the limp corpse of his swan napkin.

"That's a wonderfully inventive scenario, but it still doesn't tell me why you became a psychiatrist."

She sipped wine again, setting aside the demolished salad plate and uncovering their plates of salmon.

"I'll tell you after we eat the main course."

So they ate in silence, flake by savory flake of baked salmon, crunch by crunch of the tiny strips of potato, sip by sip of the white wine until the bottle was gone.

He thought over Revienne's imagined high-wire act.

He'd felt in that position often during his stay at the clinic and later escape. It was an apt metaphor for what he knew of his life these last few days. He watched his hands with the exquisite Christofle sterling flatware. His fingers were indeed long and strong, as his legs would be again. As other parts were rehearsing for being again.

This escape, this idyll, was almost over. He was sorry about that.

He was startled from his reverie when she poured from the opened bottle of white wine into fresh glasses, and swept the empty dinner plates together and to the side.

He took sliced fruit and cheese from the desert plate, and sat back.

Revienne nibbled on a wedge of pungent white cheese. "Why I became a psychiatrist." She sighed. "How could I be anything but, after Sophie."

He waited.

"My younger sister. Do you have brothers and sisters? We don't know, do we, Mr. Randolph? I had the one sister. There were four years between us, enough for me to feel superior. Cruelty, indifference must be educated out of the young, I believe. They are greedy, self-centered, and frightened."

He said nothing, the best way to keep a story being told, but he wondered if she was obliquely referring to him in his amnesiac state.

"Sophie trailed me and embarrassed me in front of my cool new friends. She still had baby fat, while I had breasts and boys.

Her skin was unfortunate but my parents assured her that she'd be just like me someday. Frankly, I would not want to be like I was then, vain, selfish, and stupid."

There was nothing of the seductive woman in her now, just the voice of truth and self-disgust.

"She lost a great deal of weight. No one suspected bulimia. Her skin got worse, but she was thinner than I was. She had no breasts and she never would. I came home one day when our parents were away to find Sophie outside the third-floor mansard, poised like a diver.

"I called to her from the street, begged her to wait, to hang on.

" 'I can fly,' " she told me. " 'I am finally light enough to fly.' "

I screamed for the neighbors to call the police and ran up the four flights to the roof. While I ran up step after step until my legs shook, she took flight. I arrived where she had been to see her on the street below."

She crumpled the napkin into a tight ball in her hand.

"My God."

He felt an odd kinship with her. Had he failed a brother? He felt a wave of anger and guilt, and then fury with his fled memory that forbid him responsibility for his past.

"I shouldn't have asked," he said.

"It was a long time ago. It gave me purpose. The public was ignorant then of the suffering of young people. I've specialized in trauma cases, but I work gratis with the young from poor families in Paris. Don't weep for me. I make a lot of money on my celebrity cases to underwrite my charity work."

"I'm a celebrity case?"

She smiled. "Presumed so. You have the money to afford the clinic and my exclusive time."

"This has been more exclusive than I'd imagined."

"It's been . . . invigorating for me, in a way. You are difficult. I like the challenge."

"Will I ever fully remember, do you think?

She assumed her professional face. "These cases are unpredictable. The added pressure of someone trying to kill you might choke off your memory even longer. Your best course is to reunite with your uncle. Once I put myself together again and return to the clinic, I can contact him, direct him to where you'll be. It's time you had another keeper, Mr. Randolph, and you know it."

He nodded.

"Why did you pursue me when I vanished

instead of going your own way?"

"A number of reasons."

"Yes, Mr. Randolph?"

"I panicked. Yes, I did. You were indeed my keeper. I needed you. And, I knew you wouldn't have vanished like that of your own will, unless you had an underlying motive. I needed to know why you had disappeared."

"You still don't trust me, Mr. Randolph."

"No, Dr. Schneider, I don't. Until I have my memory back, I won't trust anyone. And even then it'll be dicey. Difficult."

"And if you never do recover your memory?"

"In time, I might find people to trust. But I have to make sure I live that long."

"I don't envy your future."

"I don't envy your past." He refilled their glasses. The wine glowed.

"What of our present?" she asked.

"That's ours to determine."

"If someone doesn't kill you first."

"Apparently I'm harder to kill than someone counted on."

"I knew you were an extraordinary man five minutes after I entered your room for an interview."

"I look good in a hospital gown?"

She smiled. "You looked like hell, but you

still were — let me find the exact English words. You were wary. Proud." She made a fist, searching for the right idiom. "You were prickled, like a land mine of the mind."

"Prickly, I think you mean."

"Hard to get close to, to see into. Mental spikes all around you. Lightning snapping."

He laughed. "This from a head case with no memory and bum legs?"

"Yes."

"Am I still so prickly?"

"Yes . . . and no. So —"

She leaned forward to push him into the chair back so quickly the cane fell to the floor. His muscles automatically tensed for an attack and it was one.

She knelt before him. Looking down, he saw the gaping camisole barely supporting her rounded breasts under taupe aureoles and rose tips. Just.

She looked up, easing off his Bally slip-on ankle boots. "This is *my* restaurant. No shoes —"

She rose, her breasts pressed against his thighs (oh, God) . . .

"No belts, unless you have any kinky after-dinner notions —"

. . . to loosen and pull away the narrow Bally snake of smooth leather.

"No tie —"

Her torso pressed his as she arched upward to undo the tack and the silken Ermenegildo Zegna knot and draw them away.

". . . allowed."

He caught her hands in one of his, put his other at her nape and pressed her face to his for a long, luxurious, five-star kiss. Or several. He liked the appetizers at her restaurant already.

His free hand slipped the camisole straps off her lovely, strong shoulders, one by one. She shrugged them farther away. Seducing and being seduced felt like the most civilized parlor game in Europe.

He felt the physical and mental pain of the past six weeks melting like marzipan after-dinner sweets into the sour landscape of his soul. It wasn't just the sex, it was breaking the touching barrier. He'd needed comfort more concrete than words. This had been coming for some time, and would be worth it no matter the cost.

Mostly.

Maybe.

Oh, baby . . .

CHAPTER 56
ON THE TOPAZ TRAIL

Since it is Miss Topaz's hotel, as she puts it so firmly, I am forced to let her lead.

Ordinarily I resist a subservient position on principle, but I am not a fool.

Ordinarily an extraordinarily svelte and attractive lady of my species is not walking, tail high and swaying, directly ahead of me.

I am already checking out the surroundings for romantic rendezvous spots, but Topaz's lively mind is on other matters.

"The moment I noticed the hotel security forces converging on the theater, I knew something fishy was up."

" 'Converging'? 'Something fishy was up'?" That is usually my line. Why has the lithe Miss Topaz started talking like an ungodly combo of Miss Lieutenant Molina and Sam Spade?

"The perp was gone," she goes on, "and your mistress's significant other required lifesaving treatment. However, I concluded his attacker must have been somewhat attacked in turn, or he would not have ceased to harass Mr. Matt, as you call him."

"What do you call him?"

"Hot. Did you see that pasodoble he did? I trust we will still see his tango tonight."

Oh, no. Females are so shallow. "The show must go on," I say sourly.

She stops and turns. I find I have trailed her to the theater area, where yellow crime-scene tape warns off all comers.

Topaz walks under the streamers, tail high. I follow.

"No, Louie. 'The Shoe Must Go On.' "

Yikes! Has she been talking to my Miss Temple lately? What is it with these females and fancy footwear?

I soon discover what. The area is deserted while the forensics people are back at the lab doing *CSI: Las Vegas* film montage tests and things to music. Who would ever imagine major network viewers would be seduced into watching science how-to films in the name of crime drama? Mr. Wizard would have been proud. Bill Nye, the PBS "science guy" would have been begging for cameo roles.

Miss Topaz trots through the empty audience seating and onto the wooden set floor, bold as old gold. She stops by the velvet curtains backing the stage above the set of four risers.

I can see where the curtain has been torn and dusted for prints. Blood runs down the velvet in an ugly dark snake of color to the floor, where it has dried to a carmine color.

I come from a hunter breed. Normally blood is no big deal, even though I have not had to eat live game in years. But when it is the blood of someone you know. . . .

"He could have bled to death."

"I know," Topaz says. "But it is lucky he bled here."

I eye the many drops. I know the forensics people numbered and photographed each one. We should not be leaving pad prints on the scene of the crime. I am about to say so when Topaz darts to the side of the stage.

She has zeroed in on the last tracked blood drop of Mr. Matt, no doubt on the perp's Cuban heel, because it is moving toward the aisle to the exit.

"He stepped in Mr. Matt's blood as he was leaving," I say, shuddering.

"Now, Louie. I know you are emotionally involved, but we must keep a clear head."

" 'We' must keep a clear head? You were not in the heat of battle, rushing into the churning size-twelve footwork of two men fighting to the death. You did not take the body blows that I did, the kicks that spun me almost into the aisle. I am black and blue all over, except it does not show."

"Poor Louie," she purrs, polishing my indignantly heaving sides with her close-cropped satin coat.

Not bad.

"No doubt you are too distracted to notice the significant difference in this particular blood drop."

I put my eyes to the floor. The light here is horrible. "The blood mark sinks in the middle."

"It does not sink. The heel has a flaw. It marks the floor with a small depression, and the blood drop is uneven."

I look again. Sure enough, the heel has left a small dent in the floor. I sit. And think. I lash my tail about for effect. Miss Topaz watches me, her vibrissae shivering with anticipation.

"Mr. Matt said he was drawn onto the stage by the stamp of flamenco heels that he took for Miss Tatyana in Spanish mode," I finally say. "But the stamping sound was made by a man wearing Cuban heels. Those heels sound so sharp and loud because pounded-in nail heads pave the bottom surface. During his frenzied stomping, a nail must have been vibrated loose, and . . . bent back into the heel from the pressure of the next stomp, producing —"

"A lovely little dent that will follow him wherever he goes."

"Yes. I take it you have explored that direction."

"Down the aisle and out into the carpeted casino."

"Carpeting." I frown, fearful.

"A bent nail head leaves an indent there too, but we must hurry, Louie. Foot traffic is fierce out there and could erase the trail."

"Would a Zorro in retreat not attract attention?" I ask.

"Yes. But you say he left the sword behind and likely took the hat and gloves away in a —"

I glance at the empty bandstand to the side. "An empty guitar case would do it."

"Brilliant!" she coos. "Let us make our own tracks."

So we do the feline hustle out of there and into the noisy casino, where we must dodge the constant kick of tourist shoes to follow the trail of the bent nail.

It is not so arduous as I supposed.

The man's stride is about eighteen inches and the nail is snagging the carpet strands. In forty feet we have dodged around some deserted slot machines far from the central aisles where they are set "loose" to lure tourists.

A plain door in the wall is where they stop.

"What is this, a janitor's closet?" I ask.

Topaz looks thoughtful, then solemn, which is not hard to do with those pieces-of-eight eyes.

"Better, Louie."

I wait.

"It is an employee bathroom, opening only with a key, not usable by the public."

The truth sinks in.

This was an inside job.

CHAPTER 57
AN OPEN AND SHUT CASE

Somehow I did not expect my first date with Topaz to be staking out an employee rest room at the Oasis.

I was hoping for one of those storied Italian dinners behind the restaurant at the Venetian. Gondoliers poling tourists through the faux canals and singing "O Sole Mio," which pays tribute to a variety of fish much prized in feline circles.

My green eyes meeting Topaz's golden ones as we each chow down on the same long strand of angel-hair pasta until our vibrissae duel delightfully. . . .

Instead we are crouching under a pair of empty stools waiting for a croupier to need to take a leak.

Romantic, not!

Actually, it is a little waitress doll who unlocks the rest room door and allows us to shadow her inside. This is not good. She senses our soft furry sides on her hosed calves and looks down with a frown just as we dash out of sight into a cubicle. *Euw.* These floors are never cleaned to the demanding standards of those who have to put four unshod feet down on them.

Luckily, the waitress just wanted to repair her lipstick and quickly waltzes out again.

We return to the rest room's main area and loft up on the countertop to wash our feet in moist sink bowls. I manage to put my weight on the flipper that lowers the paper towels and we soon are high, clean, and dry.

Topaz nods to a row of metal lockers on the entry wall. All boast combination locks. These must be assigned to key personnel. We sniff around the locked doors, but accomplish nothing but sneezes from all the scented products within.

"How are we going to get out?" Topaz asks.

I can tell she has never done a stakeout before. Before I can explain that we will get out as we got in, the key scrabbles in the door again. We *whoosh* back into the cubicle, undoing all our good footwork.

"Listen!" I hiss.

Our backs arch in unison as we hear the scrape of a shoe cleat on the plain tile floor. I duck my head under the door to peek. A pair of large, black, Cuban-heeled shoes stands before the locker. We hear the combination lock spinning and clicking, the door opened and shut.

Then the shoes and wide-bottomed black trousers head for the door.

I poke Topaz in the shoulder with a rude claw and whisk out to race through the door before it closes and locks automatically. The minute I am through, I throw all my weight against it to force it to a standstill.

Miss Topaz eases out at an unruffled pace while I huff and puff from my effort. "Quick!" she says, "he is wasting no time."

All we have seen from our floor-bound rear viewpoint is that he is a tall white male with a loping stride. I was right! He is carrying a stolen guitar case, and his hands are gloved in black leather. The shirt, cape, and hat must be in the case.

We weave in and out of the forest of moving legs, leaving squeals and curses in our wake, rather like Moby Dick, only unlike the white whale, we are black. And not a marine mammal.

Black Legs leads us on a hard chase all through the casino and then the shops and then the meeting areas and then the service areas to the utter rear of the building. A last gray metal door opens at his push, a one-way exit. Before it shuts on his vanishing heels with the one bent nail we elect to eel through.

The heavy door slams shut, but we have split — literally — to either side and the shadows. He turns to check that no one is coming through the door behind him.

A Dumpster awaits; his goal all along. I hear the huge truck gears grinding a few blocks away. This one knows a fast trash pickup will swallow the evidence he deposits now in minutes.

He will leave his load and vanish. We need a way to ID him. My shivs are still throbbing from marking his rear pants. At least they were not denim, but something sleazier for dancing. I am betting he is not dumping those, because his blood is on the ass. Not enough to drip and leave evidence unfortunately.

"We must mark him," Topaz's hot breath wafts in my right ear. She has slipped into my shadow.

I explain I already have, and how.

"Something visible to humans," she insists.

"I know. I suppose I could claw his face."

"You are already bruised from fighting this man. He would smash you to the ground."

I am not afraid of taking on this literal bruiser again, but claw marks would only mean something to someone who knew and believed in my crime-fighting nature, like Miss Temple.

The light from the dim security lamp in the

distance catches on Topaz's collar.

"Duck," I tell her, nudging her behind me, with her amber crystal drops swinging like a lady's earrings.

"How do these come off?" I ask. "When the tourists collect them for the prize?"

"Something called a 'spring ring.' "

"Sit still. I am going to see if my front fang can spring one of those babies free."

"Louie! This is no time to be collecting prizes. You are cheating."

"No, but he will be. Now be patient and keep quiet."

"Well!"

But she does. Of course I am forced into some very intimate quarters, mouth to mouth almost, as I struggle to work a topaz drop free without the aid of an opposable thumb.

Our hot breaths mingle. I growl a little. Topaz unintentionally purrs a little. I could get used to this, but — *dang!* — the glass jewel suddenly is in my mouth. I mean, good!

Our quarry is squatting by the open guitar case, drawing out the black accessories of villainy: the flat-brimmed hat and cloak. Which he folds back in the guitar case. He stands and strips off his long-sleeved black shirt, revealing pale white skin. He dons a short-sleeved shirt from the case and sits on the concrete to take off the flamenco boots and pulls out a pair of simple black slip-on shoes. His folded pants are beside him.

I slip up on them soft and silent as a shadow, and tuck the pendant in the left rear pocket. Just for a backup. And because I am enough of a street cat still to believe that tagging a perp should fit the crime, I use my strongest remaining front shiv to slash an initial into the back heel of one shoe: the letter *L.*

CHAPTER 58
FENCED IN

After a not-so-jolly room service breakfast at eight, Rafi sat on the suite's sprawling main sofa manning his cell phone and jotting notes on the hotel stationery.

He was Mr. Action Center. Molina sat beside him, frowning and periodically checking her own cell phone. Forensics wouldn't have much to report for hours. Rafi's security staff was checking out the entire *Dancing With the Celebs* support staff and cast, but only after Molina had put Rafi through a catechism of where they were allowed to investigate and how they were to deal with any evidence they found. Dirty Larry was on another couch, far away, analyzing his informal footage for likely Zorro candidates.

Temple curled up on the couch opposite Rafi and Molina with Matt, who was soon to head for rehearsal with Tatyana. Mariah and EK were still sleeping in their bedroom, after the late hours and excitement of this day's very wee hours.

Louie's presence was MIA. He had exited with the waiter to go off on errands of a peculiarly mysterious nature.

Temple hoped he was getting the goods on someone.

Meanwhile, this was Rafi's operation, his hotel, his expertise.

He flipped his cell phone shut and regarded his ex. Professionally. Like they were long-standing colleagues, which they had been, long ago.

"The fencer was found safe at home in his hotel room, pretty zonked."

"That can be faked," Molina noted.

"Not with hooker twins zonked out next to him on the bed. My people roused him enough to learn his Zorro and other costumes had always stayed in the wardrobe room."

"They roused him?" Temple asked alertly. "The hooker twins?"

"No. My staff."

He eyed Molina again.

Temple watched them both. Such an interesting situation. She had her cops, he had his hotel cops. Wow. Equal again, in a way, as when they'd been rookie uniformed officers together on the streets of L.A.

Temple was torn between feeling sorry for Molina and cheering on Rafi. She wondered where Mariah would fall on that continuum if and when she learned Rafi Nadir was her father.

At the moment, he looked like an okay candidate, and her mother, wearing vintage seventies garb and fighting whatever physical problem she had been, looked pretty lame and tame.

It was always a mistake to underestimate Molina. Rafi was feeling pretty cocky now, for all the right and wrong reasons.

Matt stirred, his head on Temple's shoulder heavy but welcome.

She swallowed. Hard.

He'd been ambushed alone by a seasoned swordsman, Matt armed with nothing but his occasional martial arts workouts and his wits. He'd done a Max Kinsella job of coming out of that intact. Except for his left hand, which rested on her thigh, under the loose clasp of her contrite right hand.

Could one have a contrite right hand?

She did. She'd encouraged Matt to enter this orgy of dance, publicity, and public self-revelation. Temple Barr, fiancée, expert PR woman, and rotten advisor in all roles.

Rafi looked up at Temple. He then announced fresh info from his staff, probably just to frost Molina.

"Zorro costume's missing, all right. I guess the sword was left in the attack area because it had no fingerprints, the usual quick ditch and run for it."

He glanced at Molina, whose olive skin had flushed deeply red at that phrase, "a quick ditch."

And hadn't she done just that to Rafi, fourteen years ago in L.A.?

Temple shivered, partly from the idea of Matt's bandaged hand and wrist on her thigh, partly from watching Molina come apart before her eyes. Max would enjoy this. Or . . . would he? She was petty enough to like it on his behalf, scared enough to dread it on Matt's behalf. Someone had tried to kill him!

She needed Molina and all her homicide skills, as Molina needed Rafi and his hotel security history.

Shoot! She and Molina were twins right now, needing exactly the people they most despised and distrusted.

Temple eyed Rafi. His usual five o'clock shadow was now purely 3:00 A.M. satanic smudge and his Cheshire cat expression said that he was aware of every damn nuance Temple was.

He winked at her, then his glance moved

to the sleeping Mariah and Ping-Ponged between anger and regret.

Yeah. He had daddy genes, probably to his own great surprise.

She wondered if Matt or Max did, and could think of half a dozen reasons why either might not . . . or did. A dozen reasons why she didn't want to be her own mother, wobbling erratically between seasoned insight and neurotic overcontrol of her only daughter and youngest child.

And poor Mariah was both.

CHAPTER 59
TERMINAL TANGO

Temple had only one more night after this to don Zoe Chloe Ozone garb, the awards show on Friday.

She could hardly wait to dump the annoying little spotlight-grabber.

What had almost happened to Matt made this entire competition, for charity or not, seem trivial. She knew she should lighten up, and would later. People just want to have fun, and that's very good for the human race.

Someone, or several someones on these premises, didn't.

Temple glanced around. She saw Dirty Larry and his camcorder plying the aisles along with other pro and amateur videographers. Hank Buck stood at the far stage wing, arms folded, eyes scanning the audience. His gaze met hers and he gave a little nod. Other discreet, safari-uniformed hotel guards dotted the back of the house. One was seated almost invisibly behind the judges' table.

Molina had insisted Leander Brock give her a list of the dancers in order.

When Temple saw it, she knew she was still enough of a competitor to rejoice that Matt had been paired with Olivia Phillips again. By the fifth show and final dance, re-pairings were inevitable.

Olivia was an ideal partner for Matt. Their heights were right for the cheek-to-cheek tango, and they liked and therefore enhanced each other. Olivia's tall, slender frame was made for the tango, and Matt had proven he had Latin *cojones* in the pasodoble. (And even later in the Paso Duel with "Zorro.")

Temple wasn't sure that the dance partners were "drawn" for this final performance night. Glory B. was paired with Keith Salter, not the greatest dancer but a good height match. The tango was built on sharp head motions and close body contact by both dancers, facing each other, then apart. Matched heights made it work. So CC had "drawn" the statuesque Wandawoman and José was stuck with Motha Jonz. Giggle.

Temple eyed the "thermometer" graphics board. Despite no personal onstage mishaps and therefore no sympathy votes, Matt had edged out José. Temple would bet his working against type was winning over voters. Olivia and Glory B. were neck and neck on the women's side.

The dance order would be Salter and Glory B., José and Motha Jonz, CC and Wandawoman, and Matt and Olivia last. Some thought last was the best position in a competition. You stay on the judges' minds better. Yet mostly call-in and e-mail voters counted these days.

Zoe Chloe would only be onstage at the end, to award the junior dance studio scholarship. That vote board showed Patrisha and EK at the top.

Temple crossed her fingers for EK as she eyed "her girls."

The four wore glittery tops and short skirts, less trashy but a mirror of what older teen celebrities wore. Molina had sprung a mint for Temple to take Mariah and EK to lunch at the Fashion Show Mall on the Strip and on a shopping spree that midday, so Mariah was looking successfully "teen queen" too.

Temple had welcomed the outing. It took her mind off Matt, his rehearsal demands and physical condition. Although by early this morning he had been remarkably ready to, ah, rise and shine.

"What are you grinning about, ZC?"

Crawford Buchanan had breezed close to whisper in her ear. He loved taking these hit-and-run liberties and could play his fingers across his victim's neck if he didn't think she'd call him on it. ZC would. She was wearing the radically high, platform wedge, black satin ballet-style shoes she'd splurged on at the mall for Zoe Chloe's final appearances, so she could stomp him like a bug if she wanted to.

"Just thinking," she said, "that my junior dance corps look darling but age-appropriate. Even the Los Hermanos Brothers are giving them a new look."

"*Eh.* They're okay. A little mousy, maybe. Never your problem," he added with a patented leer at her black-and-white polka-dotted hose. She also wore a kilt-length fuchsia plaid taffeta balloon skirt and white, puffed-sleeved cropped jacket with a giant fuchsia silk peony on the shoulder that hosted a black rhinestone spider pin as big as a teacup.

On this last competition night (and because Molina and Rafi refused to watch from the greenroom), the ZCO party had seats along the front row on the judges' side.

Sitting in the audience was so different from watching on a TV screen in the greenroom. They still had their little "family" row: Rafi, Temple, Molina, and Mariah.

The final introductions began as the band played the first couple on stage.

Tango music was sophisticated, like the dance, sometimes brighter and jazzy, sometimes darker.

Wisely, Glory and Keith had been given a quick, intense routine, with lots of dips, leg wraps, and intricate steps for the agile and petite Glory. Keith wore men's formal black and she sparkled in vibrant orange taffeta. Keith pretty much functioned as the pole in a stripper club. That quieter role enhanced his dignity, so the applause was warm when the couple finished with Glory doing the splits in front of his upright figure.

"Your best dance," Danny could honestly tell Keith. "A subtle job of supporting your partner so she could perform some very demanding moves. Fabulous job, Miss B. You've come far. I expect to see you in a *High School Musical* touring company shortly."

"Really?" Glory B. radiated new confidence even while panting hard.

"Nine," said Danny, looking at Glory B. so she'd know the rating was hers, not theirs.

The audience went wild. Glory B. grinned

and waved at them as she left the stage.

"There's one contestant whose self-esteem has visibly soared during the competition," Temple whispered to nobody in particular, her eyes glued on the stage.

"Actually," said Molina, "you're right." She glanced at her rapt daughter, visibly reconsidering.

Audible breaths were drawn in when Crawford announced "José Juarez . . ."

". . . and his partner, Motha Jonz."

Their held breaths *whooshed* out like a disappointed tide at the news of his partner, a cumbersome dancer at best.

This was another dance opening that placed the partners at opposite ends of the stage.

José wore the tight, chest-baring black shirt and pants of male ballroom dancers in sexier routines. His rolled-up sleeves showcased forearms muscular from fencing. A tilted black fedora with a crimson band shadowed his chiseled features.

Motha Jonz glittered in basic black studded with bloodred rhinestones, but she still was shaped like a saguaro cactus, round and fully packed. They stalked each other around the dance floor, their steps measured between intricate twining moves and sudden hip-to-hip turns. They'd break apart to pose, then resume the tease.

The audience was whooping at every sexy move now, with pockets of applause bursting out. In this light and this dance, Motha Jonz looked like a contender for the first time.

The judges thought so too.

"Your best dance, both of you," Danny said while awarding them a nine.

Leander was almost in tears. "A terrific recovery from the sad mishap last night. Motha Jonz, you looked 'mahvelous.' And, José, you are perfection in this dance." He awarded them his first ten of the competition, which had the audience in an uproar.

"What was with the hat?" Savannah Ashleigh complained. "We want to see *all* of Mr. Juarez, don't we, ladies?" she asked the audience. "Even his *face!*" Her raucous laughter was echoed by approving shrieks from the female audience members.

The shrieks died fast when the Cloaked Conjuror strode out in a Darth Vader mask, wearing a long black leather coat slashed open along the sides and back so every stride cracked like a whip or the flap of giant batwings. Wandawoman stalked after him in a Spider Queen outfit, a spandex catsuit slashed open more than it concealed, accessorized with torn net and tattoos, working a red-satin lined cloak like combination train and tail.

Some nervous high-tech music emphasized both the robotic rhythm of the tango and the simmering passion beneath it. It was a mad, bad dance and the audience loved it.

The judges, not so much.

"Power, yes," Leander said. "Physically, you two are the most powerful of the men and women. But . . . finesse, my friends! The tango does not celebrate the birth of the Death Star but the intimate, dangerous dance of the sexes. Your footwork did indeed live up a military march, not a dance, and despite the magnificent visuals, no underlying feeling came through."

He waved a "seven," with Savannah and Danny brandishing "eights."

So far no "mishap" had marred the evening. Temple hoped Matt and Olivia would make that a record of four couples unmolested.

Tension in the ballroom was tangible. Matt's paso had knocked them dead. How could he improve on it? Those few who knew what a harrowing night he'd spent were figuratively nibbling their nails. Temple could sense the tension from Rafi and Molina on either side of her, not only for

Matt, but for knowing that if the evil luck that had dogged the contestants was to strike again, tonight, now would be the last chance.

Temple had felt the mood in the audience and among her "posse" heightening with every dance. Even Rafi and Molina stopped scanning the audience like presidential bodyguards and applauded the end of José's number. They better not be disloyal to Matt, Temple thought. Her nerves were twitching inside of Zoe Chloe's faux adolescent little body while waiting for Matt's tango.

She tried to remember her new platform shoes made her almost five-and-a-half feet tall and Crawford would look like a total shrimp when they were onstage together for the junior award later and at tomorrow's adult award show. Matt had called her cell phone before the show began to tell her he felt fine and ready to rumble. She'd semi-punned back that the rumba wasn't the dance of the day.

"And now," Crawford finally crowed, sensing his reign as emcee peaking, "our last couple of the night performing the . . . Last Tango in Vegas! The glamorous Olivia Phillips and her partner, new Latin king Matt Devine!"

Oh, wow. Temple's eyes were glued on the

staircase. She wanted someone's hand to grab. She looked right past Molina and saw that Mariah had scrunched down on her mother's other side and was staring raptly at the stage. "He's gonna be okay, he's gonna be okay," she was mouthing, as if making up for her unguarded and selfish blurt when she saw Matt streaming blood in the wee hours of this morning.

Kids have to learn to deal with shock; it doesn't come naturally.

No couple arrived at the top of either stairway in the wings.

The audience stirred, uneasy.

Temple fidgeted in her seat. Was he ill?

Then Matt was there, sliding down the curving banister as he'd first done to escape the masked attacker fifteen hours ago. Talk about capitalizing on real-life experience.

He shot off the end doing a spectacular airborne split over the four risers to the dance floor, landing perfectly in a wide-legged stance, his martial arts training coming into play. He turned and looked back up the stairs as if willing an apparition to appear.

"Oh, wow," Mariah squealed.

Temple echoed her internally. The makeup and costume crew had made a totally bold move. Matt's hair was the natural color, but gelled close to his head except for a blindingly blond high-rise top. His black leather pants and shirt were "skinfully" tight. A black leather gauntlet on his wounded left arm stretched up to his shoulder, a brilliantly kinky twist on a practical costume necessity. The recent strains had chiseled features set in the expression of predatory intensity affected by male ballroom dancers.

The effect was startling for a tango: a blond man, totally icy-hot Nazi cyborg fetish awesome.

The look made a certain historical sense, Temple told herself while swallowing hard. Many Nazis had escaped to South America after World War II, and Argentina streets gave birth to the tango and refined it later after World War II.

Mariah didn't get these nuances, but she got the one that mattered. "He is *smokin'*. The girls at school will be so freaking jealous!"

Olivia appeared at the top of the stairs in a clingy backless burgundy gown slathered with sequins. Its fluttering "car wash" skirt was slit strategically up to her hips at every opportunity.

Age did not wither, nor custom stale her utter feline sensuality.

This was the couple to beat. The audience rose in a standing ovation to acknowledge that.

That motivated Olivia to move. She glittered like a glamorous serpent as she slithered and slid down the banister, spinning down the four stairs to plaster herself against Matt's back and wrap a possessive cocked leg around his braced thigh.

O-kay, Temple told herself. She was watching Rico and Lola at the Copa, right? Music and passion were always the fashion. *Disengage, Zoe Chloe!*

That was kinda hard. The audience was clapping and hooting at every move, and there were lots of them. The tango was a deliberate dance with sharp leg flicks keeping the couple entwined in a sexy procession of moves, scissoring their lower legs in and out.

In this version Olivia was the attempted aggressor. Her sharp, spike-heeled leg flicks flirted between Matt's wide-planted legs very . . . dangerously. Throbbing, aching violin music dictated each nerve-wracking flirtatious advance and retreat of the dancers' legs and hips.

Temple couldn't even imagine *rehearsing* this dance. The guy would have to wear a suit of armor. At least an athletic protector.

On her left, Rafi was emitting a low, admiring laugh.

On her right, Molina's eyes were no longer wandering like a bodyguard's, but transfixed on the stage and Matt.

Olivia was all flashing naked leg, stretching a supernaturally long and straight gam to, uh, Rico's broad shoulder. He caught her arched ankle and turned her legs like the hands of a clock, until she slid slowly down his side in the splits, an amazing feat for her age. Grandma Gypsy Rose Lee.

Even more amazing, Olivia moved from lying at his feet by drawing herself up through his legs from the back in a torso-clinging move that defied gravity . . . and decency.

The audience frenzy was drowning out the music now. Temple glimpsed Molina quickly distracting Mariah's eyes from the stage with a whispered comment.

Temple had heard network dance show judges comment once that a routine was so hot and intense that they felt like voyeurs, like it was too private to watch. That was happening now with an ex-priest and a grandma who'd just met a week earlier. Dance was an amazing art form.

Zoe Chloe was blushing and Temple was thinking someone should call the police to shut this show down when the couple executed a series of sharp spins and Olivia sank into the splits again, clutching at . . . Rico's . . . disdainful hip. Was there such a thing as a disdainful hip? If there could be a contrite right hand, sure.

The applause and screams were overriding everything, even the couple going to the judges' table. They took bow after bow at center stage.

"Some full recovery," Rafi growled on Temple's left.

"Max certainly nailed the competition there, and practically the girl," Molina muttered on her right.

Max?

Temple stared at Molina, to find her longtime antagonist flushing. "I meant 'Matt.' God, Barr. Can't you manage to get boyfriends without mirror names?"

That's when the audience gasped.

Molina snapped her head back to the stage and a dazed Temple changed focus a split second later.

While she was ambling toward the judges' table arm in arm with Matt, Olivia's shoe had hit a slick spot on the shiny wooden surface. One high heel kicked out from under her.

She was going to land flat on her back,

the worst kind of impact. Especially for a sexy senior citizen.

Matt's knees buckled as he tried to push himself beneath her before she hit, hard.

Molina and Rafi were sprinting onto the dance floor as were a bunch of beige shirts from hotel security, not to mention Dirty Larry slinging his camcorder strap over his shoulder to rush down the aisle to the scene of the accident.

Another dirty trick — sabotage — was all anyone in the know could think. The triumphant couple went from a strut to the judges' table to being swallowed by a clot of converging security personnel.

The center of the stage looked like a football field with a loose ball.

Temple charged over, late, picturing Matt and his already disabled arm crushed at the bottom of the pile.

Feet lost purchase and skidded, bodies and arms flailed about on a floor as slippery as an ice rink.

Danny was standing, leaning over the judges' table on the dais that gave him an overview of the melee. "He's holding something! Striking. Get him!" Danny yelled with the overriding vocal command of a choreographer who could call whole chorus lines to attention.

A mantra of screamed "Die, bastard, die" came from the unseen heart of the struggle.

"Get him. Get him. *Get him!*" male voices chanted between desperate grunts. "Get who?"

"Man in beige," Danny bellowed, leaping over the tabletop to help. "He's got some kind of weapon."

Midnight Louie, long MIA, suddenly came streaking past Temple's side vision, making for the tumbled bodies in the pile.

He paused to eye the flailing limbs and feet, lifting a snarling face featuring an amazingly wide and bloodred maw lined with white, sharklike fangs.

Then he leaped onto the struggling pile of flesh, bones, and clothing with what Temple would swear later was a martial arts cry. Or the feline version, anyway.

Louie chomped down hard on one particular exposed khaki butt, ripping a back pocket clear off, so the contents scattered, including a small brittle comet that flew across the wood floor.

The accosted man screamed with pain and reared up, revealing a clenched fist.

It was the oddest sight. All the other men in the pile lifted up too, as if it was a modern dance movement, chaotic, brutal, choreographed.

The man Louie had targeted was pushed up by their pressure, one fist held high, something in it.

"Matt!" Temple cried, spotting a pool of black at the very bottom of the pile.

She charged forward, glimpsing Danny Dove on her left trying the same rescue maneuver. Her brand-new shoe sole slipped, but it wasn't an issue.

She was suddenly stopped in midleap by a blow at her midsection that knocked the breath out of her, partly because of her own rash forward momentum.

Matt! her mind screamed.

Her body was being hoisted in a lift, and then slammed back down to earth, every bone shuddering from the impact.

She couldn't move. She was held fast to a living wall and every eye was turning to her and whatever imprisoned her, the guards' . . . Danny's . . . Molina's . . . Matt's . . . a black cat's . . .

The silence in the ballroom became profound, like total deafness.

A fist shook in front of her vision. Big. White-knuckled. Clutching . . . something small and silly and insignificant.

She could hardly see it.

A thread? A hair? A cat whisker?

"Thisss," a guttural voice in her ear

whispered, and then shouted to everyone. *"Thisss* is a *sssyringe* of pure, uncut *heroin.* One jab and she's dead meat."

Temple realized that her feet in their empowering platform wedgies were dangling, that the man had again hoisted her like a Barbie doll.

Damn! She always knew there was some seriously big disadvantage to being short and slight. On the other hand, she might be able to do an Olivia and kick her Goth shoe up behind her, right into the family vault.

"Don't move," Molina ordered. *"Anybody."*

The policewoman was pushing herself up from the floor like a Greek tragedienne coming back to life, like a really pissed off Medea.

"Hank," Rafi Nadir called from the rear. "Give it up."

The guy spun, Temple's limbs flopping doll-like as he turned.

The chest she was pasted against heaved, powerful and iron-hard, like a machine. "I can't get the bastard," the voice heaved out behind her, "I can get her. Again. And again and again."

She saw his arm rising above her. He wasn't brandishing a cat whisker. It was a hypodermic needle. Heroin! No, God!

She'd seen slow-motion, damning scenes

like these in live theater. The helpless chorus writhing in joint impotency on the floor. The mad, cursed central figure lifting an arm to tear out his own eyes, to drive daggers into her innocent children's bodies, to rend garments at the cruel fate the gods decree. . . .

Temple lifted her foot in its industrial-strength Zoe Chloe Ozone Goth shoe just as ahead of her Danny leaped up, up, and *awaaay* in his beautiful balloon of a powerful dance kick, and behind her someone shouted, "Hike!"

Hike? Why not?

She kicked hard up and behind her like a tango diva with gladiator-style spike heels and a life wish.

The man screamed, tumbling away and down behind her, and she was on the floor as the flying tackle behind her hit home.

She was belly down, face-to-face with a horizontal Matt, who grabbed her hands and pulled her hard toward him in a paso move. On the slippery floor they could roll far away from the kicking feet and churning arms and legs behind them both at last.

Temple examined what she could see of herself. "No hypos?" she asked.

"God willing," Matt said, patting her limbs and torso, hunting hypos.

549

"You were way too hot in the tango to be doing that right now," she managed to huff out. "I might explode."

He pulled her up to her feet as if doing an Olivia lift and held her even closer as Molina and Rafi and Dirty Larry pulled a man in an Oasis guard's uniform away from his fellow guards and into custody.

The face was a deranged mask, but Temple was able to identify it. Hank Buck.

Rafi held the lethal hypo in his hand and moved carefully over the slick floor to show it to Matt and Temple. Empty.

"Good thing you're so short," he told Temple. "And have happy feet. And a berserk cat. Between the two of you, he missed harpooning you and did in his own shoulder."

"What happens now?" Temple asked.

"In seven or eight minutes he'll be as high as a fruit bat and we'll read him his rights and interrogate him backstage while he's euphoric before the EMTs get here. Because the horse was injected into a muscle, he'll have two to four hours before it kills him. A nasal mist called Narcan can reverse an overdose.

"Buck was obviously hoping to dose Matt during the confusion of helping him and Olivia up. Floor was probably sprayed with silicone. Being on duty here, he'd have watched the rehearsal and figured out where Matt would end up.

"If he'd gotten away before Matt realized he'd been 'stung,' or if Matt just didn't register what had happened, we'd have no idea he'd been drugged or what was used and how to reverse it. So, though Buck is the bastard who should die, he'll live to stand trial for attempted murder."

Rafi slapped Matt on the shoulder. "Lethal dance, man." He smiled at Temple. "You still have Supergirl chops, babe, and your cat rocks." He sighed. "And Molina will happily take my ass to the cleaner's because one of my staff was the wacko."

CHAPTER 60
CURTAIN CALLS

The law enforcement types had shuffled the rogue Oasis guard off the dance floor so Matt and Temple stood dazed and embracing alone at the center.

The hypo had been intended for Matt, and then turned on Temple.

She slowly realized she'd been aware of Crawford's droning voice circling the struggle. Now she could see and hear him. He was circling her and Matt now, like a media shark.

"Ladies and gentlemen, you have been hearing the blow-by-blow account of the capture of the dangerous lunatic who's been sabotaging our wonderful dancers. Tune into the KREP-AM radio 88.6 on your dial, where I'll be broadcasting my eyewitness account just as soon as I get back there this evening. By then I will have the name of the man who just tried to kill Mr. Matt Devine and my broadcast assistant, Internet darling

Zoe Chloe Ozone."

He minced carefully forward, came close, and thrust the microphone into their faces.

"How did it feel to come so close to death?"

Danny Dove came near with an expression that indicated he was close to a homicidal act, and extracted the mike from Buchanan's hands.

"This is Danny Dove, head judge." He put his free arm over Matt and Temple's shoulders and started walking them offstage. "We respectfully request that Matt and Olivia visit the judges' table to receive their scores for an amazing performance. Then, if our stalwart Miss Ozone feels up to it, she will award the junior dancer scholarship."

Applause broke out.

"We appreciate your patience and forbearance," Danny added, "and will return for the final adult results tomorrow."

He turned to hand Temple the mike and returned to the judges' dais. Olivia had been standing on the fringe and smiled tearfully as she walked over to stand by Matt. All three embraced, not with the usual euphoria of a great dance finished, but with a survivor's fervor.

Temple stood between them, holding the mike, while the judges held forth.

Danny was the evening's Iron Man. His calm control eased everyone back into normality.

"What can you say to perfection?" he began, then answered himself. "Bravo and brava! And to Miss Tatyana" — he turned to see her standing, subdued for once, in the wings — "let's have her step into view for a round of applause. She choreographed the most superbly sexy tango I have ever seen."

Applause and shouts erupted.

"And," Danny added, "though the audience and judges were unaware of it, I've been told that Matt was recovering from blood loss from a previous attack with a knife in the wee hours this morning, but he and Tatyana were able to still stage an unbelievable routine.

"As for the dancers, you completely gave yourselves over to your roles. You were precise, you were edgy, you embraced the music even more intimately than you embraced each other. You gave us an incredible experience. Ten."

Leander Brock was silent for a long, dramatic moment. "I confess that my emotions have been through a buzz saw. To go from the thrill of watching . . . no, experiencing such a dazzling tango, to the life-

and-death struggle that followed on this stage . . . to think that an event designed to raise money for deathly ill children might have resulted in someone's death on this very stage, it's too much for me. I can only thank God and second Danny. Ten."

Savannah too seemed as subdued as Tatyana. Then she threw her score cards on the floor at Matt and Olivia's feet.

"You two are off the charts. I'd give you a fifteen if I could. That was Oscar-worthy acting and entertainment. And Matt, honestly, I thought you were too nice to win this thing. Dirty dancing is where it's at these days. But you were amazingly, sizzlingly, devilishly, almost X-rated *naughty* in that dance and I loved it! Tell me you haven't sold your soul to the Devil, because I'd sure like to be next in line for it."

She smiled at Olivia. "Sistah, you give all us seasoned ladies hope! What about those sexy flicks and splits? Have you been possessed by the ghost of that leggy legend, Cyd Charisse, who just left us not too long ago? Like Fred Astaire said of her decades ago, you were 'beautiful dynamite' in that tango. Ten with whipped cream on top, because you two got me in a lather."

The standing ovation lasted for two minutes.

Danny nodded at Temple and held out a sealed envelope.

The mike was shaking in her hands and her knees were trembling. She faced the audience but her eye was on the floor director, who nodded encouragingly and held up two fingers. Two minutes to go. Two minutes to fill. She wanted to rush backstage and hear what Hank Buck had confessed to. He was just now probably reaching the euphoric spill stage.

"I have to admit that I am not up to the usual Zoe Chloe Ozone speed right now," she began. "The events tonight have been too awesome, as have been everyone on this stage, cast and crew, including the security and law enforcement personnel who averted a tragedy I would tend to take very personally no matter what had happened."

The audience laughed lightly, easing tension.

She smiled. "It's appropriate that we honor first the winner of the junior competition, for this show was produced to raise hope for the young. The scholarship will benefit . . ."

She struggled to open the thick paper of the envelope while holding the mike.

"Would you believe my hands are shaking?" she asked the audience during the lull.

More laughter and applause.

"The scholarship will benefit" — now her voice went shaky — "Patrisha Peters."

Shrieks from offstage brought an ecstatic Patrisha and her partner Brandon running to Temple and the mike.

"Thank you all so much," Patrisha said, in tears. "This has been the best experience of my life and, gosh, dancing with a Los Hermanos Brother was the coolest thing in the world."

The other Hermanos brothers and the girl contestants and their mothers came running on stage to surround the winning couple, with the judges soon joining them and the adult contestants streaming out from backstage to surround and embrace Olivia and Matt.

Temple stood alone at the mike watching the floor director's two spread hands, the fingers counting down from ten.

"And so we thank you all for your generous votes and will meet one more time tomorrow to name the winning *Dancing With the Celeb* stars. Same time, same place, and same cast, thank God."

Danny came up to hug Zoe Chloe just as the final little finger folded into the director's palm and he beamed at Temple for her perfect timing.

Even the audience came streaming down onto the stage now, dazed and happy and emotionally drained.

"Oh, Danny," Temple said, finally allowing tears of relief and joy to saturate his shoulder. "Thanks for getting me through this. I was so out of character at the end. I just couldn't conjure Zoe Chloe."

"You did it just right. Zee Cee will be back tomorrow all sass and savvy. After all, she's going to be the sole MC, if she wants to be. Buchanan is history on this show. Matt and Olivia are mobbed right now, but I bet you want to catch up with your police 'posse' backstage, so let's slip away and let you do what you do best, unravel this conspiracy."

"Yes, please."

Chapter 61
Dial M for Motive

Molina intercepted them outside the green-room, which was now a temporary police interrogation room.

"He's not happily hostile yet. It's hard to tell how much he's had and how fast it worked," she told them, as Danny slipped away to return to the love fest on stage.

"But I'm not too late?" Temple said. "I didn't miss anything?"

"This show hasn't started yet. But this is the guy."

"Why would anyone hate Matt that much?" Temple asked.

"A teensy bit prejudiced, are we?" Molina asked in turn, as Rafi joined them. But she smiled.

"It's a legitimate question," Temple insisted. "This guy is a local. The only thing vaguely aggressive Matt did since coming to town was to track down his stepfather. So this Hank Buck was a friend of that scum-ball? Really? I can't believe that. Cliff Effinger didn't have any friends. Whoever tied him to the bow of the pirate ship at the Treasure Island so he drowned could not have been Matt. If that was anything, it was a hit.

"And another thing," Temple added. "What about the Barbie Doll Killer? Could Hank Buck be it?"

"I doubt it," Molina said. "I can't deal with that issue here and now, but I have a nasty suspicion that I'm gonna get on ASAP. Right now why Buck wanted to kill Matt is a priority.

"My detectives are even now breaking down Buck's bio like he was Lee Harvey Oswald," Molina said. "They're going to his neighbors, his car mechanic, anyone. If there's a connection to Matt, they'll find it. Two attempts at murder must have a powerful motive behind them." She looked over her shoulder to Mariah's father. "He was one of yours."

Rafi shook his head. "He was one of yours first. That was on his application that my people pulled. He was hired here before I was, but before that he was on the force. We found no record of dishonorable discharge. Your detectives are trying to find out why he quit the force. He *was* seeing the department psychologist, but those records are protected."

"Not for long. Either way," Molina said, "he was one bad cop, public or private. Why'd he target this event and these people?"

"That's sure what I wonder," a new voice said.

They all turned, shocked to see that Matt had joined them, and doubly shocked by the sight of his current tough-guy tango image.

"I finally escaped my fans," he said. "I want to know why this guy almost killed me and Temple. I don't see a reason."

"I don't see it, either," Rafi admitted. "It'd make more sense if one of the celebrity dancers who was a victim of dirty tricks was the murder target. I can see it being Motha Jonz. Buck could have been hired to off her by the gangsta rappers, say, whoever Motha Jonz was involved with at the time of the Vegas shoot-out. I could see using the dance show to do that."

"Hey," Temple said. "Buck didn't have to be hired. Wasn't a teenager shot and killed during the gunplay on the Strip? I need my laptop. I could look that and all the other celebrity 'sins' right up. There are hundreds of sites on stuff like that."

Rafi had a cell phone to his ear. "Nadir here. Collect a hot pink laptop from the — ?"

He handed Temple the phone and she described it and told the guard where in the central bedroom it was. Then Rafi took back the phone and said he wanted the laptop in the dancing show greenroom "yesterday."

" 'Hot pink'?" Molina mocked. "Can you never stop being girly?"

Matt pulled Temple close to his leather-clad side. "I don't ever want her to."

"You see the benefits," Temple purred, watching Molina look away and shake her head. Temple straightened up and got back to business.

"Maybe that messenger boy shot in the rap star shoot-out was a relative of Buck's," she said.

"But Buck didn't try to *kill* Motha Jonz," Matt said. "Rafi, your gangsta rap slaying idea is interesting. Exchanging live ammo for blanks was the most dangerous dirty trick, but Motha Jonz was the *shooter.* The Cloaked Conjuror and José were more in danger from her."

Temple had sat on an empty guard's chair and now looked up and nodded.

"She might have gotten a police charge out of the incident," Temple said. "That would have hurt her career even more than it has been. And she might have been found guilty and convicted."

"What about all those other dirty tricks?" Matt wondered. "What was the point?"

"Obvious." Molina was brusque. "Diversions to mask that you were a target, *the* target. I don't know if he intended the Cloaked Conjuror to be injured by Motha Jonz's loaded gun, but the fact that he did get hurt got us police thinking the whole thing might be a follow-through on the continual death threats he gets."

"There must have been more to it," Matt insisted. "We're missing something."

"What about the shoe incidents?" Temple asked.

"You *would* get on the shoes," Molina said, rolling her eyes. "They were the most minor 'accidents.' At worst, Olivia could have twisted her ankle. As it was, her dancing through the problem and CC upholding her only enhanced her ratings with the audience. And you told me your nosy cat pretty much targeted very early on that the stage mother dosed her own daughter's shoes with the pepper spray for the same reason — audience sympathy and votes."

Molina eyed Rafi. "Now do you understand why I'm so set against Mariah getting into the kid performer stuff?"

"Wait a minute." Temple sat up straighter. "I'm getting something. I'm seeing something."

"So now you're psychic?" Molina said.

"No, I'm . . . I don't see how it relates to Hank Buck, that's all. But, what you said: the onstage 'accidents' raised the victim's scores. They got a sympathy vote. Olivia's heel was first and the rating went up. That inspired Yvonne Smith to make Sou-Sou an underdog with another, far more dramatic shoe problem. And it worked. Her daughter's score went up."

Rafi was leaning forward, elbows on knees. "That's right. It snowballed. Salter was poisoned, Wandawoman drugged, CC shot, and Matt was personally attacked by someone in Juarez's guise. That had to be Hank, but could Sou-Sou's mother have set up the other incidents to disguise the fact that her daughter's problem was staged? And then there's Temple's idea. Maybe somebody in the competition or around the competition is a relative of the people these celebrities hurt. I mean, look at them. They're quite a crew. In a way what happened to them fit their crimes."

Matt caught his drift and kept the ball rolling. "Glory B. was the first one to have

564

an almost accident even before the first show. She fell on the jungle gym and Danny Dove thought it had been tampered with. She got a DUI citation for an accident a few months ago, and a little girl has serious leg injuries."

"I just Googled Glory B. online to get the facts straight," Temple said. "There'll probably be a huge settlement for the family of the girl. I don't find anything obviously bad about Olivia," Temple said, "but Keith Salter was all over the entertainment gossip shows for some cases of food poisoning at his restaurant in Aspen. E. coli. It was especially bad. A toddler died. No one was found derelict, but the media loved broadcasting the problem because Salter had raked so many other chefs over the coals on his *Butcher's Holler* show."

Molina spoke. "The hospital said there was no way to ever tell if his poisoning had been accidental, or intentional."

"Wandawoman being drugged in the pasodoble?" Matt asked.

"Oh, my gosh," Temple said, "that could have been done to make *you* look bad too. I'll look her up."

Molina shook her head. "Who needs detectives anymore? Everything is online."

"And it stays there forever," Temple said.

"Sometimes good, sometimes bad."

"The 'bad' refers to Zoe Chloe, right?"

Temple, tapping away on her laptop keyboard, shrugged at Molina. "Zoe Chloe has her uses. I just wish I could figure a way to earn money off of her popularity."

"Everybody wants to earn money these days, especially these annoying celebrities behaving badly," Molina noted.

"Maybe even Hank Buck," Temple said.

"What are you getting at?" Rafi asked.

"Let's say he always was in this to get Matt. I know, we don't know why, but it looks like that. Let's say . . . he saw he could use the competition to get other people too. Then he went wild, was a revenge machine. All these celebrities going wild in Hollywood and Vegas, getting away with things. That could irritate a law officer, right?"

"Irritate. Not drive nuts."

"What if he already was nuts?"

"Any evidence?"

"Only in what he did at the other end of his mania."

"What are you getting at?"

"I'm getting at, who could hate Glory B., Olivia, Chef Salter, Wandawoman, Motha Jonz, and Matt enough to persecute them? Persecute. But kill? The only person Hank Buck tried to kill was Matt."

"He's the most innocent of the innocent," Molina protested.

"That before his tango, or after?" Rafi asked.

"Forget the dancing," Molina snapped. "The last thing this is about is dancing. The dancing was the pretext."

"Amen," Temple said. "And there was Hank Buck, full of whatever venom he had, having all these people on his turf, and at his mercy. Most of all, for reasons we don't know, Matt."

Dirty Larry's buzz-cut dirty blond head came through the greenroom door.

"Our boy Buck is reaching smack high. He'll be singing his soul out like Janis Joplin and I've got the camcorder and a tape recorder rolling to capture every sweet, demented syllable of it."

Hank Buck was handcuffed, wrists in front of his body, his face was relaxed and dreamy.

Temple couldn't believe this man had been active enough less than fifteen minutes ago to grab her, lift her, try to kill her.

Two young uniformed EMTs sat near him.

He was wearing hospital scrub pants. The uniform cargo pants were laid out beside him, one rear pocket torn and traces of blood on the seat and down the legs.

Matt and Temple looked inquiringly at Molina.

"Your cat removed the rear pocket when he went berserk," she told Temple. "I don't know how he ID'd Buck. Maybe by smell. When we got Buck subdued we saw the blood and the emergency people took a look."

She paused, took a deep breath. "It's like he got caught on a fence with exposed nail heads recently. He's got four infected gouges down both sides from his buttocks to his calves. Must have hurt like hell. Maybe your cat just smelled blood."

Or maybe, Temple thought, Louie just recognized a man he had marked earlier, perhaps when Matt had been attacked by Buck posing as Zorro.

But, wait, Louie had been sleeping hard in her bedroom when Matt managed to reach her cell phone, so that couldn't be.

Just another mystery to go unsolved.

"Bastard," Buck crooned gently as he recognized Matt, rocking back and forth on the sofa so many celebrities had sat on. "It would've felt so good to kill you."

"Why?" Molina asked. "Why kill Matt Devine?"

"Bastard," he muttered. "*Umm,* feels so

good. Felt so good getting those stupid, pampered 'celebs.' They all get off too easy."

Rafi stood behind Molina, a cell phone to his ear. "Alch says Buck *did* work the gangsta rap slaying case," he whispered in her ear. "Just, ah, guarding the crime scene stuff. But he saw the main players, the dead boy, the glitzy car."

"So you did the dirty tricks," Molina pushed.

"Sure. Hey, it helped up the votes and donations. I was jes' helpin' those poor little bald cancer babies, right? Good guy. Better guy than some rich, spoiled assholes making fools of themselves on the stage. I am a good guy! Bitch got it all wrong. Needed some slappin' around."

He suddenly giggled, a truly chilling sound: childish, secret, mean.

"Took her out for a few dances around the floor. Mop it up with her. Had her trained to do housework on her face."

Temple felt her stomach turn.

Molina turned to stare at Rafi.

He nodded soberly.

"Girlfriend or wife?" Molina asked.

"Wha' does it matter?" His head was rolling on his neck, his eyes not connecting with anything. "Not there anymore. I don't care now. She's quiet. So quiet. Bastard. Thinks he's God? Tellin' women things. Interferin' in my life. My wife. Leave? Leave? Tell her to leave? She's left now, bastard. She's gone. Who you gonna tell now? You gotta die. I'm gonna do it. Finish the job. It feels so good. I was so smart. Stupid, stupid cops. Turn on a brother. They do it too sometimes. Bastard. Get 'tween a man and his life. Uh, man and his wife. She's gone."

Rafi was whispering into the phone. "Check any domestic abuse trail, or gossip. Yeah? On it already? Jesus Christ!"

Molina turned, frowning at the loud expletive.

"Jesus Christ is comin'," Hank Buck crooned, "comin' on a snowy white cloud of smack for to carry me home. Why dint anyone tell me heaven was full of horse, huh?"

She nodded Matt and Temple into the hall, Rafi trailing her.

"Amateurs are out of here. You've got your answer," she told Matt.

"His wife is someone who called my 'Midnight Hour' advice line, who I told to leave an abusive husband?"

"Before you try to say it's your fault," Molina went on, "this guy was going to blow anyway. Rafi, Alch tell you what I think he did?"

"Yeah. He was already checking Buck's personnel files and in touch with any family he could find. The guy's sister-in-law reported her sister missing two weeks ago. No trace so far."

"So we've bagged a murderer?" Temple asked, appalled that a confirmed killer had been stalking the show and Matt.

"You've got all the info you're going to get," Molina told Temple. "Both of you get outa here and those so extreme costumes. I don't want to see anything more tonight but uniforms and hear anything but the location of that poor missing woman's body."

She turned to go back into the greenroom.

Rafi clicked the cell phone shut.

"Well?" Molina barked at him. "You coming or not? He's your boy too. We're not done here."

She moved on, leaving Temple, Matt, and Rafi staring after her, stupefied.

"Guess I'm on the team," Rafi finally said as he shrugged and followed her.

CHAPTER 62
TOPAZ TANGO

The audience has finally emptied the house, the crew has left, and only the ghost light is on in the wings, along with the soft ambient lighting along the aisles.

I sit center stage. Alone.

Waiting.

At last a lone figure comes slinking slowly down one aisle from a seat on the very back wall of the theater.

Legs longer than yesterday. Doing the model walk, one lean smooth gam crossing in front of the other. Eyes glittering in the semi-dark, fixed on me, not on the ladder of steps she is descending. The jewels at her neck matching their color and fire.

I was made for nights like these.

I wait. Rock solid, holding my powerful limbs in check, no longer breathing hard from my earlier heroic exertions, breathing hard from expectation.

I wait and she comes to me, crossing the

wooden dance floor surefooted, never faltering even on the slippery section.

She walks straight up to me until our blinkless gazes are only inches apart.

At the last second she veers left, brushing my side, coiling her long black train around my powerful shoulder.

I stand and look over my shoulder blade, her head is turned likewise toward mine.

She executes a sudden spin and then stalks close along my side again, brushing her face fast against mine before she is walking away.

I follow with one sharp step forward, catch her passing train and draw my mitt along it. She stops. Makes two dazzling shrugs with her sexy shoulders, then our feet are moving in the time-honored way of our kind, making impatient stuttering, kneading little steps, flicking around each other, between each other.

She lashes her train high, letting it quiver in time with her steps.

Our feet are silent, we are silent. The stage is silent for all the intense motion at its center.

She spins away again, and I follow fast. She turns. I turn.

She suddenly slides close along my side again and we turn and turn, our sides undulating together and apart, together and apart.

After another intense round of these steps, she suddenly executes a slow slide down my shoulder and rolls on her back, her golden eyes never leaving my face, her lithe body curled into calculated surrender.

I know this is the climax of the dance, that we will hold our triumphant pose for a few seconds and accept the silent applause of our kind that our routine has won for centuries.

But this is the twenty-first century. Midnight Louie may be a fearless crime-fighter, conquering hero, and primal tiger of the night but he is also a canny suitor.

I move to the side and pick up the small something I have been guarding ever since the stage finally cleared and I could find it. My many schemes to ID the perp for later plucking weren't needed when he gave himself away but that is no reason to let a jewel languish underfoot, unclaimed by the jewel to whom it belongs.

I pick it up delicately in my fangs and turn to Topaz.

Those glorious eyes had narrowed at my seeming desertion at so critical a moment, but now they flare with understanding and renewed passion.

She lies still as I approach her supine beauty. I bend down and with the most skilled ministrations of my teeth and tongue, reattach the precious topaz pendant on her collar so the set is whole again.

Now the dance is truly over.
Let the games begin!

CHAPTER 63
CIAO CIAO CIAO

Max awoke, alive and well.

What do you know?

He awoke with Revienne draped over him, asleep and looking like a Botticelli angel. Of perhaps a couple dozen positions he could recall at this point, he was only physically capable of one or two so far. Apparently they'd sufficed.

He felt . . . mahvelous. Rested. Relaxed. He'd managed to satisfy this gorgeous woman with two game legs and a memory that couldn't access High School Seduction One, much less the *Kama-sutra.*

He supposed, on reflection, that he owed an awful lot of that to her. As he owed his very survival. He felt the double afterglow of fulfillment and escaping mortal danger.

Not that he could trust her any more than before.

Still. He caressed her tousled yellow hair, kissed her pale temple.

Temple. The word gave him a twinge of something. Guilt?

Revienne stirred.

"I'm going to have to buy you clothes today," he murmured into her Venus-pink ear. "I sorta hate to do that."

"Sorta?"

"I'm reluctant to do that right now."

She stretched, using him as a bed. "We could stay like this for weeks, couldn't we?"

"Weeks," he whispered back. "I'd be getting stronger every day. You wouldn't have to work solo to satisfy me. I'd satisfy you every day from Sunday."

" 'Every day' is nice, but why 'from Sunday'? I do Sundays, Mr. Randolph. You can come with me after to church, to sanctify us."

He gazed into her changeable gray-green eyes. "You have no sense of sin?"

"Over this? No. Do you?"

He did a quick examination of conscience. Where had *that* phrase come from? Ireland, probably, and the Church. He was aware of bitter bile rising from his gut. Ireland. The Church. Examination of conscience. He knew Revienne the psychiatrist could make hay of these phrases if she knew their effect on him.

An unwelcome thought, or maybe emotion, pricked his conscience. "You mean I could have been cheating just now, cheating on an unremembered woman?"

Her fingertips stroked his frown lines. "A man like you must have at least one woman somewhere. Cheating would be a way of life."

"No. I can't tolerate liars." He frowned. "If there is such a woman, I'll have to find her and find out if she and I can fall in love again."

"And . . . this, you'd confess it?"

"Yes. If she asked."

"And if you did confess?"

"If I'd been in love with her, she'd understand."

He shook away the thought of this hypothetical woman. "What did you mean, 'a man like me'?"

"Rich, clever, with enemies. Sexy even flat on his back with two broken legs."

He shut his eyes. He was more than the sum of all those enviable things, flattering as the last evaluation had been.

If he'd been rich and powerful, as she'd assumed, his current situation had stripped any pride he'd taken in that anyway. He'd needed this encounter. Desperately. Needed her. A woman's touch, and what passed for her love. He'd been wounded in body and mind.

He would not apologize to anyone for the human connection and bliss and self-confidence he'd gotten from her this past night, whatever she was, whether her intentions toward him were for good or ill. Why did he have to have this suspicious core? Why couldn't he take anyone or any act at face value? He must be a very lonely man. Rich, yes. And with that came certain kinds of power, probably overrated.

He had the right instincts. Revienne had loved the expensive room service feast. Or had she loved his thoughtfulness, his thinking of her? That was free. That cost nothing but caring for another.

He looked at her again, remembering the moment of mutual orgasm. Thinking of hers, not his. How cool it was to be part of it, like he was rediscovering sex. Rediscovering himself.

She opened her eyes as his fingers stroked her brow. Caught him unawares.

"You are a very strange man, Mr. Randolph. You almost look right now as if you loved me."

"This is only a situational liaison," he said, smiling.

"Exactly what I'd call it, professionally.

We are two, mostly healthy, heterosexual individuals forced by danger into close quarters. It is only natural that our will to live should manifest itself in an overwhelming attraction and sex. Classic."

"I'm glad you didn't say 'underwhelming sex.' Classic feels very good."

"Yes," she said. "It does. Are you still determined to be rid of me right away?"

"What about your sexual liaisons? A woman like you wouldn't sleep alone unless she wanted to."

"And what is 'a woman like me'?"

"Intelligent, beautiful, sophisticated, compassionate."

Her smile faded. She bit her lip on his last word. "You think this was a pity fuck."

"Where'd you hear that phrase?"

"I've treated Americans before."

"In bed?"

"Americans are not usually such a treat in bed. Nor Irishmen."

"Based on your wide reading, or personal observation?"

"You think I'd tell a monogamous prig like you?"

"We don't know for sure that I'm that warped. Check it out."

"Again?"

She did.

■ ■ ■ ■

He sat in the sleek Italian chair at the Hugo Boss Black collection shop in the Jamoli department store. This was where he'd bought his stressed champagne suede thigh-long jacket, to go with his slightly glossy gray casual pants and black silk T-shirt. The army-green silk shirt and toffee tie were in the Bally duffle bag at his feet. He'd been attracted to black, so avoided it. Might be a giveaway.

He still carried the cane, more as a weapon than a crutch. Necessity and the mountain had made a molehill of the process of rebuilding his leg muscles. He'd not be do-ing acrobatics for some time, but they were definitely in his future, he thought with some regret as Revienne came out from the dressing room wearing a Hugo Boss Black silk suit. The cut and sheen were fabulous, but it wasn't pink, like her ruined one. Only Parisian designers tried something as sur-prising as that. The Swiss liked the colors of money, muted tones that whispered of great wealth.

This suit was a mossy mocha shade that made her gray eyes look almost green and her blond hair like saffron silk. It was belted, with a short, hip-hugging peplum and a neckline open to four inches above the belt. There was a large black-and-white photo of a runway model wearing it with nothing underneath, and not much of anything to show for so much exposure.

Revienne had chosen a dull violet silk T-shirt that made her glossed lips look good enough to eat.

He sighed. Enough of that nonsense. They had serious arrangements to make over lunch.

They ate at the excellent department store restaurant, their table for two well isolated. The expensive, marble-clad décor made the place a discreet echo chamber where it'd be hard to bug a conversation.

"You seem to have recovered from your scruples," she said, tucking her box and bags against the wall. "Spending all these other people's money, I mean, to see me off to the clinic."

"The credit cards I filched before in Alteberg were from tourists, maybe on a once-in-a-lifetime trip. Didn't want to mar that too much. What I've taken here has been from millionaires, and probably predatory ones at that."

"Won't it be suspicious if I come back looking like a million dollars?"

"*Au contraire.* Here's the story you tell: I'd had a bit of a paranoid episode and recovered enough of my memory to secretly call a driver. You didn't think it a good idea to leave me in such a mental condition. So you accompanied me into Zurich, where I paid you royally for your trouble and the unexpected overnights and went off, refusing further treatment. I take it the clinic collects a portion of your fee, and it was prepaid?"

She nodded.

"There you are. If everyone is paid, no one is curious, unless they're imposters. Stick to your story. Eccentric millionaire goes AWOL for a few days, treats you to dinner and a new ensemble, and drives off into the alpine sunset."

"What if I spy some suspicious behavior when I'm back there?"

"I'll get in touch with you in Paris when you're back."

"You still don't have a memory, and you're running on stolen credit cards."

"I'll be all right, thanks to you and mountain-training physical therapy school. Haven't you realized I'm a survivor by now?"

"Yes. And, more important, you have as well, Mr. Randolph, which is the only reason I can leave you in somewhat good conscience."

Their wineglasses were empty, a fresh credit card from an arrogant woman in the Hugo Boss Black for women department had paid for the lunch. They stood, and he took her hand.

"It's best," he said, "that you return to your normal haunts and routines."

" 'Haunts'?"

"Places you usually go, in the pursuit of your work . . . and pleasures."

"What if my work and pleasures have come to . . . coexist?"

Was she anxious at losing a lover, a case, or a target? *Damn suspicion!*

"The only thing that coexists between us is danger. All mine. If I peel off, you'll be safe."

"You're so sure?"

"No. So go immediately to be with colleagues. People you trust. Warn several to set up an alarm if you vanish."

"And you? Your safety? Your whereabouts, your well-being? I do not give up easily."

"I can contact you. And will. When it's safe."

"I am to wait, that's all?"

Her fingers were curled into his suit jacket. When he left her here, at the department store, she wouldn't know whether he was driving out of Zurich, or flying, or taking a train or another bus.

"Do I strike you as a woman who will wait?" she pressed.

"No, Revienne, that's why I beg you to listen to me. I'm stronger for knowing you, for knowing you inside out." That's the closest he could come to love. He sensed he didn't give love easily, to many. "You must keep yourself safe, give me a reason to keep myself safe. You understand?"

She looked deep into his eyes. "You feel responsibility so strongly you can block out love. That is both admirable, and a curse."

"You don't want to hook yourself up to a curse."

She got the "hook up" part.

"No, but sometimes that's not an option. Take care, whoever you really are. Live so that I can remember you, and not in vain. Come to me if you need to. And always remember what love we made. That was past the loss of your memory. You can never erase me and I will always remember."

He didn't let himself say anything more, but he wished he could.

"*Au revoir,* Dr. Schneider."

She smiled and leaned in to press her cheek to both of his in the French manner, and to nip one earlobe.

"*Au revoir,* Mr. Randolph," she whispered. "And if your uncle should inquire about you?"

"Tell him where you left me."

"That's all?"

"He's likely as much a survivor as I am."

He turned and strode away.

He could hear her last, agitated words, but he didn't look back.

"Wait! You've left your cane."

Yes, he had.

Both of them.

CHAPTER 64
FOR HER EYES ONLY

"I need to talk to you, privately."

Temple stared at Molina.

"The Casablanca Bar okay with you?"

"Uh, yeah, except I'm not sure Zoe Chloe Ozone is old enough to drink."

"Surely you're carrying your own ID somewhere."

Temple nodded.

"Then we'll both have to visit the ladies' room, but you to dig out your ID. You first."

Right. Separate visits. The idea of sharing a rest room with Molina was oddly appalling.

Vegas hotel bars and restaurants did have nearby rest rooms but they weren't always apparent. Temple left New Age Molina staring gloomily into the tent of exotic sheer draperies that was the bar while she went off to do her duty to her kidneys after all the excitement, and dig her driver's license out of her Miracle bra.

She paused before the mirror to make sure Zoe Chloe's blueberry-colored lipstick wasn't smeared. This would be almost good-bye to ZCO. Temple sighed. What a relief not to be "on" and in frenetic character every moment.

It would also be a relief to get past this awkward semipalsy moment with Molina. Drinks at a bar? Why would the disdainful detective want that?

Molina was waiting in the same spot.

"Your turn," Temple said.

"I'm okay. There's another rest room that way. I suggest we snag a couple of drinks at the bar and then a table. A waiter could be a good long while."

Temple nodded, reaching into her tote bag when they found a gap in the barstools.

"I'm buying," Molina said.

Temple was sure glad Zoe Chloe never betrayed surprise.

Her last offstage chance to be Zoe saw her ordering a Green Appletini. Yup, she had to produce her driver's license. Molina went the hard-boiled route and ordered scotch on the rocks.

It felt very odd to be weaving a path around tables in Molina's wake, clutching a martini glass.

The first empty table was lit by a candle

flame trembling like a caught bird in a pierced metal cage, a small draped tent of faux isolation meant to make a vast space seem intimate, or at least private.

Temple set her drink down on the glass circle that topped a swagged tablecloth.

Even sitting, Molina seemed to loom in the miniature tent.

"So what's the occasion?" Temple asked. "You surely aren't thanking me for going along with this masquerade as Zoe Chloe."

"No, but I suppose I should. You're right that this isn't my idea. Your fiancé suggested we have this chat."

"Matt? Why?"

"To clear his conscience."

"What can you tell me about him that he wouldn't?"

"Such perfect trust," Molina said, her voice brittle. "He won't be responsible for keeping my secrets any longer. I made the mistake of confiding something in him that he won't keep from you, no matter how disturbing it is."

"Disturbing?"

"Shut up and sip. I can't say this won't hurt me more than it will you."

Temple felt a cold chill curl around her innards.

Molina took a good swallow of scotch, and

began. This was obviously both a reluctant confession and a kind of story.

"As you can see, I'm a certifiably lousy judge of men," she said. "First there was Rafi Nadir, now Dirty Larry. Perhaps the colorful names misled me."

Temple's PR genes revved up. Time to soothe the anxious client. "Rafi doesn't seem so bad now, maybe to you too. And Dirty Larry was useful in this case."

"Useful," Molina repeated with odd emphasis. "Yes, I suppose he is that, among other things." She smiled. "You're always looking for the rainbow behind the rain, Little Miss Sunshine," Molina mused, gazing into the distance, her eyes unfocused. "I wonder if that's what attracts them?"

"Who?"

"Men." Molina's eyes met Temple's, blue as the bottle of curaçao on the shelves behind the bar.

"Which men?"

Molina ignored her. "I suppose I shared my . . . predicament with Matt because it was something we had in common."

"Being Catholic?"

"No. Being knifed."

Temple felt her eyes widen in a way Zoe Chloe would never allow. "So that's what —"

"That's what is wrong with me. It's been six weeks, but Matt can tell you eighty-six stitches have a way of reminding you about them for a long time."

"Eighty-six! Who? Why?"

"A moment, kiddo," Molina said in an almost motherly voice. "I gotta brace myself a little longer." She swallowed again. Then sighed, and sat back in her chair. "I'm actually glad this is just us girls," she said sardonically. "Men do require keeping one's guard up."

"Your men, maybe," Temple answered almost as sardonically. "Rafi is always edgy around you and Dirty Larry is half manipulative and half scared . . . ah, spineless."

"Is he really?" Molina asked, surprised.

"Who, what?"

"Rafi is edgy?"

"From my viewpoint, he's been coming on like gangbusters," Temple said.

"Maybe. But it's for Mariah, not me."

"You going to let him escort her to the father-daughter dance?"

"She's gone beyond gaga over the new Matt." Molina grinned. "Even I may have. Who knew? Maybe you. If I decide to come clean on this before the fall dance, Rafi will have to overcome that."

"She'll just be glad that Matt *isn't* a father

figure. By then she'll probably be into Los Hermanos Brothers. It's great that Danny Dove is giving Ekaterina a personal scholarship for classes and Mariah's ecstatic that Adam wants EK in their next video. She's been pretty selfless about this whole thing."

"Yeah. Surprise. Maturity peeking through. She's actually being apologetic to me. So" — Molina took a slug of her drink — "you don't think much of Larry."

"Don't know. He's one of those guys who could be bad news. Or not. What does my opinion have to do with your slashing?"

"Too much." Molina made a sour face as she swallowed more scotch. "It's how I got slashed that's the literal sticking point. It was in your ex-fiancé's house."

"Ex?" It took Temple a moment to identify Max as an "ex-fiancé." And then, really out of left field, "House?"

When she did, she rejected the whole phrase: "ex-fiancé's house."

"Max doesn't have a house."

"He did. No sense to deny it. He lived somewhere and it certainly wasn't with you at the Circle Ritz, at least not in residence."

"Why on earth were you and Matt discussing Max and his house?"

"That's where I got knifed."

"Excuse me, are you trying to lay another

592

bogus charge on Max? He's out of Vegas, was planning to before — I don't know where he's gone, or why, or when. Just that he's gone. For good."

"I would have said that a few weeks ago myself. Gone for good. And good for you, though you didn't want to believe it. But I'm not so sure now. That house on Mohave Way says different."

"You were there? That must have been during the Red Hat convention."

"No. I was there later."

"But . . . there was nothing there later. Nothing in the house. Why would you go there?"

"I can give you reason to stop excusing Dirty Larry. I had him follow you, and one time he followed you to Max's house at 1200 Mohave Way. That's how I knew where to go myself. Later. Alone."

"Max would have been gone by then."

"Right. And he was."

"Then how did you get in?"

"You don't have a need to know."

"You *broke* in. But what about the woman who lived there?"

"What woman? The house was unoccupied."

"The aging chorus girl."

"Really? You saw her?"

"Yes, I went to the house and she said she'd bought it. She was moved in totally, every stick of Max's furnishings was gone, even the magical props in storage."

"The opium bed?" Molina asked quietly.

"The opium bed, the trick boxes . . . wait! How do you know about the opium bed?"

"I saw it. The house was fully furnished."

"I was there on a Tuesday night."

"I was there the following Sunday."

Each was silent and each communed with her drink again.

"Then —" Temple began, choking back fear, pain, and rage.

"It was a magician's trick," Molina declared, "a vanishing act on a house-moving scale. You saw the illusions, the end result of it. I saw the stage restored to normal."

"But why?"

"He wanted to be completely out of your life, leaving you free to do what you did. Forget him, marry Matt."

"But . . . why?"

"A rolling stone gathers no moss. Maybe the same old story. The demons from his past were after him again and he wanted you out of danger."

Temple sat there feeling Zoe Chloe Ozone melting off her body like a greasepaint clown face. Was Max gone, or dead? Dead or gone? Or were they just the same thing?

"You said no one was there," she told Molina, looking for a hole in her story. "Who cut you then?"

"I have no idea. True. The house was dark. I heard someone moving around after I'd gotten in. A strange tearing sound in one of the rooms. I can tell you Kinsella's clothes were slashed to ribbons in one closet."

Temple gasped. "Who'd do that?"

"I'd had a stalker at my home the past few weeks. I thought it was Kinsella."

"Max? Stalk *you?* Are you crazy?"

Molina shrugged that one off. Temple noticed she wasn't sharing what Matt had gleaned: that she thought Max had come on to her once, during a physical showdown that had turned psychological.

"Now," Molina said, all policewoman, "I'm beginning to think that same stalker was in his house that night. That's when I began to believe that he might be 'innocent' in some ways. I almost could make a case for my stalker being his stalker. And don't ask me why, because that motive is very cloudy and twisted."

"And the stalker cut you?"

Molina nodded. "I confronted the person in the hallway. A large butcher knife was missing from the kitchen block as I came in, I recalled too late. My scar will make Matt's look like a needle scrape."

Temple nodded. "Someone hateful after Max. I'd almost think it was that woman who cut Matt, except she's dead. But her associates need not be."

"The woman from Max's counter-terrorism past that Matt keeps talking about?"

Temple nodded, dazed and almost feeling knifed herself.

"Could be," Molina said. "That's all IRA stuff, though, and they're pretty old news. Inactive. Terrorism is a wholly owned subsidiary of Al-Qaeda and suicide bombers now."

"You don't suppose Max went off to work on that front?" Temple asked with a shudder.

"Wouldn't seem his culture, but he is a chameleon of sorts. No, there's something rotten going on in Vegas tied into all this, but I have no idea what it is."

"So," said Temple, finishing her martini and actually debating ordering another. "Matt will be okay now that you told me it looks like Max stage-managed his own vanishing act and is alive and well and somewhere far away?"

"He didn't want to be the one to tell you

he knew Max had pulled another now-you-see-him, now-you-don't. But he didn't want to be the one to keep you in the dark, either."

"Matt has a pretty fine meter on his conscience, doesn't he?"

Molina nodded. "Yes, he does. An excellent thing in a man." She drained her glass. "You do realize that Max made it look like he was gone to end any hope you might have of a relationship."

"He'd been . . . drawing away lately. In a way, I wasn't surprised."

"Or . . . he could have known that he was again the target of some nasty international assassins and he wanted you out of the way forever."

"Possible. Max takes his personal responsibilities seriously."

"Or, to be totally realistic, he may have been taken out by those same shadowy figures and the scene set up to convince the one constant in his life that any search for him was futile."

Temple would *not* tear up in front of Molina. Or choke on her words. "Yes, that too."

There was a pause. Was it possible that Molina was choking on something too, like regret?

She finally spoke again. "What say we get another round and toast your fiancé."

Temple assumed she shouldn't ask which one, the old or the new.

Maybe this round they could discuss the possible sins and saving graces of Rafi Nadir and Dirty Larry Podesta. Who would ever have thought?

"Where's that pesky cat of yours, anyway?" Molina asked as they returned from the bar.

"Louie seems to have made some new friends at the Oasis. It's always good to have connections in this town."

"Skoal," said Molina, lifting her glass.

"Cheers," said Temple, wondering how Molina was ever going to sort out the guys in her life without one of them proving to be crooked or going AWOL.

Meanwhile . . .

Max of Arabia, swarthy in desert burnoose, lurking near some ancient market.

No, the land of IEDs and suicide bombers made the IRA look like Boy Scouts by comparison. Temple hoped Max was on a cushy assignment in the Caribbean, chasing tax evaders.

CHAPTER 65
CANE DANCE

The hotel was within walking distance of more than shops and restaurants. He was heading for the Bahnhof train station, one of the busiest in Europe. It was an imposing nineteenth-century building as sleek and remodeled inside as a modern airport, with yet more shopping on a lower level. And where there was shopping, there were pockets to pick.

He needed to ditch the credit cards after each use in an urban area, and Zurich was unusually small and insular even for a European city. He couldn't bury them in anything here but refuse, which was regularly accumulated and could be searched, unlike endless alpine meadows.

He rubbed his chin as he thought, surprised by the scrape of his own carefully cultivated stubble across his palm. Revienne hadn't complained, but he wanted to kick himself for forgetting about it during the heat of their moments. So, more data to process. Thoughtful lover. Usually. Add that to the list of attributes he was compiling about his habits and likes and dislikes. Faithful? Apparently. That was inconvenient.

So. What was the verdict on Revienne? If he'd truly trusted her, he'd have used her given name in bed, he'd sensed that much. Yet the honorifics were inciting in a Victorian pornography way. Close, but not completely close. Unrestrained but still restrained.

As his memory was: still restrained, in a straitjacket.

He'd been constantly and unconsciously scanning the street and pedestrians. He stopped at a shop window to examine the reflection of a slow-moving silver Audi that seemed inclined to window shop too. It moved on, and after a couple of minutes he did too.

The railway station's looming bulk was only three blocks away. It would present an array of problems for him, but mass ground transportation was safer than the airport.

A portly fellow in a homburg hat gazing too intently at the footpath brushed by. His cane tangled with Max's ankle.

Like most street mix-ups, it quickly became a bungled Fred Astaire routine. Max grabbed the cane and spun out of the way, but the man's cane slipped to the street. The old fellow was tilting off balance with no support.

Where the devil had the fellow's cane gone?

Max bent to help him look for it. Then the cane reappeared between his ankles, knocking him off balance. He fell back against the rear fender of a stopped car.

He was perfectly placed to tumble inside an open backseat car door.

Oh, no, they didn't. His arms grabbed each side of the frame as he prepared to thrust himself back onto the sidewalk and freedom.

"Max, you ass," the old man hissed, "get in and make no more fuss about it. We're attracting attention.

"Sorry, young fellow," Garry Randolph added loudly in German. "Many thanks for catching me. Come, my car will take you where you were going."

By then Max had managed to draw his long legs inside without too much pain as Garry pushed into the backseat after him and pulled the door shut.

The car eased back into traffic.

"Where's — ?" Max started to ask.

Randolph snapped his wrist and a telescoping cane unfurled in the space between them.

"I don't need a cane anymore, but my fingerprints are on the one you left behind," Max complained.

Garry Randolph jerked his head behind them.

Max rubbernecked backward. A teenage boy was bending to retrieve the cane.

"He's mine," Garry said. "I knew I could lose the walking stick in the confusion of the moment. The boy's been paid to burn it."

Max eyed the driver, who had never looked back.

"Doesn't speak English and wears earphones playing Vivaldi anyway. A long-ago associate. How is the lovely doctor?"

"Wearing a lovely new suit and en route back to the clinic."

"Do you trust her?"

"No. She did help me escape the place."

"After the attempt on your life with the hypodermic needle."

"What was in it?"

"Phenobarbital."

"Know why I'm worth so much dead?"

Gandolph scratched the bristly gray mustache, then pulled it off. "No. You're walking well. I'm amazed."

"The bones were healed, so my atrophied muscles were the problem. Running for your life makes for very motivated physical therapy. How did you find me?"

"You had to pass through Zurich. I actually located you yesterday, but the lights in your room burned all night and I was reluctant to be seen in the hotel anyway. Had a siege of sickness, did we?"

Max cleared his throat. "That was actually Dr. Schneider's room."

"I see. A rather different kind of siege." Garry shook his head. "Max, Max, Max. A deceptive woman got you into this whole counterspy mess twenty years ago. Boys will be boys, I suppose."

"Is there some reason I shouldn't have been doing what I was doing?"

"She may be employed by an enemy."

"Beyond that."

"Any reason why you should have slept alone last night, you mean?"

He nodded.

"You left the love of your life behind in Las Vegas when you crashed into the wall of a nightclub during an airborne magic act."

Max stared at this man he was supposed to know, and trust.

"Good God! I was in Las Vegas? Not on some damn mountain? I knew I was never on a mountain! Damn mountains, particularly Alps. But, Garry, I had a . . . wife? Lover?"

"Yes and no. Even you realized you couldn't commit to marriage while your life was in danger, and you finally told her that. Freed her just recently. You also told me if anything ever happened to you, I had a mission: to find the first woman who deceived you and gave you a grief you couldn't lose and set you on the path of espionage.

"You were unconscious after that murder attempt in Vegas, and then amnesiac. I used every resource I had from our active espionage days to smuggle you out of the United States to the Swiss clinic. I even set it up so that your Las Vegas love saw your house emptied of all your possessions and occupied by a stranger."

"That was brutal."

"She's a tenacious young woman. I needed to be brutal. Then I installed you in that Swiss clinic at great expense and manipulation and set about trying to trace Kathleen O'Connor. The Kathleen O'Connor from twenty years ago in Northern Ireland."

"Kathleen O'Connor. The name means nothing."

Garry's now mustache-less face grimaced. " 'Kitty the Cutter' is what your ex-

604

girlfriend named her."

"And what is the ex-girlfriend's name?"

"Temple. Temple Barr."

Max winced to remember kissing Revienne's temple and feeling an odd tenderness, a moment of fugitive memory.

"Oh, God. Why didn't I remember that there was someone?"

"You'd decided to let her go, Max. Another man loves her, one she became attracted to when you disappeared before, for almost a year. You knew it was too dangerous to associate with her when we were making inroads, finally, on uncovering the Synth."

"The . . . sinth? Is that some *Star Wars* thing?"

Garry chuckled sadly. "So odd how you remember all the minutiae of our crazy modern world and nothing significant to your current situation and life. The Synth is a presumed international cadre of spies and magicians. That's a very natural mating of interests, as you and I prove. We're going to the airport, but we have a small private jet at our disposal, so we don't risk exposure. I've got the proper forged passports. The flight will be long."

"My duffle bag —" He wasn't used to baggage and had dropped it at the scene.

"The musically inclined Hans scooped it up while we were tussling before pulling the car away. It's on the front seat. Any weapons in it?"

"Just clothes and grooming items."

"Apparently not a razor," Gandolph commented dryly.

"Don't you like my *Pirates of the Caribbean* look? It took a very expensive electric razor to cultivate this unkempt appearance."

"The question is, did Dr. Schneider appreciate it?"

Max grew thoughtful. "I don't suppose I care at the moment. How could I forget the 'love of my life'?"

"Hopefully, or sadly, you may not forever. Meanwhile, we're on the trail of the woman who ruined your life."

"To extract justice?"

"She's dead too."

"Then what's the point?"

"Closure," Garry said.

Closure.

Maybe it took a memory to see any point in that, Max thought.

CHAPTER 66
DANCING IN THE DARK

At night the underwater lights in the Circle Ritz backyard pool made the aquamarine rectangle gleam like a glimpse into Atlantis.

Temple sat in the temperate night air, on a lounge chair, watching Matt do his laps.

"Now I know what the expression 'bronze god' means," she commented dreamily. "Will that spray-on tan fade fast?"

He lifted his wet head from the water, his blond hair silvered in the moonlight.

"I sure hope so. Why do you think I'm swimming in chlorine? I want to wash that dance show out of my hair and off my epidermis."

"Why? You won."

He dived and resurfaced at the edge near her chair, crossing his bronzed arms on the edge to hold himself up.

"Yeah, and the show raised $180,000 for the kids' cancer fund, so it was worth the hassle, although not the attempts on my life.

And that doesn't include being mobbed by tween girls from thirteen to ninety-three after the final show."

"It was great that Glory B. won the women's vote. She was so grateful. You could see her maturing on the spot. What a wonderful moment. All the contenders won something — self-confidence, renewal, fresh job opportunities."

"Fresh commercial temptations."

"So your perfectly highlighted blond head hasn't been turned?"

"Lord, they want me to do spray-tan TV ads."

"You'd make more money for good causes, including a house fund maybe."

"Not spray-tan anything. I'll let my agent handle it. Tony knows my bottom line is human dignity, even though I've played fast and loose with it lately. At least my dance gig exposed and stopped one very sick man from harming more people. I never dreamed my radio advice could get someone killed."

"Your advice didn't kill her. Her husband did."

"He was insanely bitter about so much. He'd fit the Barbie Doll Killer's stalker profile."

"Hank Buck was a local problem. I think Molina got a lead on that Barbie doll case during this dance show stalking. She has to win that one. Her kid's bedroom was targeted with one of the mutilated dolls."

"Now that she knows her homegrown stalker isn't Max." Matt tilted his head to watch Temple. "You must be pleased about that. You always told Molina he wasn't the villain she thought."

"Yeah. I wish Max knew she was coming around to reason about him. If there's a Max out there to know anything."

"You think he's . . . dead?"

"I hope not."

"Why?" he asked.

"Oh, Mr. Radio Shrink! You are so not going to trick me into missing Max mode! Not now, when I want to go over the Temple tango moves as soon as you get out of that water, dry off, and dance me back to our lovely pied-à-terre."

He laughed and let the flat of his hand hit an arc of sparkling water toward her chair. "You don't like to swim."

"Not in pools. Along the turquoise Riviera . . . that's different."

"You're an expensive little sea nymph."

"Darn right." She sighed. "Rafi really wants a relationship with Mariah. He's got a head start. I hope her mother will cooperate."

"This injury has broken down her resistance to reality. Like Kitty the Cutter's slash did mine."

"Really? That was . . . liberating?"

"It's liberating to confront that some people want to hurt you, for no reason you can see, and you don't have to hurt back. 'Hurt' was too much a part of my so-called nuclear and extended family in Chicago. We don't have to keep up the tradition."

"We're supposed to head north and meet your family and mine someday soon."

"Someday soon. You don't want to come into the water with me? It's as silken and warm as unchilled wine." He lifted a hand. "Come on."

"I'm dressed."

"Clothes dry."

"My hair."

"Is perfect, dry or wet."

"I paddle like a springer spaniel."

"I'm a merman from shining, sunken Atlantis. I'll hold you up, and you'll breathe underwater."

"Really?"

"No. Don't breathe underwater. But come with me."

His hand pushed closer.

Temple sighed, stood, kicked off her slides, and went to squat by the pool's edge.

"You are a very metaphysical guy, you know that?"

He grasped her hand and pulled her down. "Shut your eyes and think two stars to the right and straight on till morning."

He pulled her forward into the alien element. The water was tepid and as silken as he said. She sank in it until her chin broke water and he buoyed her up. She gasped with surprise at the buoyancy, the way cares seemed to float up from her like bubbles.

"Take a deep breath," he said, "and don't breathe after that."

They sank down together to Atlantis, kissing until she saw its gleaming turquoise towers behind her eyelids. Her hair swirled like seaweed. They were no place on earth. It felt heavenly.

CHAPTER 67
NO GOOD DUDE
GOES UNPUNISHED

". . . and the food is *vershtunken*."

I am sitting in the parking lot of the Circle Ritz apartments and condominiums, an elegant five-story fifties' doughnut of a building wrapped in black marble, listening to my jet-black dam unleash a flood of invective about my home, sweet home.

I mean the word *dam* not as a water barrier or a swear word — cat heaven forbid! — but as the word that indicates the alma mater of myself, Miss Ma Barker.

I hasten to ease her aggravation. "Free-to-Be-Feline is highly regarded as an earth-sensitive, digestatory product, literally green, which you must admit is all the politically correct rage these days," I say, not believing a word of it.

I am known to loathe the stuff by one and all, save my devoted roommate, Miss Temple Barr. Clever as she is, she has never tumbled to the fact that her favorite feline health food is — not to put too fine a point on it — *"ver-shtunken."*

Meanwhile, Ma Barker, a pretty testy old dame who commands a feral colony, rants on.

"I led my loyal entourage all the way down from north Las Vegas to this so-called Promised Land to hand them bowlfuls of dried, army-green rabbit turds? Served in sterile plastic? Not so much as a fresh, grease-soaked fast-food wrapper for a napkin? Even the do-gooder brigade of homeless cat-trappers and ball-snappers did better by us than you, son."

"They mean well!" I cry. That was ever the best, though weak, defense for ignorant humanity. "I, ah, find Free-to-Be-Feline in my own personal food bowls daily."

I nimbly dodge admitting to actually eating it.

"You have gone over to the Dark Side, son. I understand. Mere security is a powerful lure."

"Hey! I *provide* security, I do not crave it."

"Whatever, I have been scouting the neighborhood and have found a more amenable location."

"The Circle Ritz is a very good address!"

"That may be, but I have never been an uptown girl, except geographically. Look at us, son. We are marked by the Tipped Ear. We have been trapped, 'napped, and lopped off at the ear and in other, more personal, external and internal places. The world knows us for a neutered colony, but we are not about to give up our rep as a mad, bad street gang."

"I know that, Ma. Getting free vittles is not a sign of defeat."

"I do not object to the free vittles, just the quality at your pad here. I have found a better free lunch."

"Yeah?" If I am dubious, it is because I am well aware how little the feral elements of our breed are welcomed anywhere.

"Yeah. I am talking juicy, greasy burgers. I am talking long, lank, salty fries. I am talking the dregs of thick, creamy milkshakes. I am talking doughnuts."

"Doughnuts! That is the worst of empty calorie foods. No carnivore worth its fangs would sink them into a glazed doughnut."

"That is where you are so wrong, son. Follow me."

She pushes up onto her venerable limbs and stalks off, her knife-sharp shoulder blades parting the steamy Vegas daylight like shark fins.

I have busted my derriere getting Ma and her gang to a safe house. How annoying that she spurns it. Those of our breed are masters of spurning, however, and food is the prime example of what we can achieve in that direction.

Speaking of directions, Ma Barker is heading northeast of the Circle Ritz, cross-country. She is a cagey mitt-to-mitt fighter and even vanquished a raccoon, a feat for one of her advanced years. Still, I do not trust her alone in new territory.

We finally halt in some weeds near a low, undistinguished-looking brick building. The spunky, funky Circle Ritz it is not.

Call it one-story bland.

However, my nose sniffs old, cold oil that has dripped from cars and . . . fast food. The place has a manly aura, and I am ever in favor of that.

I spot a lot of cars at rest, otherwise known as parked. They are also marked.

"This is it?" I ask. "The site you have chosen over my own premises?"

"Right." Ma Barker's still-skinned nose lifts to inhale stale oil and dead fish and overcooked cow.

"Are you crazy, Ma? This is the southeast substation of the Las Vegas Metropolitan Police Department. They have a no-tolerance policy toward gangs. They will sweep up your posse and cart them off to stir and the so-called 'shelter' death chambers faster than you can hiss Free-to-Be-Feline."

"You think so, sonny? Look, my lead agent has made first contact."

I look, and I have to admit my old lady is a pretty canny strategist.

None other than Gimpy, the gangly adolescent three-legged victim of a car accident, is hopping around the station's back door, mewing piteously. I hate to see our kind stoop to begging for what we should be given, but the cruel breaks of life on the street have made Gimpy into an orphan out of a Charles the Dickins tome.

A bicycle officer in summer Bermuda shorts uniform is leaning down to share some double cheeseburger with little Gimpy.

"She is female and an easy touch," I hiss to Ma Barker. "No way will the male cops let your gang set up shop here."

Another officer steps out the door, the burly sort just the right size to kick an inconvenient cat out of the way.

"Poor little bastard," he says. "Ear is nicked, so he has had his balls cut off too. I got some take-out Chinese shrimp he might go for." He ducks back in and soon returns with Gimpy's fish course.

"Somebody underwrote getting that leg surgically removed," Miss Bicycle Officer, heretofore ID'd as Miss BO, says. Hey, it *is* hot in this town!

"He must have been in horrid shape to need it removed," she goes on, staring into the surrounding brush. "There must be a colony around here. The trap, neuter, and release programs say it is better to keep them on the streets until all the clodder members die out."

"Clodder?" the guy asks, "like in cluttered?"

"Naw, it is the official name for a community of stray cats."

"Huh." The guy squats carefully beside Greedy Gut, aka Gimpy. He chuckles. "Look at the little fellah eat. He must still be putting on muscle."

In his dreams!

Meanwhile, Ma Barker is massaging me with her mitt, shivs out. "That clodder talk was our cue, Louie. Time to take a bow. We can hang back like we are bashful, and you lower one ear so they do not see you have two whole ones."

I gaze at Ma's face with the rakish ear at half-mast. I thought a raccoon or another cat had taken a chunk out of it, but now I see that the missing piece has been nipped off in a nice straight line.

Nobody nips the ear off Midnight Louie!

I growl and would retreat, except that Ma has her claws in me right where it could do some damage to my perfectly functional male member and satellites.

I too am politically correct in the failure-to-reproduce department, but my neutering was accomplished internally, with a human procedure called a vasectomy. That is my license to thrill in this town. I cannot strew unwanted litters anywhere, although I can distribute my personal favors hither and yon as I please.

Trouble is, my lack of littering capability does not show, and I could be whisked away and stripped of my will to love, by mistake. What a tragedy!

So when Ma Barker wants me to step forward into a lineup of two, I am hesitant.

"Move it, lad!" She whacks me in the rear, all four shivs at full extension.

We bound as one into the limelight, the bright open sunshine of a Las Vegas spring day.

"There is a couple more!" BO cries, delighted at my quandary.

Officer Shrimp Combo goes from a squat to a looming position. "Yeah. A couple more members of the Off-Strip Clodders, right? One pretty tough-looking gang."

"Oh, those poor cats. They look so ragged and hungry."

I beg your pardon, ma'am! I am sleek, well-fed, and well able to see to it that I remain so. Ma may be a bit ragged from her fight-to-the-death with the raccoon, but I am as smooth as George Clooney in a black dinner jacket for the Oscars.

"Come on, kitties."

I have not fallen for that con game since I was six weeks old, but Ma Barker inches forward, doing a pretty good imitation of Gimpy's pathetic gait.

Officer Shrimp Combo is galvanized into action. "I better see what other tidbits the crew has. That is one skinny old raggedy cat."

Ma Barker looks over her sharp-boned shoulder to shoot me a triumphant wink with one still half-swollen-shut green peeper.

I shake my head and disappear back into the scratchy brush.

How could any self-respecting feline give up the moderne comforts of the Circle Ritz under my protection to put her gang's lot in with a bunch of beat cops?

She gets up and lurches back to the bushes and me for a farewell.

"This is a superior setup for us. We are used to fast food, in fact, we prefer it. So you can continue running your fancy P.I. firm from the fancy-schmancy Circle Ritz, and we street cats will hang with the street cops. I am sure we will be able to pick up a lot of hot tips for you about nefarious goings-on, and we can help these folks in beige keep crime down. Now that we are all fixed, we need a hobby."

It is considered bad form among all species to talk back to one's mother and I am speechless anyway.

I nod and slink off, returning home to a bowl full of Free-to-Be-Feline. I must summon all my energy to perform the daily scam job that gets my Miss Temple to slather edible little nothings on top of that noxious base so a guy can eat.

Somehow, I fear that the feral crew I hoped to help has helped themselves to the better cuisine. Life is not fair.

Tailpiece:
Midnight Louie
Mulls Many
Matters

How sharper than a serpent's tooth is an ungrateful parent.

I know, I know. That line was originally aimed at ungrateful offspring.

But these relationships work both ways and I am both amazed and peeved that my grand plan to relocate Ma Barker's gang to the Circle Ritz has ended in a mass desertion.

Not that I am merely taking this personally. I am also deeply concerned that the whole clodder will now be subsisting on the worst of junk food fresh from the fast-food joints. Every day. Greasy burgers and fries. Chicken wings. Barbequed beef. All those treats that help our law enforcement personnel beef up for the job.

I have to say that the buffet at the Oasis offered a better balanced diet, when no one was slipping e. coli into the celebrity chef's private trays. I hope to sample its wares on later visits to the resident mascot. Topaz is a delightful hostess and I foresee an excellent collaboration. I am done with those snooty long-haired Persian dames. Topaz is a shorthair like me, albeit purebred.

On the human side, I must say that I have never been included on a family outing before and it was an interesting experience, to say the least. No wonder our kits are out of there in three months. These twenty-year parent-child associations can get very complicated. Perhaps soon there will be a meeting of the minds on whether and when little Miss Mariah should be told she has a long-lost father in the neighborhood.

I look upon the retirement of Miss Zoe Chloe Ozone from the public eye again with massive relief and huzzahs. Although the Goth girl's wardrobe of fishnet hose and patterned tights and fingerless gloves offer a guy like me much opportunity for ripping and scaling, one tires easily of the bizarre for the sake of it.

I am not sure which major man in my Miss Temple's life has won the sexiest man alive sweepstakes. Mr. Matt stepped out and up quite literally in the Latin dance moves department, but Mr. Max is no slouch in the romance department even on the run. Call me prejudiced, but I do not consider amnesia sufficient excuse for canoodling with a woman who is not Miss Temple.

On the other hand, a little amnesia might come in handy to a dude.

Imagine my forgetting Miss Midnight Louise. I have indeed hit my head while pursuing a criminal more than once. In fact, I took several head and body blows during the course of saving my Circle Ritz friends' hides in this latest case.

In fact . . . now that I think about it, I am having trouble pulling much out of the old memory bank, like certain feline dames I may or may not be related to, who hang out at a certain Vegas hotel and also a nearby police substation.

Sometimes forgetting family is the best way of dealing with them.

There was an exciting new development on my Vegas turf. A mystery bookstore opened in nearby Henderson that offered a vintage-flavored atmosphere and food for the body as well as the reader's soul. The enterprising couple behind Cheesecake and Crime — he whips up the many varieties of cheesecake, including jalapeño, which sets my collaborator's tastebuds tingling — hoped to make it an institution.

Since Miss Carole has had the good taste to set not one but two mystery series in my backyard, I wished it well, but the brick-and-mortar bookstore part folded soon after the 2008 economic swoon. Independent mystery bookstores are a dying breed (no matter how appropriate the phrase is to the genre), so it is a truly lamentable turn of events.

And the clerks wore vintage clothing! My Miss Temple is distraught.

You may still order their baked goods virtually at www.cheesecakeandcrime.com. (You can also grab and/or order my books wheresoever you may find them so that *I* do not end up as mouse cheesecake!)

Lastly, we received a flurry of excited mail in the fall of 2007 about a new television series, *Viva Laughlin,* set in the rising shadow city south of Las Vegas visited herein.

Why was producer Hugh Jackman playing a key hotel-casino owner named "Nicky Fontana"? Were my books now a TV series? Alas, no. 'Twould have been far better if that was the case. In fact, *Viva Laughlin* aired only two of its three filmed episodes, one of the fastest flash in the pans of that TV season or many others.

How did "Nicky Fontana," owner of the Crystal Phoenix Hotel in *my* series and in manuscript since 1985 and in print since 1990, become a character in *VL?* (Note that the initials are the reverse of Las Vegas's.)

Miss Carole suspects some script researcher came across one of my books and liked the name.

Miss Carole also avers that if they *had* used *my* series for TV, with the hunky Mr. Hugh Jackman playing Mr. Max Kinsella, it would have been a hit. Several readers of the female persuasion reacted to that scenario with sighs and swoons, but, alas, it was not to be.

Very Best Fishes,

Midnight Louie, Esq.

If you'd like information about getting Midnight Louie's free *Scratching Post-Intelligencer* newsletter and/or buying his custom T-shirt and other cool things, contact Carole Nelson Douglas at P.O. Box 331555, Fort Worth, TX 76163-1555 or at www.carolenelsondouglas.com. E-mail: cdouglas@catwriter.com.

Tailpiece: Carole Nelson Douglas Plays the Dance Card

How splendid to see you getting out of your couch potato rut, Louie, to cut a few crooks on the dance floor.

The reality TV dance show craze might look like it inspired Louie's latest adventure, and, in fact, I'm a fan of two of them, although dancing doesn't come naturally to me. My creative right brain isn't geared to the left-brain elements of complicated steps and music.

I'd taken a little modern dance in college but missed getting early childhood lessons, and was never very good at it. So I started taking tap dance lessons as an adult because I think it's always good to grapple with something that doesn't come naturally.

It's shocking to realize I've been dancing, and finally getting better, for more than twenty years now. I started by studying tap dancing, moved to clogging when I lost the instructor, and finally added the most difficult dance form of all, flamenco, which involves complex and simultaneous foot, arm, and skirt movements, and mastering the castanets too.

Here are some dance sites on the Web, for those who have access. If some sites are no longer available, you can do your own "tango" search.

For a funky montage of images illustrating the lyrics of Barry Manilow's huge hit, "Copacabana," see http://noolmusic.com/videos/copacabana_-_barry_manilow.php.

Watch the Muppets assist Liza Minnelli in a charming take on the classic number at http://www.youtube.com/watch?v=eekXeZvHno.

To play voyeur with Richard Gere and Jennifer Lopez in a sizzling tango clip from *Shall We Dance,* go to http://www.youtube.com/watch?v=bibtqDxXv1o.

A playful tango featuring a guy in gangster suit and fedora plays at http://www.youtube.com/watch?v=5E4mBoGX6Dw&feature/.

The Topaz Tango chapter couldn't have been written without the cooperation of two of my adopted cats, Midnight Louie, Jr., and the young and beautiful calico feral, Audrey.

I "met" what would become my first black

cat at Lubbock, Texas, Animal Services during the first Midnight Louie Adopt-a-Cat book-signing tour sponsored by my publisher in 1996. My husband, Sam, and I drove more than six hundred miles to fetch the petite, year-old black cat that had "picked" me during a flying tour of Texas.

We took "Midnight Louise's" shaved stomach as a sign of spaying. Once home, we were soon shown the truth. "Louise" was a neutered male. There is only one Midnight Louie, so he became "Junior." At eight, Midnight Louie, Jr., began going blind from retinal degeneration. I'd never had a cat lose a faculty before and was in despair, but he adapted beautifully and goes everywhere, jumping up wherever he desires.

He was thirteen when we brought a trapped feral calico female we'd been feeding for months into the house. Audrey was named after the carnivorous plant that pleads "Feed me," in that cult black-and-white Roger Corman black-comedy film, *The Little Shop of Horrors,* which we loved even before it became a color remake and an off-Broadway and then Broadway musical.

Audrey would come six times a day to eat a full can of wet cat food when she had a litter to nurse. Although we had Audrey fixed at once, we didn't realize her raging hormones would take time to dissipate. She fixated on the only male cat in the house: neutered, blind Midnight Louie, Jr. For the first time we witnessed the feline courting dance. *She* entices him. Poor Audrey used all her considerable wiles, but Louie, although a handsome glossy jet-black lad, is not interested in that way. Alas, it's a doomed dance of love, but now I know that cats do dance and so should we all.

The writer's brain needs to "dance" too, trying left-brain recreational pursuits that involve hand-eye coordination. That can be dancing, playing the piano, or doing crossword puzzles. Some writers play computer solitaire when needing a recess. Even with a mouse, you are moving cards and making logical decisions.

And then there's the most pleasurable hand-eye coordination of all: petting a beautiful cat (and they all are) and watching it curl up and purr with satisfaction.

ABOUT THE AUTHOR

Cat in a Topaz Tango is the twenty-first title in **Carole Nelson Douglas**'s sassy Midnight Louie mystery series. Previous titles include *Cat in a Sapphire Slipper, Cat in a Red Hot Rage,* and *Cat in a Quicksilver Caper.* In addition to tales of her favorite feline, Douglas is also the author of the historical suspense series featuring Irene Adler, the only woman ever to have "outwitted" Sherlock Holmes. Douglas resides in Fort Worth, Texas.